Penelope Douglas is a *New York Times, USA Today*, and *Wall Street Journal* bestselling author. Their books have been translated into nineteen languages and include The Fall Away Series, The Devil's Night Series, and the standalones: *Misconduct, Punk 57, Birthday Girl, Credence*, and *Tryst Six Venom*.

They live in Las Vegas with their husband and daughter.

Visit Penelope Douglas online:
www.penelopedouglasauthor.com
www.facebook.com/PenelopeDouglasAuthor
www.twitter.com/pendouglas

ALSO BY PENELOPE DOUGLAS...

FALLS BOYS

PENELOPE
DOUGLAS

PIATKUS

PIATKUS

First published in 2022 by Penelope Douglas
Published in Great Britain in 2022 by Piatkus

5 7 9 10 8 6

A CIP catalogue record for this book
is available from the British Library.

ISBN 978-0-349-43576-3

Printed and bound in Great Britain by Clays Ltd, Elcograf S.p.A.

Papers used by Piatkus are from well-managed forests
and other responsible sources.

Piatkus
An imprint of
Little, Brown Book Group
Carmelite House
50 Victoria Embankment
London EC4Y 0DZ

An Hachette UK Company

www.hachette.co.uk

www.littlebrown.co.uk

PLAYLIST

"B.Y.O.B." by System of a Down
"Dark In My Imagination" by of Verona
"Dark Matter" by Darkswoon
"Esto No A Terminado (This Isn't Over)" by Snow Tha
Product, The Newton Brothers
"Feel Good" by SAYGRACE
"How Villains Are Made" by Madalen Duke
"I Ran (So Far Away)" by Hidden Citizens
"Immigrant Song" by Trent Reznor, Atticus Ross, Karen O
"Kill Me First" by Emanuel Vo Williams, Robin Loxley,
Samantha Powell
"Problem" by Natalie Kills
"Queen" by Loren Gray
"Radioactive" by Imagine Dragons
"Throne" by Saint Mesa
"Wherever I May Roam" by J Balvin, Metallica
"Wicked Game" by HIM
"ZITTI E BUONI" by Måneskin

In addition to playlists,
all of my stories come with Pinterest mood boards.
Feel free to take a look at FALLS BOYS' storyboard
(https://www.pinterest.com/penelopedouglas/
f-a-l-l-s-b-o-y-s-2021/) as you read!

AUTHOR'S NOTE

The Hellbent series is a spin-off of the Fall Away series. These are the kids' stories.

Reading Fall Away is helpful but not necessary. The parents do appear a lot, as well as references to their past storylines, so if you wish to read those first, the order is *BULLY, UNTIL YOU, RIVAL, FALLING AWAY, AFLAME,* and *NEXT TO NEVER*.

ADRENALINE is a bonus content collection of conversations and scenes I wrote over the course of the Fall Away series as treats for readers. It was published after the series ended. You can find it on my website, as well as more bonus scenes written after its publication.

We first meet the main characters of Hellbent in the epilogue of *AFLAME,* and they appear heavily in *NEXT TO NEVER*. There are also a couple of bonus scenes on my website that take place after *NEXT TO NEVER* and kick off their journeys.

Again, none of this is necessary, but if you'd like to experience the whole world, *BULLY* is where you can start.

Enjoy!

A. HAWKE'S HOUSE   F. EAGLE POINT PARK

B. DYLAN'S HOUSE   G. FISH POND

C. KADE'S HOUSE   H. CEMETERY

E. HIGH SCHOOL   I. THE LOOP/FALLSTOWN

                 J. MINES OF SPAIN

*This map is a loose representation of Shelburne Falls to give you a basic idea of the placement of homes and points of interest. There are more streets and businesses than what the map includes.

SHELBURNE FALLS

Toward
Weston

K. SKATE PARK
L. BLACKHAWK LAKE
M. JT RACING
N. QUINN'S HOUSE
O. QUINN'S BAKERY

P. BLACKHAWK SUMMER CAMP
Q. BOWLING ALLEY
R. MOVIE THEATER
S. RIVERTOWN
T. THE DIETRICH HOUSE

U TBD
V. TBD

HELLBENT

LILIAN BRANDT

TATE BRANDT

JAMES BRANDT

KATHERINE TRENT

DYLAN TRENT

JAMES TRENT

JARED TRENT

THOMAS TRENT

JAXON TRENT

MADELAINE MOORE

JULIET CARTER

HAWKE TRENT

QUINN CARUTHERS

MADOC CARUTHERS

HUNTER CARUTHERS

KADE CARUTHERS

JASON CARUTHERS

PATRICIA FALLON

FALLON PIERCE

A.J. CARUTHERS

SERIES FAMILY TREE

To my father, who wishes
I'd write "a nice murder mystery."

This is it, Dad.

There's still going to be sex in it, though.

CHAPTER ONE

Aro

I don't know how I'll die, but God, I hope it's with a view.

The rafters above cross over my head, ascending higher and higher and only visible by the faint light of the moon streaming through the windows.

But as I stretch my eyes, trying to see deeper into the darkness up there, it just becomes a void. Invisible. Empty space. I can't make out what's beyond, and I almost like that better.

Mystery. Discovery.

Hope.

I spend too much time looking up. More so than ever now.

"I sent him!" Hugo yells into his phone. "You got a problem with that?"

I wince, dropping my eyes.

"Flaco got arrested," he explains to a customer as I look over at him at his desk. "You got a new guy now."

1

Nicholas and Axel sit off to the side, cutting lines on a small round table with a girl in the middle. Her hands clasp a beer can in her lap.

Not a girl.

A kid.

She tries to look older with the blue streaks in her white hair, but she can't be more than thirteen.

A Metallica song covered in Spanish blasts over the speakers, but I still hear Hugo as he continues to gripe into the phone. "You know what the transiency rate is on runners? You think I got a damn secretary who can call and alert you every time one is replaced? You want the shit or not?"

I'm almost amused, but only because I like to see him stressed. It's a pain in the ass for the delivery service as well as the customer. You text, and the last thing you want is someone you don't know showing up at your house with the drugs you ordered. Hugo's right, though. Runners come and go. They get arrested, deported, they O.D....

Three guys line up behind me, waiting their turn as we stand in the repurposed fire house. The bay door behind me still works too, letting cars enter from time to time. It's like a massive garage, but despite what goes on in this building, I like it. It's old and still smells like the tires of the old fire engines they used to keep here.

I glance up once more, my body—for just a moment— way up there and looking down at all of this. From high above. Away. Safe. In the quiet.

I murmur to myself, "Tranquila."

Peace.

But then someone speaks. "Come on, kid," they say.

I look over, watching Axel hand the girl a severed straw and direct her to the coke on the table.

Every muscle in my body hardens, my legs immediately moving without thinking. I close the distance in two steps, grab the straw out of her hand, and shove her in the chest, pushing her dumbass back into her seat.

Axel and Nicholas rear back, looking up at me, but I'm talking before they have a chance. "What are you wasting blow on her for?" I snap.

Axel rolls his eyes, picking up another straw. "White kids got problems too, Aro."

He plugs one side of his nose, sticking the straw into the other, and leans down. I turn away, but I hear his snort behind me.

Hugo tosses his phone onto his desk, turns down the music, and I step back up, my hands in the pockets of my black bomber jacket.

"How are you?" he asks, picking up his half-eaten hamburger and taking a bite. He washes it down with a swig of beer and rises, digging in the file cabinet behind him.

When I don't answer, he turns to meet my eyes, my keys for the night jingling in his hand.

I stare at him.

He laughs under his breath, shaking his shaved head and I eye the scar on his eyebrow that he got from a fight when he was eighteen. He'd stitched himself up after downing half a bottle of tequila that night, and I looked up to him as a role model.

I don't anymore.

"So rude to me," he teases. "You used to love me."

I was fifteen. It's amazing how quickly someone can wise up.

He takes a seat and writes down my schedule on a slip of paper. "How are the kids doing?" he asks.

3

I remain silent, watching the table to my left out of the corner of my eye and making sure they don't task me with driving the Falls girl to the hospital tonight. She needs to stay on her side of the river.

"Your foster mom staying out of your way?" he continues, folding the paper.

I hold out my hand for it, still not answering.

He pauses, staring up at me like he's waiting for something. Like for me to smile and hang on his every word like I did when I was younger and stuck in the same foster home with him.

I shift my gaze over to Axel and Nicholas, brothers we met back in the day when we were all placed together. They're both lanky and tall, but Axel's black hair is styled with a pompadour and shaved on the sides, helping to amplify his neck tattoos. Nicholas's is trimmed but messy, still looking like the same kid I grew up with in a lot of ways.

The four of us have barely gone a day without working together or running into each other, but unlike me, they're not still in contact with their real families and helping to support siblings. I have a family, just a mother who doesn't want me.

Axel's hand drops to the girl's knee, and I narrow my eyes.

"Addresses are programmed in." Hugo slips the paper and burner phone into my palm and then hands me the car keys. "Take the Cherokee. And as usual, you get twenty percent of whatever you come back with, and don't..."

He grabs my wrist, and a gasp escapes from me as he squeezes it.

"Don't come back empty-handed again," he warns. "I can get her to do it for free." He gestures to the kid sitting with Nicholas and Axel. "I keep you on because we're family, but it's getting harder to justify to Reeves that you're not better for other work now."

I clench my teeth together, yanking my wrist free and knowing exactly what he means by that. I'm eighteen now. If I want to keep making money, they may decide there's only one way I can do that and collecting rent and running stolen merchandise isn't it.

"That's not what I want to see, Aro," he tells me, his eyes softening, "but..." He hesitates, and I stuff the shit into my pocket, keeping the keys in my hand. "Maybe it's better, you know? More money, a lot less risk..."

I shoot him a look.

"You're going to get caught," he states as if there's no doubt. "It's only a matter of time. And then, what happens to Matty and Bianca?"

I turn to leave, but he takes my arm, pulls off my hood, and yanks me in by the back of the neck.

I stiffen, but I don't fight. I don't fear him. Not *him*.

"He's coming tonight," he says.

I stare into his eyes, unfaltering, except for the tiny coil in my stomach.

"He wants an assortment of young and pretty." His eyes don't leave mine. "It'll suck, and it won't feel good, but it'll keep you out of jail and you'll have a wad of cash in your fist when it's over."

I would rather walk into oncoming traffic. I can get a wad of cash without taking off my clothes.

He lowers his voice, but I know the trio to my left is watching. "You don't even have to smile for him. A él le gusta cuando a las chicas no les gusta."

He likes it when the girls don't like it.

"Let me go," I say.

5

But I don't wait for it. I whip out of his hold, pulling up the hood of the sweatshirt I wear underneath my jacket and spin around.

"Believe it or not, I do care about you," he tells my back.

Yeah, cares about me enough to turn me out. *Fuck you.*

I reach over, grabbing a fistful of the girl's purple and white tie-dye sweatshirt, and haul her ass out of her seat. Drinks topple as the table nearly falls over, saved only by Nicholas.

"Hey!" she yells, stumbling to my side.

"Aro, what the hell?" Axel barks.

But I ignore them, swinging us around and tossing Hugo a look. "I'm taking help."

If Reeves is coming, then she's leaving. I push her in front of me, following her out and not sure why I give a shit. I guess I wish someone had done the same for me years ago.

I push through the door, hearing Hugo shout behind me, "And stay away from those little Pirate shits!"

The steel door falls shut, and the kid spins around, but I grab her arm and pull her forward again before she has a chance to run.

"Let me go!" she yells, her white hair falling into her face, the blue chunks vibrant like she just redid them. Technically, she's one of those *little Pirate shits*—a resident of Shelburne Falls, that clean, picturesque, All-American, CW lobotomy, seven miles away that loves to rub their money, cars, and Jared Trent in our faces, because he is their only bragging right, as far as I'm concerned.

But for some reason, they didn't want this girl, so she came over here to Weston to find people who did. I shove her toward the Jeep. "Get in the goddamn car."

I round the rear of the old navy-blue vehicle, the remnants of a *My Kid Is an Honor Student at Charles A. Arthur*

Middle School bumper sticker hanging on for dear life on the bottom of the back windshield. Who knows how many owners ago that was, and I have no idea where Charles A. Arthur Middle School is.

I climb into the car and slam the door. "Tommy, right?" I ask. She's only been hanging out at the garage for a few weeks, and we've never spoken until now.

She throws me a look but doesn't answer.

I start the car. "So, what's up, Tommy? You got a family to support? Drughead parents? Are you starving?"

"No."

I shift the car into Drive and glance at her. "Are you abused at home?"

She turns her scowl on me, her eyebrows pinched together.

Yeah, didn't think so. "Then you should keep your ass there," I tell her. "It's so easy to slum when you have the security of knowing you don't really have to be here, isn't it? You get to leave anytime. You'll never be us."

She grabs the handle, about to throw her shoulder into the door to scurry out, but I click the locks just in time.

She glares at me. "You want me to go, but you won't let me leave!"

"Just shut up."

I take off, speeding out of the deserted parking lot, overgrown weeds spilling through the chain-link fence that separates the property from the field behind it. The August humidity makes the heat worse, and I jack up the A/C, desperate to remove my coat and hoodie, but a night of crime is kind of like riding a motorcycle. It's best to cover as much of you as possible.

"I get fifty percent of your twenty," she points out.

I turn left, watching the road. "Or you can get a hundred percent of a fat lip. How about that?"

Little punk actually thinks I want her tagging along tonight. No clue that I just saved her ass, and I'm damn-well not sharing my take on top of it.

I pull up in front of Lafferty's Liquor, park on the curb across the street, and leave the engine running. The old man who runs the place—Ted—moves past the windows from his position behind the counter.

I look over at Tommy. "Stay here," I tell her. "Keep the engine running. If a cop comes by—or an adult—you tell them you're waiting for your sister. Play on your phone while you say it, so they can't see how nervous your eyes look right now."

She furrows her brow.

I continue. "Don't stutter when you talk to anyone. And if you leave with this car, I will prank call 911 and tell them your dad is beating on me at your house. I think they know the address, Dietrich."

Her face falls, realizing I know exactly who she is. I know all the Pirates. She purses her lips, but she keeps her damn mouth shut. She's smarter than she looks, I guess.

Opening the door, I climb out of the SUV, resisting the urge to adjust the baton digging into my back as it sits just inside the waist of my jeans and hidden underneath my jacket.

Walking across the street, I ignore the Sentra honking as it speeds by and pull open the door to the liquor store. I see the top of a customer's head as they dig into the beer cooler at the far back, but tip my chin back down, avoiding the two cameras, one at the far right and one behind the counter.

8

I cast my gaze up, meeting the owner's eyes. I can just see the exhale as he realizes what day it is. As if he didn't know.

I come up to the counter but position myself a little off to the side to allow his customer to step up. I hold Ted's eyes until he finally tears his away from mine.

He rings up the beer, the guy pays and he takes his shit, walking out the door. As soon as the door closes, I grab the plastic display case of cigars on the counter, his worried eyes flashing to his goods as he sucks in a breath.

But I don't do it. I pluck a package of gum out of the box next to it and set it down, pushing it toward him. He only waits two seconds, because that's all it takes to realize what it took eighteen broken bottles of Dewar's to learn last time.

Reaching into the register, he counts out rent and pushes it with the gum toward me. I swipe it off the counter and walk for the door, spotting a rack of Hostess treats and snatch a package of powdered donuts, leaving the shop.

I tense as I cross the street, feeling it every time that I do this. The reminder that every action justifies a reaction, and this might be the day. He could come barreling out the door after me. A cop could be watching, waiting to catch me in the act.

Maybe I'll feel something hit my back, and it's the last thing I'll ever feel.

I don't turn around. I keep my head up, each step bringing me closer to safety.

I open the door, hold my breath, and slide into my seat, locking the doors like I do every time.

Sweat trickles down my back.

"Did it go okay?" the kid asks.

I toss the donuts into her lap, strap on my seatbelt, and pull away from the curb, keeping my eyes on the rearview mirror and still waiting.

I drive, feet turning into yards that turn into a mile, and I finally relax a little. I know the day is coming. Hugo is right. It's just waiting for it that's hard.

She eats the donuts, sitting lookout as we do this three more times. I hop out, collect payments, and get us out of there as quickly as possible, tackling the easy customers first, in case I run into trouble that takes the rest of the night on the harder ones.

Heading out onto the highway, I take the next exit and a couple of turns, driving into Wicked's parking lot. The club is technically in Shelburne Falls, but they like to pretend it's not within the limits of their nice town.

This is one of the harder ones. I put the car in Park and look over at Tommy. "Same as before."

I leave the car running, pull off my hood but leave my ski cap on and reach out, opening the door.

"But I want to come in," she argues.

"Stay."

And I slam the door, looking around me as I head through the cars crowding the parking lot.

Music vibrates against the walls of the club, and I pause a moment.

The smell already hits me. The scent of cheap body lotion mixed with heavily worn six-inch heels caked in sweat, spilled beer, and Coke syrup.

Sometimes there's a hint of piss or puke, depending on the time of year. Bachelor parties and frat boys home for summer vacation make June my least favorite month to step foot in this place.

But it's August now. The traffic coming in and out has finally died down, but the summer heat has baked the desperation and despair into a foul stench I can't imagine ever getting used to.

I pull the baton out of my jeans and slide it up my long sleeve, holding the cuff so it doesn't fall out. Walking for the club, I pull open the door and give Angel Acosta a nod as he mans the entrance.

"Hey, babe," he says.

I keep walking, the bass hitting hard, making the floor shake under me as I make my way past the bar and glance at the girls on stage.

Lights glow across their skin, hair flipping and barely any real dancing going on. Just slinking up against a pole and crawling all over the stage.

I give them credit, though. I can't imagine a harder job. Maybe there's no math involved or as much risk, like there is being a cop or a soldier or a doctor, but I'd rather do anything else than fake it like they have to.

"Aro!" someone calls.

I see Silver waving from one of the platforms, nearly naked, and muster a wave when I really just want to break something. We were in middle school together.

I head down the hallway, the dull thrum of the music fading a little more, but then I hear Skarsman shout as I approach. "Do you know how easily you can be replaced? Girls are aging up every year, and they don't have kids who constantly get sick!"

I sigh, slowing as the door to his office sits open.

I'm sure my mother would've gotten the same lecture years ago if she hadn't had me to worry about her kids when they were ill. She never missed work. Built-in babysitter here and all.

I round the corner into his office, leaning on the door frame and see his eyes flash to me. Short-cropped salt and pepper hair and clean shaven, he's as well-dressed as he is groomed. Black suit with a dark purple shirt underneath, he does a good job of hiding how fucking nasty he is on the inside.

He blows out smoke and snuffs out his cigarette in the tray. Some girl sits in front of me with her shoulders slumped. She's dressed in a black sequin bikini top.

"Great," he bites out, glaring at me. "Just go fucking sit down out there. I don't want to deal with you right now."

I clutch the end of the club in my hand, keeping it hidden behind me.

When I don't move, he jerks his chin at the dancer, telling her to scram instead. She pops up from her chair, her red hair curly and pulled out of her face with a barrette. She's gorgeous, which is why he hasn't fired her yet.

"Insulting that they send a kid to collect from me." He snickers, moving around his desk.

The girl brushes past, and I stay there, staring at him.

He approaches me and takes the handle of his office door, waving his hand. "Come in," he says.

I relax my hand, the baton sliding out of my sleeve, and muster every muscle, swinging it back and then forward. My heart jumps into my throat as the attack lands on his shoulder, making his knees buckle, and sending him to the ground.

"Ah!" he growls.

Fuck.

Holding the baton in one hand and his hair in the other, I bring his head down hard on my knee for good measure, a sharp pain spreading through my leg.

I hate this part.

I squeeze his hair in my fist, holding his face up as I get close. "They don't send me to handle you," I tell him. "They send me to handle everyone."

12

He wanted to close the door, and it wasn't for a single good reason. I grew up being underestimated, because I'm not a man, and sometimes it worked, but it doesn't anymore.

"Get the money." I throw him off.

He lands on all fours, sitting there.

"I mean now!" I yell, kicking him.

He scrambles over to his desk, pulls himself up and digs in a drawer, taking out his container of petty cash. He opens it, but I grab everything, not even counting it.

"Fuck you, Aro!" he gasps.

But I take the baton and swipe it across his desk, knocking over his lamp and other shit. I crumple the bills in my fist and hold it up. "Don't make me come down to this shithole again for this. Send Angel with it to the garage. You know the drill."

But he always flakes on delivering it, because he's hoping Hugo will just forget.

I stalk out, refusing to turn around but feeling the threat there like I did at all the other places tonight. Every step takes me closer to away.

I pass the girls onstage, stopping at Silver and stuff a few bills in her hand. "Share it, okay?" I whisper in her ear.

She gapes at the hundreds, a well-deserved bonus for the pennies he pays them, and nods. "Thanks. Are you okay?"

She must see I'm upset.

But I nod. "I'm fine."

I keep walking, trusting her to share it with the others. She knows I'll hear about it if she doesn't.

I slip behind the curtain, entering the back room, and seeing some counting their cash, while others talk, text, and primp.

I see Violet Leon and come up behind her. She smiles and turns in her seat. "Aro."

I bend down, kissing her cheek and feeling her mouth press against my face. Probably leaving a huge purple lipstick print.

I pass her a little cash. "Get him those dirt bike lessons for his birthday," I tell her quietly.

Her son is nine. I've babysat him here and there over the years, like she did me when I was growing up. At forty-eight, she thought she was done raising kids, but her little surprise package is more work than his three older siblings.

But he's a good kid. And he's dying to take classes at JT Racing.

She gapes at the money. "Are you serious?"

I stuff the rest of the cash in my pocket.

"Aro, I can't..." She shakes her head.

But I stand up again. "You better."

It will make Luis's year, and everyone has it hard enough. Let him have some fun.

She smiles, tears filling her eyes, but that's about all I can take. Spinning around, I walk toward the back door, pushing it open.

But for a moment, I hesitate and look back over my shoulder to the two kids playing on the floor. Blocks surround them as their mom probably takes the stage, and I look outside to the motel across the lot. Cora Craig comes out of a room followed by a trucker who makes his way for his rig. She heads toward the club, fixing her clothes and with money in her fist.

I look away as she brushes past and then watch her rub her daughter's head as she passes by.

And all of a sudden, I'm five again, except it wasn't blocks. It was crayons and a mermaid coloring book.

I open my mouth, feeling the bile rise up my throat. I dash outside, letting the steel door slam behind me as I lean back on a stack of pallets. I drop the club and bow my head as I inhale and exhale.

My body shakes, and I can't draw in a breath without feeling the sob crawling up my throat. Tears fill my eyes.

I hate her. I hate this.

I hate everything I see.

I turn around and fall into the wall, sweat dampening my body, and I close my eyes, trying to let the nausea pass.

But instead, I open my eyes and look up.

The night sky, black and wide, spreads with stars above, and I see Mars, the brightest object tonight. I like Mars. More than all the planets, because it has the most possibilities. People will go there someday. Maybe someone who's my age now, and I'll see it online.

I breathe in and out, imagining the sky looking back at me and wanting to be something worth seeing.

My blood cools a little, my shoulders square, and I stand up again, calm.

It always helps—looking up. There's only possibility. The view is never worse.

I turn to head to the parking lot, but someone appears.

I halt, seeing a male and female police officer approach, an amused look in their eyes like they found exactly what they were looking for.

Fuck.

"You have weapons on you?" the male asks.

Slowly I raise my hands, showing they're empty as the baton still lays on the ground somewhere behind me.

"No, sir," I tell him.

"Empty your pockets."

I drop my eyes to the weapons on his holster, the female closing in behind him. I soften my voice, even though my pulse is racing. "I don't feel comfortable with that, sir."

He just laughs. Leaning in, he whispers, "I can detain you without a charge for up to forty-eight hours. I can also frisk you."

I know. But still, I try. "I don't feel comfortable and I do not consent, sir." The money on me feels like a soccer ball in my pocket, and it won't go unnoticed. It has to be a few thousand bucks. "Am I free to go?" I ask.

"No."

Of course not. It was worth a try.

But I can't spend forty-eight hours in lockup. I clear my throat. "I consent to a search, sir."

The woman steps forward and pushes me around, my hands slamming into the brick wall. She pats me down, my torso, my legs, my arms, emptying everything out of my pockets. I close my eyes, a sick feeling rolling through my stomach as the weight of the cash on me disappears, and I hold my breath.

Don't come back empty-handed.

They toss everything on top of the dumpster and back away. "No weapons," she announces. "She was telling the truth."

"Aw, sorry about that, kid." The male cop leans in. "Have a good night, okay?"

My chin trembles. *Motherfucker.*

I wait for them to leave, but I don't have to turn around and look to know all the money is gone.

My white and black polka dot wallet, my house key, and my cell phone all sit on top of the lid. No cash.

I kick the dumpster, the hollow clang echoing in the silence. "Son of a bitch!"

I scream, my hands shooting to my head, and I look up at the sky again, finding Mars.

But I can't see straight. Goddammit.

Don't come back empty-handed. I can't go back with nothing. Not again. Hugo won't give me work.

Or he'll make me pay it off another way.

It's always like this. It can go either way, and it always goes wrong.

Grabbing my baton off the ground, I storm off toward the parking lot, the taillights of the cop car leaving the lot. I find Tommy standing outside the Cherokee, sipping something from a flask she must've had on her.

I take it, downing a gulp of tequila.

My hands ache, I'm squeezing my fists so hard, and I don't care if I go back with ten thousand bucks or a black eye, but I'm going back with something.

"Where would the Pirates be hanging out tonight?" I ask her. "Rivertown?"

She nods. "Yeah. Probably."

I hand her back the flask and walk around the car. "Get in."

"But I'm not allowed there, Aro," she argues.

Not allowed? I arch a brow, the chip on my shoulder getting heavier. Screw that.

I climb in and so does she, both of us buckling our seatbelts before I speed off out of the parking lot.

I jack up the radio, too loud for the kid to talk me out of this.

Back in the day, when I still attended school, Weston's rivalry with Shelburne Falls lit up the nights.

Well, a few anyway. When I didn't have to babysit or work or worry about something, I'd pile into a friend's car, and we'd cruise into their territory, only a few miles away, but a whole different world.

They have a swim team. A skate park. Charming shops and parks, and the parents and cops look the other way when the kids race Mommy's and Daddy's cars.

Or when they demolish their boyfriend's car with a crowbar. I'm not entirely sure that story is true, but it's fun to think about.

Of course, the Falls has their dumps. Their bad parts and poor people, but they also have mansions, parties, and local celebrities. Jared Trent—a former racer who's on TV a lot and his sister-in-law, Juliet, whose novels were on my high school reading list.

The Falls were always better than us, and they knew it.

There are some things we know how to do, though.

I cruise into town, winding through the neighborhoods that I remember wishing I could live in when I was a kid. Green lawns, porch lights, the scent of Dad cooking burgers on the grill in the backyard.

But when I grew up, I realized there was a vast difference between the appearance and the reality. Inside all of these beautiful bullshit houses were liars just like everywhere else. Fuck the Falls.

I turn onto High Street and slide into a spot on the curb, gazing around at all the businesses, some open but most closed for the night. The bakery, Frosted, is probably closed for the season already. The owner, I hear, is still a college student who's probably back at school by now. The sign for Rivertown glows above, the bulbs illuminating one after another down the letters and back up, and I see the place lit up inside, all the Pirates hanging out, filling the place.

"Aro, they won't let me in," Tommy says again.

Two women run past, moms jogging their kids in strollers, and I breathe out a laugh. *This place...* "Let's go."

I get out of the car, dumping the baton in the back seat,

and look back to make sure she follows. I don't know what she's afraid of, but tonight, she's with me.

We stroll across the street, and I pull up my hood. I open the door and step inside, music filling the place like a bar, someone's vape smoke hovering around the ceiling lamps in the dim light.

Rivertown is controlled chaos, and the kids are too stupid to see it. Their parents built a nice place for them to get together that looks like a bar, with booths and private seating in the adjoining tunnels in the back, a great menu, pool tables, and loud music, but it's right in the center of town in full view of traffic cams and a block from the police station.

They run around like they own the whole world, but I guess wolves born on a leash never know they shouldn't be wearing one.

I look around, seeing a few eyes turn my way like they do to see who's entered the chat, and hold back my amusement. I bet they all have names like Hudson and Harper.

Walking to the bar, I feel the room shift a little, the chat faltering and whispers rising above the jukebox. I don't belong here.

They know who I am. Now let's see what happens.

I turn, resting my back against the brass railing and survey the room as Tommy sets up position next to me.

"You want to park, you have to order," a voice says.

I turn my head, eyeing the bartender and seeing realization cross his face. "Never mind," he says, backing off.

I think we sell him weed.

I gaze at the tables filled along the wall, spotting Trent and staring until she looks up and stops acting like she doesn't know I'm here.

It's kind of fun knowing that Jared Trent's daughter owes me money.

But someone is at her side, watching us, and I feel his disdain from here.

He's not looking at me, though. His hard eyes stare motionless and filled with intolerance at the kid next to me, and I glance between her and him, seeing her eyes drop to the floor like she's trying to disappear.

They won't let me in there.

"This is your town," I tell her. "Why do they hate you?"

She just shakes her head, though, and I look back at the table, my anger rising. She's thirteen. What the fuck is their problem?

"Are you holding?" some guy asks from my side.

"No."

He walks off, and I shake my head. It's funny how they like me here more than Tommy. I guess I'm more useful.

Trent rises from the table, walking straight for me. She stops at my side, like she's ordering from the server. "I'll have it tomorrow," she says in a quiet voice. She grabs a straw and reaches over the bar, making herself a soda.

"Dylan," the bartender scolds.

But I reply, "Now."

"I don't have it," she says.

"Now." I glare at Blue Eyes, relishing this and hoping I have a reason to hit her. "Or the next time you see me, it'll be in front of your parents or at school."

"Screw yourself." She sips her drink, batting her eyelashes. "I shouldn't have to pay for bad merchandise. Keep coming at me, and you won't have a customer to speak of."

I can't stop myself. I slam the drink out of her hand and yank her down by the hair.

"Ah!" she growls. "Get off me!"

The crowd howls, people gathering around, and she grabs my legs, throwing her shoulder into my stomach. She rams me into the bar, and I crash into the stools, the wood digging into my back.

"Ugh," I growl, dragging her to the floor with me.

Scrambling, I grip her collar, holding her away as I flip her over and climb on top.

"Get off her!" someone shouts, a dozen legs moving around us.

Someone grabs at my coat, but they're gone before I have a chance to throw them off.

"You make everything worse," a man's voice says.

Trent hits my face, and I rear my fist back, so happy she doesn't have my money. This is more fun.

But before I can bring the punch down, someone grabs the back of my jacket with both hands and hauls me off of her. They shove me back and dive down, taking her by the arms and pulling her to her feet.

Dressed in long black shorts, a white T-shirt, and running shoes, he checks her face, but she pushes his hands away, looking around him to scowl at me like I'm dirt.

Brat. I push past him, going after her again, but he takes me by the collar and walks my ass backward, setting me away from her. "Back off!" he shouts.

He starts to turn away, but then I see him do a double-take. His blue eyes drop, his dark brow furrows, and he moves my hair away to look at my neck.

I shove his hand away, baring my teeth, but he's already seen what he needs to see.

He shoots the girl behind him a glare. The long green line inked through the word *RIVER* vertically down the side of my neck means Green Street.

And now he knows she asked for this.

She looks away from his stare, like she's in trouble. Like...

He's going to scold her.

Then it hits me. It's not her boyfriend. This is Hawken Trent. Her cousin.

Well, well, well, Mr. Class President. Just graduated. Now I remember. He's taller than he looks in the sports section of the local newspaper.

"Get her out of here," the blond, whom I realize is Kade Caruthers, calls out.

Both of them are football players. Or Hawke was anyway.

Someone advances on me, but Hawke rubs a hand through his short, black hair. "Wait," he grits out.

I watch him take out his wallet, seeing the muscles in his jaw flex.

He takes out some cash. "How much?" he asks, not looking at me.

But Dylan Trent bursts out, "Hawke, don't pay her a cent! She sold me a broken phone!"

"You lying little shit," I growl, peering around her cousin to her, my skin hot.

But Tommy answers him. "Four hundred," she pipes up.

I hear him counting out the cash, but I stare at Dylan, watching her pout.

She damn well hides behind him, though, doesn't she? Her friends crowd around her, some blonde girl shaking her head at me.

Hawke holds out his hand to Kade. "Give me your cash."

The kid's mouth hangs open, and Hawke arches a brow.

Finally, he sighs and digs out his money, handing it to Hawke.

He counts it out, Dylan flips me off, and I smile like I'm about to have some fun. *I'm going to cut you up so bad.*

Hawke shoves the money into my hand, and I look down at it in my fist, the dirt under my nails visible through the chipped, three-week-old red polish on my fingers.

"You got any more problems with anyone in the Falls," he says, "you go through me. I don't want to see your drugs, your shitty stolen merchandise, or your Weston Rebel bullshit in our nice town. Got it?"

The room is quiet except for the speakers still playing music, everyone staring at Tommy and me. But then...someone laughs quietly, and I raise my eyes, seeing the blonde next to Dylan covering her shit-eating smile with her hand.

The walls close in.

I'll give her something to smile about.

I fling the money back at him, and before anyone knows what's happening, I ball my fists and shoot out my leg, the toe of my boot landing right in her fucking mouth.

Screams erupt, I lunge, but Hawken Trent grabs me, lifting me off of my feet before I can reach his cousin next. He flips me over his shoulder, and I flail, trying to get free.

But I see her all right. On the floor. Blood spilling between her fingers as she holds them over her mouth and screams like a baby. People crowd around, trying to help her, but he carries me away, out to the sidewalk.

"Jesus Christ," he says through his teeth, dumping me on my feet and backing away. I tongue the coppery taste on the inside of my lip. His cousin landed one good one on me during that fight.

He stares down at me, and my stomach drops a little at the color of his eyes. "You know what percentage of people in jail are repeat offenders?" he asks me. "Is that the life you want?"

Please...

Tommy comes to stand at my side, and I pull my hood back up. "You won't be there to protect your girls this fall, Mr. Class President."

"I won't be far." He looks like he's holding back a smile as he backs up toward the club again. "I don't want to see your ass back here. Leave!"

Pulling open the glass door, he enters the club again, and I can't help it. I smile.

So arrogant. All of them.

I got her good, though. I got them both.

I grab Tommy and push her toward the car, both of us climbing in.

"Gotta be honest," she says, buckling her seatbelt. "I'm a little unimpressed. So far we have no money, and two men have succeeded in shaking you down tonight. Maybe you should let me try."

I smile, pulling out the wallet I grabbed from his back pocket when he carried me out of the bar. I hold it up, peel it open, and find exactly what I'm looking for. The key card to JT Racing headquarters.

I know all the Pirates. And what they're good for.

"You can help." I hold up the card to her. "Interested?"

Her eyes go big, she grabs the key, and she laughs. "Hell yes."

I start the car and drive off, dialing my old foster brothers. Nicholas picks up.

"I need you," I tell him.

FALLS

CHAPTER TWO

Hawke

I watch her speed off, not taking the direction home, but I don't care to worry about it.

What was Dylan thinking? Weston is bad enough, but Green Street won't stop. She doesn't want them on her ass.

I see Schuyler covering her mouth, blood dripping.

It was bad back in the day, the rivalry. But only to the point of being mildly dangerous—the clashes at the Loop between the Pirates from the Falls and the Rebels from Weston—but things had changed a lot in twenty years. Our town got richer—with people like my father and my uncles succeeding and giving back with jobs and events that brought in revenue—and Weston got poorer.

But struggle isn't always a bad thing. Only when we're desperate do we dig in, and Weston found ways to brace themselves. They've risen. Disgracefully, but still.

And all in ways that are illegal.

Bella and Socorro pull Schuyler off the floor, and I approach. "Are you okay?" I ask her.

She just turns, whimpering and running for the bathroom. Her friends follow.

She's bleeding hard. She'll need stitches, probably. Pretty sure she's never been hit in her life.

I start to follow her but stop. She broke up with me. She'll ask for help if she needs it.

Spotting Dylan, I pull out a chair at her table, Kade taking a seat next to me. He holds our cash in his hand. "We need to send a message," he tells me. "We've got enough problems with St. Matt's, and I don't want you leaving me to deal with Weston, too."

I start at Clarke University, my dad's old school, in a couple of weeks, and Kade will be a senior. He bitches about what's ahead of him, but honestly, he can't wait. Grudge Night, senior year, football, and Rivalry Week—he's waited for his chance to be in charge.

"She's not over here as a Rebel," I retort. "She's a shallow, senseless, little punk, soon-to-be inmate at Stateville Prison." And then I give Dylan a look, only her long, dark lashes visible from underneath her baseball cap as she plunges the tortilla chip into the queso. "If you all would just stop buying from them..."

She shoots her eyes up. "I had no choice," she tells me. "Every time I had a missing assignment last year, my dad took my phone. I need a spare before school starts."

"Or you could just stop missing assignments?"

"Can't." She shrugs, stuffing the chip into her mouth. "Too busy looking for you while you're skipping classes."

I shake my head.

But I shut up. She always does that. That younger cousin thing, looking at me with her mom's storm-blue eyes and her dad's big, bright smile that she uses a hell of a lot more than he does and saying that she's just following my example and she'll do as I do, not as I say. I have a perfect GPA. I can afford to miss classes.

"Here." Kade hands me my money, pocketing the rest that was his.

I take it and dig in my back pocket for my wallet. "And all that bullshit with St. Matt's is on you," I tell him. "You can deal with your own brother."

He purses his lips and looks off, knowing I'm not leaving him with any messes that I made.

I switch hands, checking the other pocket.

"Well, if we're all just too small town for you, Hawke," Dylan chimes in, "why'd you decide to go to college so close to home?"

But as I dig in my pockets and come up empty, realization hits and Dylan's words are lost on me.

"What's the matter?" she asks.

I jerk my eyes up to her and then to the door. *Shit!*

Dylan gasps. "She didn't..." She gapes at me, and then... she throws her head back, pealing with laughter. "Oh my God. That's fantastic."

Seriously? Whose side is she on?

An alert hits on my phone, and I pull it out, staring at the notification.

JT Alarm 08 Activated. Do you need assistance?

Oh, no. My wallet. My card key to the race shop.

I dart my gaze up to Dylan. "Move!" I order and then look to Kade. "Now!"

They don't ask why. They bolt, scrambling out of their chairs and follow me out of the bar. We dash across the street to Kade's truck. He tosses me the keys. "I can't afford another ticket," he says. "You drive."

We climb in, and I start the engine, shifting into *Drive* before speeding away from the curb. The seatbelt alarm sounds, but I ignore it, turning left and then right. The shop is less than two blocks away.

"I'll text Dirk and Stoli," Kade says, tapping away on his phone and messaging our friends. "We may need help."

I hope not. She'd better not be bringing more of them over here.

I jerk the wheel, barreling into the parking lot and hear the alarm. I slam on the brakes.

Dylan's phone rings, and I jump out of the car, looking for the girl.

Or Tommy.

For a light, a movement. Anything.

I spot the broken glass, one of the panels on the front of the shop shattered on the floor inside, and I peer up to the second floor, still not seeing her.

Fuck it. I step inside, not caring if she has a weapon on her.

"Hi," I hear Dylan say behind me. "Code 9556732, last name Trent, password Madman."

She follows me, her phone pressing over her light brown hair to her ear underneath, but Kade pulls her back. "Dylan, no." He points to the glass and her flipflops. "Stay here."

She nods, trying to listen to the security company on the phone. "Yeah, send the police."

My parents and Dylan's are out of town tonight, but they'll still get the alert. They'll be calling any minute.

I look around, the whole place dark and not a sound. I scan the first floor, taking inventory of my uncle Jared's equipment, my dad's computers, the bikes and cars—everything in the same exact state as when I left earlier today.

"I don't see anyone," Kade says.

"Okay," Dylan says into her phone. "Thanks." She hangs up, looking at us. "Cops are on their way."

Other than the broken window, everything's fine. There's no sign of her or the Dietrich kid. What...? Did she really just come here to break a window? Why steal my wallet then?

"She had to know there'd be a security system," Dylan says. "This isn't smart."

No, it's not. Why—?

Then it occurs to me. I pat down my pockets again, noting both my missing wallet and my missing keys.

My chest caves. "It's not smart," I exhale. "It's a decoy."

Kade and Dylan glance at each other, but I run. "Stay here!" I shout, racing to the truck. "Handle the police."

"Hawke!" Dylan calls.

Followed by Kade. "Hawke!"

But I'm gone. Slamming the door, I take off, flying out of the lot and speeding home. Son of a bitch.

She knew we had a security system. She's not smart. She's a diabolical little shithead, who knew exactly what to do to get me and the police anywhere but where she was going to be.

"Goddammit." I lock my jaw, more disappointed in how I let this happen.

When did she get my wallet and keys? It had to be when I was carrying her. How did I not feel that? "For Christ's sake," I hiss, feeling stupid.

I drive down Fall Away Lane but kill the headlights and pull over to the side, a few houses down from mine. I don't want her to know I'm coming.

She was alone—or only with the kid anyway—at the bar, and I'm not scared of Tommy Dietrich. As long as the Rebel didn't call in backup from Weston, I'll get her out of my house before she has the chance to fuck anything up.

Climbing out of the truck, I walk down the street and look around, but I don't see any cars I don't recognize. She would've kept her getaway car close, but not obvious.

I stop on the sidewalk, turn right, and look at my house with Dylan's next to it on the left. My dad and uncle went to Chicago to meet with an engineer they're looking to hire for the business. They took my mom, Tate, and James.

Which they've been posting pictures of all day on social media.

Fucking hell. She knew the houses were empty when she saw Dylan and me at Rivertown.

I approach the tree situated between the two homes, watching the windows for any sign of the two girls.

And then movement catches my eye, and I jerk my head left, seeing a flashlight in the second-floor hallway of Dylan's house.

I race up the tree, the branches of the old maple spreading between Dylan's bedroom and mine. I hop up onto the thick arm leading to the French doors of her room and see them cracked open.

Slowly, I swing my legs over the railing and then dig out my phone, texting Kade and then silencing the ringer.

"Shhh!" I hear someone say from somewhere in the house.

Everything in my body tenses.

I step inside my cousin's room, glancing around as I make my way for the door.

A small laugh drifts in from the hallway, and I have only a second to hide as the door opens and Tommy Dietrich walks in.

I grab her.

She yelps, but I cover her mouth, wrapping my arm around the kid and holding her tight. She doesn't fight, though. She barely breathes, like a frightened, little rabbit.

I lean down, whispering into her ear. "You're going to go home, understand?"

She nods quickly.

"And you're going to stop choosing losers as friends just because they're giving you a bit of attention," I tell her.

She nods again.

She's hanging in Weston because they're the only friends she can find.

"Leave," I tell her. "Quietly."

I release her, slowly stepping away and watching her climb back out the French doors. She doesn't look back as she hurriedly climbs into the tree, and I turn, grabbing the door handle and pulling open Dylan's door.

But then Tommy's scream hits my back. "He's in the house!" she shouts.

I blink long and hard, resisting the urge to curse at a thirteen-year-old. *Goddammit.*

I move into the hallway, closing Dylan's door behind me, and pause a moment. She might have a weapon. I peer over the railing, not seeing any sign of her, and look around at the doors on the top floor. My aunt and uncle's room, James's room, a spare room, bathrooms, and closets. The downstairs office and Jared and Tate's bedroom would be the primary targets. They have the most valuables.

I step down the stairs, heel to toe, and keep my eyes and ears peeled.

I open my mouth, hesitating, but she knows I'm here. "So how did you know my cousin's windows were the only ones without an alarm?" I call out in a loud voice. "Maybe you've been simmering on this job for a while?"

Did she come to Rivertown with the purpose of getting my wallet and keys? Or Dylan's?

"Or maybe you just got lucky," I add.

I stop at the bottom, taking in the dark kitchen to my left and turning toward the living room to my right. The TV is too big to carry, and they don't collect antiques or art like Madoc and Fallon. I turn around the banister, looking down the hall toward the home office. That room is worth raiding, especially since Jared has a safe he's never developed the patience to open, so there are things laying everywhere.

Like petty cash for the house and bank registers he brings home from the shop every night if he gets lazy and doesn't take time to deposit them.

I step toward the office. "You could've robbed the race shop, you know?" I call out. "I would've let you steal anything." The floor creaks under my feet, and I pause. "It's insured and not worth the risk."

I take another step and then another.

"But coming to our homes was a mistake, Rebel." I approach the door. "Drop what you took. And leave."

I reach out to take the handle, but footfalls hit the floor above me, and I hear the whine of Dylan's door hinges.

Shit!

I bolt back into the foyer, and I grab hold of the banister, launching myself up the stairs three at a time.

I run back into Dylan's room and see the girl Tommy was with climbing out the window and into the tree.

"Stop!" I yell.

She may not have been able to steal a lot, but she took something.

Chasing after her, I jump up, grabbing hold of the limb above and swinging my body, landing on the lower branch I climbed up on.

She swings around, I stop, and so does she, both of us watching each other.

I look down. A fall won't kill us, but it could definitely break a leg.

"Drop what you took," I bite out, taking a step.

She does the same, backing up slowly as I advance. Past the trunk and onto the limb leading over to my house. And my window.

I flex my jaw. "If you step one foot in my room..."

"I know," she says, and I can't see her smile, but I hear it. "I've heard about you."

I'm sure she has. People love to talk shit, and everyone believes everything they hear.

But that part's true. I don't like people in my stuff.

Her boots, the right one with duct tape wrapped around the toe, move steadily over the limb, one behind the other. I don't know if anyone other than family has ever been in this tree. At least not in the last thirty years or so.

"Dylan's mom grew up in this house," I tell her, stalling and keeping her attention on me as I tilt my head toward the window behind me. Then, I gesture to the one she's moving toward. "Her dad grew up over there. This tree connected their bedrooms as kids."

I step and so does she.

"You've heard the stories, right?" I stalk her. "The girl who fought back? Childhood best friends who became enemies who became lovers?" Jared and Tate stories still circulate around my old high school. Dylan's getting really sick of it, poor girl feeling like she has to crowbar a car to prove whose kid she is. "Tate was kind of lonely as a child," I tell her. "So was Jared. This tree was their bridge to each other when they needed a friend. When they needed the sadness to go away. When they needed a different view."

A black bag hangs across her body, one of her hands on the strap, and the other holding the branch above her.

I keep going, keep moving. "I guess that's why our parents opted for no alarms on our windows," I explain. "They wanted us to have each other if we were ever afraid to talk to them. This tree is family. It'll never die. But you will, kid. And probably young, too."

Because you do stupid things.

She stops, and the light from my porch just reaches her midnight eyes.

"Don't you want to enjoy a little more freedom first?" I tease.

Before you inevitably get arrested.

But she's not smiling. Her gaze hardens. "Freedom?" she whispers. "What is that?"

Her eyes shimmer, and I realize they're wet. I go still.

"Is freedom having no responsibilities? No job?" she asks me. "Or a job that pays enough to feed and shelter you for longer than just today?"

Chills spread all over my body, and I open my mouth to reply, but I don't know what to say.

"I'm not a kid." She snickers like I'm so naïve. "You are."

And she spins, yanking up my bedroom window and diving inside.

I chase after her, climbing into my room and racing through my door as she thunders down the stairs and into the foyer of my parents' house.

I come up on her tail, just as she's about to reach the front door, and catch her, both of us crashing into the wall.

She growls, whipping around to get out of my hold, but she pulls too hard, and we both tumble to the floor. Pain shoots through my elbow, and she flips over onto all fours, scrambling to her feet. But I grab the hood of her jacket and yank her back down, coming down on top to straddle her.

Ah!" she yells, her arms flying out, trying to hit me.

I grab her bag and pull it off her, tossing it to the side before I pin her hands above her head and glare down.

She opens her mouth, but she doesn't say anything. Just fixes a snarl on her face and glowers back up at me. I almost smile, liking the nice, hot shot of adrenaline running through my chest. My dad on my back, Schuyler—it's been weeks. I appreciate the distraction. I'm blowing off more steam than an afternoon at the gym.

I cock my head. "Need a ride home?"

She raises her chin, getting all tough, and I almost laugh. Her black eyes under long lashes promise pain and suffering if I don't get off her, but it's a good look on her.

"I'll give you one, if you want," I taunt. "My cousins will help. A whole escort of Pirates back to that shithole, Weston."

I see her jaw clench, but still, she doesn't spit any vitriol back at me. She's used to not giving an inch. She's used to people taking it.

I pat her coat, feeling a lump in one of the pockets. I dig inside, and she tries to fight me off with her one free hand. "Get off!" she shouts.

I pull out her wallet and flip it open. I read her driver's license. "Aro Marquez. 686 East 3rd Street, Weston." I close it and stuff it back into her jacket. "It's up there forever now." I gesture to my head and then pin her other hand back down. "Stay out of the Falls, or I will make trouble for you." I lean down, and she tries to jerk her face away, but she has nowhere to go. "And I won't even need my daddy or my credit card to do it."

I know what their preconceived notions are about the Falls. We're all spoiled trust fund babies to her, even though she's lying on the floor of my house and can plainly see it's not a mansion.

I roll to my feet and grab a fistful of her coat, pulling her up with me.

I stare down at her. "You shouldn't have come alone, honey."

But a honk sounds outside, and we hear shouts. "Aro!"

I look down at her. She smiles.

Oh, what the fuck?

She shoves me in the chest, and I stumble back, crashing into the entryway table. The dish of keys falls to the floor, shattering.

The next thing I know, the alarm screams in my ear, and I flinch, watching her run out the front door.

I follow, seeing cars in the street, headlights blinding me as I dig in after her and watch her legs disappear ahead.

"Hawke!" I hear Kade, his pounding footsteps approaching as Dirk and Stoli flank him.

I look over. "Where's Dylan?"

"At the shop with the cops," he says.

I'd texted him to get him over here, but I'd wanted to make sure Dylan wasn't alone first.

A small group of people enter on my right, and I look over, seeing the girl, all tall and brave now that her boys are here.

I lock eyes with Hugo Navarre. He was a senior when I was a freshman. We never met on the field, but he's stayed involved in the bullshit between our towns.

"Well, well, well..." He strolls over, leading his pack—Nicholas behind him and Axel on his right. "How old are you now, Trent?"

Old enough to do serious time if I hurt you, if that's what you're asking. Which is what he's asking. He wants to make sure I know that I can't hide behind being a minor now.

"I need to search her," I tell him.

I felt something else in her pocket.

He grins, looking at his lapdog. "Did you steal something?" he asks her, but it sounds like he's talking to his puppy who can do no wrong.

She doesn't answer, just looks at me, a gleam in her eyes.

Hugo just laughs. "Sorry about that, man."

But I look directly at her. "Empty your pockets."

She doesn't.

My phone vibrates in my pocket, and I pull it out, checking the screen. "That alarm triggered the security company, which is calling my phone right now," I warn her. "When I don't answer, they'll send the police. Empty your pockets and then run. You have about four minutes."

Her gaze doesn't leave mine.

I step toward her, Hugo and his boys shifting to be ready. "Don't touch her," he says.

Her crew inches closer. "Not unless you want to pay," he adds.

Her eyes flash to her boss, and I see the alarm.

Hugo walks up to me. "I'll let you pat her down all night for the right price." He looks over his shoulder at her. "You ready to start working like a big girl?"

"Hugo..." Their friend Nicholas moves forward, like he's about to intervene, and I almost smile. Not all is well on Green Street.

But Hugo knows who's in charge. "I know she's not much to look at," he tells me. "But maybe a street girl is exactly what you need. It gets better once she bathes. I promise."

Some of the guys behind him break into laughter, and I glance at the girl, her expression not so steel anymore. She stares at the ground, her lips tight.

You ready to start working like a big girl?

39

Is he trying to turn her out? How old is she?

My father would kill these guys.

Axel saunters toward me. "Weston girls are hotter anyway. You know that."

"But if there's more than one of you, it's extra," Hugo adds, looking around at Kade, Dirk, and Stoli.

I hear Stoli speak up. "Nah. I don't want any of that."

"It'll be too much work hosing her down," Dirk says.

"Shut up," I grit out.

I move toward her. "Come here."

Her eyes flick up to mine, and I hold out my hand.

She looks at it, and I know she won't take it, but I have to try. She shouldn't be with these people.

"Come here," I say again.

But she just shakes her head. "Fuck you."

I pull the money Kade gave back to me out of my pocket and offer it to Hugo. His eyebrows shoot up, a gleam in his eyes.

He takes it.

"Come here now," I order her.

She shakes her head, backing up to run, but Hugo takes her by the collar. "No!" She fights, and I take a step, ready to help, but this is what I want. I want him to force her to me.

"I told you not to come home empty-handed," he says in her face.

He pushes her over to me, but she bites down on his hand, his growl piercing the air. I lunge for her, but she stumbles backward, out of Hugo's hold and fumbles to get out of my reach.

Sirens blare, lights flash down the street, and she looks at me, fear written all over her face.

No, not fear.

Fright.

She's afraid of me.

Did she think I was actually buying her? I take a step, but she whips around, running away. I spot something green hanging out of her pocket, the police close in on us, and I watch as she jumps into a black Mercedes and speeds off.

I swing around as she zooms past, watching her go, and something nips at me as the wheels in my head turn. *Something green...*

Hugo chases after her. "Aro!" he yells. They all run in her wake, but she charges away, turning right, and peels around the corner, out of sight.

"Fuck!" Hugo rages. "Aro!"

"The trunk!" Axel shouts at him as if reminding him about something.

They go after her on foot, disappearing down the next street, and I realize...

That was Hugo's car she took. She left Rivertown in a Jeep Cherokee. I turn my head, spotting the old navy-blue vehicle way down in front of Mr. Woodson's house.

She took the wrong car.

Guilt hits me. *She took the closest escape.*

But then, it hits me. *Green...*

"Shit," I whisper.

It was a ribbon hanging out of her pocket. A tattered. Green. Ribbon.

I turn to Kade, pointing to his truck. "Go!"

We run, Stoli and Dirk following, all of us piling into the cab. I start the engine and take off. "She's got Jared's charm," I spit out, racing around the corner.

"The thumbprint?" Kade asks.

"It was in Dylan's room." I hit the gas, not caring if I get a ticket. "The Rebels would love to have that fucking trophy."

41

The thumbprint belongs to Dylan's mom. She made it when she was a child, and there's a whole story about it between Dylan's parents. It's special. Jared always had it on him for races, and last year, he gave it to Dylan for luck on the track. It's worth five cents and our family's most valuable heirloom.

"Goddammit." I zip around a car and speed up on another. Hugo and his guys appear ahead, and I fly past, watching them in my rearview mirror.

"I don't see her," I pant, searching the road ahead.

But Stoli speaks up. "It's just a piece of clay, Hawke."

"And the only thing of value to Jared, other than his family," Kade fires back. He looks to me. "Don't lose her. I want it out of her dirty, thieving hand."

Where the fuck did she go? I spin around the corner, race down the empty street, and look left and then right. Taillights catch my eye, and I jerk my head, seeing a car enter the park.

Those aren't Mercedes taillights, but I recognize the vehicle. I hit the brakes, a screech filling the air around us.

"Ugh, there goes ten dollars' worth of tire," Kade grumbles.

Reversing, I turn and hit the gas, driving into Eagle Point, around the bend, and up the lane. The chain-link fence lays across the road, the back entrance of the park only for people entering on foot.

Did she do this? Is she trying to get arrested?

I drive in, the fence grinding under my tires, and survey the area, looking for any sign of her. Picnic tables and playgrounds decorate the landscape, along with a pavilion and amphitheater, and then there's the...

I glance left, seeing the pond.

The Mercedes is there, driven to the edge of the bank that overlooks a fish pond about ten feet down. The driver's side door hangs open.

I turn, hurrying over.

"Where is she?" Kade asks.

I pull up to the car, leaving it running as I jump out. "I don't know."

I stop at the edge of the basin, looking down into the water below. Dylan's parents were married here. It's a small body of water, man-made, surrounded by a rock deck and rock walls. A small waterfall spills below me, a tiny stream leading to the water. It's blue-green in the sunlight, but tonight it's black.

Where the hell is she?

I head back to the Mercedes, searching the car, but there's no sign of her.

The trunk.

That's what Axel had said. He was worried about the trunk. I pop the lid and look inside, two black duffle bags next to each other and stuffed in the back.

I pull one out, unzipping it.

Stacks of cash sealed in Ziploc bags cover the bottom, two large, red bricks of coke on top.

Son of a bitch.

Kade peers inside. "Is that...?"

"Yep."

"In Shelburne Falls?" he blurts out.

I shake my head. He doesn't let himself see things he doesn't want to see, including the fact that our nice, little town has a dark side.

I yank out the second bag, finding more money.

I don't give a shit about the cash, but if these drugs belong to who I think they do, turning them in to the cops is useless. My gut twists, knowing what my dad would do. Especially after what happened a few years back.

All this shit does is hurt people.

I snatch up the two packages of drugs and head down the small hill, digging my pocket knife out.

Kade jumps in front of me. "Hawke, what are you doing?"

"Move."

But I don't wait. I veer around him, unsheathing the blade.

"Hawke!"

I stop at the fence that separates us from a hundred-foot drop off a cliff that overlooks the river with barges, the dam, and Weston on the other side.

Stabbing the package, I slice through it, white powder clouding the air, and I rip it open, holding my breath as I spill the fucking shit over the side of the cliff. The wind picks it up, and a cloud of white sweeps over the tops of the trees below, drifting south.

"No!" I hear a girl's howl and footsteps pounding toward me.

But I already have the second one torn open, and I shake it hard, emptying the contents.

"Shit!" she cries. "Stop!"

I spin around, chucking both packages over the side and see the girl, grabbing her collar as I shout at Kade. "Go! Take the guys, and go now!"

"Hawke—"

"Just go!" I yell. "Don't leave Dylan's side. I'm right behind you."

He hesitates, looking like he wants to argue, but then he twists around and runs. Stoli and Dirk follow him.

I take hold of her with both hands, backing her up to the tree behind her.

"I'm dead," she murmurs. "What did you do?"

Reaching into her pocket, I pull out the charm and hold it up. "That's all I wanted."

She slams me in the chest, baring her teeth. "Don't touch me."

I almost laugh, because not once did it ever occur to me to touch her how she thinks I would.

But it's not funny. Nothing at all is funny about the situation she's found herself in. "You shouldn't go back to them." I tuck the charm away in my pocket and meet her eyes. "Go get yourself a real job and re-evaluate your friend-ships, honey. Have a nice life."

I turn to leave, but someone is there. I halt, seeing Of-ficer Reeves.

Shit.

He stands there, out of uniform and alone, approaching us. "Hawke."

I feel the girl at my side, and my legs are suddenly too heavy.

"You okay?" he asks me.

I steel my jaw. His Challenger idles behind him, the headlights off, and he slides his hand into his leather jacket. He's not on duty. I wish he was. He's more of a problem when he's not.

"Miss Marquez," he says, nodding. "Quite the mess you've made. Are you armed today?"

I glance at her, but she stares at him, not responding. That look is in her eyes again. The fear. Just a bit, but it's there.

Reeves's Challenger is the car I saw entering the park, and I followed, because he was probably looking for her too. Hugo would've called him, because Hugo's not the one in charge. Not ultimately.

I've known about Reeves and Green Street for a while. And who really runs it.

"You can go home," he tells me. "Your parents will be worried with all the commotion over there. I'll take it from here." He walks toward us. "Tell your mom I said hi."

I see the girl out of the corner of my eye, and I know...

She's going to take punishment for this. I don't know what I was thinking.

"I should come with you both," I finally say. "Give my statement. I dumped some drugs I found."

He stops, his gaze hard. "You destroyed evidence?"

Evidence. I want to laugh. *No, I just cost you thousands of dollars.*

But I just say, "Yes, sir."

"No," the girl blurts out. "He didn't. He's just trying to be the hero. It was me."

I look over at her. Why is she lying? He's going to hurt her. Or worse.

"That's...unfortunate," he says in a low voice, eerily calm.

Goddammit. Is she actually trying to help me? I'm not in danger from him. All of my friends know I'm here. I'll be missed if I disappear into an unmarked grave, and my uncle is the best attorney in the state. I'm not in any real trouble.

What will he do to her?

"Hawke, you can go," he says again.

No.

He calls her over. "Come here, girl."

I hear her breath shake, but slowly, she passes me, lifting her chin.

My mind races. Something's not right. He's not taking her in, and even if he does, he'll have time to do anything he wants to her first. No one believes kids like her.

46

Like my dad when he was her age.

I walk past him, away from the pond, leaving her behind, and knowing there's nothing I can do. I can call more police. Make sure she's not alone with him.

But then he has her in jail. With full access.

And if she's released, she's a target.

It happens. Shit happens every day, all over the planet, and you know there will be more. More people like her who make all the wrong decisions and get used. It's just life.

It's her fault anyway. She robbed us and stole her boss's car. She got herself here. She's a mess.

And she took the blame for me. *Stupid girl.*

I walk past his car, and I'm moving before I think too hard. I yank open his car door and climb in, pushing away all the panic of what I'm about to do. I shift into gear, look ahead, and see them, his hand caressing her face just before it slips up her ski cap and fists her hair.

She winces, and I flip on the headlights.

Reeves twists his head, seeing me in his car, and I hit the gas. I'm not letting some rat punk from Weston take the fall for me, even if everything else tonight is her fault. But even more, I'm not letting him use kids to make money.

"Hawke!" he shouts.

I ram the Mercedes, hitting the gas until it tilts, falls, and rolls down the incline to the pond. It crashes below, all of his fucking money in the trunk, and he releases her, running over and slamming his fist on the hood of the car.

I stop, push open the door, and step out. "Run!" I tell her over the hood.

Her dark eyes stare at me as she breathes hard.

"And that's the last time I help you," I growl at her. "Get out of here!"

I'll get out of this, but she won't.

47

She sidesteps like she hasn't found her legs yet, but then she runs, her hair flying against her back as she disappears into the night.

You're welcome! But I don't say it out loud. No idea if she has a chance, but at least she has tonight.

Reeves starts to go after her, but I swing around the back of his car and shove him to the ground.

"You little shit!" he spits out.

I put my hands up, surrendering, but he climbs to his feet and grabs my head, pulling me to the ground.

We tumble, rolling over the side of the incline, falling over the rocks, and I separate myself, scrambling backward to get away from him.

"Just like your fucking father," he says, advancing on me. "Always in the way."

I flex my jaw as he comes at me with his hands, but then his foot shoots out, taking me off guard. He kicks me, and I plummet into the pond. I gasp, going under, but it's only a few feet deep. I find my footing and rise back up.

I just open my eyes, but he's there, his hand fisting my hair and pushing me back down. What the fuck?

I open my mouth, bubbles rising in front of me, but all I hear is my own muffled yell under the water. I grapple at his hand, trying to free myself, but just as I'm about to pull him in with me, he's gone. My head is free, and I pop up, drawing in a deep breath, sputtering.

What the hell?

Wiping my eyes, I look up and see the Rebel standing over me. To her side, Reeves is on the ground, holding his bleeding ear and shuffling away from her.

She holds a rock in her fist, and for a second, I'm frozen. She didn't run.

Stupid girl.

48

"You're dead," he tells her, almost a whisper.

I climb out of the pond, she looks up at me, and I look at her.

And we move. Slowly away from each other. She drops the rock, running right, and I gaze down at Reeves one last time before I take off to the left.

"Stop!" he bellows after us.

But we're gone, each going our own way, and I know we're both in a shitload of trouble right now, but I just need a second to figure out what to do.

I leap down some more rocks, racing through the park and out the front entrance, going the only place I know I'm safe right now. I just need to catch my breath. I need to think.

Fuck! What the hell happened? What did I do? It went so fast.

I hit a cop. I destroyed his property, and even if my family can protect me from him, they can't protect me from Green Street.

And she'll be dead no matter what.

I whip off my wet T-shirt, slipping it into my back pocket, and keep my eyes peeled as I cross High Street.

Reaching up, I pull the ladder down and climb up the fire escape, hopping up onto the roof. I go to the door in the ceiling that sits between Quinn's bakery and Rivertown. It's only been an hour since I was here last.

I take a moment, trying to calm down. I'm safe up here. The entire roof of this strip of businesses is shielded by the trees on High Street, and I breathe in and out, thoughts racing through my head.

It's okay. I had to do it.

Or maybe I didn't. Maybe there was another way.

Either way, I'll be fine. I can handle this. I'll get out of it. I'll figure it out. When I tell them about Reeves, he'll roll

49

over on his lackeys. They'll get arrested and Green Street will be gone. I won't need to watch my back.

I can buy myself time and get this handled.

Blue and red lights flash in the night, and I head over to the edge of the roof, looking down. Cop cars race down High Street, Reeves probably realizing he had no choice but to report this. He'll need to control the narrative now.

And then, I see her. Running down the sidewalk and more cop cars down the street, about to be on her tail.

She stumbles into the alley, and I follow her around the roof, looking down as she struggles. I hear her breaths from here.

I raise my eyes, seeing the patrol cars close in, slowing as they approach the side street she disappeared onto.

They saw her.

She's about to give out. She can't run anymore.

They'll have her soon.

CHAPTER THREE

Aro

"**I**'m not dead yet," I gasp. "Not yet."

I pull at every door in the alleyway, knowing I'm wasting my time. It's late. Everywhere is closed.

But one gives way, and I don't bother to wonder why. Slipping quickly inside, I search for a lock to keep the police out, but it's dark and all I feel is a deadbolt as my fingers graze the keyhole.

Shit. I choke back my fear, breathing hard as I back away from the door, watching it and knowing. They're going to come through. They will. I don't think they saw where I went, but they'll figure it out. This is it.

Matty. Bianca. Everything will hurt them, and I won't be there.

"Check every door!" I hear a muffled shout.

I draw in a sharp breath, realizing they're right outside. I stumble back, bumping into something, the legs of a table screeching across the floor.

I whip around, seeing I'm in some kind of kitchen just as a cop shouts, "Here!"

No.

I bolt, pushing around the steel worktable and past the ovens lining the wall, the lingering smell of cherries and sugar drifting around me. I dash through the two-way door, into the shop with coffee machines, a display case, and a counter—dishes, cups, and other supplies are stacked underneath.

Frosted. I catch the name of the bakery on one of the paper menus sitting by the register.

Racing to the front door, I yank at it, but it doesn't open. I run to the windows, squeezing between small round tables, and hesitate, gauging whether I should use one of the chairs to break a window. But then lights flash, a cruiser's lights approaching down the street, and I spin around, hiding myself behind the patch of wall between the windows.

"Goddammit," I grit out.

The back door slams shut, and I hear a sharp voice bellow. "You have nowhere to go!" he says.

I stumble off to the side, my eyes planted on the two-way door. I shake my head, my eyes stinging.

"We're coming through the door!" he warns. "Put your hands above your head! Say 'okay' if you understand."

I back up, slamming into the wall, but my palms press against something smoother. Something cold.

I hear their feet shuffle, the walls closing in and at my back. There's no way out. I drop my head, knowing Hugo was right. It was only a matter of time.

The hinges on the two-way door creak as the cops start to come, and I close my eyes, ready.

But then...my stomach drops, and I pop my eyes open as I fall backward.

What?

I gasp, a hand covering my mouth and an arm wrapping around my waist as my body is hauled backward, just as the kitchen door opens.

What the hell?

We stop, they hold me to their body, the entrance in front of me closes, and I watch as the cops enter the eatery, flashlights scanning the space.

No. I jerk away from the hand, but they hold me tight.

"Shhh…" he bites out next to my ear.

The cops approach on the other side of the window, and I jerk to escape, because they'll see me, but the arms won't let me go.

"Don't move," he says in a quiet voice.

We watch the police flash their lights around the shop—around us, over us, but never on us. They pass, never seeing, and search the space, not seeming to notice us here.

Can they not see us?

I remember seeing a large mirror with a gilded frame on the right wall when I burst through the door. I stop breathing for a moment as one of the police officers approaches, two feet in front of us, flashing his light on the glass.

He sees something. I shake.

But then I see it too. Blood. My blood is on the mirror. When did I get hurt? I try to take inventory of my body, but my blood is pumping too hard to notice anything else.

The stranger's hand falls away from my mouth, but I don't move, waiting for the cop to see us.

He stands there, his breath fogging up the glass as he inspects the stain, confirming what he already knew. I was here. Now I'm not.

He backs away, all them making their way through the kitchen door again and disappearing. Off to look for me wherever I'd gone.

Arms release me, and I jerk my head around, seeing Hawken Trent glaring down at me. "This is awesome," he gripes. "What the hell do I do with you now?"

As if I'm his problem and he didn't one-hundred percent escalate what went down tonight right along with me.

He turns and walks away, down a long hallway that's too dark for me to gauge its length or have any clue about where the hell I am. I follow the white of his T-shirt before I lose sight of him.

"What is this place?" I ask. "How do I get out?"

He says nothing, and I stay on his tail, going deeper and deeper into a black void until we come to a short set of stairs leading down. A small, wrought iron chandelier hangs at the bottom, finally giving the space some light.

"How do I get out?" I shout, chasing after him.

I got the cops off my tail. Now I want to leave.

"And where are you going to go?" he retorts.

We descend the stairs, and I follow him as he veers right and steps into a room with no windows, cement walls, and an array of monitors posted above a desk, camera footage displayed on the screens. I catch sight of intersections, the ticket booth for their movie theater, the lanes inside the bowling alley. Rivertown.

"You just lost what...?" he challenges. "Eighty, maybe ninety grand from the looks of what was in that bag, not counting the three-dozen bags of blow hidden underneath." He takes a seat at the desk, observing the screens. "If Green Street doesn't get to you first, that cop will, because I'm guessing it was his. They'll already be staking out your house."

"You think I'm going to sit around here and wait for you to turn me over to them?" I reply. "Or use me for whatever bullshit you have planned? Pinche gringo pervertido pedazo de mierda..."

He glances at me. "Up the stairwell," he says, typing away on his screen and inputting some kind of code. "To the roof. There's a fire escape." He pushes his keyboard away from him, shoves his chair back on its wheels, and rises, reaching behind a hard drive and yanking out cords. "Bye."

I hesitate for just a moment. I didn't expect him to let me leave. Why the hell did he grab me in the first place then?

Spinning around, I stalk out of the room, run back up the stairwell we just came down, but instead of heading back down the dark hallway, I turn right and see a faint light from the other end of the tunnel. I make my way over, coming into a great room, and I stop in my tracks, my mouth falling open a little.

Jesus. I tip my head back and gape at the high ceiling, the night sky visible through the windows above. Couches sit around the space, a TV set up as well as a few industrial-looking chandeliers. A kitchen sits to the back, countertops and appliances making it suitable for someone to live here long term, and I see a spiral staircase leading to a door in the ceiling above.

I rush over, grabbing the railing and launching myself up the stairs, around and around until I come to the top. I hunch over, the space small as I push my weight up onto the hatch and lift it. The welcome fresh air of the evening breeze caresses my face, and I see the tops of the trees that line High Street loom past the expanse of the roof.

I start to push the door all the way open but then stop.

Where will I go? What if I want to get back in?

Does the mirror open from the outside?

I drop the hatch, closing it again and descend the stairs until I can stand upright.

I stop, thinking. He's letting me leave. He's not a threat.

Yet anyway.

And he's right. The police won't be the only ones after me. If I get taken, I'm no good to Matty and Bianca. Right now—maybe—I still have a chance.

I descend the stairs, glancing at the brick wall to my left, in front of the couches, and see words written in large white script. The paint looks a hundred years old, and I don't know what language it is. I don't care.

I search out the rich kid, finding him still in the surveillance room or whatever he calls it. I don't know why he helped me, but I know it wasn't just because he wanted to.

"There will be a warrant out for you," I tell him, staring at his back as he works. "But unlike me, you can just call Mommy and Daddy. The Trents own this town, don't they?"

His father's and uncles' names are everywhere. Billboards, newspapers, businesses...

"Green Street won't come after you," I point out, "especially since you can identify Reeves. I mean, I'll go to jail, but you'll be fine."

He still doesn't turn to look at me, and I stuff my hands into the pockets of my jacket, leveling my gaze on him.

I've seen him plenty of times. I don't think he's ever seen me before tonight. He wouldn't notice someone like me. Unless he's ordering his caramel Frappuccino.

I step up to him. "Give me my phone."

"Give me my wallet."

The image of it plummeting into the pond pops into my head, and he must've seen it happen, which is why he knows I don't have it.

"You can sleep on the couch," he says as he checks the monitors, probably for police. "And there's food in the kitchen. If you leave, you can't get back in without me. Don't tell anyone about this place, and stay out of my way."

And he leaves the room, not once looking at me.

A flashlight sits on the desk, and I grab it, heading out of the room. Going back the way we came in, I climb the stairs again and walk down the long hallway, able to see the route more clearly now. The walls are cement, like the floors, but they're painted black, the ceiling of the tunnel rounded like an arch and cords run along the walls, attaching to lamps overhead every twenty paces.

Coming up to the mirror, I look through the two-way glass and see the bakery is still empty and dark. I push on it, but it doesn't give. I flash my light around the frame, feeling with my hands until I run across a latch. I press it, the mirror giving way with a quiet click and opening into me.

That's what he did. My stomach drops a little, remembering the sensation of falling backward. I step into the shop, casting my eyes and light around one more time to make sure it's empty, and keeping my eye on the street outside the windows for movement.

I search the outside of the mirror, looking for a way in from this side, but as I paw around the ornate gold frame, all I feel are the same straight lines, leaving no space between the mirror and the wall. How many people know about this? Are there more entrances to the hideout?

I pull my sleeve down over my hand and wipe my blood off the mirror. Headlights reflect on the store windows across the street, and I dive back through the secret entrance, pushing it closed. Looks like he didn't lie about that. There's no way in that I can see. He must access it through the roof normally, but then that raises the questions... Is he the only one who knows about this place? How'd he know that it was here to begin with? Is it part of the bakery that his family owns?

I jog back down the hallway, coming into the great room again and see the stars dot the night sky out of the windows. The room is large, but it's long, not wide. Narrow. Sandwiched between two businesses, the pastry shop and Rivertown. This place isn't accessible to either the street or the alleyway, but you can tell it's here from the outside. Unfortunately, most of us and our untrained eyes would just assume the windows belonged to one of the adjoining businesses.

Up the stairs again, and through the door in the ceiling, I step up onto the roof and turn off my flashlight, doing a scan of the empty space. The roof connects to others.

Fire escape. That's what he meant. Over the side of the roof.

Trees dot the curb on High Street, giving me cover from anyone who might be up high enough to see me, but I peer over the edge, noticing the sidewalk is in full view. It's a good spot. I can see whomever would be there. They wouldn't be able to see me.

Taking one more look around, I dive back into the hideout and close the door over my head.

I don't have a phone. I have to get one. I walk as quietly as possible back into the surveillance room, catching sight of Golden Boy on the monitors. He must have cameras inside this place.

He's jump roping. How cute. We're running for our lives, and bro-for-brains is pursuing inner calm with endorphins and green tea.

But I linger on his image for a second, finally forcing my eyes away and kind of wishing the image of him without his shirt was clearer.

Using the mouse, I load the Internet, bringing up my account and type out a message to Hugo. A rare car streams past a few of the screens here and there in front of me, activity dying down in town, and I spot a patrol car turning onto

High Street and hold my breath as it slowly cruises past the bakery and then Rivertown, not stopping.

Don't let him hurt anyone, I type out to Hugo.

Reeves will get his money one way or another. He may not tackle Hawke's high-profile family, but mine is fair game.

I've never asked you for anything, I write. **I'll get the money back**.

I know you will.

Desperation breeds motivation, right? I remind him of his words to me years ago.

But are you desperate enough? he asks.

I stare at his words on the screen, understanding the implied threat.

Leave them alone.

I would never hurt them, Aro. Come home.

I stand there, leaning over the desk and my fingers hovering over the keyboard. This is the part of being in trouble I hate. But it's the part I'm good at. There's never been a decision for me that's as easy as right and wrong. It's simply finding the choice that leaves me with the most options and the least consequences.

If I go back, there are two outcomes with Reeves. A bullet or a bed.

You're only prolonging the inevitable, Hugo types when I don't respond. *Put yourself out of your misery, baby.*

But bullet or bed, my siblings would be safer than they are now. I have to go back.

I log off, close out the screen, and back away like he's about to reach through the monitors and take me.

Why did I do that tonight? Why did Hawken Trent help me? Twice? And why did I help him? I should've let them have him.

I lower my eyes, dazed as my head swims. An array of shit lies all over the desk, and I slowly take it in.

A couple of fake IDs with his picture on them. Newspaper clippings of his dad and uncles, his beautiful family smiling at the opening of some speedway or dining at some restaurant or golfing. A stack of college brochures and so much computer and electronic equipment, books and manuals, information and ambition and possibilities pouring off every shelf and out of every drawer.

He's smart. Educated. Rich. Connected.

He didn't need my help. In a couple of weeks, he'll be starting college, and I'll only be worth the money Hugo and Reeves can make off of me. I'll be dead in five years, and he'll be skiing.

A sound, like singing, breaks through my thoughts, and I look up, seeing movement on the monitors. Two bodies close in around the door on the roof, two more climbing up over the ledge from the fire escapes and coming this way. My heart rate speeds up.

They all stop, looking at something, and I take the mouse, zooming in on one of the faces.

"You know you can't leave now, right, Rebel?" he says, and I notice it's Kade Caruthers.

62

He smiles, and one by one they all disappear through the hole in the top of the roof, entering the hideout.

Can't leave? What? The door in the roof closes, and I suck in a breath, realizing they're inside, and then...

Two clicks reverberate inside the walls, echoing all around me, and I dart my eyes back to the screen, seeing the word LOCKDOWN in a red box at the bottom of the center monitor.

I run, back up the stairs, to the left, and down the hallway to the mirror, knowing I'll run into them if I go the other way. I grab the latch at the top and press it, but nothing moves. Not the latch. Not the mirror.

I press it again. Nothing.

Laughter echoes behind me, no less than five Pirates somewhere in the hideout locked in with me.

I fall back against the cold, cement wall.

I should've left when I had the chance.

FALLS

CHAPTER FOUR

Hawke

"**W**hose phone are you calling from?" my dad asks.

"Mine."

"You have a phone I don't know about?"

I keep my smile to myself, drying the sweat on the back of my neck with a towel and toss it into a bin. "Of course, I have a phone you don't know about," I reply.

Jaxon Trent doesn't raise idiots.

"I can trace it," he tells me.

"You can, but you won't find me."

I hear an exhale over the phone and can just picture my father shaking his head like he does when he realizes the apple didn't fall far from the tree. I wouldn't say I'm smarter than him, not by a long shot, but any solution to a problem I come up with will have the least number of variables. My father is different. He likes variables. Loves surprises. I don't.

"Get home," he says, his voice harder and more urgent. "Goddammit, Hawke. You hit a cop."

"I can explain."

"It's online!" he barks. "People are making up their own explanations. It's too late."

I know. And I know he's right. The longer I hide, the worse it looks. But I don't tell him that getting myself out of trouble isn't all I'm interested in. I have cousins in this town. Little ones who will have to go to school with the shit Reeves is quietly pumping into every pool party, skate park, and soccer mom. My dad and Madoc can help, and I might let them, but I'm not ready to make that decision yet. Not until I know what I'm doing.

"I'm okay," I assure him. "I'm safe."

"Your mom is frantic."

They're probably home from Chicago by now. I'm sure they rushed out of there as soon as they got wind of what happened.

A pang of guilt that I probably should've felt with my dad finally eats away at me when he mentions my mom. She never really did anything to make me feel like I needed to protect her, but I always do.

"I'm in Shelburne Falls," I tell him, knowing he'll tell her, "and I'm not leaving. But I'm not coming home. Not until after Grudge Night. I need time. I'll turn myself in then."

In eight days.

He's quiet for a moment, and voices echo from down the hall. I turn toward it, watching the door to the gym.

"One decision can change your life, Hawke," my dad says in my ear.

He's done nothing but raise me with that thought in mind in everything I do.

"What do I tell the police when they come looking for you?" he asks, just as Dylan, Kade, Stoli, and Dirk burst through the door.

"In about two minutes, you mean?" I tease my dad.

Home is the first place they'll look.

"Just tell them the truth," I reply, turning away from my friends and cousins. "You talked to me. I'm around. You don't know where."

He won't have to lie.

"And the girl?" my dad asks. "Who is she?"

I look behind me again, seeing the Rebel enter the room and looking pissed. He saw her on the video? How much footage is online? Jesus. I need to go back to the monitors and do a deeper sweep.

"She's a nobody," I tell him.

And I hang up, sticking my phone into my pocket as I turn around and grab my water bottle.

"I knew I should've kept this place to myself," I grumble, not meeting Kade's eyes.

"I just had to make sure you were serious." He casts the Rebel a look. "What the hell are you thinking?"

I'm not sure I was thinking at all. I texted him and Dylan a bit ago to let them know the situation. Of course, they rushed over.

The Green Street punk advances on me. "Open the door."

But I ignore her. Looking at Kade, I uncap my water. "I was thinking that I might not know what I can use her for, but I'll keep her for a rainy day. I never throw anything away. You know that."

Laughter echoes around the room.

"Open the door." Her tone deepens, like she's trying not to yell.

"Well, she's here now," Kade goes on, "and she's not going anywhere until you're safe. Can you comprehend the shitstorm she'll bring down on this place if she's let go? They'll know exactly where to find you. Keep it on lockdown and don't let her out."

"Open. The. Door," the Rebel growls.

"Christ…" I wince at her irritating voice. I can only handle one of them at a time. "You make everything worse, you know that?" I tell Kade.

Granted, my actions tonight weren't my best, but he antagonizes every situation, and him and her in the same room is just going to piss me off.

"Open. The. Door," she says again.

But Kade moves into me. "No one asked her to come into our town."

"No one invited her," Stoli adds.

"I kind of invited her…" Dylan mumbles, and I arch a brow, because that's the fucking truth.

Of course, it's not entirely her fault. One way or another that Weston shit always rolls over into Shelburne Falls.

"Did you talk to your dad?" Kade asks me.

"Did you talk to yours?"

I mean, his dad's a lawyer. He can help with the cop.

But Kade whines. "Do you want me to? I'm kind of trying to make him forget how much trouble I am."

"Hello!" the girl yells. "I'm talking to you."

I glance over. "Sit," I tell her. And then I look back at Kade. "I don't want to involve our parents."

"You think they're not already mobilized?" he shouts. "I'm surprised Jared doesn't have an ankle monitor on her by now."

He gestures to Dylan who simply laughs under her breath. Dylan's father is my dad's half-brother. Kade's dad is my dad and Dylan's dad's step-brother. Dylan and I, technically, are blood, but Kade and I are just as much cousins, even though we don't share DNA.

"Open the door," I hear.

I look at Dylan. "Did you bring clothes?"

She holds up a small duffle bag and launches it over to me.

I open it up to see a couple changes of clothes I asked Dylan to bring for the girl. I don't want this chick looking for excuses to leave.

"Like she's going to fit in your stuff, Dylan," Stoli replies with a snide smirk, and I shoot him a snarl to shut the fuck up. I don't need to hear comparisons regarding the size of my cousin's breasts to another girl's.

But Dylan is quick to respond. "But I thought football jerseys are one size fits all."

Kade, Stoli, and Dirk burst into laughter. "You didn't," the latter says, impressed.

Dylan shrugs but can't hide her own self-satisfied smile at bringing a Pirate jersey for the Rebel.

I shake my head, holding up the bag and seeing the delinquent's black attire out of my peripheral vision. "Go find somewhere to sleep," I tell her and toss the bag over.

"You'll look good in our colors," Kade jokes.

"Black and orange Pirate booty, baby!" Dylan howls, Stoli rushes over and lifts her high, everyone laughing.

I can't help but smile at my cousin and how she keeps up. The women in my family are incredible. Not one of them waits for an invitation. Some peoples' ceiling is Dylan's floor.

"Under a black flag we sail!" Dylan boasts as the others cheer.

But then something slams into my chest, and I lose my footing. I step back to right myself as the duffle bag I just threw toward the girl lands back at my feet.

My smile falls, the fun stops, and I see Kade step toward the Rebel. "What's your problem?"

But I hold out my hand, stopping him.

I stare at the bag on the floor. Here comes another fight. I knew she was going to be a waste of time.

"Look at me," she says.

And I hate wasting time.

"I said, look at me, hijo de tu puta madre."

My heart skips a beat, but I do it.

Raising my eyes, I look at her. Her hood is off, her dark brown hair hanging down her back and over her chest where it spills out of the cap, and I see a trail of blood running down her neck. I falter. I didn't notice that before.

There was blood on the mirror, though. It must be on her clothes.

She moves toward me slowly. "You need me, I don't need you," she states. "You have everything to lose, I have nothing. I'll be in prison in two years anyway, right?" She cocks her head at me. "Or dead?"

"Or pregnant," I add.

But I want the words back as soon as they're out. I...

I close my mouth as Dylan shifts off to my left, the room so quiet I can hear the town clock chime through the cement walls, one level up, and two blocks south.

She doesn't say anything, only tips her chin higher as she holds my eyes, but I want to look anywhere but at her. "I didn't mean that," I murmur.

"No, no..." She stops me. "Stick to the narrative. It makes all of this so much easier."

I narrow my eyes, tearing them away. I'm not letting her turn this around on me. Poverty is no excuse to do the things she or any of her pals do. She can make her own opportunity. My dad did.

"Open the door," she says again.

I hold still.

Now she shouts. "Open the door!"

And I do it. Fuck it. I pick out my phone, tap in the code, and I hear the locks release.

Pivoting on her heel, she makes her way toward the door, but I hear her boots halt. She turns her head to look at me. "My name is Aro Marquez," she says.

I meet her eyes.

"Aro Teresa Marquez," she tells me. "And you may not remember me years from now, and maybe no one will think of me and no one will want to, but I was fucking here."

I freeze.

She holds my eyes for a moment, and then...she leaves, disappearing through the door.

The others turn their eyes on me, and a few moments later, I hear a ceiling door slam shut.

"Hawke..." Dylan whispers. "What the hell?"

I don't look at her, the scold in my cousin's voice shaming me enough.

CHAPTER FIVE

Aro

The excess water hangs at the corner of my eye—I feel it wet my skin—but I blink two more times, slow and calm, and it's gone. Staring up, through the steel of the fire escape over my head, I find Vega. From it, I trace a straight line and locate Arcturus. The two brightest stars tonight.

I expand my gaze, taking in both, as well as the other glowing point in the sky, Mars. We can see it every night until next Monday when its orbit takes it out of view again.

I picture the dunes and the rocks I've seen in pictures, the vastness and silence, and even though I'll never view the planet any closer than this, it's the most beautiful thing I'll ever see. It reminds me that I don't matter. Not really. It's been spinning for billions of years, and we've been spinning for billions of years—millions of me's have come and gone. Nothing I do makes any difference.

Seems depressing, but it's really not. It lightens the load to know all I have to worry about is what I'm eating next and where today takes me.

I blink again, making sure the tears are gone, and push off the wall of the alleyway outside Frosted. I can't remember the last time I dropped a tear, but I just came closer than I have in a long time.

His haircut, the smell of his clothes, how they were cut just a little bit better than other guys' to fit him in a way that you could tell why designers get away with charging sixty dollars for a fucking T-shirt...

I barely know what any of that stuff in the surveillance room is or how to work it. He's smart. And he speaks like he's never not been the center of attention.

He has people and college and cash in his wallet. He knows he's important. Why does it bug me so much? I know what they're like. They can't hurt me. Why did I feel so small in there?

I had to get out.

I pull up my hood and stick my hands in my pockets, rounding the corner and jogging down the alleyway between Rivertown and a hardware store. I swing over to the dumpster, kicking away some boxes and crates to make sure Tommy isn't still hiding there.

It's empty. Hopefully she went home, and hopefully, she keeps her ass there, because I can't go back to the garage.

I grab a crate and throw it. "Fuck," I whisper, the weight of my dilemma finally sinking in. Trent is right. I have nowhere to go. My old foster mom still lets me crash at her place since I aged out and quit school months ago as long as I pay rent.

But that's the first place Hugo will look for me.

Resisting the urge to run, I put my head down and exit the alley, making my way down the deserted sidewalk. I quickly dive down a side street.

I cut through the park and turn onto Orange Hill, seeing a car parked in front of the house ahead, its engine running.

I glance up the hill, seeing movement through the side-lights on both sides of the front door, so I approach the car, seeing it's empty, and just go with it. I'm already in enough trouble to make me disappear for a decade. What's one more thing on my record?

Quickly, I open the door of the 2008 BMW, climb in, and slam the door, shifting into first gear.

I hit the gas, speeding off before anyone comes out the door. Pressing the clutch, I shift into second, and then third, racing through the neighborhood and ignoring stop signs. It's late, no one's around, and I need to get on the highway where I can go faster. There are no street cams in the residential areas, but with a posh little town like Shelburne Falls, everyone is on community watch. Someone will see the car, but I'm on borrowed time anyway. I need to see them once before...

I hang a left, maintaining the speed limit as I go, passing businesses and the elementary school, and more homes. More homes with people like Hawken Trent who think they know what real problems are.

With people like his cousin Dylan with her black leather Keds she wore the first time we met, because she wants to look like everyone else but be respected for being just different enough by rebelling against the standard Chucks or Vans that all the other kids are wearing.

With people like Kade Caruthers who show you everything they are in the first five minutes of knowing them and will never be anything more.

I glance out the windows, to the houses on both sides of me, and know I would never belong in any of these places.

But...

I'd love to see Matty and Bianca safely asleep in one before I go. I pause my gaze on a light blue Victorian with navy shutters and a wrap-around porch. Trees sprout out of the front yard, a swing swaying from a branch. Matty would love that one.

I pull out onto the dark country road, kicking up my speed to fifty-five and cruising the short distance to Weston. We may not be far from the Falls, but it's a different world.

Instead of rounding the hill toward Chicago, I turn right, cross the bridge and the river, and continue down the wooded road, broken from years of disrepair. Houses mixed with trailers sit on both sides of the road, spaced sporadi-cally by a gas station or an autobody shop.

But then the forest gives way, and the town opens up ahead, mills and factories and old warehouses-turned-apartments decorate the view ahead, and at this time of day, in the dark, it's almost pretty. The old brick. The lights.

I don't know what the hell possesses Tommy Dietrich to venture over here to brighten up her life, but just about the only thing we have going for us is a good football team and some well-preserved history. Being a river town, we were one of the first settled when the pioneers crossed the plains, and so many of the old structures have survived, if not worse for wear. We have character. Just no money to take care of it.

Still, though...come winter, those Falls kids find them-selves here for the ice racing on Duck Pond when their track is no good in the snow.

I turn at the coffee shop, speed down the street to where I know there are no cameras, and park the stolen car in front of an abandoned house.

Pulling down the sleeve of my sweatshirt, I clean the steering wheel and stick shift, using the same hand to open the door and clean the outside handle.

Walking away from the car, I go south one block, turn left, and jog up the hill to my real mom's house. Her car isn't in the driveway, but the lights are on, and equal amounts of dread and relief hitting me. I don't care who's home. As long as it's not him.

I need money, clothes, and some sleep. Tomorrow, I'll come up with a plan. I'm not dead yet.

Sneaking around the back, I remove the screen from the window of my bedroom but catch a flash of movement inside. I stop, peering through the opening in the curtains.

Bianca sits on her bed, smiling at something. I search the room with my limited vantage point, a guy coming into view. He pulls on his shirt, covering his scrawny chest and then leans over, kissing my fifteen-year-old sister on the mouth as he fastens his belt. I straighten, dropping my hands from the window.

...or pregnant, Hawke's words come back, ringing truer than I want to admit.

"Goddammit," I murmur, continuing around the house to the back door.

My sister's boyfriend is her age, but for some reason I let myself believe they weren't sleeping together. Of course, they are. That's what poor Weston kids do when they don't worry about going to college.

I open the screen door, turning the handle slowly and hearing it squeak. I wince but push the door open, seeing Matty standing at the kitchen counter and trying to spread peanut butter on some saltines.

His fingers are covered as he struggles to stay on his tip-toes, the nails of which I see are still painted black from the last time I was here. That's a good sign. My stepfather must be in lock-up, or else he'd have wiped the kid's toes clean.

I slip in, but before I can close the door, Matty turns and sees me. His five-year-old eyes light up, and he drops the butter knife. "Aro!"

I press my finger to my lips, kneeling down in front of him. "Shhh..." I kiss his forehead. "Where's Mommy?"

He scratches his nose, getting peanut butter on his face. "At work."

I swipe my thumb across his face, wiping off the mess, and then grab a paper towel, cleaning my own hand. I pick up the knife, helping him with the crackers. "Why are you awake?"

It's after midnight. I remember counting the chimes I heard from the town clock in Shelburne Falls right before I left the hideout.

But instead of answering me, Matty takes one of the finished crackers and starts eating.

I watch him hold it with both hands, taking bite after bite. Like it's something he's afraid to lose.

My throat tightens.

He swallows as I finish the rest. "Are we going shopping for school supplies soon?" he asks.

"I promised, didn't I?" I tell him.

And I've never broken a promise, because I never guarantee things I can't deliver. Like a trip to Hawaii or a car or a college fund. I want to laugh at how gullible I was when she told me I actually had a savings account from when I was little.

I don't care if I'm in prison. I'm taking him shopping for school supplies.

"Draw me anything lately?" I ask him.

He takes another cracker, shaking his head and not looking at me.

I narrow my eyes. He always has a picture for me. "Where are the pencils I gave you?"

"Daddy—"

"He's not your dad."

A cough drifts in from the living room, followed by the sound of an empty beer can knocking into another, and I tense. I don't know why I ever give that little sliver of hope air to breathe. My stepdad's not in lock-up, and she'll never kick him out. He pays rent, after all.

Bianca and I have the same father, but Matty is the product of a fling that lasted about three months, six years ago. Not long after, John Drakos swooped in, finding a nice, comfortable support system of people to do his laundry, cook his meals, and clean up after him. My mom doesn't want to go back to paying all her own bills.

I hand Matty his plate and squat down, telling him, "Go to your room and eat. Close the door."

He nods, well-conditioned not to ask questions. I wait for him to go, hearing the TV play gunfire and explosions, laughter echoing afterward.

Another door shuts, and I hear footfalls hit the stairs, "Have fun up there, boy?"

I creep to the end of the wall, just on the other side of the living room. My sister's boyfriend must be leaving.

"That headboard slams any harder, it's gonna pound a hole right through the goddamn wall," John says, chuckling. "Must be some good stuff."

"Jesus, man," his friend laughs.

I peer around the corner, seeing Bianca's boyfriend whip open the front door and walk out. "Sick asshole."

He leaves, level-headed enough to know who's bad news, and yet, he still leaves his girlfriend and her little brother with a guy like that.

Hawke comes to mind again and how he carried me away from the people he cared about inside Rivertown. Somehow, I don't think he'd leave his girlfriend in a house like this.

I open the drawer next to the fridge, sifting through nails and screwdrivers of varying size and finding the long wooden handle. I pull out the hammer and shield it behind my leg, entering the living room. I stand in front of my step-dad, blocking his view of the TV. "Matty is awake. No one made him dinner," I tell him, ignoring his friend to my left.

John stares up at me, unfazed. He's only seven years older than my mother, but he's lived hard. Lines crease the skin around his eyes and forehead, he perpetually needs to shave, and his hair is always greasy. But it's still black. He's not fat, and he has a job, so in this neighborhood he's considered a catch.

"Where are his drawing pencils?" I demand.

But he just laughs, emptying a beer can. "I think you've got bigger worries right now, girl." He reaches over, setting the can down on the table at his side. "Get out of here."

And I can't stop it. Fire spreads up my neck, heating my face, and I'm sick of everything the way it is. I hate him. I hate all of this!

I swing the hammer, bringing it down over my head and right onto his hand.

If I'm going, I'm going. I've been wanting to do this for years. I grab the gun he has sitting there, drop the hammer, and cock the weapon.

"Motherfucker," he growls, wringing out his hand, and I see his middle finger bleeding. He glares up at me, suddenly very sober.

"This isn't your house anymore," he tells me. "You got nowhere else to go, do you?"

I will fucking sleep on the streets. It wouldn't be the first time. But I know I can't take them with me.

"You're dead." A sick smile curls his lips as he tries to catch his breath. "You know you are. I'm all you've got. That's why you came back."

My hand shakes, whatever pain I caused gone from his eyes and a calm settling as he closes in. "I'm all you've got," he whispers.

I was a year younger than Bianca the only time he ever tried something with me. Half of his earlobe is missing as a result, but I was the one removed from the house, arrested, and psychologically evaluated for weeks before finally discovering that my mom didn't want me back. It was the second time I was removed from her house. Neither were my fault. I just fucking reacted when she didn't.

In the end, she chose the one who could pay bills.

I don't really hate her for it anymore. I honestly think there was a time when she loved me. I remember it.

I just think with some parents, after the kid isn't cute or little anymore, they realize it's a huge fucking job, and a huge expense and for what? What do they get out of it? I mean, really? A dog is cheaper and it doesn't talk back.

I don't hate her for myself. But I do hate her for having two more kids she has no intention of raising.

John rises from his recliner and approaches.

"Go into the garage, Aro."

I stare at his chest, the letters on his T-shirt swirling together until I can't actually read them.

"Her mom will be home soon," his buddy says off to my side.

John keeps his focus on me. "Her mom knows she's old enough to start earning her keep."

Not sure what he means, but I'm certain it involves the only thing anyone thinks women are good for.

It's all my mother thinks she's good for until she's too old to work at the club, and it's all Bianca is learning she's good for right now.

I exhale as he takes my hand with the gun. He tries to pull the weapon, I meet his eyes, and I squeeze the trigger.

Fuck it.

A pop fills the air, I jump, and he flies back, a flash of red spilling from his hand. His friend scrambles from his seat, the shot echoing through the house and making my ears ring.

Screams sound from upstairs, his friend runs, and a sting registers on my right arm. I look down, seeing blood and spot the hammer I had in his hand now as he crashes into the wall and collapses. His hand is covered in blood—not a fatal wound, but enough to send me packing for a few years.

It's over.

This is how I end. It's almost a relief.

I just worry about Matty. Bianca will understand all the shit that will happen to her in life. Matty still just wants hugs. He won't understand why no one wants him.

"Aro!" I hear my sister cry. "Aro, what are you doing?"

She stands in the hallway, staring between our stepfather and me, my brother behind her looking like he's about to cry.

"Aro!" someone else calls.

But I can't focus. I fall back, slamming into the wall, sliding down until I'm nearly seated.

"Oh my God!" I see the blur of my mother sweeping in, dropping to the ground near my stepdad and sobbing. "What have you done?" she screams over her shoulder at me. "Get out! Get out now! How's he going to work now?"

How's he going to work? I almost laugh.

But then there's another voice. Deeper. "Get the kid outta here," someone orders.

Out of the corner of my eye, I see Bianca spin Matty around and lead him back into the bedroom.

I look around at what's happening, but everything is blurry.

"We have a shooting victim, non-fatal. 875 Burnes Avenue," the man's voice says again. And then...he touches my face. "Get up."

I blink, raising my eyes. *Hawke?* But then the pain hits me and before I know it, something circles my body, and I'm swept up into his arms.

"Who's going to pay?" my mom cries. "Huh, Aro? We can't afford an ambulance. Why don't you just leave us alone?"

My hand shakes, and I can't stop it. Hawke carries me out, and I rest my chin on his shoulder, looking back into the house but not at my mother crying on the living room floor.

I want to take Bianca and Matty. "I'll be back," I whisper, my vision going black like I'm sinking further and further down a tunnel.

But then I faintly hear his voice. "You are never coming back here."

And I'm not sure if it's a dream, but in a moment, the fatigue and nausea from the pain takes over my thoughts, and I wrap an arm around his neck, holding on as he puts me into his car.

FALLS

CHAPTER
SIX

Hawke

She's a mess. And I mean that in every conceivable way. Not once since tonight began has she made a single choice that wasn't the complete opposite of something I would do.

As soon as she left the hideout, I remembered that I had no way to get in touch with her if I needed to, so I chased her down to give her phone back. What I saw when I got to her, was her seizing the first opportunity to commit another crime. I watched her drive off in Mr. Leong's BMW, just as Dylan drove up behind me on her way home. She gave me her car, finished the last block home on foot, and I had no choice but to chase after the little thief. If she could leave a trail of shit on her way out of Shelburne Falls, she'd find her way back the exact same way.

She's a time bomb. The police will be after her more than ever now. I can't leave her to her own devices. Not when my ass is on the line too.

"Let me look at that," I tell her, lowering myself to the stool in front of her and opening the first aid kit.

Blood drips from her fingers as her hand drapes over the side of the desk, her forearm resting in front of my keyboard.

I'm surprised I got her back into the hideout, but I'm not sure she even realizes that what just happened—what she did—was real.

"Aro?" I say, keeping my voice soft as she stares at the desk. Past it. "Let me see your arm."

Gently, I take it and rip the small gash in her hoodie wider to see. The cut from the hammer's claw is small but deep, and I waste no time, pulling on some gloves, washing it with wipes, and uncapping the skin glue. She doesn't flinch in the least when I pinch the skin and apply the medical glue to close the wound.

"Was that your dad?" I ask her.

When she doesn't answer, I search for her eyes, but they're hidden behind her hair as her head dips down.

"The only people who know about this place are family," I tell her. "You're safe here."

I haven't had a chance to research her, so when I followed her to Weston, I didn't assume she was going home. I hoped she was going to the Green Street garage. Thought maybe I could learn something that I could use against them, but when I spotted her with the little boy, I realized he was family.

I couldn't hear what was going on, but I could see the tension in her posture when she spoke to the man in the living room, and when she pulled the gun on him, I knew she was in for it. Is that all she does? Fight?

I hold the skin together, giving it a moment to bind, and I still can't even tell if she knows I'm here.

"I didn't mean what I said earlier," I tell her, but then backtrack. "Or maybe I did."

At the time, I meant it. When I assumed I knew her just because she's Green Street, poor, and from Weston.

I look at her eyes again. "But it's a shitty thing to think, and I was wrong."

Dylan had nearly kicked me in the nuts, and my mother definitely would have if she'd ever heard me say anything so ignorant. My parents dragged me around this entire planet to teach me how to see people. To teach me to listen twice as much as I talk. They knew that our environments shape us and that hurt people hurt people. They had such a life that I would never have to experience being that hopeless, so they showed me a world of people from the time before I could even walk, so I would know things even if I had never lived them.

What came out of my mouth was not the son they raised.

"But you're not stuck in this life, you know that, right?" I tell her, wanting to know more about that man in her house. "You don't have to do the things you do. Whenever I think it's bad or I'm feeling like shit, I remember it can always be worse. Always. There are refugees fleeing wars. People starving. Dying of disease..." I apply some adhesive tape over the glue. "I'm not one to lecture, but my dad is. He came from nothing. He had to fight for his life as a kid. Like you." I try to meet her eyes again, but she still has her head bowed. "He knew it was all on him to get up and get out, and blaming anyone for his lot wasn't going to solve anything." I clean up the rest of the blood on her arm. "And now, he has everything. All on his own. No one helped him."

She says nothing, and I hate putting my dad's business out there but I didn't tell her everything he went through. I'm not sure he even knows how much I know.

But he's proof that it's possible to get out.

I take off my gloves, throw them away, and stash the supplies back into the kit.

"It should heal okay," I tell her, handing her a bottle of Advil. "Some ibuprofen, if you need it."

But then I notice the left hand resting on her thigh, blood on the side of the pinky. I pick up her hand, and she lets me turn it over, palm side up.

It's not blood. It almost looks like a birthmark, but it's not.

The red-pebbled flesh looks like it still blisters in certain areas as it spreads across her palm, over the protruding bone on the outside of her wrist, and up her arm just a little, but the burn is ages old, long healed. Even if the scar will never go away.

What the hell is this? It must've been painful.

I dart my eyes up, and when I do, I see she's looking straight at me. Big, dark eyes, suddenly alert.

"There are refugees fleeing all kinds of wars," she whispers. "Wars without soldiers. Inside the houses you pass every day."

I watch her.

"Inside all the prisons around you that you don't notice," she murmurs, "because you can't see the bars."

I glance down at her hand again just before she takes it back, curling her fist.

"I could never leave them behind," she tells me.

Them. Her friends?

And then it hits me.

The kids. At the house. I saw them—heard them— through the window. They must be her brother and sister.

She doesn't want to leave them behind with their parents.

"Thank you," she says, holding her injured arm to her body and rising out of the chair.

I don't look at her, because I feel like I just acted as if I know some shit about life again when I really don't.

"There are rooms to the right," I tell her. "Food in the kitchen if you want."

She moves away, walking for the door, but then I hear her voice. "Your father didn't do it on his own."

I turn my head, looking at her stopped in the doorway, her back to me.

"Someone helped him," she tells me. "Ask him."

She leaves, and I continue staring at the empty doorway and thinking.

I guess it was easier for my dad. His only sibling was my uncle, and my dad was the younger one. He didn't have it like Aro does. He didn't feel responsible to take care of anyone else but himself. He could've easily been stuck forever in hell with his father, but he was able to escape it.

I don't have any brothers or sisters, but I have my cousins. If I were Aro, I couldn't leave them either.

And I know my dad wouldn't have left his brother if situations had been reversed.

I watch her, disappearing from one monitor and appearing on another as she slips down another hallway and enters a room. One far away from mine.

Once inside, I drop my eyes and move my hand to the button on the side of the monitor, seeing her inside her room out of the corner of my eye. I didn't install cameras to be a voyeur, per se. After all, I'm not sure how many people I was ever going to invite in here, but...

I glance up just as I'm about to turn it off and stop, watching her struggle to remove her hoodie. Her bomber jacket still lays on the floor at my feet.

Holding her arm close to her, she works her body out and pulls the hoodie over her head, a white tank top underneath.

Her dark hair is longer than I thought, seeing it fall down her back, but her breathing is ragged as she limps over to the bed, and a line of blood stains her shirt from her neck to her waist.

I dig in my eyebrows.

Why didn't she tell me? I'd forgotten that she was hurt elsewhere.

She didn't look in pain when she sat here.

I watch her stumble to the bed, lower her knees to the floor, and bury her face in the blanket, her heavy breathing visible from here as she finally lets herself give in to it.

I start to get up and go to her, but she would've asked if she'd wanted more help. She'll just fight me.

I reach up, turning off the monitor and give her some privacy.

I was wrong. A bomb is loud—only good for mass destruction and only good once.

She's not a bomb.

She's patient, quiet, unyielding, and permanent.

She withstands. Like steel.

Like an ax.

CHAPTER SEVEN

Avo

A figure looms over me, blurry, and I blink, but my eyelids are so heavy. It moves, growing closer, but it never comes into focus. What is that?

But then I snap my eyes open, realizing I'm not dreaming, and bolt up into a sitting position, jerking my head left and right.

I scan the room, something crawling my skin.

But there's no one. The closed door sits ahead, and the only things in the room other than me are furniture.

Hijo de puta.

I push my hair out of my face and throw off the blanket, wincing as pain burns through my arm. I look down at the bandaged wound and last night comes flooding back.

Shit.

I climb off the bed and walk to the wooden door, twisting the handle.

It's still locked. I exhale, turning around and checking the room again.

The bronze cage holding four, small candle-shaped bulbs hanging by a matching chain overhead, the lights still bright from when I entered the room. I must've fallen asleep with them on. I gaze around, noticing the faded, antique rug partially hidden underneath the bed, and the desk sitting kitty-corner and facing the door. A large mural of chipped paint decorates the wall to the right of it, a pastoral scene of a jungle and animals I can barely make out. I sift through the drawers in the desk and then lower myself to the ground to look under the bed, flinching at the pain in my body.

But the room appears to be empty. And unoccupied by a permanent resident too. No clothes. No receipts. Nothing of value.

I unwrap the bandage on my arm and inspect it, seeing a little blood dried around the wound. It's not discolored, seeping, or as swollen anymore. It's sealed better than any time I've ever had stitches.

He's probably certified in advanced CPR. *Boy Scout.*

I pull on my hat, my sweatshirt, and yank the hood over my head, but the world tilts in front of me, and I have to lean into the wall. I bow my head, inhaling and exhaling, and I'm not sure if I'm dizzy or sick, in pain or hungry. I haven't eaten since yesterday morning.

I stumble over, grabbing the bottle of Advil he gave me and tap out a few pills, popping them into my mouth. Swallowing them dry, I toss the bottle onto the bed and twist the lock on the doorknob, opening the door.

Music greets me with a draft of cool air just as I step into the tunnel.

It's metal music. Not Spanish but not English, either. I can't understand what they're saying, but I hear the guitars screech and the drum beat to my left. Why did he bring me back here?

A thousand more questions race through my mind, things I thought last night in passing but didn't give a shit enough to ask.

He followed me. Why did he follow me home?

He doesn't trust me. That must be it.

Will he force me to stay?

He can try.

A sound catches my ear, like a step shuffling behind me, but when I turn my head, I don't see anything down the dark tunnel. Moving forward, I walk back toward the surveillance room, passing it, and veer right, into the kitchen.

Trent stands at the stove, music blasting as he scrapes eggs across a pan. The scent of the butter hits my nose, and the nerves in my jaw twitch, making my mouth water like it does when you know something is going to taste really good.

My jacket lays on the cement-top island, and I take it, pulling it on. I slip my hands into my pockets, still not finding my phone.

I level a look on him. I'm going to need my phone.

The volume on the music lowers, and he sets down a cup of coffee in front of the empty stool, locking eyes with me. "Are you vegan?" he asks.

I arch an eyebrow. Does he know the price difference between a black bean-pumpkin seed burger and a McDonald's Value Meal? Jesus...

I take a seat as he bites back a smile. "Sorry," he mumbles. And then he sets a plate down with a piece of bread, fried in butter and topped with scrambled eggs and chopped bacon.

I pick it up, not even hesitating. I'll need energy when I run.

I sink my teeth through the egg and toast, the crackle of the bread like music. The butter hits my tongue, and for a second, I'm seven years old and in Clara's—our neighbor's—kitchen, making treats for Christmas as the music plays. Savory and warm and everything smells good.

A good moment.

When I think about myself happy someday, it's not me traveling or buying a nice car or working somewhere important. It's having a thousand moments just like that, where I'm exactly where I want to be. The next moment may suck. I still have to go back to the same foster home or deal with the same problem or not know what I'm eating tonight, but in this...one...moment, I love the view.

I fold the toast in half, smashing all the food together inside and finish it quickly in four more bites. Clearing my throat, I swallow and gulp down the orange juice he put out, and then sip some coffee.

Hawke makes his plate, and I speak before I lose my nerve. "I need about ninety-thousand dollars," I tell him. "And you need to not be arrested, so I'd say that makes us a team."

He turns, unfazed, and scrapes his eggs onto a piece of toast. "And we need to shut down Officer Reeves," he adds.

I'm kind of relieved it seems that he's agreeing we should work together, but his goal is loftier than mine. I would love to shut that asshole down, and it's cute that he thinks he can.

"Where are the goods?" he asks, setting the pan in the sink. "The drugs? His operation? At the garage?"

I fist the mug, warming my hand. "You want to steal from him?"

"It's what you're good at, isn't it, Rebel?"

"Aro," I remind him. I stopped being a Rebel eight months ago.

He nods, still not looking at me. "And my name's Hawke," he says. "As opposed to 'you motherfucker'."

I hold back my grin, watching him dump Tabasco onto his eggs. So he understood that, huh?

I gaze around the great room, sipping the coffee and noticing small reflections of light in the corners near the ceiling. Lenses catching the sun coming through the high windows. Was there a camera in the room I slept in last night?

"You have a shitload of surveillance around town," I state, judging from what I saw on his monitors last night. "Is it yours, or are you tapping into the county cameras?"

He leans a hand on the counter, picking up his open-faced sandwich with the other. His stomach flexes just above the apron, and I blink, taking another sip. "Where is his operation?" he continues instead.

"What makes you think I know that?"

He takes a bite, chews steadily as he sets the food back down.

"You're my age," he says, "which means you should've graduated this year but didn't."

I listen.

"You haven't been in school in eight months," he goes on, "not that your foster mom cared as long as the checks kept coming, right? But even those don't secure you a home anymore, since you've aged out."

The heat from the mug burns, but I press harder.

"You were removed from your mother's house when you were nine and again when you were fourteen." He sprinkles some salt on his eggs. "But your siblings weren't, so I'm guessing they believed your mom when she claimed you attacked your stepfather for no reason."

I steel my spine, watching him as he focuses on his task and the shit coming out of his mouth.

"But you never told the social workers why," he tells me, "because no matter what was going on at home, you knew being in the system was worse, and you didn't want that for your siblings. Hugo, Nicholas, and Axel were your foster brothers. You met them when you were fifteen, and you've been with them ever since."

He takes another bite, glancing at me and thinking he knows me when he knows even less than I assumed he did. We're nearly eye level, but somehow, he manages to look down like I fucking work for him.

"You're the one they send to collect protection money, rents, loans..." he continues. "You've been doing it for a few years now. They send you alone." He pauses for effect. "A girl."

And now I see what he's getting at.

"They trust you." He pours himself some coffee. "They know you get shit done. You have to be thinking about the future, and since education doesn't seem to be a priority, I'm guessing this life is all that's next for you."

Which means I'm invested. Which means he knows he's correct in assuming I'm a significant part of Green Street.

He raises the mug to his lips. "How often does Reeves come to the garage?"

I hesitate. He may not trust me, but there's no reason to trust him, either. He's not in any danger. Not really. What's to stop him from cutting and running any time he wants? That job is all I have. All I had anyway.

I place the mug between us and look up at him. "Here's what we're sitting on, Pirate," I explain. "You crashed two of his cars and dumped his shit. I attacked him. Worse comes to worst, you can come up with the funds to repay him and get him off your ass. Your family is rich."

"They're not rich."

"They could come after the people closest to us," I continue, ignoring him. I'm not splitting hairs right now. "In which case, you'll just pay up. I can't. I have a knife to my throat. That puts us on uneven ground, so I don't trust you."

In one swift movement, he twists the laptop around, showing me the screen.

I watch, seeing the two of us at the pond last night, none of the audio catching what really happened. Just showing us, looking like criminals, for the entire world to see.

On the other half of the screen is a data feed with his name, personal information, and charges he's under arrest for.

It looks just like the ones I see flit across the officer's screen every time I'm in the back of a squad car.

I take another sip. He could have gotten out of the warrant, but the video changes things. It makes Green Street look stupid. That could be bad for Shelburne Falls. "So, you're stuck now," I say.

But he just shakes his head. "I was never going to let that motherfucker get away with it. But if it puts your mind at ease, yeah, I'm in the same boat you are." Taking my plate, he spins around and puts the dishes into the sink. "We have until Grudge Night to get rid of him."

"Why Grudge Night?"

"Because I start classes the next week, and it gives me just enough time to clear my name, in case the administration revokes my acceptance for having a warrant out."

Guess he's not traveling far for school if he can drag this out until the last minute. Grudge Night celebrates the end of summer and the anticipation for the football festivities to come. The parties, the Prisoner Exchange, Rivalry Week... It's a high school thing, but I never cared much about it even when I was in high school.

"And if we succeed, what do I do?" I ask him.

He turns, clearing away the rest of the dishes. "What do you mean?"

"My foster brothers also work for him," I point out. "What will they do when I take away their cash cow? I still won't be completely safe."

He shakes his head. "I'm not here to solve your whole life." He tosses balled-up napkins into the bin. "Some of this mess you got yourself into, you can get yourself out. You did steal his car in the first place, after all."

"You tried to buy me."

"I was trying to get the charm back," he spits out. "That's it."

And he takes off the apron, leaving him in his jeans as he sets it on the counter. He busies himself with something on his phone, tapping away, his thumbs moving like lightning strikes.

So very important, he is, isn't he?

"Why don't you look at me?" I ask.

The words come out softer than I intended, but he hears me. He pauses, his thumbs suspended above the screen, and it takes him a minute, but he raises his blue eyes, meeting mine.

They're actually quite striking. His eyes. They're an azure shade, like aqua with a purple light in it that's there one second and gone the next.

But the eyes themselves are almond-shaped.

And then I notice other things. The long nose, the high cheekbones, the thick, dark lashes, the brow...

I hide my surprise. God, he must love being him. Passes for white but he probably gets to check that little box that lets him apply for college money that should go to other American Indian students who actually need it.

I clear my throat, looking away. "I don't know where he gets the drugs or how they come to us, but he does collect his money in person."

"When?"

I can't stop my sneer. "He's too smart for habitual. It's always different." I glance up at him again. "But he just collected, so it's going to be at least a week. Get me a camera, I can plant it, and then we wait."

He folds his arms over his chest. "You can get through the garage unseen?"

"No, but I know someone who won't be noticed."

He laughs. "I'm not using a thirteen-year-old."

Since when? They certainly use Tommy Dietrich for a laugh when they need.

"She's a lonely kid, and I'm guessing it's your family's fault," I retort. "Not much happens in this town without the knowledge of the Trent-Caruthers empire. That kid is treated like shit. Give her something to do."

He stands there, staring at me.

"Give me my phone." I hold out my hand. "I'll call her."

"We'll go to her house," he replies. "Her father will be leaving for work."

"How do you know—?"

He shoots me a look, and I shut up.

Cameras. Right. He probably knows everyone's schedules in this town.

And for what? Why does he watch people?

I want to know, but I don't want to talk to him to get the answer.

"If they catch her, we need to go in," I say. "And she's coming back here to hide with us."

"No one is coming back here...except us."

He walks around the island, passing me, and for some reason, I don't stop myself. "What is this place to you? How did you find it?"

I look up at him as he stands near me, but when he turns his eyes down on me, I stop breathing for a second.

101

I blink, turning forward, toward the stove.

"Why do you look away when I look at you?" he asks instead.

FALLS

CHAPTER EIGHT

Hawke

I should've asked about her arm, but I'm pretty sure she would've hit me. People like that would rather boil to death than let anyone know they need help. There's no talking to her.

I take out my phone and check the time before dialing. It's after six.

It takes four rings, but I hear my cousin clear her throat and say in a groggy voice. "Yeah, I'm here. Are you okay?"

I head into the surveillance room, shaking my head as I switch one of the cameras over to our street, Fall Away Lane. "So worried about my safety that you're sleeping?"

"It passes the time," she mumbles.

I see her car parked in front of her house, which means her dad needed to get out of the garage early this morning. He's up already, and I pan over to the house next to theirs, seeing my parents' porch light still on. They probably haven't been to bed, but I hope that they have. I don't want them worrying.

Of course, they will anyway, but they can at least sleep.

"Go to my room," I tell her, bringing up the local news on the monitor to my left and my social media on the right. "Get my laptop and my spare key in my nightstand. Bring my bike and park it in the old High Street garage."

"Your parents are going to know I took it, Hawke," she argues. "They'll corner me when I get back."

"Not if you move now," I reply, typing with one hand and holding the phone with the other. "Wheel it to the end of the block and then start it up."

"But it's raining."

I keep my laugh to myself. I'm fucking running for my life, and she's whining like she did when I used to steal her Oreos. It's actually comforting. Helps me suspend the belief that I'm in more trouble than I want to admit. "I love you," I tease.

"Ugh..." And she hangs up, not satisfied with my response.

Aro appears on one of the cameras, washing her dish and drinking a full cup of water before refilling it and downing another.

I move to my left, scanning the screens and seeing mention in the local paper of access to the pond suspended due to construction but no further details about why. I sift through article after article—my uncle's case to keep some big developer from buying the old hospital out on Highway 6 and turning it into a casino, the minutes from the PTO meeting, and the exposé on "How Cooperative is a Co-Op? Really?"

But nothing about me. Or her.

Drew Reeves doesn't want the public's help finding us.

Great. That can't be good.

I pull my keyboard up on the riser and stand in front of the monitors, bringing up the county database. I force my fingers to move before I have too much time to think.

The girl is unpredictable. And she has baggage. Lots of it. If she goes back home for those kids, Reeves will have already established footing with her stepfather. He'll know the second she steps in that house.

Not sure her mother can be trusted. Not many people would turn in their own kid, but I can't take away both parents right now anyway. Putting those kids in foster care won't make Aro Marquez more cooperative with me.

But her stepdad needs to go.

240 – Assault, I type out. I add in *Domestic Violence, Person with a Gun, Child Abuse, Shooting at Inhabited Dwelling, and…*—I think and then shrug—*Dead Human Body*.

He'll be in jail a couple of weeks on several bogus warrants before they figure any of this out. And hey, I might get lucky. Some of it is certainly true, and they might be able to prove it.

I link his last known location to the hospital after the gunshot wound last night, and pause over the enter button like I always do when I know I'm about to do something that's either incredibly clever, or really, fucking stupid. I exhale and hit the key. "Screw it."

Hitting my social media pages, I see that the story there is the exact opposite of the official news stations. Videos of Aro and me circulate, tagging her and me, and our involvement, which is as clear as day. When I check out her pages, just an Instagram she hasn't used in over a year and a TikTok account with eight followers and no videos, I fight back a small smile. I'm relieved she's not transparent about her comings and goings like everyone else on the planet, but she probably doesn't broadcast her life because what's there to broadcast? She's never really had a chance to be a teenager.

I pause a moment, lost in thought. My mind trails from the pond to the gunshot to her hand, and to everything else in the eight hours since we met. I run my hand through my hair, rubbing my scalp and feeling like I want to laugh and puke at the same time. This partnership is going to kill me.

"Whoo!" someone screams.

I blink and look up, realizing it's a TikTok video.

"When your boyfriend won't touch you AND runs off with the girl who kicked you in the face tonight..." Schuyler shouts on the screen as I stare at the video of her in front of me. "At least now I know he's not gay."

I straighten, locking my jaw as liquid heat runs under my skin.

Laughter erupts around her as she straddles Asher Young reverse cowgirl and lets him paw her. "He's just an asshole who's forgotten in 3...2...1..."

He reaches around and slips his hand underneath her crop top while she leans back into him, laughing like I'm so easy to replace.

Son of a bitch.

And before I can stop myself, I scroll down, knowing nothing good comes from looking at the comments, but I do it anyway.

Queen! several commenters tell her.

Get 'em, girl!

Sounds like a piece of work. You're better off! another one says.

He's gettin' it somewhere else. I told you!

"Jesus Christ," I mumble, continuing to skim the comment section like I don't know better. "Fuckin' people."

Asher covers her mouth with his, and my ex is practically dry-humping him. I pick up my phone and dial.

She picks up on the second ring, but neither of us say anything. She just breathes.

"Are you okay?" I almost whisper.

I shouldn't be calling her. Everything inside me tells me that I'm the one who's mad. What does she have to be mad about?

But still, she remains silent. Four months ago, I really liked her. Two months ago, I thought she might be the one.

This isn't my fault.

I swallow through the sandpaper in my throat. "Don't go somewhere you can't come back from just to prove something to yourself," I tell her. "Or to get back at me."

The video was a shit move. Putting me on blast when she knows I'm not hooking up with anyone else, even though she didn't say my name, is childish. As if people aren't talking about me enough. They know who she's referring to.

But I know what she's really doing, and I don't want her to fuck someone and regret it.

"Are you safe?"

"You're not my brother," she spits out. "Act like my boyfriend and get jealous."

I lower the volume on the screen, but I let it repeat over and over again, watching him do all the things to her that I did with her, the only difference being he probably didn't stop like I did. "Are you with him now?" I ask.

"Are you with her?"

"It's not like that," I snap, spinning around from the video and pacing the room. "There are so many other things going on that you don't—"

"I blew him."

I stop, falling silent. Images of him getting her like that flash in my mind, and I grip the phone so tightly I hear it crack.

"I kept expecting him to stop me like you always do." She speaks softly—clear and steady—like she wasn't drunk at all last night and meant to do everything she did. "But he just gripped my hair harder and shoved himself down my throat again and again, Hawke."

I don't breathe.

"I liked it," she whispers, and I hear the smile in her voice.

I have nothing to say. Am I really that mad? Is that what this is? This brick turning in my stomach? Did I want her back? I let her go weeks ago, knowing she'd find someone else eventually. Does it just hurt more than I thought it would?

"You know why I'm telling you this?" Schuyler says. "Because I know it's safe with you. You won't tell anyone. You won't shame me on social media. You're a perfect gentleman, which is why I feel like I've dodged a bullet." She laughs a little. "Your fucking would've been so polite. I'm glad I realized now how boring you would be in bed."

I close my eyes, the line of girls all through high school piling up to this fucking cherry on top. Every single one who wondered what was wrong with them when I didn't try, bitter when I stopped, and some unapologetically toxic when I said no. By my senior year, they stopped blaming themselves and started laughing together about it.

I look over my shoulder, watching her on his lap just like she was on mine last month and knowing she wouldn't have given him the time of day if I'd given her what she wanted.

"And yet," I taunt, finally finding my voice. "I'm the one you want, aren't I?"

She's quiet for a moment but then finds her words. "I did."

The corners of my lips turn up in a smile, and I walk back to the monitors, watching him but seeing myself. Seeing myself holding someone I can't let go of.

"I think about sex," I say softly. "All the time. I want it."

I close my eyes again, going deep into that fantasy.

"I want to be in a dark place with someone," I tell her. "A tight space. Touching her and not being able to put two words together because I can't see anything else but her." My breathing turns shallow again, and blood rushes to my groin. "She's got me on a leash. Time freezes. I need it. Again and again. The warmth between her legs. Her mouth." I wet my lips. "How every inch of her body is pressed against mine, and still, I need her closer."

She sucks in a breath, and I grow harder.

"I want it so bad."

"Me too," she murmurs.

"Pull up your shirt."

She hesitates. "He's sleeping next to me."

I smile again. "Pull up your shirt."

I hear her swallow. "'Kay," she whispers.

I imagine she's in bed, warm and soft.

"I'm hard." I breathe in and out slowly. "I'm always so hard when I go into my head and pull down her panties, feeling her lips brush mine. The skin between her thighs. So warm and wet."

I tip her chin up—the girl in my head—making her look at me, because she's scared too and she needs me to be strong. She needs me like I'm the reason her heart beats, and what she gets from me, she can't get from anyone else.

It's sex and more.

"I bet you're all muscle, baby," Schuyler pants. "So hard."

"I am." I draw in a breath, aching. "I want that girl who's in my head so badly. She's always there. So hot. So good at everything she does to me. I feel like I never want to fuck anyone else. I need her."

"Yeah..."

My muscles tense, but I relax them, opening my eyes as the images disappear. Schuyler groans on the other end, masturbating, and all the anger I felt a few minutes ago cools.

Sweat dampens my chest, and I look down, seeing the bulge in my jeans.

"The thing is," I tell her, my tone growing hard, "when that little animal in my head looks up at me and I look back at her... It's never you I see, Schuyler."

She stops her little mewls, and I steel my spine, closing out the video on the monitor.

"Your lip looks like it hurts," I tell her, remembering how swollen it was in the video. "Try a cold compress."

She sucks in a breath, and I hold back my smile as I hang up.

Every muscle in my body hardens and then relaxes, a shot of warmth seeping into my blood.

She's lying. She didn't blow him. That's why she posted the video. She's pushing me to react. If I won't take what she offers, then she's saving her pride. She's at home, in bed, alone.

The truth is, I don't see anyone in particular when I dream of *the one*. The girl in my head. It's never a face. It could be Schuyler. Who knows? What I do have, though, is a feeling. Just a feeling. I want what I feel with the girl in my head. Something strong. Something only for me.

Lowering my eyes, I stare at the green drawer of the old steel military desk left behind by whoever was here last. I reach out and open it, seeing a tray of cell phones I found inside and have kept there since. Nokias, Motorolas, flip phones... A lot of eight, once dead until I plugged them in, replaced batteries, worked a little magic... I have no idea who left them here, but I think I know who one of them belonged to.

I grab the black Nokia, the weight about the same as my iPhone, but I flip it open and hit the key pad, bringing up his—or her—last conversation.

Don't kill her, the owner of the phone messages someone they don't have added to their contacts. Which means this was either a burner phone or a new one they hadn't gotten around to setting up yet.

Someone has to, the other replies.

Soon, they assure.

Today.

Tonight, the owner replies.

Both of us, the other one says. **Together.**

I remember how my heart pumped the first time I read this. I was in this room, finding this place for the first time.

My skin crawled, feeling like I was being watched, but that was over a year ago when I found the place, and if anyone in this text conversation is still alive and knows I'm here, they're letting me be.

For now.

You watch, the other says.

Why?

Because I want her to look at me.

I brush my thumb over the screen.

Only me, he clarifies.

Their phone's owner responds, **Understood.**

It ends. There are no more messages that day. That night. Or in the twenty-two years since.

I'd searched all the other phones, half of which were unsalvageable and the other half had no connection to this one that I could find. What the hell happened that night? Did they kill her? He wanted her to look at him. What did she do? Was it revenge?

I want to know, and I want to know how they got here. Who they belonged to. Whoever owned them would be about my parents' age.

And whoever left them here is probably still out there. I'm not the only one who knows about this place.

But before I can get sidetracked too long, a light pierces the screen to my right. I look up, seeing Dylan turn my bike onto High Street.

"You sure about this?" she asks, handing me my helmet. "Our parents can have this dealt with today."

I take the backpack with my laptop and the keys, setting them down in the abandoned garage before tossing her a hoodie. "Stay around people," I order her. "Okay? I don't know what to expect, and it's safer to be on your guard. No practicing at Fallstown by yourself."

She chews on the corner of her lip. "Fine." And she immediately closes her mouth after the one-word response.

"I'm serious," I bark, knowing that's her tell when she's lying. "You know I'll see you. I will lock you down in here with me if I have to."

She knows I have access to all the cameras in town.

"I got it," she blurts out. "I'm not stupid."

"Not when you take the time to think, no."

She overcompensates, because she's Jared Trent's daughter. If she's not as good as him on the track, then they say it's because she's a girl, and that's the message she picked up on really early in life. It's been balls to the wall ever since to prove everyone wrong. Hopefully it doesn't get her killed someday.

The door creaks behind me, and I look to see Aro enter, having followed me. The old fire house is three roofs down from the hideout, so we just climbed up, out, and back in. All without being seen.

I pull out my laptop, examining it to make sure it didn't get wet, and then pull out my phone, texting Kade.

Be careful today, I tell him. **Don't make anything worse.**

"Here," I hear Dylan say. "It's what I owe you."

I glance up and see her hand Aro a roll of cash.

I make it fun, he replies.

I shake my head, rubbing my face.

I start to type, but then I hear Aro curse in Spanish, followed by, "Now that I'm on the run and you feel sorry for me? I don't need your charity, Trent."

I cock a brow as I crack my neck. *I've had enough fun*, I type.

"No, you need a bath." Dylan scrunches up her face as she plugs her nose, looking at me. "She smells like the fish pond."

Oh, Jesus.

Aro launches for her, but I grab the hood of her jacket and yank her back. *Dammit*. Can I have just five minutes here?

You need to be the responsible one now, I punch the buttons on my phone, telling Kade. *Please.*

I grip Aro's coat as she tries to squirm out of my hold, but I wait for Kade's reply.

Fine. And I don't feel at ease with his one-word reply any more than I do when I get it from Dylan.

I tuck my phone away and release the Rebel, but I move forward before she can rearrange my cousin's face.

"Talk to Hunter," I instruct Dylan. "Tell him to keep St. Matt's away this year. We've got enough to deal with from Weston, and I don't want him involved in all this, too."

Grudge Night is a huge draw for all the high schools in the area, but everyone needs to lay low this year.

Dylan purses her lips, looking away. "Like Hunter cares. Grudge Night is so far off his radar, I'm sure he's not the least bit interested in our petty games." She folds her arms over her chest. "He left me on *Read* the last two times I texted."

"That's fine," I tell her. "He doesn't have to respond to get the message."

Hunter is Kade's identical twin, but he's not a Pirate. He was, but now he's a Knight. He transferred to our other rival school last year—he and Kade never got along, and I guess he just needed distance. He lives closer to Chicago with their grandfather.

Dylan peels off her wet hoodie and puts on the dry one. "Hunter has forgotten we exist," she says. "You should be worried about Kade."

"When am I not worried about Kade?" I slip my arms through the backpack.

She doesn't know I was just texting him, but we both get the message. Kade looks for any reason to fight. He revels in it, and he doesn't much care that he constantly stresses me out.

A honk sounds outside, and I jerk my head.

"Relax." Dylan pulls on the hoodie as we both peer out the garage door windows. "It's just Noah."

"Like that's going to make me relax."

Noah Van der Berg idles out at the curb, straddling his motorcycle, a custom, top-of-the-line piece of machinery built by his dad and brother as a gift to him when he signed to be on Jared's racing team.

The guy is super nice, like being dashing is his fucking job.

I glare. Jared is the most high-strung, rage-infused, alpha male I know. Worse than my dad. How can he let a twenty-two-year-old blond with a six-pack sleep across the hall from his daughter?

Dylan laughs under her breath, dropping her voice into a pouty little coo. "Aw, poor Hawke, having such an attractive cousin like me," she teases, not taking my concern seriously. And then she rolls her eyes, "Not everyone wants to have sex with me. Lighten up."

Whatever.

She pulls open the door and saunters out to her new housemate in the rain. I guess I should be thankful. He was nice enough to pick her up and save me the trip of taking her back home.

He's like a brother. Yeah. That's what a brother would do. It's fine.

But I scowl as I watch him drive off with my cousin.

A second later, Aro comes to stand next to me. "The Garmin on her wrist," she says, looking out the window with me. "Does she know she's being tracked?"

My face falls. *Fuck.*

The only person who recognized my Christmas present to Dylan last year—and that it does a lot more than just count your steps—was my dad.

Aro glances at me. "You're funny."

And then she turns, walking away.

CHAPTER NINE

Avo

I grab the helmet his cousin wore and fit it onto my head as he slips on a leather jacket. I try to look away, but I keep glancing back, watching him zip it up.

Funny. I don't know what I meant by that. He's not funny. He's...

A hypocrite. It's fine to break the law as long as it serves his purpose. Crime isn't a choice when he does it. Then...it's justified.

Yeah, he's funny all right. Funny how he thinks his rules apply to everyone but him. That makes him no different than any other privileged Falls kid I've ever met.

But there is a little something different. He's harder to anticipate than I thought he'd be. With people like Dylan Trent and Kade Caruthers, they're easier to read. They want people to know them.

Hawke is purposely cold. Rigid. And not just with me. He keeps his guard up. I noticed it last night when his cousins and friends showed up. He takes the lead with everyone.

He climbs on the bike, pulls on his helmet, and starts the engine, not even bothering to look over his shoulder to signal that I'm invited before hitting the remote and opening the garage door. I swing my leg over the bike, climbing on behind him.

"Won't people recognize the motorcycle?" I ask, reaching behind me to grab hold of the safety bar.

But it isn't there.

He kicks the bike into gear, it jumps, and I grapple for his jacket just as he speeds out of the garage. *Asshole.*

We turn right, and for a moment it feels like I'm going to fall as I press my boots into the rests. I grip the leather at the back of his jacket in my fists, leaning forward but not too much. I don't like that I have to touch him, and I'm pretty sure he doesn't like it either.

We ride, the town still not fully awake on a Saturday morning, and I kind of like it. Obviously, we don't want to be seen, but I like early mornings. You feel like you have the world to yourself in a way you don't at night. It's different when the day is starting rather than ending. As if something is about to happen.

He skids to a halt, putting his feet down on the ground to steady us as the light turns red above. We wait at the stoplight, the cool rain welcome on my hands and neck because it's hot already.

Plus it washes away the dirt. I pull the collar of my hoodie away from my body and dip my nose inside, sniffing.

Then I drop my hands from his jacket, scooting back as far as I can go as if he still won't smell me. I don't stink that bad. Maybe I can sneak into my foster mom's and get some clean clothes today.

"Hold on to me," he calls out.

He revs the gas, speeds off, and I squeeze the bike with

my thighs as tightly as I can, but the motorcycle kicks into the next gear and lurches. I grab onto him, leaning into his back. "Slow down!" I growl.

But then I see the cop.

Oh, shit.

He switches gears, and I wrap my arms around his waist and tuck myself into his back as he swoops right again, down a side street, and then left down the next block.

I hold my breath like we all do when we're driving and see the speed trap too late. You're sure you're caught, and you're just waiting to see their fruit basket light up in your rearview mirror.

I grit my teeth together, my arms tightening around him like I don't have control of it.

I wait to hear the siren behind me.

But I can't take it. I glance over my shoulder.

They're not there. The street is empty.

I tap him in the shoulder, yelling, "Go!"

Let's get out of here before they change their minds.

He cuts right, speeds down a couple of blocks, and then takes a left and then another left, kicking it into gear and letting loose. We race down the highway, the rain splattering my helmet, and I relax my hold on him, just gripping his jacket.

But I stay tucked behind him, the drops cutting like darts when they hit.

This is kind of fun, to be honest. I've never ridden on a motorcycle before. And for a moment, I let myself pretend. For a moment, I have parents and a house and a manicure, and we're not on the run. I have a guy who makes love to me, and we're free.

But the thing is, when that little animal in my arms looks up at me and I look back at her... It's never you I see.

I'm paraphrasing, because I can't recall his exact words, but I'd smiled when I'd overheard him earlier. I followed to get my phone back, but then I'd stopped just before the door to the surveillance room when he told whoever he was talking with to pull up her shirt. I peeked in and saw the blonde I'd kicked last night on the screen in some video. Is she his girlfriend? He'd called her Schuyler.

I'd heard rumors about him—that he never has sex—but it surprised me, how he talked. It was kind of hot.

Has he really never slept with anyone? I try not to notice the feel of his body flush with mine. My thighs hugging his. He's tall and broad, trim and strong. It's a shame he only ever sweats in the gym.

I glance over his shoulder, noticing his grip on the handlebar, the veins bulging through the back of his hand. What does he feel like when he touches someone?

Heat pools in my stomach, and I blink a few times, looking away.

He was right to be cruel with that girl, though.

It was the kindest thing, and I'm glad he's incapable of pretending. How many men in her life will tell her they love her to get what they want? How many will say they're single when they're not? I don't think he'd ever take something he wasn't willing to give. She's luckier than she realizes, because in that respect, he's rare.

He pulls into a lot, parks the bike, and I don't ask questions as I follow him to a car parked on the side of a warehouse. I glance behind me a couple of times, finally relaxing and letting out a smile.

I'm used to evading police. Not sure if he is, but he's not bad at it. I'm not going to tell him that, though.

He yanks open the driver's side door and climbs in, and I follow on the passenger side, both of us tossing our helmets into the back seat.

I look around, the smell of leather and cologne surrounding me, from the black seats to the polished dash, but that's not how he smells. He smells like the air in October, cool and clean but there's still a hint of something left over from summer. Very subtle. Is this his car?

It's an old Pontiac GTO—silver—and it kind of looks familiar, but I can't think right now enough to place it. I thought he had an Audi or something. I thought I'd seen him in it. Maybe it belongs to someone in his family.

He starts it up, and I stuff my hands in my coat pockets, slouching down in the seat. We head out, bouncing over the curb before turning onto the highway.

I stare at the wet road ahead, some System of a Down song playing as the weight of the situation sinking in. His motorcycle, his car, his gear, his hideout, his food, his friends, his town...

Everything relies on him. I feel like luggage.

"I need my phone," I say.

"No."

I jerk my eyes over to him. "I need *a* phone." Any phone. I really don't care. "Give me one, or I'll find one."

Is he that afraid I'll screw up? Or does he need to control where I go and who I talk to like he apparently does with every woman in his life?

I watch him, his eyes zoned in on the road, his face expressionless. "What if I need you?" I ask in a soft tone.

Who else am I going to call? He knows I don't have anyone.

He presses his lips together, gazing at the road like he's about to take a math test.

Finally, he sighs, reaches over and opens the glove box, and I see at least three smartphones inside. Digging one out, he dumps it into my lap.

"Charge it," he says, pulling out a cord between his seat and the console.

I plug it in. In a moment it beeps, signaling it's powering up.

"You can't contact anyone," he instructs.

"I need to make sure my family is okay."

I have no idea if my stepfather's been treated, and not that I really care, but I do want to know if he's been discharged and is back at home.

But Hawke just says, "They're fine."

"How do you know?"

"I issued a warrant for your stepfather's arrest."

"What?" I blurt out, snapping up in my seat. "How...? What...?" I shake my head, not sure I'm understanding. "You can't do that!"

How the hell did he pull that off? *Jesus.*

"I don't know what my mom will do if she can't pay the bills," I bite out. *Goddammit.*

I don't want the motherfucker there either, but she can't keep a roof over their heads without him. Without me.

Hawke keeps his gaze on the road. "The devil you know versus the one you don't, I get it," he says, "but he was forcing himself on you. I got that much from his body language when I showed up last night. I can't let him stay in a house with kids."

You can't *let* him? "I had it under control."

He just laughs.

"I had *him* under control," I say more clearly.

Finally, he looks over at me. "You're funny."

What the hell does that mean? Flinging my own words back at me with his condescending, little smirk...

I open my mouth to retort, but he jerks the wheel right, and I grab the door to steady myself as the road under the tires switches from pavement to gravel, and the trees overhead provide a canopy.

We drive down a long road, but I can make out a clearing at the end. Is this where Tommy Dietrich lives?

He turns down one of the adjoining paths, parking off to the side, and we get out, me pulling up my hood as we jog through the woods toward her house. I'm not really quite sure why we don't just drive up and knock on the door, but if he explains, then I have to listen to it, and I have a headache from him already.

I follow him but race ahead, veering toward the side of the house and taking the lead. But he grabs the collar of my hoodie and yanks me back.

I whip around and punch his hand away. "Stop that!"

That's the second time today.

"Shhh," he whispers hard, and I know to close my mouth immediately.

He pulls me down, and we hunch behind a bush, watching a man with short-cropped brown hair carry a lunchbox to his truck, his white T-shirt advertising some bar and stained with grease. Tommy has his eyes.

"I thought he was gone," I ask Hawke.

"He's leaving now."

I hope no one else lives there besides her and her father.

"Ugh, you do smell like the pond," Hawke grumbles. "And wet potato chips."

Wet potato chips? What the fuck? I was caught in some rain last night.

The rusty, blue Ford coasts out of the driveway, and I move to stand up, but Hawke stops me.

I glare at him.

"No one knows about the hideout, outside of that little group last night," he warns. "And now you. Don't tell Tommy."

"Why?" I ask.

But of course, he doesn't answer.

"It's not yours, is it?" I ask.

He doesn't own it. He confiscated it.

"It's not about keeping it to myself," he tells me. "No one else can know about it. Just not yet. Okay?"

"Why? What is that place?"

His brow arches, and I can tell he's losing patience with me, but oh well.

Instead, he leans in, and I smell his breath, still minty from brushing his teeth.

Which I haven't done in almost forty-eight hours. I clamp my mouth shut as he gets closer.

"The only thing we have going for us right now," he says, "is that no one knows where we are. It's in your best interest to delay your inevitable twenty-five-to-life for as long as possible, isn't it?"

What a goddamn douche. "Eat shit," I say.

He smiles. "Let's go."

We approach the house, watching the windows for movement, and I dip down, slipping around the side toward the back.

"There could be other family here," I tell Hawke. "Does the dad have a girlfriend?"

"A new one every week," he deadpans. "Stay with me."

But I don't. I jet around the back porch, crouch down near a basement window, and peer inside, trying to see past the crud and mud caked all over the glass. I try to pull it open, but it doesn't give. Whipping off my jacket, I press it against the window and punch, hearing the slight shatter of glass crashing onto the cement floor inside.

I reach in and unlock the window. It's best to enter this way. Out of view of the road with only a forest to our backs. We are wanted by the cops, after all.

"That's how you break into houses?" Hawke teases. "The skill..."

I lift up the window and slide my body in, feet first. I jump down into the basement, him following right behind.

I look around, double-checking no else is down here.

He closes the window, and I silence my phone.

"The skill level changes based on the income bracket of whose house you're robbing, okay?" I reply. "Did you see his yard? He has the type of job that pays daily."

Hawke snorts, surprising me. Did he actually just express genuine amusement, and not at my expense?

I go on. "And nine times out of ten, people don't investigate strange noises because they're lazy. They don't want to find something because then they'll have to deal with it."

It's true. And sometimes smart. Don't go looking for trouble unless you have to. The people who die in horror movies are always the nosy ones. I mean, if you live alone and you hear footsteps in the attic, do you think for a second that you're gonna like what you find? Stay in your room.

We creep up the stairs, Hawke taking the lead and I let him. He inches the door open, and it creaks too loud. I wince. *Dude...*

I shove him out of the way. Holding the handle, I lean my ear in, hearing the TV somewhere. I open it another inch and listen. Satisfied that I don't detect any movement, I open the door, quickly scan, and pull him through, closing the door behind us.

She's probably in her bedroom, which I'm guessing is upstairs.

Looking behind me, I signal for him to follow. I step toward the banister, seeing light from the TV in the living room reflecting on the wall, just making out the top of the back of a head in the recliner.

"She has a couple of uncles," Hawke murmurs.

Good to know. Lightly, we jog up the stairs and spot a baby blue door with hot pink birds spray-painted on the surface.

I open it, exhaling when I see her pop off the bed. We hurry inside. "Get dressed," I tell her.

She shoots up, her joggers and T-shirt wrinkled from sleep, and she looks at us both, frozen. "What are you doing here?" she whispers. "I..."

"No time." I grab some jeans laying across her desk chair and toss them to her. "We need you. Now."

She holds the pants, her eyes flitting between me and Hawke before looking behind us as if she expected someone else with us.

She hesitates a moment longer and then nods. "Turn around," she tells Hawke.

"Take your time." I peer at Tommy through the rearview mirror. "Sit down, talk, relax, and then...say you're going to the bathroom or something."

I've repeated the process to her four times already, which isn't like me. But Hawke's reluctance to use a kid for this makes more sense than it did earlier this morning. I still get nervous going on a job, and I've been doing it longer.

Eighty percent of it is just going off a feeling. *Is it too noisy? Too quiet? Everyone's looking at me. They know. Do I create a distraction? Do I just act normal? Is this normal? Is that normal? Am I doing it right? Maybe I should wait.*

I learned that whenever possible, blend in. Be there. Talk. Laugh. Drink. Take the time to get out of your damn head. She could be in there for two hours, waiting for the opportunity. There's no rush.

"Text me every five minutes," Hawke tells her. "You don't text, I'm coming in after you."

I look over at him as he hands her something. "It has to be metal," he says.

I look down, seeing a small object with a lens. He points to the magnet on the back. "Make sure it sticks and—"

"I know what to do," she cuts him off.

Before we can say another word, she climbs out of the car, and Hawke spins back around in his seat, shifting like he's debating if we should be doing this.

"Don't do anything until you're relaxed," I call out just loud enough for her to hear.

We watch her head down the empty street, toward the garage, and I look around me—around the car and neighborhood—making sure no one is watching. With any luck, most of Hugo's lackeys will be sleeping well into the afternoon. Very little happens in the daylight—the occasional runner dropping off and picking up—but this could take a while. Less people in there means it'll be harder to blend in.

I slide my hands into my pockets, trying to crack my neck as if that'll get rid of this uneasy feeling in my stomach. Hugo wouldn't hurt her, would he? He'd never been violent with me, but then I'd never done anything that could send him upstate for life. Like plant a camera in the middle of his operation.

We shouldn't have involved her. This web will get out of control, and who's to say she's not using her phone to call the cops and let them know where we are right now? I don't really know her that well.

I watch her get farther away, her long white hair with blue streaks easy to see before she disappears inside. "This is a mistake," I say.

"Wasn't my idea."

I look over at Trent, seeing him stare at his phone. I drop my eyes to the screen, recognizing the girl in the guy's lap. "Is that the blonde I kicked last night?"

God, that seems like a year ago.

"She did a nice editing job on that fat lip." I smile and prop my foot up on the glove box. "You can barely notice it."

"She could've lost teeth, Aro."

I laugh, tipping my head back on the headrest and closing my eyes. That would've been awesome.

But he loses his temper. "It's not funny," he tells me. "I mean, what's the matter with you? None of this is funny."

None of this. My life, he means?

I tighten my fists inside my jacket. "Oh, I realize that nothing about me will be funny in five years, Rich Boy." I almost say it through clenched teeth. "You really don't have to remind me as much as you do."

In his head, it's a series of mistakes that got us here, and he knows very well it's not a habit for him.

"Nothing escapes me about my reality, Hawke." I turn my eyes out the window. "Her lip will heal."

He falls silent, and I think about her five years from now. His cousin Dylan in ten. Him in twenty. They can allow me my brief entertainment.

"There's ibuprofen in the glove box if you need it for your arm," he says.

He shuffles in the back seat and hands me a bottle of water to wash it down, and I take it, pressing the button to roll down the window, and fling the bottle outside before rolling it up again. He can take care of her, if he's so worried about someone.

We sit in silence, me forcing my eyes closed when I really just want to watch the door of the garage. He taps away on his phone before turning on the music.

But after a few, he's antsy. "This doesn't feel right," he murmurs.

"It's only been three minutes."

"We shouldn't have sent her in there," he tells me. "Another fucking mistake. All I'm doing is making mistakes."

I open my eyes, staring ahead at the garage down the street. "I'm going to remind you one last time before I beat it into you," I grit out and then look at him. "No one needs you. Reaction is still action, and you broke the law too. Don't put this all on me. I'll use you like you're using me, but make no mistake, I'd get it done without you."

"You'd be in jail already or dead if I didn't show up last night," he says, looking down at me.

I just snicker. "This isn't my first adventure, Pirate. I got along before you, and I'd still be kicking the shit out of your cousin and your girl right now if you hadn't come along and stuck your goddamn nose into everyone else's business, like I'm quite sure you have a habit of doing because you're a control freak who needs to insert himself to feel superior."

He just laughs, shaking his head. "This conversation is tedious."

I tip my head back, staring up through the sunroof as I mock back. "This conversation is tedious."

"Stop acting like a child," he growls. "And I'm not a control freak."

I turn my head, gazing over at him. "You watch everyone in town. Like God."

He can't argue that, can he?

"Do you get hard when you do it?" I ask.

He goes still.

"Knowing where everyone is at any moment?" I go on. "Who's skipping classes? Which spouses are cheating? Who stopped off at a liquor store, three sheets to the wind, before climbing behind the wheel of a car? Having the power to ruin a life whenever you want?"

He's clearly smart if he knows how to gain access to that surveillance, but it's still not clear what he's doing with it. Or with that place. I searched the rooms. There's only one bedroom with clothes, personal items, and a bed that looks like it's been slept in. He's not sharing it. He stays there alone.

"I wouldn't blame you," I admit. "It would feel good to have some power like that. But don't worry. I know it doesn't turn you on." I lay my head back again and close my eyes. "That's not why you do it."

It takes him a few moments, but eventually he speaks. "Why do I do it?" His voice is soft, like it was last night when he patched me up.

I smile, not sure I'm ready to play that card yet. Or that he's ready to hear it.

When I don't answer, he exhales hard and then I hear him open his door. "She hasn't texted," he says. "She's supposed to text every five minutes."

I open my eyes, immediately spotting something ahead.

"I'm going in there." He starts to climb out of the car.

I grab his arm. "Wait."

He looks back at me, but I'm looking out the front windshield. "There she is," I tell him, sitting up.

She taps away on her phone, looking at ease like I told her to, and then she passes Hawke and climbs into the back seat.

"What's the matter?" I ask her.

"Are you okay?" Hawke slams the door and turns in his seat, looking back at her.

She just nods, pulling on her seatbelt. "Yeah. It's done."

He and I exchange a look.

"Already?" I blurt out. "I told you to take your time. To relax. To blend in."

"Are you sure no one saw you?" he questions.

She just laughs under her breath. "Most people don't."

We both stare at her, but I glance behind me to make sure no one's following her. Hawke turns and loads the camera onto his laptop.

"Don't worry," she tells me, relaxed. "We're good."

But I'm still on the fence, looking behind me once again for any sign that she was followed. Just walking in and out like that is suspicious.

But then Hawke just laughs. "Well, shit."

I follow his gaze, seeing the workroom appear on his screen, the camera positioned just like we told her. Two guys play pool, but the flood of activity that usually happens at night has quieted. It's a pretty clear picture. I look up at Hawke. Where else does he have his own hidden cameras posted? I would post them everywhere. This is kind of fun.

Tommy clears her throat. "You're welcome," she sing-songs.

I smile, and Hawke flashes her a warm look in the rear-view mirror. "Thanks, Dietrich."

If that was this easy, we might use her again. One camera might not be enough.

"So, what do I get?" she chirps, doing an excited little bounce in her seat.

Hawke meets her eyes again, like he hadn't expected her to demand anything other than the pleasure of hanging out with him today.

She looks at me. "I mean, I should get paid, right?"

"Yep." I cast a look at Hawke.

Like the Joker said, if you're good at something, never do it for free.

She grins, gazing at Hawke again. "I want to go to the Loop."

FALLS

CHAPTER TEN

Hawke

The Loop—now dubbed Fallstown, because it's a lot bigger than the single track it started out as—is where everyone will be today. Everyone who knows me.

The fact that Tommy is one of the few people—including some in my family—who still refer to it as the Loop is a reminder of her connection to us. She gets that name from her father, as Dylan, Kade, and I get it from ours.

It's old school.

And I should absolutely not go. I could've said 'sure, I'll take you next week' or 'yeah, sometime this fall'.

But I didn't. I told her I'd take her. Why? Because I want to go too.

I want to know who's out there, what's going on, and maybe I'm also not excited about being bored with Aro Marquez back at the hideout for the next several days.

I glance at her out of the corner of my eye, holding my tongue as her filthy boot, complete with tattered duct tape, rests on my dash.

Well, Madoc's dash. This is still technically his car, although he hasn't driven it in years.

Her lip will heal, she'd said.

Like she was telling me something I didn't know. Of course, Schuyler's lip will heal. It was everything after that statement that she didn't say but I still heard.

Her lip will heal.

Her life will go on.

She's popular.

Desired.

About to go to college.

And everything about her life will be charmed and perfect.

Because nothing about Aro Marquez's life will be. She knows that no matter how many times or how hard she kicks, people like Schuyler have the last laugh. Aro knows she's invisible.

I glance over again, just slightly, studying the burn on her left hand. It peeks out of the cuff of her hoodie, the pinky dark and the skin rough, the injury covering the entire finger and spreading over half of the back of her hand like something that spilled on it and stained.

I want to ask her what happened, but I close my mouth instead. That conversation is for people who trust each other. She'll just get defensive.

I pull onto the dirt road, leading to the Loop, immediately pressing the brake to slow.

"You'll tell the rest of them I'm allowed here?" Tommy asks.

The car rocks over the uneven terrain, and I meet the kid's gaze in the rearview mirror. Her eyes are big and round, and I feel like she's going to hide behind me the whole time.

But I nod anyway. "Yeah."

I know why she's scared, and she should be. Not that it's her fault, but she'll be in high school in another year, and it's about to get worse. She needs to start fighting.

Aro looks back at Tommy and then at me, tucking her hands into her pockets. "Is it because she's poor?"

What? I shake my head. "Gimme a break."

"Then what is it?" she presses. "Why is she the one Falls girl not welcome in the Falls?"

It's complicated. And not worth explaining.

But most people know it has nothing to do with the kid. She's just the casualty of a situation that started when our parents were in high school with her father.

When I don't answer, Aro starts mumbling under her breath in Spanish, loud enough for me to hear and assuming I don't know she's talking shit about my family and me.

I ignore it.

"It's so bright," Tommy says, smiling as she looks into the distance beyond the trees.

It's just after noon, but the lights under the cloudy sky make it look like a carnival. Has Tommy *ever* been here? Her dad used to race here, but since my family now owns it, he doesn't step foot on the property.

"How many tracks are there?" Aro asks.

"Four." I pull into a secluded area between two trees. "Back in the day, it was all just dirt. My uncles will barely show up anymore now that it's so different."

I would've loved to have seen it back when it was new. Back when it was dangerous. Illegal.

"They say it's because they're too old. 'It's time to let new blood rule', but I think they just couldn't deal with saying goodbye to a place they loved. They prefer to remember it like it was."

"But your dad changed it," Tommy points out. "Are they mad at him?"

I smile. "No, kid." I glance up at her in the mirror. "Everything changes. That's how the world works. People change. Communities change. And you have to change with it. Just because it was the right way for one group of people doesn't mean it's right for everyone for all of eternity. My uncles know that."

I turn off the car, pulling my wallet and phone out of the console. "We learn. We change. We grow. If you don't grow, you die."

I close the sunroof and move to get out of the car, but everything is too quiet. I look over, seeing Aro watching me.

What? What did I say?

I shake my head, remembering better than to initiate a conversation that will just end up making my head hurt. "Slouching is bad for your back," I point out, eyeing her posture. "It strains your spinal discs."

Something happens to her face—the creases between her eyes soften and her lips move.

Is she smiling? I turn away, climbing out of the car.

"Why are we doing this?" she calls out. "I mean, I'm not excited to go back to that secret chamber either and be bored out of my mind while you continue to critique my posture, but we shouldn't be here." She and Tommy exit the car and meet me back by the trunk. "Your dad will be here," she points out. "He'll interfere. Not to mention, you're the class president, son of a semi-famous writer, and what...six foot three? You don't blend in."

Six-one.

And she's right.

But my parents need to see me, and I...

"Everyone has a camera phone and then there's the drones," she goes on. "What if we're spotted? What if they follow us back to the hideout?"

I open up the trunk, digging out the hoodies left over from skiing last winter. That was the last time I used his car. I toss a blue one to her and take a red one, and then I grab three face masks and dole out one to Tommy and then to her.

She stares at it. "I've been vaccinated. And boostered," she snips. "You mean you haven't? Doesn't sound like you. Figured you for someone who doesn't even drink diet soda because it's carcinogenic."

"It's to cover your face, moron," I tell her. "Get it on before I stumble over the realization that you know the word carcinogenic and start to think you have a brain."

She snatches it out of my hand, while Tommy pulls hers on. "It's actually smart." She poses. "Protesters in Hong Kong have been using these for years to hide their identity. Besides, they're also becoming a fashion accessory."

And then she does that old dance move where you form a V with your fingers and move them in front of your eyes.

Aro and I stare at her. Hong Kong?

"I *do* have a brain, on the other hand," she teases Aro.

I keep my smile to myself and pull on my sweatshirt, Aro doing the same, and then I grab Tommy's hand and put it on the waist of my hoodie for her to hold onto.

"If we get separated," I tell Aro, "I'll meet you on the roof at High Street. Keep the phone on you."

"And be ready to run," she adds.

It's a warning, because she knows this is an unnecessary risk, but I'm not making her be here. She can leave if she wants.

We walk, Tommy holding onto me as we make our way for the racetracks.

"So many Mustangs," Aro coos like she's dying of starvation.

I look over, seeing my uncle's old Boss 302 displayed off to the side. Ancient, but the car is a legend here. Dylan will be racing it tonight.

"You like Mustangs?" I walk, pulling Tommy.

"Love them," Aro sighs. "They're the easiest cars to break into."

I falter in my steps. *Jesus Christ.* I shoot her a look, but I don't say anything.

Honestly, back in the day, I'm sure my uncles would've loved her. I can't tell anyone who my dad is—or who my uncle is—without someone in this town telling me a "oh, wait till you hear about the time we were arrested" story. I think that's why I hate mistakes. My dad risked too much in order for me to live this way.

"Don't get into trouble," I tell Aro.

I can't see her mouth, but I feel like she makes a face before veering off and walking into the crowd. I almost call after her, but fuck it. It's not like she'll be able to hide a Mustang in her sweatshirt.

I pull my hood down over my eyes and keep my head down, filtering through the throngs of people coming and going. Saturdays at Fallstown, especially at the end of summer, are always packed. People are coming home from vacations, getting ready for the school year to start, and this is where they go if they want to catch up with friends. There will be events all day and into the night.

The bike track sits far off to the right, a few sets of bleachers starting to fill in anticipation of the one o'clock event, while another track roars with the engines of old muscle—Mustangs, Chargers, Camaros, Challengers, and GTOs. Drivers who appreciate a little nostalgia and history, like my uncles.

Howls and cheers ring in the air, and I look ahead to track number one—the main event. I move closer, slipping around the crowd, Tommy at my back.

I spot Kade under the hood of Dylan's car, while Noah, my uncle Jared's protégé, sips a beer and talks to some women. My dad stands up in the tower on the other side of the track. I can always tell which outline is him. It's the one hunched over the desk filled with computers and surveillance, and he's probably on high alert, keeping an eye on the crowd. I'm sure he considered canceling, but he knows I'll show up.

I scan a hundred-and-eighty degrees, looking for anything.

Aro.

Green Street.

The rest of my family and friends.

"Are you crazy?" I hear someone hiss.

I turn my head just enough to see Dylan at my side, her shoulder touching my arm as she faces whatever's behind me, trying to look like we're not talking.

"What the hell, Hawke?" she breathes out.

"Long story," I murmur.

Dylan eyes Tommy. The kid moves a little, probably tempted to hide herself.

"Green Street is here," Dylan says. "They're watching Kade and me, hoping we'll lead them to you. They can't see you with me."

I glance around quickly. "Are you okay?" I ask her.

"I'm fine," she replies. "My parents are around, and Noah is here."

I watch Noah pull up his T-shirt and use it to wipe off his face, two women about to piss themselves at the view.

143

I don't care if her mom and dad are home. If I'm not next door, I'd rather she not be there. There's a glimpse of her in those videos online too. Green Street could target her.

"Stay at Madoc and Fallon's," I tell her.

"Why?"

"They have a gate. It's safer."

Just then Noah climbs into her car, revving the engine for Kade as he works on something, and cheers go off all around him. Mostly girls. I wince, not sure if I have a reason not to like him or I'm simply jealous he can give multiple orgasms at the same time without touching anyone.

Dylan follows my gaze and snickers. "Dude, stop worrying about him and me in the same house."

That's not my concern. It's just—

"I'd be more worried about him around your mom," she jokes. "He doesn't look at me like he looks at her."

"Ugh..." Really?

"I think your dad's about to kill him," she muses, smiling a little.

"I'll help."

"Well, be careful." She looks over her shoulder at him. "Mountain Boy can swing an ax pretty good."

Whatever. I hold out my fist. "Text me when you're home safe."

She bumps me with hers. "Same."

She keeps moving, and Tommy and I head for the bleachers, but I see Aro come up carrying two beers. She keeps one, handing me the other. I stare at it, knowing she's not twenty-one and she has no money. "Do I want to know?" I ask her.

She holds my eyes, sipping her beer again as my answer.

Great. I shake my head, handing it to Tommy. "Go sit down and watch."

I'm driving tonight, and she's owed some fun. What the hell...

She smiles and pulls down her mask, sipping it like it's cocoa on Christmas.

Music starts blasting over the speakers, riling up the crowd, and I feel sweat trickle down my back.

Aro drinks the beer and looks around. "It's like a movie."

"What is?"

"What you all do for fun."

I drop my gaze down to her. "Have you ever raced?"

"Not for fun."

It takes me a second, but a snort escapes me before I can hold it back. She doesn't look at me, but I see a smile cross her face as she downs another gulp.

I take in the cars—old or new, that cost money to modify—and the teenagers, the drama, the rivalries...

I feel it too. I always did. Kind of hollow.

I never connected to this like Kade and Dylan do. I don't think Hunter does either. This was our parents' thing. I grew up with it.

I'm tired of it now.

I want something that excites me as much as this does them, but different. Something new.

I see my mother hand my little cousins, A.J. and James, some popcorn as they sit on the bleachers, and then she walks away, back to the concession stand.

"Don't cause any trouble," I tell Aro again before walking away.

I follow my mom, texting her as I go.

Behind you.

I see her drop her head and look at her phone. Her spine goes straight, and she starts to turn but doesn't.

Behind the food truck, she tells me.

I see her walk for the field, trees dotting the area, away from the noise and eyes.

But then arms slip around my waist, and I go still, fear stunning me for a moment.

"I didn't do anything with him," a girl's voice says.

Schuyler. I let out a breath, realizing it's not trouble. "You let him do something," I reply.

"We're broken up, Hawke," she says into my back. "It's not cheating."

No, it's not, but still. I don't know why I'm mad, though. Am I that jealous?

Or is it pride? Am I pissed because she let someone else touch her, or because she's giving me an easy target to blame for why it ended? *It wasn't me. It was her. She did this. She's the sole reason we failed.*

I used to be able to say that, but after five or six Schuylers, I know it's not them anymore.

"I want it to be you," she says.

I shift, feeling walls around us that aren't there. Squeezing us in, tighter and tighter.

I'm sick of sex. I'm sick of talking about it. I'm sick of thinking about it. Is that all anyone wants?

I pull her arms off me.

But she comes back in, grabbing me. "I'm sorry," she says. "I'll go as slowly as you want. I want to be your little animal."

I wish she could. I wish anyone could at this point. I want to feel it. All of it. All of *her*. The vision in my head.

So fucking much.

But I keep stopping.

I pull away. I can't do this right now. "I gotta go."

I head off into the brush, around the truck, and see my mom standing near the generator.

She rushes up and hugs me, and I wrap my arms around her, feeling her head lay on my shoulder and remembering when I was little and mine rested on hers.

"Your father told me you were safe but thank goodness." She shakes, and I hear the tears in her voice, but she doesn't cry. "Jesus, Hawke."

I release her, knowing I'm about to be yelled at now that she's satisfied that I'm safe.

"It's too late for a lecture," I warn.

"You're coming home."

"Not—"

"It's not a discussion!" she whisper-yells.

Her green eyes catch fire, and I flinch, because she scares me. My parents have a knack for getting everything they want. I didn't inherit that trait, unfortunately.

I take a moment to gather my thoughts. "That asshole has a warrant out for me," I tell her.

"You know we'll take care of it."

"I don't want it taken care of," I retort, hardening my voice more than I know I should. "I want him gone."

She drops her eyes, shaking her head. "Hawke—"

"Ricky was high on his shit when he crashed the car," I say.

She stops, slowly raising her eyes, and I can see the sadness over the loss five years ago. My parents used to take kids in. Kids like Aro. Ricky was sixteen, and the last foster they did. He's gone, and they still feel like it's their fault.

We stare at each other in silence as I wait for her to understand. I can't let this guy go. He's terrorizing a community that's too comfortable to challenge him.

"What am I supposed to say here?" she asks. "If you were me, would you just let your son take matters into his own hands?"

"No."

Of course not. I understand her position. She doesn't want anything that puts me in danger. I get it.

But I stop, Aro popping into my head and the sudden understanding of how different our lives are. I mean, I knew it, but I didn't fully get it until now.

No one will come and save her. I have a dozen ready to stand in front of me and block danger.

I made a deal with her. I should stick to it.

"There's nothing you can do to stop me," I say as gently as possible.

She looks at me, her chest caving a little and looking deflated. Like she can't believe I just said that.

It's true, though. I'm eighteen. She's not wrong, but neither am I. I'm doing this.

"I think that no matter how good your parents are or how rich you are, kids are going to get into trouble," I tell her. "You did everything you were supposed to, but I'm not backing down."

I kiss her cheek and turn to walk away, but then I hear her call out behind me. "What can I do?"

I look up, seeing Dylan climbing into her car and Noah handing her a helmet.

I turn, relief flooding me. "Can you ask Madoc to talk to the police? Find out where I'm standing with all of this?"

I need to know how much trouble I'm really in.

She nods, and I continue. "And antibiotics from Tate."

Her eyebrows touch her hairline, but I assure her, "It's not for me. Just in case, though."

She relaxes.

"And, um..." I pull out my phone, texting her again. "Can you have someone check on this address?" I know she has contacts with CPS. "It's two kids and a mom. Don't...do anything yet. I just want to make sure they're okay."

Not all foster kids are lucky enough to be placed in homes like my parents', and if they're sent farther away, that could trigger Aro. But I don't trust her mother, even if I did remove the stepdad.

"Are they relatives of that girl?" she asks.

I nod.

"I'll make a call today," she says.

I approach her and hug her again. "Thanks." I pull back. "I'll be in touch. If you don't hear from me in forty-eight hours, drag the river."

Her eyes go round, and I just laugh. "I'm kidding."

She slaps me on the arm, about to cry. "It's not funny!"

I kiss her forehead, still laughing. "I'll be in touch. Tell Dad I'm fine."

I pull my mask back up and head through people again, making my way to the bleachers where Tommy still sits by herself at the top. Looking over, Noah still talks to Dylan as her engine starts, and I see Kade chatting with friends nearby.

I wish he'd show some damn concern. I can't be the only one watching out for her around these guys. He used to be pretty protective, but after Hunter left, things changed.

I round the side of the bleachers and jump up on the side, climbing up and slipping onto the top bench so I can avoid all the eyes.

I take a seat behind Tommy, her beer cupped in her hands, still half-full. She stares out at the track, barely noticing as I take the drink from her hand and down a gulp. Following her gaze, I see Kade staring at her and not looking happy that she's here.

Her head bows a little.

"You know why he does that?" I hand the beer back to her. "Because it works."

On the one hand, I get it. Her dad fucked up in a way that'll never be forgiven and accepting her would be saying we can look past all of that when we can't. It's not her fault. It just sucks.

Kade and so many others in this town don't have to go out of their way to make her life worse, though. We don't all have to be friends, but we can be kind.

"Girls with blue hair aren't afraid of anyone," I tell her.

She laughs, and I see her head bob in a nod before she takes a drink.

"Hey, where's my purse?" someone says down below.

I look over the railing and notice Kelsey Smith spinning around and searching the area.

Her friend moves her chair, searching underneath it. "When did you see it last?"

"It was right here," she blurts out.

I raise my eyes a little, seeing a blue hoodie slink through the people.

I blink long and hard. "Wait here," I tell Tommy.

Dipping under the railing, I jump off the bleachers and push through the people, keeping my head down.

But they notice anyway. I see them do double-takes when I pass.

We have seconds.

I reach out and catch Aro's arm, guiding her beyond the crowd and keeping my voice as low as possible. "I told you not to cause trouble."

I reach around into the center pocket of her hoodie and pull out the cash I knew I'd find. I glare down at her.

She shakes her head. "Did you see her shoes?" she asks. "She can afford it."

"You don't know that."

"What do you think I'm going to do?" she argues. "Gamble with it? I'm buying fucking food, since you took away my mom's meal ticket."

I advance on her, because she's fucking yelling and we're gaining notice. I growl down at her, barely unlocking my jaw. "You should be grateful I took him out of your house."

She laughs. "All you did was take away one problem and create another. Morals are for people with second bathrooms."

"Then I'll take care of it."

"I will take care of it!" she shouts. "I feed my family. Not you!"

Everyone's looking at us, and I gaze down at her, too tired and too frustrated to figure out what to say to make her shut up and behave. She escalates everything.

She's too inconvenient. I've never known someone who repeatedly does the exact opposite of what they're supposed to. And for what? Eighty bucks? Why take unnecessary risk? Why look for trouble?

"We're going to get caught because you do stupid things," I tell her.

"Oh, like venture into a public place so you can check on your girlfriend?"

What? That's not...

I straighten, staring down at her. She must've seen Schuyler and me just now.

But I'm not going to explain myself to her. I don't explain myself to anyone. The longer this goes on, the more trouble I'm getting into, and she refuses to listen. I'm not going down for her.

"This isn't working," I say.

"Yeah, you ain't kidding."

Screw this. I still have a chance, and no matter what I do she'll end up in jail one way or another, because she only thinks from one minute to the next. Never tomorrow.

"I'm turning myself in in the morning," I say. "And I wish you the best of luck."

I walk back to the bleachers to get Tommy, but I hear her behind me. "I'd say the same, but you won't need it."

I stop, glancing behind me, but she's already gone.

And I stand there, feeling like I'm sinking and I can't get to the surface.

What will happen to her?

Where will she go?

The men in her life are predators.

My gut clenches, and I dart my eyes around, searching for the blue hoodie. Where the hell did she go?

I don't see her.

And as I take Tommy back to the car, I can't stop saying Aro's name over and over in my head, and I don't know why.

Maybe so I never forget.

So, I'll remember she was here.

Aro Teresa Marquez.

RIVER

CHAPTER ELEVEN

Aro

It takes me two hours to walk to my old house. I should probably swing by my former foster mom's and get a change of clothes, but I need to check on Matty and Bianca. Plus, I don't have the rent money I owe her.

Only my stepdad's car sits in the driveway as the place comes into view, which makes sense. My mom would probably be at work by now, and if he's in jail like Hawke said, then he's not here even if his car is.

I walk up to the house, gazing at his '79 Dodge Dart as I pass. I should steal it. It's worth a good chunk of change.

But Hawke's words ring in my ear. It would just cause more trouble, blah, blah, blah.

Of course, he's right. There's no way Hugo will take it as a payment on what I owe. Not a car stolen from someone we know.

The only thing I can do is run away with it and hope I don't get caught. *I could do it. I should.* I know how to get by. Food, fuel, shelter... I could be in Chicago tonight. Seattle by Wednesday. Canada by morning. I could start over. Even if I got caught, it's so tempting just for the hope of seeing a different view for once.

I could go.

I veer around the house and slip through the back door, something strong wafting through my nostrils before I even close it.

Vinegar. I inhale, also noticing a hint of baking soda and dish soap. Goosebumps spread up my arms as I recognize the scent. Bianca cleaned.

We could never waste money on store-bought kitchen and bathroom cleaners, so we always made our own. The bulb over the stove lights the kitchen just enough to see, but the house is quiet, and I immediately relax my shoulders at the shine on the counters and squeak of the clean floor under my shoes. Too many times I've come home or woken up to chaos. The stench of cigarettes and weed. Puke on the stairs. Strangers crashing on our couch after a party. Holes in the walls from a fight.

When I smell vinegar, I know everything's okay.

I dig in my pocket and pull out the few small bills I'd found buried in my back pocket, counting them.

I scoff and roll my eyes at myself, throwing the money on the counter. That won't help buy what they need, but I'll figure it out. I always do.

I open the fridge to see where they stand on the necessities, but as soon as I pull the door open, individually packaged Jell-O cups and cheese sticks spill onto the floor.

I dive down, narrowing my eyes as I try to pick up the mess, but I see all the food on the shelves and hesitate. What the hell?

The packed fridge overflows with milk, juice boxes, lunch meat, snacks... I drop the stuff in my hands and pull open the drawers, seeing it filled with fresh produce. I stuff the contents that spilled out back onto the shelves and rise, pulling open the freezer. Treats and meat and pre-packaged pasta and stir-fry meals...

I straighten, realization hitting. My mom rarely stocks the fridge, but sometimes she'll get a big spender at the club, and she can afford to buy some fun stuff. I pull open cabinets, seeing cereal and Pop-Tarts and canned soup.

But she would never buy this much. And never the high-end brands. Whoever did this isn't in this family. We don't shop this way.

Bianca enters the kitchen and stops when she sees me. She has a trash bag full of garbage she's probably carting outside.

"Where did all this food come from?" I ask her, but I think I already know the answer.

She smiles, setting down the bag. "Instacart. Someone had it delivered this morning."

Someone, my ass. I slam the freezer door and pull off my hood and hat, running my hand through my hair. He let me panic when he told me he had my stepdad arrested, and he'd already sent a month's worth of food. He didn't want any pushback, so he didn't tell me that I had one less thing to worry about.

And I would've pushed back. I don't need him showing them a life they'll never have and getting their hopes up.

Filling up a glass of water, I drink until it's empty.

"Aro, what were you thinking?" Bianca asks behind me.

I stay quiet, not because I'm avoiding her, but I'm not sure which stupid thing that I did she's referring to.

Probably the gunshot.

Instead, I change the subject. "Are you okay?" I turn around. "And Matty?"

She nods, a wistful smile crossing her lips. "We're fine. I don't know who sent the food, but it helps. He's in heaven." She laughs, turns, and I follow her, both of us peering around the corner and watching his feet bouncing over the side of the couch as he hugs a bag of pretzels and Flynn Rider sings on the TV. "Been watching Disney all day and snacking," she tells me. "I should cut him off—"

"No," I say quickly, loving this view the most. Him, belly full, and lost in the fun he's having. "Let him eat what he wants."

She nods and we slip back into the kitchen.

"They've been looking for you," she says. "You really shouldn't be here."

"I just wanted to make sure you all were safe. Where's Mom?"

"Working." She opens the back door, tossing the trash into the can right outside. "Asshole got arrested for some outstanding warrant, so they picked him up from the hospital. She's trying to scrounge money together to bail him out."

"Of course, she is." But I fight to hold back a smile. They don't seem to know the warrant is fake. Hawke's trick is working, and no one is onto him. Yet.

I dial her on my phone and then hang up. "That's my new number," I tell her. "Don't give it to anyone."

"Are you okay?" she asks.

I almost laugh, not sure how to answer that. She's a little clueless sometimes, but she's kind.

"I won't be if you get pregnant," I snap, shooting her a teasing look but not really. "You're taking your pills?"

She looks away, embarrassed.

"Bianca?"

"Yes!" she whispers a yell. "Damn!"

Telling her not to have sex with her boyfriend is useless. He's all she really has.

"Take care of Matty," I tell her, spinning around.

"I will."

I open the back door, taking a step out, but suddenly, someone is there. I rear back. Hugo's eyebrows shoot up, surprised, but then a smile curls his lips like his job just got a lot easier.

Shit!

I shove him in the chest, he topples backward, and I run, leading him away from the house.

Yanking up my hood, I tuck my phone inside my clothes and dig in my heels, powering as fast as I can.

Climbing over the chain-link fence, I jump down into the next backyard, and instead of turning right toward the street, I race left, toward the dirt road, behind the houses.

"I'm not going to hurt you!" Hugo yells. "Why do you run from me?"

Bullshit.

I halt in the alleyway, looking left and then right. Axel stands in front of his red Mustang, and I spin around, rushing the other way.

I shouldn't have come. I could've called. What good am I, if I can't help them?

I take a right, down a small pathway between houses, and leap over the fence, scrambling into the wooded area that borders Weston.

Footfalls pound behind me, and I look back, seeing Hugo on my tail. I whimper, unable to stop the noise from bubbling up my throat.

He lands on my back, taking me down into the tall grass, and I jerk my elbow back into him. He falls off, and I scurry to my feet, but he grabs me and comes up, wrapping his arms around me.

"Shhh..." He sounds like he's handling a child. "No one is going to hurt you."

Tears spring to my eyes, and my legs nearly give out. He squeezes me, the wound on my arm aching.

"Killing you doesn't make him money," he says. "Thank God, right?"

I growl, thrashing in his hold. "Hugo, no."

"Shhh."

He brushes my ear with his mouth, and I shake, my gaze slowly rising upward. I see Orion in my head, pinpointing in the sky where the top left corner star of the constellation might appear when it becomes visible every winter.

Betelgeuse. One of the brightest stars in the constellation. I picture it looking back at me. *Do you see me?*

"Just let her go, man," Nicholas shouts.

He never had the stomach for this.

But Hugo just tsks. "We all serve our purpose." And then in my ear, "This is the only way. You know that."

Then he grips my jaw, twists my face around, and covers my mouth with his. I cry out.

"Hugo!" Nicholas growls.

See me.

I bite down, tasting his blood, and he screams. So do I. I drop like dead weight, feeling his hold loosen, and I run. As fast as I can. Past the tree line and into the darkness of the woods. I run and run, slipping into a pool of mud, but before I can get out, they're nearly on me. I dip down, my body nearly covered in the sludge, and I go still, trying to make like a stone.

"Bianca is growing up nice and pretty," Hugo yells.

I shake.

"I'll get my money back on your ass or hers."

I squeeze my eyes shut, my stomach roiling.

"I don't want to do that," he says, looking around the trees and into the distance, past me. "But *he* will if he has to."

Hugo is a piece of shit, but I don't fear him, not like Reeves. Hugo would coerce me, but he'd never force me. And he knows Bianca is all Matty has right now.

He doesn't want that.

"The clock is ticking," he calls out. "Come to your senses."

A moment later, footsteps retreat, and they leave.

I crawl out of the little pool, mud spilling from my clothes as the rain kicks up again. I tip my head back, but I don't look. I just let the water wash away the dirt.

If you don't grow, you die.

I don't want to die. I don't want to be this anymore.

I stay there a while, making sure they're gone as I try to let the despair and worry work their way through me—out of me—so I can get my head clear. So, I can figure out what I need to do.

After a while, I walk slowly, staying on side streets and between houses, checking my phone and seeing it's dead. Probably from the water.

I walk and walk forever, down a dark country road that slowly starts to brighten with streetlights as the sun sets, and I don't know where I'm going, just away.

At least it seems he doesn't know about the camera at Green Street.

Thoughts race through my head—solutions that won't work and people who can help me but won't. Is this what my mother thought once upon a time? Where the pressure got too hard and the options too little, and she just decided that was it? All she'd ever be.

So, she pays the bills she can, lets her kids raise each other, and carves out a moderate amusement for herself here and there until she dies.

Did she want more? Ever?

They wear you down. All the shit, all the time, and all the disappointment until you just stop fighting. You let it happen to you. You let everything happen to you, and you just act grateful it's not going to kill you today, so you can enjoy a few more beers. You don't fight it, because if it's not one thing, it's another, so what's the point?

What's the point? What are we here for?

I take a step, climbing a fire escape, when I realize I'm back at the hideout. I'm in Shelburne Falls. It's dark, and I'm soaked from rain that still pours.

I look around me, seeing I've ascended three stories of the building, making my way for the roof, and I'm suddenly so tired. I stop, my legs shaking.

My muscles harden like they're filled with knots, and I grip the railing before stumbling backward. I slide down the edge of the landing and drop to my ass on the steel grate of the third floor. I'm done. I got nothing left.

My muddy hair hangs down my chest, and despite the August air, I shiver in my soaked clothes.

Grow or die. I don't want to die. If I went back to Hugo, it would kill me. I can't do what he wants me to do.

I hear him before I see him, his steps coming down the stairwell. He stops at my side, and I see he's wearing running shoes. He was probably exercising when he saw me on the cameras.

I'm about to tell him I'll take a hike. I'm just resting.

But he takes a seat next to me, and for some reason, I feel tears burn my eyes.

"Are you injured?" Hawke asks in a soft voice.

I shake my head.

Rain spills between the grating, and I don't know why he stays there, getting just as soaked as me.

I don't try to talk, though. Whatever comes out of my mouth seems to make everything worse. Yesterday I didn't really care. Today I do.

"My parents took me all these places growing up," he says. "They had a hard time of it when they were kids. They didn't get to see the world. Learn what they were capable of." He bends one knee up and drapes his arm over it. The vein in his hand bulges, disappearing underneath his watch. "And when they got pregnant with me long before they were really ready, they decided to not let it stop them. They were getting out there. Together. They strapped me on their backs and went."

I try to picture him as a child, but I can't.

"Camping, hiking, hunting," he goes on, "broke down bus rides through the Andes, and we even had to hitchhike once. My mom was really scared." He laughs a little and then continues. "They taught me to ration food and forage for supplies. How to do a lot with very little." He pauses, and when he speaks again, he's quieter. "But it never really occurred to me until today..." I see him look over at me out of the corner of my eye. "I did all of that with the knowledge that I was never in any real danger."

My chin trembles, and I clench my teeth to stop it.

"I was never going to starve," he says, "because I was never going to be alone in the world. I have a huge family. All of whom are ready at a moment's notice to be there for me."

Unlike me, he means. But despite the warmth I feel that at least he's aware of how lucky he is—how he might not be the guy he is if he'd been born into my world—I fight to stay hard.

"I don't need your pity," I tell him.

But he's quick to respond. "I don't feel sorry for you, Aro." He falls quiet, and I almost can't hear him when he says, "I think you're amazing."

My heart skips a beat, and I freeze.

Amazing? Did he smoke something? Not enough oxygen getting into the hideout, maybe?

"You can do a lot for an eighteen-year-old," he muses, and I hear the smile in his voice. He's still looking at me. "What can you do at nineteen, I wonder? At twenty-five and at thirty?"

A lump lodges in my throat, and I turn my eyes out to the alley, blinking away the water on my face.

"Let's do this." His voice is gentle. "I don't want that piece of shit to win, okay?"

I want to. I want to do this with him. To finally win.

Never give up the fight.

Hawke stands up and holds out his hand for me. I don't hesitate. Taking it, I let him pull me up, my body no longer weak, just tired.

And hungry.

I face him, and he faces me, and it occurs to me how small I feel suddenly. Like my giant ego has deflated a little, and I'm just now realizing how tall he is.

I don't look at him. "Thank you for the food," I say. "I'll pay you back."

He's quiet for a moment, and I know he's not asking for his money back. He wouldn't.

But he knows I can't owe him.

He simply replies, "I know you will."

And it's done. We talked and didn't fight, and it's strange how I'm suddenly glad I don't have to leave him.

"Here," he says and reaches over, pulling my jacket off my shoulders. "Let me wring it out. We'll wash it."

It takes a moment, but I agree. Nodding, I let him pull my coat off, and I slip my hoodie over my head, the hat coming with it.

I drop everything to the landing and kick off my boots, not wanting to track mud into the building. Finally, I look up at him to see him staring down at me.

I stand there a moment. My drenched hair hangs in my face, mud coating my black pants and arms, turning my white tank top a grungy brown. Drops of rain hit my feet and spill down his chest that I didn't realize was bare until now.

Something warms, low in my belly, and for just a second, I'm a teenage girl. Something throbs, and I suck in a little breath, looking away.

"Astronomy," I say.

I look up, and he cocks his head, looking puzzled.

"I like...astronomy," I tell him something about me. "I used to dream I'd be an astronomer when I was twenty-five or thirty."

Since he asked.

His smile is small but beautiful, and I dive down to gather up my nasty clothes before he touches them.

FALLS

CHAPTER TWELVE

Hawke

She doesn't need anyone to save her. Maybe that's why we've been fighting so much. I resent that she'll always find a way to eat. To pay the bills. To get out of one scrape before she gets into another, even if it means lying, stealing, and conning.

I resent that there's a right way to do things and a wrong way, and she always seems to choose the wrong way.

But I stare at the footage recording from the garage—drugs and young girls and a toddler running around on screen in the worst possible environment...

And maybe I don't know everything. Maybe there is no right way. You eat or you don't.

I log onto social media, sweeping the sites and seeing my hoodie and hers visible in several videos from Fallstown—a few comments noticing me too.

I came back to the hideout a few hours ago and tried to track her phone, but there was no signal. She probably threw it away.

You okay? I text Tommy as I walk for the kitchen.

I dropped her off after Aro left the race, but there's still no certainty that they didn't see her at the garage today.

A text rolls in. *Yeah, why?*

I almost laugh as I open the fridge and dig out a beer. For a kid who looks like she's going to cry every time someone looks at her wrong, she pulled off a dangerous job today with amazing ease.

Thanks for helping, I simply reply.

Ur welcome.

I set my phone down, but then it beeps with another text.

I'm free tomorrow, Tommy writes.

And I chuckle, shaking my head and mumbling under my breath, "I'll let you know, kid."

I drop the phone onto the island, but then I hear Aro's voice behind me. "So, does your cousin not have boobs or something?"

What?

I turn my head and see her standing there, freshly showered with her wet hair fanned around her and hanging down her arms.

My face falls a little.

Something flips inside me, and I draw in a sharp breath, looking away. I close my eyes for a second. "I..." I shake my head. "I have no idea. I never looked."

Jesus Christ. I open the drawer and pull out the bottle opener, my neck sweating.

"I mean, the jeans are fine," she explains, "but the shirt is..."

I swallow and glance back, seeing her pull at Dylan's white JT Racing T-shirt, the curves of her breasts creating two half-moons that are still visible even as she tries to keep the fabric from clinging to her body.

A sliver of skin peeks out above the waist of her black jeans, tears and holes in the pants giving an eyeful of her tawny skin and shape.

I pop the top of the beer and take a swig, trying not to look, but she was hiding a lot under that hoodie and hat. Hair hangs in her face, rich, dark eyes—almost black—peering at me through the wet strands. I drop my eyes to her mouth...

I take another drink.

She continues to tug on the shirt, trying to keep it away from her body. When I don't say anything, she shifts on her feet, an awkward silence filling the room. "So, you said there was a washing machine?"

I look down, noticing she has a garbage bag in her hand. Her muddy clothes. Right.

"Yeah." I lead her away, thankful to have something to do. "Follow me."

We head up the small staircase, down the hallway, and I open the mirror into the bake shop.

"And the Pirate jersey is baggy, if you'd prefer that," I tease, remembering Dylan included another option.

"My tits look horrible in orange," Aro says. "Everyone looks horrible in orange, Hawke."

Tits? Did she really...? Ugh.

I step through the mirror, feeling her follow me. "Don't women hate the word tits?"

My mom would never say that.

But she jokes, "Oh, I'm sorry. My *breasts* look horrible in—oh, nope, 'breasts' is still pretentious. I'll just keep saying tits."

I wince. That sliver of attraction I might've felt a moment ago is suddenly gone. Thank God.

"Or hooters!" she chirps.

Jesus…

"Knockers, maybe?" She won't stop. "How about 'my bosoms'? Mammary glands! Udders!"

I push through the kitchen door, hearing it slam into the one of the stoves behind it.

"I can make this so much worse, Hawke."

"God, you're vulgar." I walk over to the combo washer and dryer Quinn installed here to take care of dish towels and aprons. I open the washer lid.

"Just keeping it real," she taunts behind me. "We'll never be friends."

"And I might cry about that eventually." I turn to look at her. "Once it sinks in." I point to the shelf to the right of the machine. "Tide PODS are there. Don't eat them."

I walk away, hearing her snort.

She dumps her clothes into the washer, takes a pod, tosses it in, and starts the machine. Her right arm stays at her side as she does everything with her left, and it hits me. The injury from her stepfather. I forgot.

I should've checked it when she came inside. She looked like she'd been in another fight.

I doubt she's eaten since this morning either.

My stomach growls, too.

"You hungry?" I ask, hearing the water start to load inside the washing machine.

She faces me, and I blink, trying to hide the fact that my gaze dropped. To her shirt.

I clear my throat. "I'm starving." I turn and get to work, pre-heating the oven and digging a pan and some utensils out. "There's a container of sauce in the cooler. Can you grab it?" I ask her. "And toss me the pepperoni too."

She smiles small, and I can tell she's hungry. It's after midnight, but she doesn't look any more tired than I am, so we set to work, making pizza in the sealed-off kitchen that's supposed to be empty until next May.

I stream some music, both of us relaxing a little. It's late, and if anyone passes by and hears us or smells the oven, they'll think it's coming from Rivertown.

It's kind of nice—seeing the world but not having them see you. Like we're the only two people left.

I watch her pull her hair up into a ponytail, long bangs hanging in her eyes as she kneads the dough I made. I chop toppings, and I can't stop the heat warming my body. I don't know why this feels good, but it does.

She's the first non-family member woman I've been around in a long time who's not expecting me to make a move. Being around her isn't hard or pressuring.

She's easy.

For a little while anyway.

"You are such an idiot!" she barks ten minutes later as I spread sauce over the dough.

"Chicago-style pizza is not pizza," I retort, sorry I ever got into this dumbass discussion with her.

"And who determines what pizza is?"

"Italians." I place pepperoni slices, keeping my tone calm, even though she's about to spit fire. "Pizza is not something you eat with a knife and fork. Now the pliable New York pie that you can fold in half? Hell yeah."

"Would you have some fucking regional pride, for crying out loud?" She scowls at me. "We're basically Chicagoans."

"It's not pizza." I flex my jaw. "It's a meat pie."

"And Chicago is tougher," she snaps, getting in my face. "Windier, colder, snowier—you need more substance in your pizza."

"Oh, please."

She continues. "The rest of the country just can't handle four pounds of heat and meat in their mouths, Hawke."

Oh my God. I gape at her for a solid four seconds and then...

I can't contain it. I laugh, having to turn away. "What the hell..."

I laugh so hard my eyes tear, and I hear her behind me. "Haha," she teases. "Gotcha."

I plant my hands on the counter, bending my head and still laughing. "Okay, okay...I got nothing on that."

She beams, and I get the rest out as I walk over and take some of the cheese she's shredded, sprinkling it on.

"Now, how do you feel about the Chicago *pub-style* pizza?" I ask.

She follows suit, sprinkling on cheese. "Pizza should not be cut into squares."

"I agree."

"That's not pizza."

I shake my head. "Not pizza at all."

She finishes while I search the cabinet for the oregano and sea salt I left here. Quinn's bakery ovens are even better than Grandpa Jason's brick one, so whenever I want perfectly baked crust, I just come here. Or when I want to cheer Quinn up. She loves making pizza.

I toss some seasoning on top, a quiet settling over the room, and I glance over at Aro, seeing her watch me. She looks away. "Um...is the camera still working okay?" she asks.

"Yeah. I checked the footage while you were in the shower. Nothing so far."

I'm recording when I'm not watching, so whatever is going on there, we'll catch it. We just have to be patient. For how long, is the question.

"I need to go out tomorrow," she tells me. "I need to sneak into my foster mom's house while she's at work and get some clothes."

I look over at her, studying her. They'll be looking for her there. Even though she's technically no longer in the woman's care, Green Street will know she still crashes at that house. They might not be staked out there, but the neighborhood will be told to keep an eye out for her to show up.

"That's not a good idea," I tell her. "I'll have Dylan bring some bigger shirts."

"And underwear?" she presses. "Bras? I mean, I can't wear hers. I need things, Hawke."

I drop my eyes but raise them again, realization hitting. She's not wearing anything under her clothes right now. Whatever she had would be in the washer.

She stares at me, but I pick up the pizza, not saying anything. Underwear isn't that important. She's not risking being caught for that.

The silence that settles is more awkward than the last, and there are a million things I want to ask her, but she's in a good mood, and I don't want to ruin it.

Thankfully, she steps in. "You know, your girlfriend being jealous isn't out of line." she says, sipping my beer. "I probably would've keyed your car by now."

I laugh under my breath, visualizing that perfectly. And I know she's right. Holing up with another woman looks like something it isn't.

"How about I sneak out to get clothes," she says, a playful tone in her voice, "and you sneak out to see her and explain the situation? It's a win-win."

Yeah, right. I'm not letting her out of my sight. She'll do something stupid.

Plus, the issue with Schuyler started long before this weekend. It has nothing to do with Aro and will take a lot more than an explanation to fix.

She picks up some leftover shredded cheese and tips her head back, dropping it in. Everything feels warm as I watch her.

I don't want to go out. I like it here.

With her.

She asked what this place was and what it meant to me, and I'm not entirely sure yet, but I do know it has a name.

And so many stories behind it. Stories of people who were here before us.

Most of the town doesn't even think it really exists. But they like to believe it does. They want to believe the stories are true.

I stare at her, realizing something. *We'll be one of them.* One of the stories that people will tell one day. Aro and me.

I don't want to leave. Not for underwear. Not for Schuyler. Not just yet.

I pull myself away, pressing buttons on the oven and setting the timer. "Let me look at your arm," I tell her. "Come on."

"It's really okay," she argues, but I'm already walking away, untying the apron around my waist. I toss it back onto the worktable and lead her back into the hideout, sealing it closed again, even though I know no one is coming into the bakery, and I'll have to go back out to get the pizza anyway.

Taking her into the other kitchen, I pull out the first aid kit and some cooling lotion. She just took a shower, so it's clean, but I don't have anything for the pain other than ibuprofen.

Sitting down on a stool at the island, I take her arm and pull her over. She stumbles, coming to rest between my knees.

"I just don't want this to get infected," I tell her, inspecting her wound. "If we're going to get caught, it's not going to be because we had to go to the hospital."

She looks down at me, but I don't meet her eyes. I spray the cut with disinfectant, apply some ointment and wrap a bandage around her arm, trying to keep it clean.

"I didn't think you'd have a tattoo," she says.

I look up as she eyes the script across my shoulder, above my chest. Really small. Most people don't notice it at first.

I continue wrapping her up. "It's the only one I have."

"What does it mean?"

These violent delights have violent ends.

"I don't know," I tell her honestly. "I'll let you know if I figure it out."

She cocks her head, studying me, and I'm thankful she doesn't ask why I got a tattoo I don't understand. I've been staring at the same tattoo on my father my whole life. I know it means something. I know it's important.

"Why didn't you think I'd have one?" I ask. "Too much of a mama's boy?"

"No." She smiles, and she looks five. Sweet. "It just seemed like you were different."

Different? When has she observed me? We've never met before yesterday.

She draws in a breath and clears her throat. "Weston was looking forward to a rematch with you last fall," she says. "But you quit the team mid-season. I saw you play once. The year before, actually."

So that's when she might've seen me. I secure the tape around her arm. "You don't strike me as person who goes to pep rallies and football games."

"I was delivering weed to a cheerleader."

I laugh, despite myself. It's not funny, but it's comforting. I'm kind of glad football's not her thing.

"Ten seconds left in the fourth quarter," she tells me. "You caught a pass and tumbled right into the end zone, securing the victory."

Yeah, I remember.

"I didn't really care until I saw that you weren't celebrating." She stares at me, but I don't look as I tap her out some medicine and pour some water. "That's when I noticed you. Your teammates crowded around you, the stadium exploded in screams and cheers. You just walked back to the sidelines, even as they tried to hang on and congratulate you. You acted like none of it was there."

I can't believe she saw that. Did other people pick up on it? I didn't mean to be a prick. I just...

I sit there, pulling her short sleeve back down. "I found this place a week before I quit football." I glance over at the gray brick wall, gesturing as I read the words in white paint. "'Vivamus, moriendum est.' It was there when I got here," I tell her and then translate. "'Let us live, since we must die.'"

She looks back at the words, and I can't tell if she's breathing. I've probably stared at those words for hours in total.

"I don't really like football," I tell her.

She jerks her eyes back to me, now understanding. I didn't want to be on that field that day. I hadn't for a long time.

She rubs her arm, looking down. "I don't like a lot," she almost whispers. "Some things you have to put up with."

"Some things you do."

I understand what she's saying. I could quit football, because I don't need a scholarship. I can quit jobs, because I don't need the money. I know I'm lucky. I have choices.

"And sometimes you can just quit. Leave. Hide," I say. "Sometimes that's okay."

She raises her eyes to me, and something fills my chest in a way that's new. I like that she's here. I'm glad she came back.

When I saw her enter the alley tonight, soaked and hurt and in so much more pain on the inside than she was on the outside, I went up to get her. She really had nowhere else to go. It wasn't right. How does a kid get to be that alone? What did she do? What could she possibly have done to have no one?

She'll never need saving. She'll always get up. I already know that about her.

Let's see what two loners can do together.

I rise from my seat, grabbing my workout gloves on the counter and pulling them on. "And she's not my girlfriend anymore. We broke up two weeks ago." She looks up at me as I look down at her. "We're not leaving here. No unnecessary risk. I'll have Dylan bring you something tomorrow. What are you...thirty-four C?"

Her eyes go wide. "I thought you never looked."

"At my cousin, dumbass." I pull the strap tight with my teeth. "I can look at you."

Her eyebrows rise.

"Twenty minutes on the pizza." I step to the side and head for the gym. "Come and get me when it's ready."

CHAPTER THIRTEEN

Aro

I *can look at you.*

Does that mean he likes to?

Two days later, and I'm still obsessing about it.

I gaze down at the T-shirt, grinding a thread from one of the holes in the thigh of my jeans between my fingers before I take in my reflection in the fish pond.

He looked at me.

I guess I told him to when I thought he was avoiding acknowledging me that first night, because he thought he was so much better. But maybe that wasn't why he wouldn't look. Hawke is complicated.

The debris from the crash has already been cleared, but there are still some shards of glass here and there, and significant damage to the rocks. Koi swim just under the surface of the water, what's left of the foliage broken and smashed.

Cones and a construction fence block off the entire area, but I hopped it and descended down the small walls to the water. The reflection of the moon shimmers on the pond.

It's been a day since his cousin brought me more clothes, but I'm trying to wear as little of it as possible. The undergarments are new, and I told him I could easily get mine, but he doesn't trust me to stay out of trouble.

I take in my appearance once more and then shake my head. Guys look at girls. It doesn't mean anything. That girl I kicked in the face is pretty perfect.

Or was. Before I kicked her in the face.

And she's not my girlfriend. Hearing him say that kind of delighted me. Probably more than it should. At least I don't have to feel guilty about living in such close proximity to her man.

I jog down the path, away from the pond, to a fire pit in a secluded, wooded area. Climbing the three rock steps, I cross the circular gathering area and lean over the side of the rock wall, pulling away the shrubbery. Buried underneath is the black duffle—or one of them—from Hugo's trunk. I pull it up, rise to my feet, and slip the strap over my head, the bag hanging at my side.

I should just leave it here, but the bag isn't waterproof, and the park crew will be repairing the pond, and they could find it. I jump down from the platform and run back up the path. I really hope they don't have cameras here. I wouldn't put it past Hawke to be regularly scanning footage of every corner of town. He'll lock me up for good if he sees I snuck out.

But a shape appears ahead, and I halt, my boots grinding over the dirt path.

Shit. I stare, seeing three figures walking toward me.

I back up, and they stop.

"Don't touch me," I say, gripping the strap of the bag.

The one on the right tries—and fails—to hold back a small laugh.

"Where's my son?" the middle one asks.

I take another step back, staring at him. Son?

I take in the height, the black hair and blue eyes, and the stoic stare like everything's an inconvenience and he's far too busy. *Jaxon Trent*. Hawke's father resembles him in more ways than just looks.

I recognize the one on the left. Jared. His older brother. Hawke's uncle. Dylan's father. He put Shelburne Falls on the map and practically invented Fallstown. The Pirates have lived under a lucky star ever since. Fuck him.

The one on the right looks familiar, but I don't remember from where. Blondie looks like a frat boy and a little out of place with these two.

Frat boy...

And then it hits me. He looks like Kade. Blond, blue eyes, lean but muscular build, and a cockiness in their eyes, because there's nothing they don't win at. That's why this guy looks familiar. He's the mayor of Shelburne Falls. I've seen him on posters.

"How did you know I was here?" I ask, ignoring Mr. Trent's question.

A gleam hits his eyes before they dart up to the tree, and I notice a security camera.

Jesus Christ. I scowl. "You're all creepers. Your whole family."

The blond one shakes with a laugh, and I dig my eyebrows in deeper. No wonder Hawke is a little voyeur.

They approach, but I don't move this time. There's three of them. I won't get away.

"We can protect you," Hawke's father says.

"*I* can protect you," Mr. Caruthers clarifies.

He's not only mayor, but he's a lawyer. I'm pretty sure he prosecuted my stepfather on one of his many run-ins with the law back in the day.

These are the last people I would trust.

They don't give a shit about me.

"I was a foster kid, too," Hawke's dad says, inching closer. "I know how it is. You get used to nothing feeling like home, but then you're not even sure what that ever felt like anyway, right?"

I look ahead, his chest coming into view.

"Maybe you don't remember something warm and safe," he continues. "You just reminisce about a time when you didn't know there was anything better."

Like my brother. Some snacks and some Disney are all he needs to escape. He isn't aware of everything happening around him.

"You get pushed around by people like us—adults—and you realize that no one really wants you." His voice is almost a murmur, and I wonder what memory plays in his head right now. "You're just a job. They feed you. They don't talk to you. You get used to distrusting everyone."

My throat grows thick. I force it down.

"But I was lucky," he tells me. "I got out."

"You're lucky, because you're a man." I meet his eyes. "You can make kids and leave. One pregnancy, and a poor girl stays a poor girl."

I harden my jaw, breathing hard. Men walk out of their lives every day. My father did. My stepdad comes and goes when he feels like it, knowing someone will take care of Matty and Bianca. *That someone always ends up being a woman.*

Jaxon Trent nods. "I know."

He comes to stand in front of me, and I hold his gaze, trying to control myself. Why am I so upset?

I want to go back to the hideout.

But Hawke's dad goes on. "The problem with relying only on yourself is that someday you'll burn out."

I don't blink.

"You'll get tired of the fight, and you'll give in." He looks down at me. "You'll let everything happen to you, because you just don't have the energy anymore. You're tired of everything being so hard."

Yes. Exactly.

I can already feel it coming. I don't know how, but he knows.

"Is he safe?" his dad asks.

I drop my eyes, nodding.

"Does he need me?"

I want to say yes. It surprises me. I don't want Hawke hurt in any of this. Maybe I should just end it. Let him go.

"I could take you right now, you know?" he says. "To the police. He'd come out of hiding if I did that."

"I know," I murmur. In that instance, I know Hawke wouldn't let me take the rap alone.

I should tell them where the hideout is. I should get Hawke out of this.

"If he was your kid, what would you do?" Jaxon Trent asks.

I'd do what you're doing. I'd order my kid home or find them and drag them by the ear if I had to.

I promised him, though. He made me promise I wouldn't tell anyone.

I shift on my feet, picturing his face at the police station when he knows I ratted us out. I don't want to give up.

"Trust him," I tell his dad. "He's a good person."

He bugs me a lot, and I've only known him a few days, but I know that much.

His dad sighs, and I see him glance at his brother on one side and the mayor on the other, but no one says a word.

I nearly glance at Jared Trent, suddenly remembering the stories of how he married the girl he bullied in high school.

They have no room to talk, quite honestly. They would do what Hawke's doing.

"If I don't get back soon, he'll wake up and know I'm gone," I blurt out. "He'll yell at me again."

Mayor Caruthers chuckles, and I look up to see a small smile on his dad's face.

"And why did you come out tonight?" Jared presses.

But I clamp my mouth shut. Dream on, douchebag.

They're quiet for a minute, and I know Hawke's father is debating whether to make good on his threat to drag me in to the cops in order to force his son home.

"Please take care of him," he finally says.

I look up, all of them standing there, and for the first time it hits me how truly better Hawke's life is than mine. His dad loves him. Which is why he's doing the hardest thing right now and trusting his kid.

It isn't until I'm out of the park and circling High Street for the third time that I know for sure I'm alone—that no one followed me—and it's safe to re-enter the hideout. Sneaking back up to the roof, I climb down into our place and shut the door. I run down the hall, peering around corners for any sign of Hawke, but it's after two in the morning. He should still be asleep.

I stash the bag under the cushion of the recliner in the sitting area, plop down on it a couple of times to even out the lump, and then I jet back down the hall, seeing Hawke's door is cracked. I don't see any light coming from inside, though.

Tucking my hair behind my ear, I push the door open until his bed comes into view.

My skin crawls, feeling like I'm being watched. Like he's up, ready to pounce and yell at me for going outside.

But his bed sits ahead, the headboard against the wall and Hawke lays in the middle, the sheet draped up to his waist.

"Hawke?" I whisper.

Is he really not up? I thought for sure I'd get caught.

I tiptoe into his room and stand at the foot of his bed, the glow from the hallway lighting up his form. The sheet sits just below his stomach, his torso bare, and I inch in, trying to get a closer look.

Heh. You can see his abs even when he's not flexing. One arm drapes over his stomach, the other lays on the bed at his side, his head turned and his chin down. His lashes don't move, and the steady rise and fall of his chest is like a metronome you can't hear. He's so peaceful.

I rise back up straight, about to leave, but I drop my eyes to the sheet and the way it hugs his legs. The upside-down V between them perfectly pronouncing every curve. Every muscle.

Every muscle.

Heat spreads up my neck, and I spin around, leaving the room. God, he's got a nice body. Too bad he doesn't know how to use it.

I head to the kitchen and make myself a sandwich, standing at the island and eating.

Vivamus, moriendum est. I stare at the words on the brick wall across the room in front of me. Stars glow outside the windows above, too high for anyone to see in and for us to see them, but I can see the stars from inside, and that's good enough for me.

Hawke still hasn't divulged what this place is exactly. What's his plan? He's known about it for a while and hasn't really shared it with anyone other than a select few.

And me.

But someone else knows about it. Possibly several other someones. I stare at the inscription on the wall again, gauging the age of the paint, but I'm not sure. It's definitely not new. Hawke didn't paint it. He even said so.

Taking my sandwich, I stroll through the door to my left and down another hallway I haven't explored yet. This may have been a speakeasy back in the day. Room after room, windowless, cool, and with the smell of oak and bourbon. The feel of wet hanging in the air. Dark.

How can the city not know that shops and eateries occupying this strip of building take up less space than what's actually here? Don't they have blueprints? Deeds with square footage?

Chicago isn't far. I can imagine Al Capone and Bugs Moran using this as their black market storage for the illegal liquor they were bringing into the city.

But there's furniture too. Pictures on the walls.

I stop and peer in closely at one of them—a girl, her blonde hair blowing in her face as she walks in a field. The sun wanes behind her, and I can almost make out her eyes behind her hair, but not quite.

These things are newer than the 1920s. People have been here since.

A small light glows ahead, and I walk toward the glass. I look through and crane my neck, trying to see as much as I can of the business on the other side of the hideout. On the other side of a mirror just like the one leading to the bakery.

Rivertown.

I smile. "You've got to be kidding me."

I'd bet my life Hawke was in here, watching the cameras, and saw Dylan talking to me the other night. He showed up out of nowhere to save the day, just like Superman.

I laugh and take a bite of my sandwich, turning away. I'm not really mad, although it does aggravate me that he uses his superpowers against me.

But then realization dawns, and I stop. I cease chewing my ham and cheese.

If he has cameras everywhere else, then he has them inside here. I forgot to check.

Ugh. I run back down the hall, into the great room, and throw off the seat cushion, grabbing the duffle. Hugging it to my body, I spin around, looking everywhere. Every nook. Every corner. Around every piece of fucking furniture.

And then I see it. The small fiberoptic lens on top of the kitchen cabinet.

Another sits on top of the door frame, and there's another on top of the window latch high above.

Oh, come on. Seriously?

But I'm madder at myself. I know better. I'm great at reading my surroundings and seeing threats. I toss the sandwich onto the counter and take my bag to my room, stuffing it under a chair and then scan every surface of the walls.

I know he has one in my room. "Come out, come out, wherever you are."

A tiny glare hits the corner of my eye, and I shift back and forth, seeing it and then not again. Taking a chair, I climb up and slide my fingers into the light fixture, pulling out the little lens.

I turn it around in my fingers and then crush it in my fist. "I'm going to kill you." I leap off the chair, yank open the door, and run to his room.

I kick the door wide, step inside, and pitch the fucking camera right at his sleeping form.

"Ow, shit!" he growls, jerking up in bed.

He grabs his cheekbone, and the lens bounces off him, to the wall, and then to the floor.

I breathe hard, glaring at him.

"Goddammit, what the hell?" he shouts, seeing me. Pulling his hand away from his face, he checks for blood, but there isn't any. "Are you serious?"

"That was the camera in my room!" I shout.

I rush over and stomp on it, grinding it into the ground.

He grabs my arm, pulling me onto the bed. "Do you how expensive those are?"

Who gives a shit? I climb on top of him, straddling him, but he grabs my wrists before I can attack.

"I turned it off when you arrived!" he yells. "Stop!"

I twist my arm free and flick him in the forehead twice.

He flinches, trying to turn away. "I said I turned it off!"

"When I arrived?" I challenge him.

He hesitates, and I flick him again.

"After you went in the room!" he finally answers.

Likely story. I flick him on the nose.

"Ow!"

I wrap my hand around his throat, pinning him to the bed. "How long after I went in the room?"

"You weren't undressed, if that's what you're asking!"

Yes, that's what I'm asking. But I squeeze his throat for good measure.

"I promise I haven't seen anything," he rasps, trying to inhale. "I'm not spying on you."

I stay there, glowering, because I believe him, but I don't want to. Sometimes it just feels good to be mad.

When I don't get off him, he shifts underneath me, grunting. "Can you..."

He takes my waist in both hands and tries to move me, and that's when I feel him. Hard through his pajama pants. All the way through my jeans.

"Aro, please." He throws me off. "I..."

I fall onto the bed at his side, and he sits up, grabbing the sheets and bunching them up to cover his erection.

Heat rises to my cheeks, and to his too. I bite back a smile, loving how embarrassed he looks.

My anger dissipates, and everything warms. "I thought you were..."

He props himself up with one hand and keeps trying to cover himself with the other, pushing it down.

He glances at me. "What?"

"Nothing."

But it's not nothing. His narrow waist disappears under the covers, his hair hanging in his eyes, and he's actually more handsome this way. A little vulnerable.

Since I met him, he almost hasn't seemed human. Like he has a database of the most optimal responses to any given situation, and he's never wrong.

He doesn't always have the right answer, though. He has problems just like the rest of us.

"I thought maybe women didn't turn you on," I broach. "I've heard the stories."

He points to the door. "Get out."

I laugh under my breath. "No, now come on," I beg. "Don't be mad. It's okay to still be figuring yourself out. Maybe you're attracted to both. I just kind of assumed..."

"Yeah, everyone assumes," he fires back. "Why can a woman be picky, but a man's sexuality is questioned if he's not diving into every short skirt like an animal who can't control himself?"

He crashes back to the bed, the back of his hand resting on his forehead as he stares at the ceiling.

His body responded to mine. Like I'm sure it did to all the women he turned down.

I didn't mean to imply that chasing every short skirt is normal. But his sudden anger implies this is a sore subject.

"What's wrong?" I ask him.

He chews the corner of his mouth, still not looking at me.

"She's really pretty," I say. "She won't stay single for long, you know?"

I don't know why I'm encouraging him to get back with his ex. I'm sure she treats him fine, but she's kind of bitchy.

But then, so am I, so whatever.

I sit there for a minute, and he lets me, the wheels turning in his head.

After a few more moments, his breathing calms. "I just can't get out of my head," he says. "It happens every time. A thought and then a thought and then a doubt and then a worry, a concern, a dread, until my head is swimming, and I want to scream." He closes his eyes, and I can tell he's trying to control himself. "It's so loud, and then I've lost it. The moment."

He sits up, resting on his hands behind him, and I watch him wet his lips.

"What do we do after?" he says, thinking out loud. "What's next? Is she going to expect me to be a certain way? Will she be forever? What if I get her pregnant? What if she doesn't like it? What if I finish too soon?" He pauses and then says a little quieter, "What if I don't love her?"

I know these questions aren't for me, but I don't know what to say, because I think it's amazing that he thinks like that. So many of us seize immediate gratification, but he wants it all to mean something.

"I just..." He searches for his words. "I want what my parents have." He finally raises his eyes to mine. "They have to have each other, because the only other option is unthinkable. There's no choice. He can't be in a room with her and not touch her." He looks down at his lap. "I've never felt that. Not ever."

I wait, listening.

"I mean, I should've felt something like that with some-one, right?" he asks. "Some kind of overwhelming need? Even for just a moment?"

I haven't. I don't know if that happens for everyone. I'm not sure I'd want someone to own a part of me that much either. That kind of passion really is overrated. Like some unrealistic expectation films give us that end up making us feel like we don't have something good if we don't end up with someone willing to rip apart the world to kiss us.

I clear my throat. "I do know someone who...can maybe help."

He arches a brow. "'Help?'"

I wiggle my eyebrows.

"A prostitute?" he shouts.

"Just to get you over the hump," I explain quickly. "Maybe if you just do it—get the pressure off you for the first time—you'll feel a lot better and more relaxed."

He points to the door. "Get out."

"I have her number right here..."

He falls back to the bed. "I don't believe I'm having this conversation."

I laugh, turning toward him and crossing my legs. "I'm teasing. Relax."

I wouldn't want his first time to be with her anyway. It would take a month to get the glitter off of him.

I let my smile fall and look down at him. "Sex is a big deal," I say. "Especially for women. It's easy to feel degraded. Abandoned. Forgotten. Worthless if you're a virgin. Worth-less if you sleep with 'too many' people." It's different for him, but I know he doesn't want it to be. "When you brought me in here with you, I thought you were going to try to take what you wanted from me—use me—because I'm poor and living on your good graces and vulnerable."

"Have people done that to you?"

"But you didn't," I continue, avoiding his question. "You've left me alone, and for the first time in a long time, I feel..." I look up and around, trying to put it into words. "Like I don't have to keep my guard up every second."

He listens, his eyes on me.

"I'm glad you don't try to hop in the sack with anyone at any time," I say. "I like that about you." I force the words out, because it's hard to admit I actually think really highly of him. But he needs to know he's worth the wait. "You're a different world, Hawke. Whoever it ends up being, I hope she knows she won the lottery."

His expression softens, and he looks like he wants to smile, but he just looks back up to the ceiling.

"I was patient with myself at first," he explains, "thinking it would eventually happen and everything would be fine, but it still hasn't happened, and the more time that passes, the more nervous I get." He laughs at himself. "I want to do it. Obviously." He gestures to his body that was very hard a minute ago. "I think about it. I like to think about it. None of them ever feel like I'm home, though. I never feel safe."

"And that's why you watch people," I say.

He looks at me.

"You asked me a couple of days ago why I thought you watched the town from your room with no windows where no one will see you." I hold his eyes. "It's control. A sense of security. You feel powerless with sex, and it's a way to have power. Power that no one else has."

Except maybe his dad. The apple didn't fall far from the tree there.

"But you're giving her too much of it, Hawke," I tell him. "Power, I mean. She's just as nervous as you are. She just wants to know she's wanted. It's not that hard." I fall to the bed beside him, sighing and feeling a yawn come on. "Turn off the cameras, except the one for her. Tell her to do what you want her to do. She'll do it."

My head sinks into his expensive pillow, and I already feel lightheaded like I'm drifting away and completely conscious of it. My stomach drops, and I think I smile.

"You have your own bed," I hear him bite.

I yawn. "Watch me sleep there or here. Either way, you're a creeper."

FALLS

CHAPTER FOURTEEN

Hawke

I open my eyes, instantly at ease in the windowless room. I love sleeping here. It's cold and dark, and I never feel guilty about sleeping late because I can't tell if the sun's out or not.

The scent of the old furniture fills my room, and I reach over, switching on my lamp.

"Mmmm." I hear a sweet, little whimper next to me.

A jolt hits my heart, and I jerk my head, seeing Aro. I forgot she was here.

That's weird. I usually wake a couple times every night, but I slept straight through. I fall back to the bed, relaxing as she sinks back into her slumber, barely shifting with the soft light in the room now.

She's kinda cute. When she's quiet.

Her black lashes drape under her eyes, her skin smooth and her lips full and cherry, like candy. Her feet hug each other, and she's balled up like she's cold. I sit up, reaching down and pulling the blanket I never need over her body.

In a minute she'll be awake, mocking me, fighting me over something that doesn't need to be an argument, or making my head hurt.

For now, I can enjoy the sound of her small breaths. I've never slept in the same bed with anyone before.

One of her hands lays on top of the other, the pillow tucked tightly under her head, and a need washes over me to see her sleep for as long as she wants. To not have to get up and worry or work. I'd like to watch her play a video game or play with a dog or ride shotgun on the rare occasion I race. She'd love that.

And that's why you watch, she'd said.

Last night comes flooding back, and I whip off the sheet, swinging my legs over the side of the bed. I rub the back of my neck.

Why the hell did I tell her all that? Goddammit.

She woke me out of a dead sleep. I wasn't thinking straight.

She must think I'm fucking crazy.

She didn't act like it, though. It was nice to talk to someone. No one around me is very easy to talk to—not about sex. Madoc just gives me tips on her erogenous zones, my dad says there's nothing wrong with waiting, and Jared has panic attacks when anything uncomfortable comes up.

I thought about talking to a woman, but it's embarrassing. Pretty sure Dylan and Quinn are still virgins, and the others raised me, so no.

I liked finally getting it out, and she's probably right. There are other things we can do first. Things that will help me get attached to someone and need more.

"You move too much at night, Pirate," Aro says, and I hear her yawn behind me.

I rip my phone off the charger, seeing it's after ten in the morning. "And you have your own bed, Rebel," I grumble. I move to get up, but I'm swelled and poking through my goddamn pants. I sit back down. *Christ*. I rest my elbows on my knees, pretending to check my phone.

The bed bounces under me, and I struggle to hide myself as she jumps to the floor. "I'll make coffee," she announces. "You check the camera."

Thankfully she leaves, every curve of her ass pronounced like a second skin in Dylan's jeans. My cock twitches. "Shit."

I rise, grabbing my towel and heading for the shower. If she sees me with another boner, she'll start thinking they're because of her.

I wash, taking a minute to cool down and get my head straight again. I told her some stuff last night, and she was kind of cool about it.

Friends can talk to each other. I'm not trying to date her. Or get her into bed. I don't care if she's impressed or thinks I'm weak, so it's easy. No pressure.

I certainly know her problems. Maybe confiding in each other just builds trust. That's a good thing.

I dress, grab some coffee, and check surveillance on the garage, while she takes her turn in the shower. I glance back at her as she heads down the hallway, remembering her grabbing the underwear and bras from Dylan like they were top secret. God only knows what that troublemaker bought her.

"Supposed to be packing for college," Schuyler says on her video as I scan social media. "But the incoming seniors need a little help."

And then the theme to *Rocky* starts playing as she plucks packages of streamers, balloons, and party masks and throws them into her cart.

The senior party. A beginning-of-the-year celebration hosted by the captain of the football team, which is Kade.

But he has no interest in doing the planning, so he usually pawns it off on some girl or, like last year, the entire cheerleading squad. I guess Schuyler is helping him this time.

Aro's words from last night come back to mind. *She's just as nervous as you are. She just wants to know she's wanted.*

I look at the date on the video. *Last night.* I check her Instagram.

The water. The lake. It flows through our veins, and there's nothing we can do about it... It's like venom. – Karen Katchur

And there's a selfie of her at Blackhawk Lake, the sandy beach and water and her in a red bikini top. Harrington Hill, the little island in the middle of the lake, visible behind her.

Turn off the cameras. Except the one for her, Aro had said.

I stare at Schuyler's IG, getting an idea.

She's having a lot of fun, isn't she?

She's thinking I was a waste of time.

I lean down, planting my hands on the desk. "You should've been patient with me."

I grab my T-shirt and pull it over my head. Taking my phone, my hoodie, and sliding into my sneakers, I duck out of the hideout before Aro leaves the shower.

She's right. I give people too much power. What am I worried about? Kade doesn't care if they're happy. The more confused he makes women, the more they want him. And if they leave, there are others. He doesn't sweat about it.

I don't want that, though. I never did. Everything is important.

But it's time to get over it. Sex is sex. I don't have to be in love to like how her hands feel and get pleasure from it. And there are enormous health benefits to having sex that I'm missing out on. It lowers your blood pressure, improves sleep, eases stress, and it definitely counts as exercise. It's bad for my body not to have sex. I'm actually hurting myself by holding off.

I sneak into the High Street garage, pull up my hood, and duck out the back door, jogging all the way to Madoc's car that I left parked in the alley. I jump in, start the engine, and hit the gas, cranking up the AC full blast as I head out.

The lake is most busy in the summer, of course, and usually busiest this time of year. The weather will be cooling down soon, so it's the last chance before school starts to soak up the sun.

My parents reopened the old summer camp there about ten years ago, but the cabins will be empty now, the summer sessions all completed and the kids gone home.

It's a beautiful spot, the falls visible from the south shore, and we're all usually up there at least twice a week in the summer.

When we're not working for free at the camp, that is.

The rest of the year, my mom writes, and my dad helps run JT Racing and his own security company. They like to keep busy.

I know my parents are hoping one of us kids takes over the camp someday, though. She loves writing, and he loves working with Jared. Once James and A.J. are grown, they won't feel as connected to the camp or feel such a need to be there anymore.

They want it to survive, though. They want kids to have what they didn't.

I head out onto the highway and speed around the curves that give way to cliffs, and under canopies of trees filtering the sunlight. The lake comes into view, and I pull onto a side road, running parallel to the water.

Parking off to the side of the road, I climb out of the car and run across the path and into the wooded area next to the lake.

"This is creepy," I mumble to myself.

Aro is right. I'm weird.

I'm also pissed, Schuyler's leaving for college soon, and my pride wants to make her come before she goes.

"No, wait!" someone yells.

Girls laugh, and I step behind a tree, feeling fucking stupid now. This isn't worth getting caught for.

Schuyler appears, a flash of red as she runs to her car in the lot. "I'm coming!" she shouts as Holly Blake and Millie Bukoski race to the bathrooms.

Schuyler digs something out of her car, the same shade of red as her swimsuit, which I'm sure was entirely planned, and slams the door, locking it.

She reaches behind her and tightens the strap tied at the back of her neck. I pull out my phone.

I see you.

I hear the notification go off and watch her check it. Her head pops up and she starts to look.

Don't turn around, I text.

She goes still. But she doesn't leave.

I lean against the tree, watching her.

"I'm here with someone," she calls out.

I type. **No, you're not.**

She could be, but I'm calling her bluff.

"What are you going to do?" she asks. "Maybe I should turn you in."

I grin, tapping away on my phone. **Well, then, shouldn't you give me a proper goodbye before they lock me up?**

She turns her head to the side just enough that I can see her smile. Reaching up, she pulls the clip out of her hair, every blonde lock spilling down her back, and I can feel how warm the tan skin is from here. I can imagine what it feels like.

She pulls the strings of her top, dropping it to the ground right there in the lot, and I draw in a sharp breath. She swipes her hair over her shoulder and off her back, letting me look at her naked skin, and I know she's trying to push me. To get me to come and get her.

I know how much you like to watch me, her text reads.

I breathe hard, forcing my legs to move. I walk toward her, seeing her turn her head at the sound of my steps on the gravel, and I slide my hand up the back of her scalp.

I squeeze her hair. She moans. "Not just watch," I whisper.

I want this. A light sweat covers my body, I'm swelling, and she wouldn't stop me if I pushed her up against the car and just did it.

I bow my head to her, running my mouth over her temple and into her hair.

"God, I've waited for this," she pants.

She turns, wraps her arms around me, and kisses my neck, gasping and biting.

"Stay with me," she whispers, rubbing my dick through my jeans. "I need you."

She goes faster, moving my hand to her ass, and nibbling my jaw and licking my lips.

I breathe out, shaking my head clear. *I want this. I want to yank what's left off of her and see her on top of me. I want it all.*

She whimpers, moving my hand to her breast, but the skin feels rough, or maybe it's my hand and not her, but...

She fiddles with the door behind her, and before I know it, she's opened it and is crawling into the back seat. Her breasts sit exposed, and she rubs the inside of her thigh, drawing attention to what's underneath her bikini bottoms. Between her legs.

She licks and bites her lips, and I lean down, taking her face in my hand.

Kiss. I swallow. *Inside her. Do it.*

I can't breathe.

Her mouth. Her breath. Wet. I envision it in my head. The image of me on top of her, kissing her and moving between her thighs, but...

Then it's over and what then?

She kisses my mouth, sticking her tongue in. I go still. It's cold.

I can't fucking move.

No. Not in a car. I don't want to just fucking throw down in the back seat of a car.

I yank her hands off me and stand up, closing my eyes, because I can't do this anymore. I can't look at these girls and see that pathetic look back.

I'm fucking broken. There's something wrong with me. There's so much I can't...

"Get the fuck out of here," I hear her say, interrupting my thoughts. Her voice is completely calm as if she knew this would happen again.

My eyes are still closed, but I know the look on her face. I've seen it ten times already.

I want to explain to her, but there's nothing I can say I haven't already said. She wants to have sex with her boyfriend. Like normal people do.

I can't. I'm never gonna be able to do this.

I feel sick.

"You're pathetic," she says.

I turn and leave, the heat of her eyes, or my own fucking shame burning my back all the way to my car. I just want to be back at the hideout. Why did I leave? I shouldn't have done this.

I thought I could prove something before she left for school.

I race home, park the car, and dive back into the hideout, the familiar cool of the cement walls and darkness a small comfort.

I can see. They can't see. I'm safe.

I stalk down the hall, whipping off my hoodie and tossing it on the floor.

I need to get drunk. I don't say that much, but fuck...

What happens if I can never do this? I want it. I know I fucking want it. I want a woman and kids and a life with someone someday. I don't want to be alone forever.

Goddammit. I walk into the small kitchen, seeing Aro playing *Grand Theft Auto V*, doing that newbie thing where they move the controller in the direction they want their character to go. She holds the device above her head, jerking it right a few times, and I roll my eyes. I'm shocked she even knew how to start the PlayStation.

I grab a water from the fridge.

"Hey," she says, hearing me and looking over her shoulder. "Where'd you go?"

I take a drink, swallowing half the bottle as she sets down her controller and walks over. She's back in her black pants and T-shirt again, the outfit she wore underneath her hoodie and jacket to Rivertown that first night. Except now the clothes are clean.

Her eyes fall, and I follow her gaze, noticing the red lipstick on my collar.

"You saw her," she says, but there's something in her voice I can't read.

"I was careful," I assure her.

She stares at me, and I turn, digging an apple out of the basket on the counter.

A kernel of popcorn flies at me, hitting my chest. I look at her. "What?"

"What do you mean, what?" she argues. "What happened?"

She wants to know if I fucked her? "None of your business," I say.

She swings around the island, teasing. "Oh, come on. If you're going to sneak out and put us in danger, at least entertain me."

Put us in danger...

I set the apple and water down and move away from her, planting the island between us again. I place my hands on top of it, staring at her. "You first."

She stares at me.

"Saw the cameras this morning," I tell her. "Where'd you go last night?"

She clamps her mouth shut and turns away. "None of your business."

Motherfucker. And I don't know why, but I swipe my hands across the island, sending the metal bowl full of popcorn flying to the floor. It scatters, the bowl clanking across the cement, and she spins around, her eyes flaring.

I let loose. "We need to be able to trust each other or this doesn't work!"

"Oh, back to your condescending bullshit, I see," she taunts. "I'm not a child. I come and go as I please."

Yeah. Of course. Without regard to anyone else.

I'm not even entirely mad at her. She's back and appears to be safe. And from what I can tell, she didn't cause any trouble or get seen.

I just want to yell. I'm mad.

She approaches me. "What happens after we get evidence on Reeves?"

"We go back to our lives."

"Wrong," she fires back. "You go to college and a string of friends and girlfriends born under lucky stars just like you, where you don't need to be reminded that people like me are one town away. I go back to nothing. Not a damn thing changes for me."

What does that mean? I take a step, closing the distance. "What did you do?"

"I don't have to explain anything."

"What did you do?" I yell.

She gets in my face, growling, "I looked out for me."

Goddammit. She has her own agenda, and we were never a team. I should've known. Another mistake.

"I'm not letting you drag me down with you." I glare at her. "I'm sick of your shit!"

Mischief hits her eyes, and I swear I see a smile. She leaves, stalking down the hallway, and I almost go after her, but I'm not entirely sure what I want to do. Kick her out? No. This argument is my fault. I'm taking my anger out on her, and I already know I'll have to apologize.

I take in the popcorn all over the floor. I shouldn't have gone to see Schuyler. My sex life is the last thing I should be worried about right now.

Aro walks back into the room, and I turn, facing her. She carries a black duffle bag, and it's like the one I threw over the cliff.

She opens it, showing me stacks of cash, and I dart my eyes up to her.

"Really?" I ask. Now I am a little pissed.

That's where she was when Kade and I got to the park. She was off stashing this.

"You're so careless," I laugh, but I'm not amused. "Money comes and money goes. You can't hide this from them! Stop thinking about tomorrow and think about what happens in five years! This isn't the most important thing!"

"Spoken like someone who's never had to worry about not having it!" she shouts back. "That cash will feed my family for the next five years, asshole."

I rear back, about to lose my mind with her. "Like they're not going to figure out that they're the ones paying for your shopping sprees and pizza deliveries!"

Is she really that dumb? She's not old enough to get her brother and sister away from her mom, and her mom will fucking talk when she sees Aro bringing over groceries every week. When she sees her paying for toys and clothes and settling the electricity bill. They're going to figure it out.

I open the bag and look inside at the stacks of hundreds, gauging it's probably no more than fifty thousand. Five years? She'll blow through this in six months.

"You brought this shit in here?" I ask, but it's an accusation. "What happens if I get caught with this? What happens if they come in here and see this and assume we were both in on this? How much fucking trouble are we already in, Aro, and you go and do this? Don't you get it?"

"Oh, don't worry, Pirate." She taunts me. "I'll take the rap for everything. This is all my fault anyway, right? I don't have a future anyway, right?"

She steels her defiant chin, but I see the tears she tries to hold back.

I didn't say that.

Did I?

I didn't mean it if I did. And it hits me how much I want her to have a future. Everything she does—good or bad—is never for herself. I see that. She has good intentions.

"It was always over for me." Her voice drops to a whisper. "Since the moment they were born. All I can do is what I can do." She turns, sliding down the island until she's sitting against it on the floor. "For as long as possible."

A tear spills, but she's trying so hard not to crack.

"What happens after we get the evidence?" she drones on. "What happens if you get caught with the money? What happens, what happens..." She laughs to herself, shaking her head. "It all happens." And she looks up at me. "Don't you get it? I don't care what happens next week. They need to eat today."

She drops her gaze again, resting her arms on her bent-up knees, and I grind my teeth together, feeling the sting in my own eyes. My throat grows tight, like needles are poking me, and I thought I understood, but I don't.

I'll never know the things she knows.

I lower my body, squatting in front of her, and I want to touch her face.

But I don't. Instead, I choke out, "What happens when I don't know where you are?"

She sits there, her face barely visible behind her hair, but I see more tears spill.

"I like you," I tell her. "Everything has changed for me."

I can't go back to my friends and live like none of this ever happened. And my heart hurts, thinking about her out there, living as if I never existed. Will she forget me?

"What would've happened if you'd needed me last night?" I ask.

She can't just go out alone. If they'd caught her, I would've never found her. She'd be gone. At the bottom of the lake, or in a lonely lump of wet earth out in the middle of the woods that no one ever found, because no one would look for her.

I don't stop myself. I take her face and bow down, pressing my forehead to hers. "I won't stop you from doing anything, no matter how much I hate it," I tell her. "But you have to tell me what you're doing."

Her body shakes a little, but I don't hear any sounds as she cries.

"I can't help you if I can't find you."

I blink away the burn in my eyes. I'll be damned if I let that piece of shit erase her like she doesn't matter, or use her like she's a commodity. I don't know if we'll win, but I can make sure she's not alone anymore.

I dive in, tucking her head into my neck, and she starts crying harder. But she wraps her arms around my waist, hanging on, and I tighten my hold.

We stay like that for only a minute before she calms again, and I have a feeling those tears were a long time coming.

She sniffles, pulling back and wiping her face. "Those windows aren't big enough," she says, tipping her head back. "You need a skylight in here."

"Why?"

"I like to look up," she says. "When things hurt."

The stars. *Astronomy.*

I break into a smile and stand up, an idea popping into my head.

I hold out my hand. "Come on."

"Where are we going?" She takes it, and I pull her up to her feet.

Keeping her hand in mine, I pull her after me. "This is worth the risk."

"What is this place?" she asks.

I feel my way up to the control booth and turn on the system, an atmospheric sound drifting loudly out of the speakers. A tinkling starts next, and I turn down the volume, loading the screens.

"Hawke?"

"Stay there," I shout down to her.

She stands in the middle of the dark aisle, and I see the domed ceiling fade from black to purples and blues, the background music beginning.

The theater lights up, casting a glow over her, and I look down, seeing her eyes tilt up and her mouth fall open.

Leaving the booth, I walk down and lead her into the chairs, both of us taking a seat.

But I don't think she knows I'm here anymore. She gazes up at the fake sky, stars you can only see out in the middle of nowhere, lighting up the night. The image rotates in a circle, but it feels like we're the ones moving, and she watches. Her mouth sits open a little, and I don't think she blinks.

"Have you ever been to a planetarium?" I ask her.

She shakes her head, and I smile, because she looks like everything just changed for her. Like she's starving and there's a feast.

"Look." She shoots up in her seat, pointing. "That's Sirius. It's the brightest star."

"Right, the Dog Star."

She twists around, taking everything in. "Yeah, because it's part of Canis Major. We can only see it right before dawn, but you can see the Milky Way really well if you get far enough away from all the light pollution."

She rises, looking at the screens behind her, too impatient to wait for them to rotate to us.

I laugh quietly.

"And Betelguese." She points. "Orion will be over our heads in a few months." She points again. "And there's Mars. It's visible a lot. Can you imagine what it's like there?"

"Cold."

She sits back down. "Quiet," she says instead. "Mountains of rock and sand dunes, winds and storms and ice..." She continues staring up at the sky. "None of it we can touch, just look at."

She smiles, and my chest tightens a little. She looks so amazing right now. Peaceful. I suddenly wish I could put that skylight in the hideout.

"There are so many stars," she whispers. "So many suns. And so many with their own solar systems like ours."

I pull my eyes away and slouch in my seat, resting my head on the back of the chair. "What's your favorite part of astronomy?"

She follows, both of us relaxing and looking up as we leave planet Earth and enter an interstellar cloud.

"I like the theory stuff," she says. "Black holes and worm holes and all the crazy things physicists are afraid we won't understand."

"Why do you like it so much?"

"Astronomy or theoretical physics?"

"Both, I guess."

She shrugs. "Possibility. Perspective." She sits up again, tipping her head back and smiling. "It's kind of comforting to realize how truly insignificant you are."

I watch her.

She goes on. "I see the star, but the star will never see me. It'll still be there long after me. Through millions of me's." She pauses and then whispers, "Life goes on, no matter if I pay the bills or not."

I ache, looking at her, because she's right and I hate it. Life goes on.

So, we live. As hard as we can for as long as we can, and we feel everything, because if it doesn't kill us, something will.

But she's too busy fighting for things I've never had to fight for.

And I hate that.

My throat is tight, and I clear it before taking a breath. "Should we go?"

She jerks her eyes to me. "Already?"

I laugh again, because she looks devastated.

"Live on other planets, I mean?" I tell her. "Instead of fixing this one?"

She turns back to the screens. "We can do both," she replies. "But we'll definitely have to leave. Having all our eggs in one basket here on Earth didn't work out well for the dinosaurs, you know?"

I nod. "Yeah."

We watch the film, traveling through space and time, galaxies and the birth of our own, and I feel it down to my bones. How lucky we are to be here.

"You are significant," I say quietly, still staring up at the screen. "Scientists say that nearly all the atoms in our bodies were made in a star. And many of those atoms have traveled through several supernovas." I pause, seeing her look over at me out of the corner of my eye. "You weren't born here. You were born billions of years ago, Aro. You're stardust." I look over, meeting her eyes. "The stars don't need to see you. They know you."

CHAPTER
FIFTEEN

Aro

The tears streaming down my face mix with the spray from the shower, and I lean my forehead into my arm against the wall as the water warms my back.

What is he doing to me?

Making me think I'm special. That I'm important. That kind of thinking is a disease that slowly kills people who are tricked into believing they have a chance. You can't give hope to someone who can't afford it.

But I can't stop the sobs. They wrack my body harder, because I want to believe him. I want to think that I'm more than this and that anything is possible. That high school dropouts can all of a sudden have completely different lives, but that shit is for the movies.

Hope breeds disappointment, and disappointment eats you.

I don't want to want things I'll probably never have. It'll hurt too much. I don't want to know about the things missing from my life. I'm happier that way.

I wipe the water off my face, feeling the ache inside me. The ache from the damage he'd done just by telling me that I'm stardust. *Such a sweet, stupid boy.*

I shut off the water and wrap the towel around me, stepping out from behind the tiled wall. I dry my feet on the mat he has there and step toward the sink, the mirror foggy from the steam.

I stare at the counter. "He's sweet," I murmur to myself.

He's self-righteous, a little uppity, condescending, and his playlist could use a serious update, but...

He's responsible. Honest, compassionate, smart, driven, and he pays attention. He sees things and takes the time to process them.

And he's sincere. He may have been telling me things I shouldn't hear in that planetarium, but he meant every word. He didn't like me thinking badly of myself.

He's a good man. He won't hurt anyone on purpose, and he won't make kids and abandon them. The other men I've met in my life—would-be-fathers and classmates and neighborhood assholes—flash in my mind, and none of them are worth a fraction of him.

Whoever he finally falls in love with will have the best.

But I frown, thinking about him finding love and knowing how hard someone like him can fall. She better deserve him. He would never hit a girl, but I'd look forward to doing it for him if she hurt him.

I dry off and pull on a pair of the new underwear his cousin brought. I'm glad she didn't get cocky and bring me thongs or some shit. Just straight black bikini briefs that actually look great with my skin tone. Not that I worried about that, but I'll have to thank her. I'll take it out of what she owes me. I should've just taken the money she offered, but I still intend to collect.

I pull on a white T-shirt she loaned me and grab the pair of Hawke's pajama pants I stole, but before I slide a leg in, I stare at them and then look at my still barely visible reflection in the mirror.

I'd hurt anyone who hurt him. It's the only thing I'm good for, but I'm good at it.

He needs to toughen up, though. Women are going to roll all over him if he doesn't stop worrying so much. He needs to learn. To stop overwhelming himself with these panics and just feel it. To know what it's like to want nothing else but her.

And maybe I want that, too. For just one thing to feel good in my life.

I set the pants down on the bathroom counter, pull my hair out of its clip, and smooth it down around me. It's still a mess, and I don't really care.

I head out into the hallway, turn left, and enter the great room. The scent of popcorn lingers in the kitchen, and I see him, slouched on the couch with his back to me, playing a video game.

Above the screen, high on the wall, the painted words reach out and grab me by the neck.

Let us live...

I'm a blip in the universe.

But I'm here.

We're here.

For now.

"Hawke?" I say.

"Yeah?" He battles hordes of enemies for supremacy of some old, Gothic city.

I inch closer, stopping at the island behind him. "You said you never feel at home with them. With the girls you date, you never feel safe, right?"

His character stops on screen just as a beast charges him.

My heart pounds, but I force out the whisper. "Do you... feel safe with *me*?"

FALLS

CHAPTER SIXTEEN

Hawke

Huh?

I turn my head, my fingers paused on the controller as she rounds the sofa and comes into view.

My stomach drops, and my chest caves. *Um...*

Her dark hair spills around her, mostly swept over one shoulder and hanging over her right breast, and I drop my eyes, seeing black underwear, no jeans, and the tight, white shirt that doesn't cover much below her belly button. Glowing skin, big, brown eyes, lips pink and clean of lipstick or gloss.

"It looked like it didn't go well with your ex today," she says, "so I was thinking..." She looks down, struggling to breathe. "Do you... I mean, would you like to...touch me?"

The controller slips out of my hand and into my lap, but I don't move. I can't speak.

Is she...?

Blood rushes between my legs, and she climbs over the arm of the couch and sinks into the seat. "I realize I'm not

221

blonde. I'm not content on the sidelines, and I don't fucking giggle," she tells me, "but I've got girl parts and I'm sleeping down the hall from you, so it makes it easy."

"I..." I don't know what to say.

I mean, in a different situation, I might like to touch her. Sure. But I'm pretty sure this is a bad idea.

"No sex," she says, turning toward me. "No pressure. We're not dating. That's not what I mean."

I listen.

"You don't have to worry about impressing me," she goes on. "And I don't have to worry about impressing you. We can just...practice."

"Do you need practice?"

I feel like she's doing this because she feels sorry for me. She's trying to help, but I don't want to use her.

And I definitely don't want pity.

But she tells me, "I don't really like sex."

I narrow my eyes.

"I want to like it," she says. "I want someone who explores. Someone who lets me explore. Someone who's patient. And nice."

Has she never had that? How have people treated her? I want to ask, but I'm not sure I want to know about some guy not treating her right.

"I just want to touch you." She stares off, not looking up at me. "And maybe see if I like it."

Is she lying? I feel like she's thinking she'll act like she's the one who needs help when she's actually just handling me.

But I don't have time to voice my doubts before she's reaching over and picking up the controller off my groin and tossing it onto the ottoman.

Rising up, she swings a leg over my lap, and I rear back, sucking in a breath as she straddles me.

Oh, shit.

She places her hands on my shoulders. "Turn off the game," she says. "Turn on some music."

"I'm not sure—"

"Do it now, Hawke."

Yeah. Okay. I grab the remote control, press the Input button until I get to the home screen and find the music streaming app. A playlist starts, "Throne" drifting out of the sound system.

She holds my gaze, and warmth spreads underneath every inch of my skin. Her weight settles on me, the heat between her legs carrying through her panties, through my jeans, and over my thighs, down my legs.

God... My eyelids start to flutter, but I stop it.

She smiles just a little—sweet in a way she never really is—and presses her forehead to mine, holding me there.

"You can touch me," she whispers, her breath falling on my mouth. "If you want."

I...uh...

She shifts up, sliding her hands up my bare chest, grinding against me. Or maybe she just brushed me and didn't mean to, but my cock stretches against my jeans, and I'm sweating already. I...

She drags her mouth across my cheek, and I don't... I can't. "Stop," I say.

And she does. She stops.

Fuck.

I inhale slow and then exhale. It's just going too fast. She didn't give me any warning. Just walked in here, dressed in almost nothing, and...

Ugh, this is such a bad idea. I'll fuck it up. I always do. What then? We're starting to be friends. She's going to leave.

I put my hands on her hips, about to move her off, but she stops me. "I just want to touch you." Her temple rests against mine, the smell of my shampoo in her hair.

"I just want to feel you." She hasn't moved her hands a centimeter since I told her to stop. "I don't want more."

"Why?" Is she not attracted to me?

But she doesn't falter. "Because what you want is right," she replies. "It should be with someone you love. I wouldn't take that away from you. I don't deserve it."

I go still, keeping my hands on her but not moving either of us.

"Just touching," she murmurs.

Someone who's patient. Nice.

Someone who lets me explore.

A lump stretches my throat, but I nod. "Okay."

I trust her.

She brushes her lips across my cheek, and I hear her inhale through her nose as she moves slowly down to my neck. Sliding her hands up, she wraps one around my neck and slips the other up into my hair. Parting her lips, she runs them over my ear and then rises up on her knees, gliding her mouth over my forehead and making my blood race.

God, that feels good. I let my eyes fall closed as she comes back down and buries her nose in my neck and inhales deep.

"I thought you wanted to touch me," I say.

She's barely moved her hands.

But she says, "I am." And she continues to move her mouth over my skin, feeling me with her lips.

Her chest rises and falls, heavier against mine, and I don't know if that means she likes it or not. I can't read her body, and I don't want to ask.

I move. Digging my fingers into her waist, I hear her suck in a sharp breath, and I almost stop. Did I hurt her?

But then I see the goosebumps all over her thighs.

I smile to myself. "Get up," I whisper.

"Hawke..."

"Get up." I nudge her, and she pulls back, scrambling off of me and rising. I stand with her, seeing the alarm in her eyes as she backs away, but I pull her back in and spin her around.

I want to see what else gives her goosebumps.

I hold her hip with one hand and cover her back with my body, reaching up and touching her hair.

"Hawke..."

"Shhh."

I thread a lock through my fingers, pulling lightly until I've reached the end.

Chills spread down her arms.

"That feels good?" I ask.

She nods. "I guess so." She breathes out a laugh. "I like my hair touched."

"What else do you like?"

She hesitates, and I'm glad I can't see her face.

"Your skin on mine," she says in a low voice.

She crosses her arms in front of her, taking the hem of her T-shirt and pulls it up, over her head.

My head feels like it's floating ten feet above my body as I gaze down at her bare shoulders. She drops the shirt to the floor, waiting for me.

"Is this okay?" she asks.

My voice is barely audible. "Yeah."

I only hesitate a moment before I press my body into her back and look down, over her shoulders.

Beautiful, tight skin covers her torso, her breasts pert and full, making my groin ache.

The brown flesh of her nipples pebbles and hardens, two points jutting out.

I put my hands on her shoulders, my thumbs running up the back of her neck. "Cold?" I tease.

"A little."

Digging in my fingers, I drag my hands down her arms, feeling chills rise again. She falls into me, tipping her head back and closing her eyes.

She likes it.

I wrap one arm around her waist and another around her chest and hold her tight, burying my face in her hair.

Everything, her gentleness and scent, her fear and innocence, I like seeing it.

I kiss her hair and feel her shudder, but it sounds like a sob.

I look down, seeing her chin trembling.

"What's wrong?" I start to pull away, but she holds my arms to her.

"I feel pretty when you do that," she whispers. "Like you like the way I look."

I close my eyes. It doesn't take much, does it? How could no one take their time with her?

She turns and slips her hands around my neck. "Pick me up."

I smile, reaching down and grabbing the backs of her thighs. I lift her into my arms, her legs circling my waist.

Her breasts press into my chest. "Let me see," I tell her.

I drop my eyes, and she leans back, her body coming into view. Her breathing turns shallow, her breasts rising and falling, and I'm dying to lay her down and touch her like she touched me. With my mouth.

"Take me to the couch." She watches me as I stare at her, my heart starting to thump harder in my chest.

I want to.

But this is how it always is. I want it, and then I don't, and I don't want to see that look in her eyes. That look that says I'm not a man.

I...

I try to catch my breath, but everything's on fire. My body, my head, my hands...

She leans into my ear. "I'm almost done," she murmurs. "I just want to do one more thing."

I exhale, swallowing through the dryness in my mouth. *Okay.*

I step back, her in my arms, and drop to the couch, right back where we started.

She leans back, letting me take in the view a second longer, and then... she explores. She presses into me, gliding her hands over my shoulders, down my arms, her eyes following the trail of her fingers as she traces the muscles and cords in my arms, one after the other.

I watch her study me like she's learning what a man looks like for the first time, and then her eyes and hands go to my chest. She feels my collarbone, grazes her finger over my tattoo, and rubs her thumbs over my pecs before she sits up and lets me stare at her while she traces my abs, the slight tickle of her fingertips making me flex.

My dick swells so goddamn hard, and I gasp.

Fuck.

She climbs off, dropping to her knees between my legs and brings her mouth down on my stomach. Not kissing. Something like it, though. Pinching me so softly between her lips, up, down, over to the side of my torso, her hands moving up my arms and her head turning left to right, leaving no inch untouched.

I bulge, rushing with blood between my legs, and I know it's pressing into her tits.

"Oh, God..." I can't help it. I take her head, pressing her mouth to my stomach and watching her tongue dip out, licking me. "Again," I tell her.

She does it again, and I blink long and hard, every fiber in my body about to explode.

"I can't believe I'm licking the class president of Shelburne Falls."

I laugh, dropping my head back.

She climbs up, wrapping herself around me and kissing my jaw. The warmth between her legs makes me ache.

She whispers over my skin. "Say 'you make me hard, Rebel.'"

I grab her ass in both hands, grinding us together just once as I hover over her mouth. "You make me hard, Rebel."

And I do once more so she feels it.

Circling my neck with her arms, she hugs me tight, squeezing me with her thighs and laying her head on my shoulder.

She's done.

My dick hurts a little, needing release, but I know it's time to stop. And I'm grateful she's the one who stopped it, so I don't have to feel guilty. I wrap my arms around her, too, holding her tight.

I close my eyes. Everything she did felt good. I didn't do much for her, though. I want her to feel good.

"You have an amazing body," she says, her head on my shoulder facing away from me.

I smile to myself. At least all the working out pays off. I have to do something with all of my pent-up energy. No one ever said that to me before, though. I think most girls feel like it would be shallow—like they only notice how you look, but it's actually nice to hear.

If makes me feel pretty when you do that. Like you like how I look.

"I like the way you look," I tell her.

"I like the way you look, too."

We sit there a while, her holding me as much as I'm holding her while we try to cool down.

But I'm more relaxed than I thought I'd be. She stopped. Like she promised. There was no pressure. No agenda. No secret bet like some of the girls did in high school to see who could get me into bed first.

She didn't want more anyway. I can stop.

I can explore. And then I can stop.

"Can I..." I start, feeling braver all of a sudden. "Can we do a little more? Can I see...more?"

I slip my hand inside the waist of her underwear, and her body goes rigid. She rises up, the heat gone from her face, and climbs off of me. She swipes her T-shirt off the floor and covers herself, lifting her defiant little chin.

"I'm, um..." She hurriedly pulls the T-shirt back on giving me one last nice view of her breasts. "No," she states. "Not on the first date, Hawke. I'm shy."

And I smile as she leaves, following her with my eyes as she disappears down the hallway.

CHAPTER
SEVENTEEN

Aro

This isn't good.

My sheets stick to my legs, and I slide my hand down, pressing between my thighs. I feel the slickness through the fabric.

I just want to crawl into his bed and wrap myself around him right now.

And that's the worst part. That it's not about sex. I don't need that.

He just feels good.

Smells good, tastes good...

Looks good.

Seriously. The day I'm attracted to such an upstanding gentleman is the same day I puke money. What the hell am I going to do with a good boy?

I go still a moment, the feel of him last night drifting through my mind. How hard he was. How the muscles in his arms flexed under my palms when he rubbed himself up into me.

I close my eyes, losing my breath. *Such* an upstanding gentleman. Except the one place he shouldn't be.

He'll be hot in the bedroom.

Lucky girl, whoever she is.

I rub my thighs together, sweat covering my brow, but then I let out a hard sigh and spring up, swinging my legs over the side of the bed.

"Ugh." I pat my hands on my cheeks, trying to snap myself out of it. I just need to get myself off. What time is it anyway?

I look around, forgetting there's no clock in here, but I spot a small, green light and reach over to my nightstand. Flipping on the lamp, I see a cell phone on a charger, a Post-It attached.

Take care of it.

I smile. How does he know me so well already? He didn't even ask where the other one was. He just knows everything.

But he came in here while I was asleep. I hope I wasn't snoring.

I check the time. *8:59*. I tap out a text to my sister.

Everything okay?

It's Wednesday morning, and school hasn't started back yet. She might still be asleep, but I doubt it. If she doesn't get back to me within an hour, I'll have to go there with or without Hawke's permission.

I sit there a moment. *Should I call my mom? A neighbor?*

I probably should know what's going on. See if she's told the police the truth about what I did to my stepfather.

But I assume she did. Protecting me gets her nothing. What's done is done.

Exiting out of my texts, I log onto social media. My accounts have been dormant for a while, but I still like to browse.

I remember the video playing on Hawke's phone, the way he stared at it, and the lipstick on his collar. *Her* lipstick.

I give in to my curiosity, typing in her name and Shelburne Falls.

That video is one of the top suggested ones for those keywords. I don't click on it. Instead, I go to her account and scroll her posts, trying not to but looking for pictures of him. With her. Just to see what they look like together.

I'm not a stalker. I'm just curious.

I spot one of her from a few days ago, the same lipstick on her mouth that was on his shirt. I read the caption:

The water. The lake. It flows through our veins, and there's nothing we can do about it... It's like venom. – Karen Katchur

Oh, Jesus. "There's less plastic in the ocean," I grumble.

I don't see any pictures of him with her, though, which isn't unusual. It seems common practice to do a mass delete after a break-up. I search his profile and find him, but there are only three posts on the account.

I smile to myself. He's not much for broadcasting every move he makes. I like that.

There's only one picture with him in it—a wide array of kids in the photo. Dylan Trent stands on one side, Kade on the other. A small girl poses with her legs wide and hands on her hips in front of him, while Hawke holds a boy, about the same age as the little girl, upside down over his shoulder.

His hair is wet, and his chest is bare, a pool in the background, and something that feels good, like bubbles, pop under my skin. The good son and cousin to everyone, but he can be so different when he's got you alone. Like he flips a switch.

My cheeks warm, and I shake my head. "Oh my God," I breathe out, tossing the phone down and standing up. "What am I doing?"

I should be worried about Hugo and Reeves. About Green Street.

But I'm not. The butterflies are too nice of a distraction. I thought it was a good idea. A little something good in all the bad, but I can't let myself think about him. It's just physical fun. He's nobody to me.

I pull off my shirt, a text rolling in, and I pick up the phone again, reading.

Come find us, Hawke writes.

Huh? Us?

I pull on some jeans, a bra, and one of the T-shirts Dylan brought, and take my phone, leaving the room.

Heading down the hall in my bare feet, I check his room, the great room and kitchen, and the tunnel leading to Rivertown. I look through the mirror, but the place is dark, closed until lunch time.

Where is he?

And then I remember. *Frosted.*

I jog back through the kitchen and down the other tunnel, seeing the bakery come into view through the glass. Tables and chairs sit around the room, the shades drawn and the light dim. But as I peer to the left, I spot the kitchen door propped open and a light on inside.

I hit the latch and step through as the mirror opens.

Laughter goes off from the kitchen, from more than one person, and I move toward it but stop. Doubling back, I pull the mirror closed, leaving just a crack open in case the owner comes through the front door unexpectedly. Or the police.

Walking across the shop, I enter the kitchen, seeing Matty and Bianca with Hawke.

My heart leaps and drops at the same time. Bianca stands at the work table, still looking like she's dressed in her sleep shorts and top, while Matty sits on his legs on a stool, flattening a circle of dough with his hands. Flour covers his arms, and he laughs. Hawke stands behind him.

Bianca sees me in the doorway and smiles. "Hey."

"H-hey," I say in a shaky voice. I slowly step inside. "What are you doing here?"

I look to Hawke, but Bianca answers. "Hawke came and got us," she replies. "Knocked on the door this morning and asked if I wanted to bring Matty to see you."

She runs over and puts an arm around me, pulling me over by the neck.

"And you just jumped in a car with someone you didn't know?" I mumble.

I glance at Hawke, and he looks at me, amusement in his eyes.

"Well, I know he's the mayor's nephew," she says, rolling a piece of dough into a little ball on the counter. "And Matty loves his car."

Hawke leans over, taking a cloth and dusting off my brother's hands.

Bianca gapes at me, mouthing. "And he's cute. Like soooooo cute."

Then she side-eyes me, like I need to get busy with that. I purse my lips, looking away as Hawke heads over, wrapping an apron around my waist.

"Are you sure you weren't followed?" I ask him.

If they saw his car in my neighborhood, they could've tailed him.

But he assures me, "I wasn't followed."

He ties the strings around my waist, my arms hanging at my side. "So, that's how it is then?" I inquire. "You can leave without telling me where you're going, but I can't leave without you knowing where I am?"

"Exactly." He comes around my front, smiling. "Are you seriously going to pick a fight right now? I can take them home, if you want—"

"Shut up." And I make my way over to my brother, hearing Hawke's quiet laugh behind me.

I wrap my arms around the kid, pressing my cheek to his. "What are we making?"

"Pizza!" he cheers.

"It's nine in the morning!" I gasp, and growl playfully as I nibble his cheeks. "You can't have pizza!"

He squirms from my tickling, pealing with screams and laughter.

I meet Hawke's eyes, softening, because I'm glad he did this. It's been a long time since Bianca, Matty, and I got to have fun together.

"And then we get to have sundaes!" Matty shouts.

But Hawke holds up his finger, giving my brother a stern look. "On one condition," he says.

Matty hesitates and then yells, as if on cue, "Chicago-style pizza sucks!" And then again, "It sucks! It sucks! It sucks!"

Oh, Christ.

Bianca laughs, Matty giggles, and Hawke grins, so satisfied.

"Preying on innocent minds that don't know any better?" I ask him.

He shrugs. "Just setting him on the straight and narrow while he's young."

I throw a ball of dough at him, Matty laughs and follows suit, doing the same.

Hawke flings one at his nose, and Matty giggles, grabbing for it on the table to throw it back, but when he whips out his hand, the plastic container of sauce tumbles and spills down the side of the table.

We all watch it drip to the floor.

"Aro?" Matty cries, turning to me, his eyes darting between Hawke and me.

"It's okay," I say, grabbing a towel to catch the sauce before it spills more. "It happens."

His fingers go to his mouth. "Is he mad?"

I look to Hawke, who's already grabbing some paper towels. He hears the question and turns, confusion in his eyes.

But I just smile at my brother and stay calm. "No."

It doesn't stop him from crying, though, and he keeps looking at Hawke, waiting for his temper.

I pull my brother in, his breaths short and fast, more scared than anything, and I look up at Hawke, watching the realization start to hit.

Matty's waiting for Hawke to blow up. His experience with men is that they don't want to be reminded you're there.

"It's okay," I tell him gently.

But Hawke approaches, squatting to his eye level. "Hey," he barks.

Matty jumps, and I tense.

Hawke scowls. "You know what I do to cute kids like you?"

Matty is still.

"I...eat them!" he howls.

And he grabs my brother in both arms, hurling him up and gobbling his tummy through his shirt like a lion.

Matty breaks into squeals, kicking his legs.

But all smiles.

Tears fill my eyes, but I turn away, busying myself cleaning up the sauce.

"That was the main course and the vegetables," Hawke announces. "Now for dessert!"

I look over my shoulder, watching him pretend to devour the kid as Matty thrashes in his arms and laughs.

"All right," Hawke sighs. "I'll save some for later, I guess. Come help me choose more sauce. I have extra." He carries Matty over to the cupboard and opens it. "Which one? Tomato and basil or marinara?"

"Marinara!" Matty shouts, but I'm not sure he knows the difference. Just enjoys being asked to choose for everyone.

I clean up the rest of the mess, kind of sorry Hawke's homemade sauce was wasted. It actually tasted really good the other night when the two of us made pizza.

Hawke sets Matty down, shaking the jar and then opening it. "Here." He hands it to Bianca. "You guys put it on."

She gets busy pouring some on the dough, letting Matty spread it, and Hawke moves to my side.

Lowering his voice, he asks, "Did he hit him or something?"

Our stepfather. I don't want to talk about it. I just want Matty and Bianca to have a good day.

But Bianca speaks up. "No," she tells Hawke. "He only hit Aro."

I close my eyes for a moment. *Dammit.* Matty doesn't need to hear that.

I feel Hawke's eyes on me, and I glance up at him. "It's fine." I unwrap the wedge of cheese, ready to grate it. "It didn't happen that often."

He watches me, but I'm not letting anyone, including my stepdad, into the kitchen with us today. For now, it's just us four, and I get to pretend we're normal kids, on a carefree summer day, making pizza for breakfast.

We sit in the bakery, the shades shielding us from the view of the people on the street, as Matty plays waiter and serves us drinks and food.

Other than that, he doesn't leave Hawke. Riding on his shoulders. On his back. In his arms.

He refuses to sleep until he just can't keep his eyes open anymore, and when it's time to go home, he tells me I can't come. He wants Hawke to himself. And I let him take them alone because I'll cry if I have to watch them go back in that house without me.

I know my sister has it under control, but I don't want her to have to. She's not his mother, any more than I am.

But for a minute, it felt like we were a family. The four of us.

I liked pretending. They're ours. We protect them.

And he's mine.

"Damn him," I whisper, but I still smile. Giving me glimpses of something better, and I'll be chasing that useless hope for the rest of my life now.

Slipping back into the hideout, I slide into some shoes and pull on my hat and jacket.

I dial on my phone, still remembering her number from when she tried to evade payment. Dylan Trent answers almost immediately. "Hello?"

"It's Aro Marquez," I tell her. "I need a favor. Do it, and we're square."

"Did you take ibuprofen?" she asks, fidgeting in the seat next to me.

"Yes."

If there's anything Hawke has a lot of in that place, it's first aid supplies.

And food. I know where I'm going when the zombie apocalypse hits.

"Juliet says it hurts," she tells me, "but it goes fast."

I look over at her as we sit in the Zen lounge of the day spa, complete with a giant Buddha and a bowl of water chimes. "You've never done this?" I ask her.

I thought all rich girls were perfectly groomed.

But before she can answer, a woman calls us. "Ladies?"

We rise and follow the technician, who's dressed in dark blue scrubs into a room, bamboo flutes drifting out of speakers from somewhere I don't see. Two massage tables sit parallel, separated with a privacy screen.

"This'll be my first time too," Dylan finally answers.

I take off my jacket, another woman turning down the sheet on each bed.

"Remove everything," the short-haired blonde one tells us. "Wrap yourself in the robe and then lie on top of the sheet."

Both of them duck out, closing the door, and I kick off my shoes. "You don't have to do it with me," I tell her, seeing her shadow on the other side.

But she chirps, "I want to. You know, just in case."

Just in case...

We strip, and I spot the shadow of her wrapping the robe around her body and hopping up to the table. I follow suit.

I bob my feet as I lie there, my pulse picking up speed. She'd texted me right after we hung up and told me to take a painkiller, but it can't be that bad, right? People do this all the time.

But they also give birth all the time too.

"Juliet," I repeat the name she'd said. "Hawke's mom?"

"Yeah."

Juliet Chase writes Young Adult novels about a world happening right under our noses where ninjas, pirates, knights, and other elite warriors still exist. It usually centers around young women finding their power and leading, no fear, strong, etc.

I try to picture someone like that raising Hawke, and how he is makes total sense and then none at all. Does he like her books?

"She and my mom are besties from high school, but I don't dare tell my mom about this," Dylan continues. "She'll tell my dad, because she tells him everything, and then that's going to be a tantrum I don't want to deal with."

"Your dad seems like a baby."

She laughs quietly. "He's set in his ways, but it's more than that." She pauses and then continues. "He was a right asshole at my age, you know? Now that he has a daughter, he knows he'd kill anyone who treats me how he treated my mom at first. I'm pretty sure he still thinks he doesn't deserve her."

Well, regardless of what their parents were like, it's clear they're a big family. All three of those men I ran into at the park helped raise Hawke. They must've done something right.

And Dylan, I hate to admit, isn't all that bad. "They seem like good parents," I tell her.

"I'm not complaining."

A knock hits the door, and then the dark-haired one pokes her head in. "Ready, ladies?"

"Let's pluck!" Dylan calls out.

Pluck? Not with tweezers, right?

I flinch a little, dread curling my insides. *It goes quick*, she said.

"Okay, lift this leg," the lady tells me, opening my robe.

I don't, tempted to pull the garment closed again. I don't know what I was thinking, but she's staring at all my business.

She scrunches up her face in sympathy. "First time?"

A rip that sounds like a Band-Aid the length of my leg getting torn off goes off to my left, followed by a long, sharp intake of breath. "Oh, motherfudger," Dylan pants.

I blink wide eyes at my tech.

She just smiles. "I'm fast. Don't worry."

She takes a Popsicle stick of wax and smears it in the crease between my leg and hip, and I stop breathing for a second. "Ohhh, that's warm."

Hot, actually, but it's getting better.

"So, why did you want to get waxed?" Dylan asks.

Another rip from her side, and I hear her whimper.

I gulp, but then blurt out. "None of your business."

I'm not going to tell her that her cousin might want to take off my underwear next time.

"Why do you want to get waxed?" I lob back at her.

The tech smooths over a piece of cloth or paper towel, I'm not sure.

"It's cleaner," she shouts. "No shaving rash. Makes exfoliating easier. I'll look great in a bikini..."

I nod. "Same."

Good enough answer for me.

242

But then she starts to peel the paper up, and everything inside me tightens. Then, riiiiiiiiip...

Fire spreads over my tender skin, and it feels like two dozen pairs of fingers are pinching me simultaneously.

I growl. "Ow, what the fuck?"

"Are you okay?" the tech winces, like she's the one in pain. "I know the first time is rough."

"The first time?" I look down seeing a clear strip of skin. "Screw this."

It's going to be at least twelve more before she's completely done.

I start to rise, but Dylan's voice stops me. "Well, look who's the baby now," she teases. "Run, Rebel, run. I got this."

I arch a brow, hearing her third strip being pulled.

I slam back down onto the table, balling my fists. "Hurry," I tell the tech.

Dylan's a year younger, and Weston women can handle anything.

The techs do their work, and I get the hang of it, really only panicking when they start to peel up the tape. The pain dissolves pretty quickly. Not sure I'd want to put up with this every few weeks, but we'll see what happens.

"Almost done!" Dylan calls out.

"Who are you..." I stammer, waiting for the strip to get pulled off. "Who are you trying to look good in a bikini for?"

I hear the smile in her voice. "Me. Just me."

Either she doesn't want to say, or she's experimenting. Nevertheless, I'm kind of glad I didn't have to do this alone.

"Do me a favor, would you?" she asks.

Another rip. I suck in air through my teeth. "What?"

I groan as the pain fades.

"Be kind with him?"

I go still, something in her voice giving me pause.

She goes on, "Hawke probably wouldn't be as nervous as he is, or held off this long, if girls hadn't fucked with his head so badly in high school."

I barely feel the next strip, and I don't move.

"They started pushing so hard, like he was an obstacle or something to achieve," she tells me. "They wanted him, but they didn't love him, and when he didn't take what they were offering, they saved their pride by talking shit."

Oh, they did, did they?

Anger curdles in my stomach.

"He just became a locker room joke." Her voice drifts off. "He counted the days until graduation, Aro. He couldn't wait to get out of there."

My fingers hurt. I uncurl my fists a little.

"And I can't get in another fight, defending his honor with bitches," she says. "My nose still doesn't look right from the last one."

I smile, trying to keep my laugh to myself. I'm not ready for her to know I kind of like her.

He's lucky. His dad, his uncles, his cousins... They've all shown up for him. If I ever hurt him, I'm not sure these people and their love for him would be any less of a threat to me than Green Street.

And suddenly, I'm a little jealous, because I want to be the one protecting him.

She drives me past the bakery, into the alleyway, and I sneak up the fire escape and back into the hideout.

Hawke is still out, but I'm kind of glad. I climb into the shower, opening his body wash and inhaling the scent. The black-tiled walls make me feel hidden, and the feet of cement between us and the street above keeps this place so quiet most of the time.

It's like another world, but it's starting to feel as if I belong here. Like I'm shedding a skin.

Reeves will be collecting soon. We'll have proof, and we can leave.

I can't help but hope that Reeves never comes.

Then I never have to go.

FALLS

CHAPTER EIGHTEEN

Hawke

I slip inside the back door, walking through the kitchen and seeing heads turn toward me. They don't say anything, though. They're used to seeing me sneak in and out of places.

Getting back to work, the servers load trays, and I push through the next door, the rolling thunder of balls hitting pins filling the air.

I scan the bowling alley, spotting Aro's "brothers", sitting there bold as brass, right in the middle of our town.

Which one of them has been with her? No idea why I care, but all of a sudden, I do. She said she didn't like sex. Did they not take their time with her? Did they take advantage of a kid when she needed a family?

Charging over, I pull my hood down, not caring who sees me. I swipe a chair from Hugo's table, watching his gaze pop up, and I plant my ass down. "You're on the wrong side of the river," I say.

Axel swipes his phone off the table, but I level him a look. "Don't bother texting Reeves," I tell him. "I'm not staying."

I spy the cameras positioned at each corner of the lanes and know there are more behind us. They know the cameras will see me. But they'll see them too.

Hugo settles his gaze on me from across the table, and I look at his leather jacket that probably reeks of cigarettes and his dirty nails, but... I spot a larger version of Aro's tattoo on his neck and know young women flock to him. Reeves got the perfect asshole to reel them in and get them to do what he wants. There's no way Hugo kept his hands off her.

"It'll cost a hundred-and-fifty thousand to pay for everything you destroyed," he tells me, laying down the situation. "Not to mention the missing bag of money. We only found one in the trunk."

I keep what I know about the second bag to myself.

"So, let's say two-hundred-fifty thousand," he states.

"Added a little interest on, did you?"

"Just a little."

Yeah, their loss is maybe one-seventy. At best.

"You know this won't go anywhere good," I tell him. "Take the loss."

Shelburne Falls may seem like a Hallmark village, but it wasn't always like that. My family knows people, too. Jared's popular, Madoc's powerful, his father-in-law is more dangerous than Green Street, and my dad is scary smart.

"You don't want our attention," I remind him.

"And you want to go to college." His eyes dance. "If you want a deal, I'll need her back."

I stare at him.

"He doesn't want you," Hugo tells me, and I assume he means Reeves. "I mean, he does, but he knows better. We're well aware *you're* untouchable. But I need my girl back."

"She's not your girl."

"I've known her a lot longer than you," he taunts. "I'm the reason she's stayed fed the last three years. Aro is special. I have plans for her."

"Oh, I know you do."

"Don't give me that look," he fires back. "I'm sure she's taken a bath by now, and you know what's underneath those clothes."

Axel breathes out a laugh, and I feel Nicholas shift in his seat.

Hugo leans forward, a gleam in his eyes. "Does it look as good as I think it does?"

Fire flows under my skin, but at the same time, I exhale a little. He hasn't seen her. He hasn't touched her.

When I don't answer, that seems to be answer enough. "Then she's safe," he says in a smooth tone. "I'll keep her for myself, if that's the case. It's time I started a family."

I steel my spine.

"She'd be a great mother," he continues. "It's a good life for her. She'll be taken care of, I promise."

I rise, done with this conversation. *She likes astronomy*.

And if I have anything to say about it, she's done raising kids until she's damn well ready.

I start to leave, but I hear him behind me.

"Or..." he says, stopping me. "She can be yours and then she's protected, too. No member of Green Street touches another member's woman."

What?

"Think about it." His tone is soft and seductive. "The tattoo would look great on you."

I walk away. *Jesus*.

So, I give her back or I claim her by putting that shit on my neck? I'm not doing either one.

I dive back into the kitchen and exit through the back door. Hitting the alley, I step just inside the rear door of the Chinese restaurant, in case they decide to follow me.

Dishes clank, someone is using a hose to spray them clean in the basin, and I wait just a minute before leaving through the front. Pulling up my hood, I circle back around to High Street and climb the fire escape.

She's not my woman. That's not what...

I reach the roof, pulling off my hood, and walk for the door.

We're friends. Kind of funny how it happened, but I like her. She's a good person—or wants to be—and I want to know what she can do someday. She deserves more.

But I'm going to college, she's not. At least not yet. She'll go her way, and I'll go mine, and I hope she gets the life she wants, but we'll lose track of each other. It happens, but it's unrealistic to think this is more than it is.

We're rivals who were forced to find common ground. It'll be a cool story someday. Maybe I'll run into her again, and we'll laugh about this.

We'll laugh, because it all ended up okay. Life worked out for her. She got out.

And I'll turn out normal, hopefully.

I lean over and pull on the door, thinking about the years ahead.

College. Travel. Work.

A woman and my children.

And it takes a moment before I realize the door on the roof isn't opening.

CHAPTER NINETEEN

Avo

I stare at the old phone, scrolling through all the texts on one of the devices I'd found in Hawke's desk drawer. There were several outdated phones and only two of them worked. The other had texts just as dark, but this thread feels different. I've read through it at least five times.

Do you see her? the sender asks.

The person who once owned the phone I'm now holding replies, **I'm looking at her now.**

What do you think?

Pretty, they say.

I'm so hungry for her.

I know you are.

I hold the device, navy blue and heavy, with a stubby antenna and no touch screen. There were several others in that drawer, different brands but all equally as old.

I hold it in both hands as I lean against the wall of his surveillance room.

I want her naked, the first says.

I promise, comes the reply.

Who are they and why is one helping the other? And who are they after? Did they bring her here? Hawke had these phones. He'd been hiding them. Why?

He's also not been forthcoming about the story behind this place.

Sweating in my bed, and able to do nothing but take what I give her, the prick writes as his friend watches her.

She'll like you.

Yes.

I read it, but I hear it as a whisper instead.

And then she'll bleed for you.

Yes.

This text conversation is different than the others I read, because it feels like this conversation is happening now, and they're talking about me.

This Saturday, his friend promises. *Carnival Tower.*

And the discussion ends. These must be burner phones, because in every one I read, the sender and recipient seem close, but there are barely any exchanges, and they feel like the same people talking from one phone to the other.

Carnival Tower. It sounds familiar.

Ringing pierces the silent room, and I know who it is before I even pull out my phone.

I answer, holding it to my ear as I look up and see him on the screen. He stands on the roof.

"Aro?" he says.

I watch him. He looks around him, nervous.

After I got back from the appointment with Dylan, I showered and thought about making something to eat for us. He was so nice with my brother and sister this morning.

I didn't mean to find the phones. I just wanted to be somewhere he was. Look at his books. See what was happening around town on the screens. It was an accident.

"Aro?!" he yells.

"What's Carnival Tower," I ask instead.

He turns his head, looking straight at me through the camera posted to the air duct rising out of the roof like a chimney. I can tell by his silence that locking down the hideout might've been a good idea. He's got a secret.

"How did...?" He breathes hard and then hardens his voice. "Open the door."

"I found your phones."

"You mean the ones as old as us?" he barks, yanking on the latch. "Open the door."

"No."

"Aro..."

"I like it here," I tell him.

I'm surprised by how soft my voice is. It feels like I'm changing.

He goes quiet, unable to see me through the lens, but still, he tries.

"I feel safe," I continue. "But it's more than that. In a world full of people who prey and lie and stare and take—who force you to do things you don't want to do—they don't exist in here, do they?" I move toward the desk, looking at him and seeing the wind shake the trees behind him and the lights from below.

But it may as well be a million miles away. Nothing out there is real. At least not like it is in here.

"I can't hear the traffic or their voices or their music," I say. "I feel everything in here. It's so quiet, Hawke." I close my eyes, barely murmuring. "What is this place?"

He hesitates, but before I can open my eyes, he replies. "It's Carnival Tower. I found the phones when I found it."

As I thought. So the phones were left here. Did they succeed then? Was she here too? Whoever they were talking about in those texts...

"How did you find it?" I ask him, looking up.

He meets my eyes. "I looked for it."

"Why?"

"Open the door, Aro."

But I don't. "What happened to her?"

He's quiet for a moment. "She fell though the mirror," he says.

The mirror. *Carnival Tower*.

Now I remember. Something about not leaning back into mirrors. A superstition in the area. They're portals.

It's bullshit. Mirrors aren't dangerous. It's nothing supernatural, like ghosts or parallel dimensions.

The phones exist. The texts are real.

This urban legend started with a true story.

"What happened to her?" I ask him again.

But he demands, "Open the door."

Part of me is a little wary. None of this makes sense, and his part is unclear. What if that's what Hawken Trent was after the whole time? Snatching me up to relive *Carnival Tower*.

Where did he go today? He's been gone for hours.

"You're not alone in there, you know?" he taunts. "You've felt it, haven't you? Like you're being watched and not by me?"

A smile pulls at my lips. *Maybe.*

But darkness does that to you.

"Open the door," he whispers.

I reach up, my heart thundering inside my chest. I tap the screen, hearing the mirrors and the roof release their locks.

A moment later, the ceiling door slams to a close, and I know he's inside.

"Where are you?" he asks in my ear.

I flip off all the monitors, killing the last remaining light in the place and shielding us in darkness.

"Somewhere," I tell him.

He's quiet, and I walk, turning left and up the short staircase to the great room and kitchen, but I don't go there. I hear his footsteps on the iron grating as he descends from the roof, and I veer left, toward the mirror and *Frosted*. He doesn't see me.

"The lights are off," he says.

"Yeah."

"You want to hear a bedtime story, is that it?"

I hold back my smile; but excitement, anticipation, and a sliver of fear fills my lungs and heats my blood.

I back up toward the bakery, keeping an eye on the tunnel.

"It's one of our urban legends," he tells me. "But as with most stories, it's rooted in fact. Something that really did happen once. I didn't start researching it until I noticed the unaccounted for space on the bakery's blueprints. Once I found my way in and found the phones, pieces started to come together."

His voice is sonorous—calm, gentle, and steady—as it drifts into my ear and through my head, like he's close. Like he's behind me.

"But stories change and take on a life of their own over time," he goes on. "And every version is different every time it's repeated. I can't be sure what's true and what's not."

This story can't be that old. They had cell phones at least.

"Tell me," I beg.

"Are you sure?"

My whisper is barely audible. "Yes."

The hideout is so quiet I hear the clock chime in the square. The hair on my neck rises.

"One night," he starts, "it's always at night in these stories, isn't it?" I hear the smile in his voice. "A babysitter was watching a kid in a big house. Secluded. All alone. Dark."

"Is this the, 'The call is coming from inside the house?' one?" I tease.

"Close," he replies. "It was Grudge Night, and her friends were off having the time of their lives. Pulling pranks. Drinking. Racing. Getting wild."

I see a shadow pass the hallway ahead and turn my back to him, hiding the light of my phone behind my hair. His footsteps fade as he goes down toward the surveillance room and the bedrooms, not noticing me at all.

"But not Winslet," he tells me. "She knew they'd come for her. She stayed put that night so that they could."

I turn, heading back toward the great room that he had just left. "Who was coming for her?" I ask softly.

He's quiet, and I pass by the couch, barely visible in the moonlight streaming through the windows above, but I spot the hoodie he was wearing laying across the arm. A white T-shirt lays on top.

It warms in my stomach, the thought of him getting comfortable.

"During this week every year," he says in a low voice, "a group from the rival school in Weston broke into houses. Not for anything valuable. Just for fun. They called themselves the Marauders."

I grin. "We did, did we?"

"Most of Shelburne Falls spent the night at parties," he explains. "Together. In groups. Safety in numbers. But she wanted to be alone if they came.

"What did we do when we broke into houses?"

"Whatever we let you do," he says.

A shiver shoots up my spine.

"The Marauders would come, in their '72 Dodge Charger that was scarier than any mask, and when you saw it enter town, you knew what was about to happen. You just didn't know to who," he tells me. "Sometimes, they'd give chase. Sometimes, they'd tie some people up as hostages for an hour to humiliate them. Everyone would laugh. It was good fun." He pauses before continuing. "Sometimes, they'd do other things if people were into it. Behind a closed door, so no one would see."

He makes Weston sound a lot more interesting than it is. Or maybe I've just had my head up my ass feeding kids and paying bills for most of my teenage years.

"You don't have these stories at school?" he inquires.

"I never paid much attention." I open the door to the Rivertown tunnel and close it behind me, satisfied I'm hidden for now. "Kind of wishing I had."

"Where are you?"

My skin feels like it's vibrating. "I'll let you know when you're getting warm."

I walk, hoping he hasn't turned on the interior cameras, because that would be cheating.

"Winslet was the popular girl here," he continues his story. "Stunning eyes, confident, money... The ultimate cool girl, living a charmed life, despite the parents who left her alone all the time with nothing but a housekeeper and a credit card."

Sounds like me, except for the housekeeper and credit card. And the cool, charmed part.

"And that's why she knew they'd come for her." His voice sharpens with an edge. "Because of everything they lost that she didn't."

"What do you mean?"

"Their best friend was dead," he states. "He killed himself earlier that year...because of her."

I stop. So, a Shelburne Falls girl rejected a Weston boy, and he lost it. I don't know what started the beef between our towns, but that sounds as good a place as any.

"Some people say they were a couple," Hawke adds. "They were in love, she broke his heart... Others say he barely knew her. He was just obsessed. Sick in the head with his madness for her."

I approach the Rivertown entrance, seeing a girl on the other side. She faces me, smoothing her hair and ruffling her long bangs, and I step up close as Pirates fill the little caverns off to the side behind her, talking and laughing and carefree, because they're only aware of what they can see.

I could flip the latch, grab her, and close the mirror before they even knew where she went. I mean, just for shits and giggles, of course. Being a Marauder must've been fun.

"Over the next several months after his death," Hawke tells me as the chick applies lipstick. "She worked hard to escape the shadow of being the callous girl who'd driven a man over the edge. But she soon realized that in that shadow was exactly where she wanted to be. She became notorious. Powerful. Feared. She wasn't letting his 'stunt' ruin her life, like I'm sure he hoped it would, when he blamed her in his suicide note, but..." A hint of pride laces Hawke's voice. "She also wasn't going to let anyone forget her part in it. She twisted it to use it."

By making his memory a joke. "She threw him under the bus to save herself, didn't she?" I turn and head back down the hallway, grazing the wall with my free hand as I go. "Made a joke of a sad guy. Must've made her school proud. Must've made Weston angry."

"Yes," he agrees. "On one occasion, she even invited her whole class over to her house for a party."

I pass vacant rooms, too dark to see what's inside, and even though I feel something crawl on my back, I press forward. It's the dark. Fear is worse in the dark when you don't know what's there.

He goes on, "She'd made a pile consisting of every love letter and present he'd given her and joined them in fucking it all up."

"I'm not going to like Winslet, am I?"

The guy was dead. There was no need to be cruel.

"They broke everything that was breakable," Hawke explains. "Tore up every letter and smashed every trinket. And then threw everything into a bonfire in her driveway."

"Do you think she was *trying* to provoke his friends?"

"It's possible. His best friend wasn't a lover like him. He had a reputation for being violent on the field. And in life. She knew Grudge Night was his. He would come for her to get revenge."

"Now that she was of age, of course."

I hear his quiet laugh. "Very good."

Yeah. They waited until she was eighteen, because when it's a minor, she was kidnapped. When it's an adult, they can just say she ran away.

"Did he find her that night?"

The texts roll through my mind, thinking about them approaching the house? Did they wear masks? Face paint?

I leave the hallway, feeling him everywhere as I step back into the great room.

"She waited," he whispers. "Made some popcorn with the kid. Watched a movie." Wind rattles the windows above. "Put him to bed and then put on some lipstick in the hallway mirror."

My skin chafes on my T-shirt, and the needles of carpet under my feet spread up my legs as I cross the room.

"Lipstick?" I ask. "Why?"

"Because she was a weapon he needed to fear."

Hawke's breath spills out of the phone and down my neck. A lock of hair sticks to my skin.

I look around, searching the dark corners of the room. The shadows. Where is Hawke?

"She walked through the house," he murmurs, "feeling him. Feeling all of them. His friends." I drift down the hall, knowing he's here. He's watching me. "In the wind against the doors. The creak from the second floor. The shift in the air from an open window she hadn't left open."

"What did she do?"

"She walked," he says. "Slowly stepping past darkened

doorways and billowing drapes, peeling off her sweater. And then her bottoms."

Warmth trails down my arms, my head starts floating, and I feel it. Scared for him to catch me but needing him to come. My chest caves every time I exhale. I can't catch my breath as I peel off my shirt, feeling the air hit my breasts.

"Did he have a moment when he was scared watching her?" I ask Hawke. "A moment when he didn't know what to do?"

"He knew what to do." His voice is like velvet, and I curl my head into it. "He wasn't a fucking coward."

I hear a step behind me, and I smile. "Getting warmer," I tell him in the phone.

"His heart pounded," Hawke tells me, "but his hands never shook. He wouldn't be shaking when he touched her."

A body covers my back, and I break out in goosebumps, gasping a little.

He takes my phone away from my ear, and the skin of my nipples tightens as his fingers graze my back and he sweeps my hair over my shoulder.

"What did she say when he cornered her?" he asks me.

He fists the back of my jeans and hauls me back into his body, burying his nose in my hair.

"'Am I supposed to run now?' she said." I moan, arching into him.

He pushes me left, pressing me into the wall, the cement cold on my nipples.

"I'm not running from you," I tell him, playing my part. "I don't want to. You wanted this conversation."

His fingers reach around, find the button of my jeans, and I gasp, curling my toes into the floor.

"A hunter appreciates its meal more than anyone," he whispers.

"And a big game hunter needs help," I taunt. "Is that why you brought your boys? I'm flattered."

He snickers in my ear, and we're them, but we're also us. The rivalry and the river, and he hates so much about me, but he wants me.

"You have a big mouth," he says. "But I'm so glad you're not all talk."

He pushes Winslet's jeans down over her ass—my ass— and I let him do all the work. He glides them down off my legs, and I step out of them.

"How do you know?" I ask, making my way around the corner and into his room. "Been watching me?"

He's quiet, but he follows. Is this what Winslet wanted? Him? Was he the one she really desired?

Is he the reason she acted out? To get his attention?

"What have you seen?" I press.

Was he a watcher like Hawke?

But he pushes me in the back, and I crash onto the bed. I pop out my knees to get myself up, but cool air hits me between the legs, and I feel his eyes down there.

When I try to flip over, he comes down on top of me, threading his fingers into my hair.

I whimper.

"Shhh," he says in my ear, but it doesn't calm me.

I fist his sheets.

"I saw some things that surprised me," he says. And then he slips his other hand underneath me, covering my breast with his hand. "Some things I liked."

My stomach quivers. Hawke...

He squeezes my flesh over and over, moving it around, and then...his hand leaves my hair and he's yanking my panties down.

"And some things y...you didn't," I pant.

He takes my hand and pushes it down between my body and the sheets. A groan escapes before my fingers are even between my legs.

Lifting my knee to the side, I open myself up and roll my fingertips over my clit. He pants into my neck and squeezes the curve between my thigh and hip.

"And then he pressed her into the mirror..." Hawke says, and he thrusts himself behind me.

The hard muscle in his jeans rubs so close, and I'm wet on my fingers as he does it again and again.

"No one will question it." He rolls his hips, dry fucking me as I play and grind my pussy into his bed. "You know that, right? Just a girl, overcome with guilt, joining the boy in death that she couldn't love in life."

"Will you hang me?"

He bites my neck. "If you leave a note, I'll do it any way you want me to."

Yeah, I don't think so. I don't think he killed Winslet at all. She was his match.

"Aren't you scared?" he gasps, and I feel heat drip out of me.

"Always."

He holds me so tight, one hand on my breast and his chest covering my back as he breathes in my ear.

"Hawke..." I moan. It almost feels perfect. There's something I can't reach, though. More. Deeper.

I whimper into the pillow. *Hawke.* I'm always scared, but I can't think about anything else right now. Just more. And more and more and more.

"Kill me," Winslet taunts him.

He squeezes my neck, and I can almost feel the mirror pressing into my body. She watched him on her. Every second of it.

"I want what you never gave him," he growls low.

And I want everything you've never given to anyone else, Hawke.

"Watch me," I whisper, begging.

He stops thrusting, rising back up, and I squirm on the sheets. I rub circles, feeling the heat of his gaze on my ass as he kneads the skin.

Hawke needs this. He likes a view, and I'm lost. Blissfully lost, fucking for him.

I feel a bite on my right cheek as he squeezes a fistful of my ass and sucks the skin.

I cry out.

"Pay me for my pain and suffering," the boy breathes over my skin. "Pay me."

Coming back down on me, he thrusts so hard—my cunt aching for him—and I know he's right there. Trying to feel me and get inside me, but not ready to take off his jeans.

"Kill me," Winslet begs.

He reaches down, taking over fingering me as he mimics fucking me, rolling his hips again and again. "I could never." He bites my earlobe. "You're far too pretty. I have other plans."

I whimper, Hawke pumping on top of me, and I know I feel the head of his dick, but then his tongue comes down, trailing up and down my back, and I burst open, coming. I arch my ass up into him, needing everything, and then he groans, not holding back, because there's no one here to disturb us.

His fingers slide inside me, deep, and I cry out as he thrusts them in again and again.

"Hawke," I gasp, squeezing the sheets with my forehead buried in the bed.

I move into his hand, riding it out.

Oh, God.

He pulls out, gliding his wet fingers over the skin between my legs and lingering as his forehead rests on my shoulder. For a minute, we both catch our breaths.

"Was that okay?" I ask him. "You don't feel badly about it?"

I wanted to tell him to get his clothes off. If he'd wanted me, I wouldn't have stopped him.

As our orgasms ebb away, though, I'm glad for his control. He doesn't want his first time to happen like this.

"No, uh..." He rolls off me and onto his back. "The story, maybe? I don't know. It took me out of my head. It felt good." Then his eyes dart over to me. "Are you okay?"

I smile a little, nodding. "Que cuerpazo te cargas."

But I don't say it in English, because he doesn't need to know how attracted to him I am.

I can barely move, though. I'm tired. Slowly, I roll over, sweat covering my stomach.

Hawke's abs flex as he stares at my body, and then he sits up, sliding a hand down my belly to my...

"It's smooth down there." He's so gentle as he touches, and I want to turn away, a little embarrassed now. "Do you always keep it that way?" he asks.

I want to laugh. "Dylan helped me with something today."

His eyebrows shoot up, and it's amazing how he can go from hot to stern in less than a second.

"Don't be mad," I tell him. "I just wanted..." I look away. "You said you wanted to see, I just..."

"You did this for me?"

"No," I reply, sitting up. "I wanted to feel you better. That's all."

I try to cover myself, but he just continues to touch, his fingers drifting over my center and inside my thighs, making the skin of my nipples tighten.

It was a good excuse, even if it wasn't the truth. I can feel everything now.

I can't stay here, though. I can't get attached. I sit up and climb off the bed, and I see him still sitting there, staring at me as I get dressed.

"Leave your door unlocked tonight," he says quietly. "In case I want to taste what my fingers touched."

My stomach drops, thinking about his tongue inside me, but I steel myself and pull on my jeans.

"Baby steps, Hawke," I tell him. "You still haven't kissed me here."

And I grin playfully, covering my tits with my arms and twisting in a little dance.

But he's not smiling. He pushes up and comes over to the edge of the bed, taking my face in his hand. "And I still haven't kissed you here." And he brushes over my lips with his thumb.

I stare at him, my heart pounding so hard I hear it in my ears.

Oh. That.

I'm not sure he's tried, but neither have I, and I think we both know why. It wasn't part of our mutual 'touching and let's pleasure and distract each other' agreement.

He doesn't press, though. He backs up and rolls off the other side of the bed, grabbing his bath towel and some clean clothes.

I pull on one of his T-shirts. "He was behind the mirror, wasn't he?" I ask him. "He was watching them."

Hawke stops and looks over at me.

"He wasn't dead," I clarify. "The guy who was obsessed with her and prompted their revenge."

It's an urban legend, after all. There's always a catch.

Hawke finally shrugs. "Some people say," he tells me. "And others think he's the one who fucked her."

I widen my eyes. I hadn't thought of that. If they wore masks, like thieves and criminals do, she wouldn't have known.

Hawke just sighs. "I don't know if we'll ever find out which one pinned her that night and which one was watching."

But we do know one thing. If he wasn't dead, and his friend didn't kill her, then the story didn't end there.

He didn't come into my room that night, but the next day, he wanted me with him nearly every minute.

"You should be safe here." Hawke turns off the bike, and we both climb off. "You can walk around a little if you want, but keep your hat on and your head down." He speaks extra slow like I'm five. "I'll call when I'm on my way out."

I nod once, a small smile spreading his mouth as he turns and heads for the administration building.

Or at least that's what he said it was called.

College starts for him soon, and he needs to meet with his advisor, which he was tempted not to do, but we needed to get out of the tower. The silence this morning was awkward, after last night.

Has he never dry-humped anyone? Maybe it went too far. But I don't think I should ask. I mean, it's not like we can take it back.

And what did he mean by 'You know you're not alone in there, right?' At first, I thought it was a joke, but after that story, I'm not sure what to think. Those phones are more than twenty years old, and Rivertown—or Frosted—could have easily been townhomes then. She could've been baby-sitting a family who lived there all those years ago, but there are so many questions. Was the hideout part of the house or something the owners didn't know about? And if they didn't know, how did the boys from Weston know about it?

Why call it Carnival Tower, and if these people are still alive, they'd only be in their late thirties or early forties, so are they still out there? Do they still think the tower is theirs?

Was that picture of the blonde on the wall in the tunnel Winslet?

And what does Hawke want with all of it?

I step onto the grass, the summer breeze rustling the leaves, and a few groups of students lounging on the ground and trying to catch some rays.

Maybe Hawke wishes it wasn't me last night. Maybe that's why he likes that story and it helped. Because Winslet is untouchable. He can idolize her, because he'll never achieve her, and it's a goal that he'll never have to reach.

He'll never be faced with failure.

Or maybe it's me.

In my head, I know that's stupid. Hawke's not like that.

But some people have hang-ups they don't realize. *Mexican girls aren't worthy, and girls who aren't virgins are dirty.* People wish they didn't feel this way, but they do. I feel it when they look at me sometimes. It's not how they look at people like his ex or his cousin.

I'm a body, built for service. His ex is a prize, built for position.

Maybe he wishes he'd never touched me. I can tell he doesn't want to touch women he can't picture honeymoon-ing with. Or bearing his children. Hawke wants to love every woman he has sex with.

I stroll, keeping my hand tight around my phone in the center pocket of my hoodie. Which he insisted I wear to protect myself, in case we fell off the bike.

Pulling my hat down, I walk around the green, the bell of the clock above ringing and signaling it's four in the afternoon. A few clouds dot the sky, a Bluetooth speaker plays "Dark Matter", and I inhale, the air smelling different here.

We're technically still in Shelburne Falls, but it's like a different world. Still beautiful, but a community within a community. Without the Trents, the Caruthers, and High Street.

I enter the library, the tables sparsely filled with students in the summer session and the smell of books, coffee, and sad obligation lingering. Most of them don't want to be here.

A guy pushes past me. "Sorry," he calls back.

But I barely notice him as I stumble. I gape up at the mural on the ceiling and the solar system sculpture spinning over my head. So many books on the floors above.

I picture myself, dressed in a Clarke sweatshirt and carrying books back to my table, like I don't have Matty and Bianca and I'm not completely broke.

I back out, slowly turning and leaving before I venture in any farther. A different life, maybe. I don't think I would even know how to study anymore.

The building across the quad says *Saber Science Building*. I walk over and enter, letting myself forget for a minute like I do when I'm with him.

I let myself pretend.

Clarke University has an astronomy department, and I don't know if this is the place, but I pass classrooms, some still empty and some filled with students. I climb one floor after another, stopping when I see a video of the Sun on an instructor's board. I hide behind the door, peering in the window just enough, and watch the star flame and burn as it zooms in and out. Text appears on the screen, too small to read, and I wish I was in there. With my laptop and my ponytail and preparing for the work I want to do someday. Maybe Hawke is texting me as I sit in class and begging me to stay the night in a house he shares with some other guys.

What a life it would be, to only have to worry about my boyfriend unable to keep his hands off me.

"Hi," a voice says.

I startle and step back, out of view of the door as a girl stands in front of me.

"Hawke meeting with his new advisor?" she asks.

What?

And then I see her lip, a cut hidden behind the makeup from when I kicked it.

I straighten my spine.

"Me too," she replies, not waiting for me to speak. "And you? Getting your schedule, maybe?" She smiles, smug. "Books? Meeting your new roommate for lunch?"

I look at her, not giving her an inch. She's in shorts and a T-shirt, but I see the red bikini strap tied around the back of her neck. The same one she was wearing in that Insta-gram picture.

The day Hawke let her kiss him.

"I'm excited," she says. "My parents think that since I'm so close to home, I'll be back all the time, but I think as the weekends go on, more of my life will be on campus. I won't want to miss study sessions, parties, athletics…"

Like Hawke, she's telling me. I won't be here with him, and he'll eventually move on, making a life here.

"I don't think I'll be back to town much at all, once school starts," she muses.

I'll be here with Hawke and you won't, she doesn't have to say it out loud for me to understand.

She leaves, descending the stairs, and I stand there frozen for a minute. Hawke isn't my boyfriend.

We're not dating, and we're not falling in love.

I should've just told her that, so she knows I'm not losing anything.

But for some reason, I don't want her to know all that.

I follow her out, seeing her on the grass, T-shirt gone and tanned body playing in the sun as water balloons fly in the air among her and her friends.

Water splashes, and she laughs before they notice me.

They exchange looks, whispers, and I feel like my clothes are ten times too big or wrong or…

"Aro?" Hawke says.

I look up to see him on the motorcycle.

He holds his helmet in his hands, his gaze flashing between them and me. "Get on the bike," he says.

I stand there.

Why did he bring me with him? I could've stayed at the hideout. Why's he showing me all this?

He stares at me, and I know he knows where my head is going. He gets off the bike, I back up, and he grabs me, pulling me into him. His lips press into my forehead. "Let's go," he whispers.

A lump stretches my throat, but when I look ahead all I see is his chest. A white T-shirt of the softest fabric, and a chest I've kissed nearly every inch of.

I let him take my arm and pull me back to the bike, both of us climbing on.

I put on the helmet, wrapping my arms around him, and I'm not even tempted to look at her as we drive off, speeding down the highway.

She'll get him in a couple of weeks when they're alone at school together, but for now, I just want to enjoy a few more minutes. A few more days.

Hawke hits the brakes, coming to a stoplight, and I only hesitate a second. "I don't want you talking to her while we're messing around," I tell him. "It'll make me feel bad."

He turns his head just a little, and I feel stupid for asking this, but he'll be hers soon enough.

"It'll feel like I'm not important," I say. "I know I'm not your girlfriend, but we're friends, right?"

He nods, so quiet. What is he thinking?

"Just not while we're doing whatever we're doing, okay?"

"Okay." There's a crack in his voice, but it still sounds firm.

The light turns, and he puts his foot on the rest.

"Aren't you going to tell me not to mess around with other guys?" I ask, holding him close.

He revs the engine. "I already know you won't."

He speeds off, the bike jerks, and I tighten my arms, whispering, "Because you know you're the one I like."

Great.

I gave it all away right off the bat, didn't I?

FALLS

CHAPTER TWENTY

Hawke

"**W**hat are we doing here?" Aro asks.

I take her helmet and mine, leading her past Madoc's front door, to the side of the house. Less people will see us if we go through the kitchen.

"Kade's having a pool party," I tell her, opening the door. "Want to go?"

She steps into the mayor's house, and I set the helmets aside, taking her hand and walking her up the stairs.

"You'll really have to explain to me some day how your rules only apply to everyone else," she grumbles.

I grin to myself. She's got a point. The difference is I trust me. I don't trust anyone else with me. If she goes out and puts my safety in danger, that's a chance I'm not willing to take.

"Weston knows about the party," I explain. "Green Street knows about it. If there's action, I need to be here."

Kade broadcasts every fart on social media, and if he doesn't, someone else will. Pirates can't have a senior party without it being public knowledge.

We head down the hallway, her hand in mine, and I resist the temptation to tighten my hold. Her skin is soft. Her hand slender. It feels good in mine.

"But they're *your* friends and family," she points out as we approach the last guest room on the right. "They might not turn you in, but they'll turn me in."

"No one will recognize you when I'm done with you," Dylan says.

We both stop at the doorway as she stands there dressed in some gray swim shorts and a blue-and-white-striped bikini top. She grabs Aro's hand and pulls her into the room.

"My palette is a little different," she says, pushing Aro down into a seat at the vanity and taking out a square case, "but we'll make do."

She opens the container, picks out a brush, and I spot a bag sitting on the bed, hopefully filled with suits for Aro to try.

Dylan pulls off Aro's hat and leans in with the makeup.

But Aro grabs it from her. "I know how to apply eye shadow, thank you." Then she arches a brow and glares at me. "I don't want to swim."

"You don't have to."

She twists her lips, giving me a half-scowl.

I just laugh. "Have fun."

I leave, closing the door, about to double-back and tell them not to fight, because when Aro gets mad she doesn't care about making a scene, but I let it go. If getting waxed together doesn't guarantee a bond, then I don't know what does.

Annnnnnd, I stop, realizing Aro got waxed to feel me better, so who the hell did Dylan get waxed for? *Goddammit.*

I pull off my shirt, keeping my shorts on and not bothering to change since I don't plan to swim. Unlocking the basement door with the spare key kept inside the red oven mitt, I jog downstairs and swipe one of Madoc's beers, pop the lid, and run back up, locking the door again. If it's family, our parents are confident we know not to drink and drive, and if we have too much, we're comfortable here to spend the night. If it's someone else's kids, the mayor can't be seen supplying alcohol.

But he also acts like he doesn't know people are sneaking it in in their Gatorade bottles and Hydro Flasks.

Opening the French doors onto the patio, music blasts from the fire pit beyond the pool, laughter and screams filling the air as one of the last parties of summer promises that the fun is only beginning as everyone looks ahead to the new year.

I'll miss high school. But only because it was familiar. It'll be hard, leaving Kade and the guys, but I've got my own plans.

And if I'm lucky, my cousins will join me in a year.

"Dude, you like walking on the edge, don't you?" Stoli gives me a look as he takes position at my side. His Solo cup is filled with something red, but I smell the Tito's he added to it.

Kade kicks a beach ball into the pool and makes his way over to me. "I bought him some time," he tells our friend, taking a sip of one of his dad's beers. "Eli is collecting phones from everyone at the door, and I've got the cameras set up on alert."

He holds up his phone, wiggling it.

I take a drink, murmuring, "Thanks."

"If anyone comes, we'll know," he says.

Stoli gulps down the rest of his drink and runs off, cannonballing into the pool. A girl squeals, turning away as the cold splash douses her hair.

I check the patio door, wanting to be here when Aro comes down. If she comes down.

She won't feel comfortable here, and I don't know why I brought her. I just didn't like the thought of her stuck back at the tower, alone.

Maybe I wanted us to come tonight, because if we went back to the tower, I'd just want to do more of what we did last night.

And then, when I freaked the fuck out like I always do, I'd disappoint her.

God, I wanted her. Last night. This morning. Now.

Even now, I just want to be alone with her.

My groin rushes with blood, and I draw in a long, deep breath.

I need another drink. I tip back the bottle, finishing it in one swallow and not remembering when I drank all the rest. "Where are your parents?" I ask Kade, trying to get my mind off my little delinquent.

He stares out at the party. "Hunter."

I glance at him. Kade and his brother are like two pieces of paper stuck together. Attached, they're useless. There's a whole side you can't see.

But try to separate them, and that's bad too. The print tears. Again, useless. They've always been this way.

I grip my empty bottle. "How's he doing?"

"I don't give a shit."

"Yes, you do."

"No, I don't," he grits out, turning his eyes on me. "It's bad enough he broke my parents' hearts and moved out. That he rarely visits and enrolled at a rival school, but he does it because he hates me. So no, I don't give a shit."

I stare at him, Kade's anger is always quick and his defenses are always up, but there's something else. The shake in his words. The staggered breathing.

The clipped words and how it's obvious he's had them on the tip of his tongue for the entire year since his twin transferred schools. He's not just mad. He's upset.

For whatever reason, Hunter felt he needed to leave. Kade is loud, popular, bold, he always has the last word, and he looks good in everything he wears. Hunter is the exact opposite. Quiet, awkward at parties, hates small talk, and he won't remember to cut his hair until it's hanging in his eyes, obstructing his view of the computer he's building or the abandoned building he's exploring or the cave he's rappelling into.

He had a hard time at our school, just like I did.

"He doesn't hate you." I gaze out at the partygoers but don't really see them. "I loved being an only child, you know? I hated every time my parents fostered a new kid in, because the kid needed a lot of attention, and as much as I didn't want it to happen, I knew I was going to get attached to someone who was just going to leave eventually. It sucked."

Kade and Hunter's sister A.J. is only nine. The age difference between Kade and her means they're both growing up alone basically, and with his twin living near Chicago with their grandfather, Kade is essentially an only child now.

"But something I learned was that when they left," I tell him, "I wanted them back. I resented these kids because I had to share, not only my toys, my house, and my parents, but I also had to change my behavior to accommodate them." He doesn't move next to me. "So when they were around, I didn't feel like myself. Sometimes, I didn't feel like I knew who I was in the house."

I had to be different around them. More gracious. More compassionate. Aware. It was hard for a ten-year-old.

"I was confused a lot about my role, my worth..." I say. "But when they left, I missed them."

"So?"

I feel the emptiness of my bottle and set it down on the table behind me.

"So what?" he asks.

"So Hunter left because he wanted to love you," I tell him.

Hunter was sick of being compared to Kade, and Kade didn't really help. After a while, he started feeding his friends. Like they always had to know he was better than his brother. A comment here. A comment there. Just a hint of condescension when he'd speak to Hunter, so Hunter always knew who was really the stronger one.

Hunter had to leave, so he wouldn't hate Kade anymore.

Kade clears his throat, but he doesn't reply. Just simply says, "I gotta check on something."

And he walks away, back into the house.

I miss Hunter, and I wish Kade would admit that he does too. Dylan is the only one who's made a huge effort to see or talk to Hunter, but even she's given up now. If someone doesn't make a move—and I mean a move that goes off like a bomb—we may never get him back.

"Who is that?" someone says.

"New student?" I hear Stoli ask, a hopeful hint in his voice. "Please tell me it's a new student."

I look up as "Queen" by Loren Gray starts playing, seeing Stoli and Dirk chuckling. I follow their gazes over to the patio door where Dylan strolls onto the deck, followed by Aro.

I draw in a breath.

Dressed in an electric blue bikini top, she slips her hands into the pocket of her rolled-over jean shorts, strings of the frayed fabric brushing across her golden thighs. Her dark hair is parted in the middle and hangs straight, and she licks her red lips as she inhales a breath and looks around, searching for me.

A lock of hair blows across her neck, and I curl my fingers, wanting to touch it. Tight tummy, long legs, and... I gaze at her body, still feeling all the parts I squeezed last night.

My shorts get tight, and she finally turns, meeting my eyes. She holds them as Dylan takes her hand and pulls her to the food, and I can see the smile in her eyes. Her shoulders relax because she knows I'm close.

"I don't know, she looks like Amos Cahill," Dirk says. "Does he have a sister?"

"No idea," Stoli says, mischief in his tone. "But I'll take Homecoming."

"And I'll take the senior ski trip."

They both laugh, and I turn, swiping my empty bottle off the table and into the garbage can. "Shut up."

They dart their eyes to me, tensing. Dirk squeezes the cup in his hand. "Sorry, Hawke." He looks to her again and then to me, realizing. "Jesus, man, I had no idea."

Does he really not recognize her from the other night?

She doesn't look different. She was pretty then.

But I'm guessing they're not looking at her face.

I head over. I need another beer from the house.

But I don't go to the house. I walk over to her, about to put my hands on her, so they all stop thinking they're going to get near her, but I see her smile as she tips her head back and watches a flock of birds pass overhead.

Swooping and soaring, high and flying away, but I wouldn't know for sure, because I'm just looking at her.

God, she's so cute.

"What?" she says.

I blink, realizing she's noticed me.

I collect myself and reach over, grabbing a Gatorade. "Those clothes don't seem like you."

"Well, I wouldn't call them clothes."

I try not to laugh, but she's right.

"I covered myself out of necessity, not because I like to, Hawke," she explains, looking back up at the birds. "It's not wise for women to draw attention to themselves at Green Street."

Right.

I guess I thought she liked her clothes. Abhorred feminine stuff. I didn't even think of how she shields herself, not only for Green Street but for home, as well. I wouldn't like the idea of her walking around in stuff like this in front of her stepdad.

"Hawke, let's play!" Kade calls.

I look up just in time to catch the football he throws, his pissy mood now gone, probably thanks to a couple shots of bourbon.

I flash her one last glance, and she nods, telling me to go. I won't stake my claim just yet. Let her just be Dylan's friend for a while.

"Blue thirty-two!" Kade shouts. "Blue thirty-two! Go!"

Kade catches the football, scrambles backward, looks for an opening, and I dart around Dirk, running and checking my tail.

Kade locks eyes with me, my heart pushes up my throat, and the ball flies, through the air and spinning toward me.

I catch it, running past the tree line with cheers going off behind me.

Like riding a bike. I slow, grabbing my shirt out of my back pocket and wipe my face off before I pitch the ball back to Dirk who catches it.

I wish I liked football more. I'm not terrible at it.

And it's not that I hate it, but I didn't understand the point. There are more fun things to do in this town.

I look over at Dylan and Aro, sitting in a tree with their cups of Dylan's special, secret concoction she makes from Madoc's liquor cabinet.

Kade laughs, holding out his hands. "Haven't lost your touch."

"No matter how hard I try," I mumble.

I walk over, getting into position, calling up to the tree behind me. "You guys should back up," I tell Aro. "You're enough trouble. I don't want you injured."

She looks down at me, her lips twitching with a smile she doesn't let out. I glance at her bikini top, picturing it buried in my sheets later. I should've brought the damn car. I'll borrow Dylan's. I'm so going to take her somewhere secluded and leave marks with my mouth. *Jesus Christ.*

I groan and squat down, one hand on my knee and the other on the ground.

"Hard eighteen!" Kade bellows down the line. "Hard eighteen! Go! Go! Go!"

I run down the field, Stoli blocks me, I double back, and I catch the ball. It's only in my arms a second before Stoli and someone else crash into me. I stumble, trying to stay upright, but then I fall into the bystanders at the sideline, the three of us tumbling to the ground.

My shoulder grinds into the grass, burning, but we all laugh.

We get up, Stoli hauling me to my feet, and a girl brushes off my back. I turn, seeing Schuyler smiling and then wiping off the drink that splashed onto her chest.

"Sorry," I tell her, turning to leave.

But she stops me. "Why? You always looked best when you were on the field."

285

I stop and look back, her flirty tone unexpected. I nod and start away again.

"Hawke," she calls.

I stop.

She comes to my side, Stoli takes the ball and runs back to the game. "I wanted to apologize," she says.

"It's fine."

I check the tree, seeing Dylan and Aro still there, Dylan gabbing away as Aro watches me.

I step away again.

But Schuyler pulls my arm.

I look down at her, dressed in the pale pink crop top I had my hand under the night she snuck into my tent during the senior campout.

Seems like years ago now.

"If a man wants you," she broaches, keeping her voice low. "He'll go for it. That's what I learned, I guess. My pride was hurt. I'm sorry."

She gives me a sad smile, and she sounds genuine, but something's off.

"You're worth waiting forever for," she tells me.

I don't know what to say, so I don't say anything. She wants to make up.

But I don't know. I don't. Touching her is nothing like touching Aro.

Aro is like climbing a Sequoia. You know the fall will kill you, but it's the only way to get that view.

"If I need help moving some boxes, can I text you next week?" she asks.

I start to walk away. "They'll have volunteers on-site."

"I'm not moving into the dorms," she calls, and I stop. "I have a house with some other girls. My own room."

And I don't miss the glint in her eyes, thinking of all the promising nights when we're both off at college.

Great.

I motion to Kade that I'm going to get a drink and head into the house and down to the basement. I pull a juice out of Madoc's cooler and drink it down halfway. I really want to add vodka, but I have to drive us home on the motorcycle. May as well let her have some fun.

I tip back the bottle, the chill burning my throat.

"Hey," I hear Aro's voice.

I swallow and pull the bottle away from my mouth, seeing that she has her clothes back on already.

"Dylan's going to give me a ride back to the tower," she tells me.

I check the time on the clock hanging on the wall. *Seven.* "Already?" I put the bottle down. "I'll take you."

"No, stay."

I look at her. I don't want to stay.

"Have fun." She smiles small, placing her hand on my stomach. "Just...be careful if you get lucky, okay? You got protection?"

Excuse me?

"What?" I spit out.

She shrugs. "I'm sure Kade does." She takes my hand and pats it, smiling softly. "I won't wait up."

Did she just seriously pat my hand?

She turns and starts to leave, one last look like she's my sister, with a mixture of protectiveness and pride as she sends me out into the world to be a man.

"Whoa, whoa, whoa," I say, pulling her back by the arm. "What the fuck are you talking about? You told me not to touch anyone while we're messing around."

She saw Schuyler talking to me. Is that what this is about?

"I was an idiot." She sighs, shaking her head. "Don't mind me. I don't know what I was thinking. Just girl shit,

I guess." She inches closer, the expression on her face so sweet I can smell the fucking frosting. "If you're feeling it, go for it. I was being stupid. You don't owe me anything. We're friends. I want you to be happy."

"Aro—"

"I want you to," she assures me, and I look down at her hand on mine. "Have fun, okay?"

What?

She leaves, and I follow her upstairs to stop her, but Dylan runs past, grabbing her keys and kissing me on the cheek.

The next minute, the front door slams shut, and twenty minutes later, I'm drunk.

CHAPTER TWENTY-ONE

Aro

I snap my eyes open, the entire front of my head aching in that way it does when you're not getting good sleep. I rub my face, Hawke popping into my mind. I jerk my eyes to the bedside table, seeing the time is after two in the morning.

I pop up, the light in the hallway that I'd left on for him still illuminated.

Is he back? I didn't hear him come in, and it's not like I was really waiting, but I do want to make sure he's safe.

I slip off the bed and rise, stepping toward my door. I hadn't meant to fall asleep, but after Dylan dropped me off, I tried to find something to do.

I played *Grand Theft Auto V*. Went into the bakery and snooped around. Called my sister, but she and her boyfriend were putting Matty to bed.

I went up onto the roof and tried looking at the stars, but all I kept doing was watching the street for him to come home.

Finally, I gulped down two of his beers and crawled into his bed, but then I remembered that it wasn't my bed, so I crawled into mine instead.

I leave my room and step quietly down the hallway to the other side and see his door wide open.

My stomach sinks, and I peer inside, the bedside lamp on and his bed still made.

Dread sits like a brick in my stomach. *No...*

I turn, trying to control my breathing, and check the gym, the great room, the other tunnel leading to Rivertown, and the bakery.

Where the hell is he?

I squeeze my eyes shut, grinding my teeth together. *Where the fuck is he?*

I thread my hands through my hair, ready to go out there and find him. Why is he still out? What's he doing?

I race back to my room, grabbing my phone and checking for missed calls or messages, but...

There's nothing.

Not one single thing.

What if Green Street showed up like he anticipated? What if the cops raided the party and Reeves got him?

What if he found someone to go home with?

I drift back into the great room, my fingers paused over his number, but if something bad has happened and he's capable of answering the phone, he would've called or texted to warn me already.

And if he's with someone, I don't...

I sink into the couch, sick to my stomach.

I don't want to remind him that I'm here. It would be humiliating.

I throw my phone down and drop back, slouching.

I just want him to have fun. I want him to find something good, because he's amazing, but these girls...

I mean, he's super particular. And picky! They don't know how to roll with that. How he always lets you know there's a better way to do something, really doesn't like to be dirty, and if I put away the dishes, he sweeps through again and makes sure they're all facing the same way on the rack. It's kind of cute, but most women would want to kill him.

And they're not going to be gentle the way he needs them to be. He's kind of fragile. You just have to be there and not pressure him, and before you know it, he's holding you so tightly you can't tell which limb is his or yours.

And the way he breathes into your neck when he holds you... It's absolutely incredible. But you have to earn that from him with patience. Trust.

No one deserves him.

I tip my head back, whimpering. Why did I tell him to hook up with someone? I should've stayed. Vetted her, who-ever it was, because I know what he's like, and I can help. There's no point in him wasting his time on someone like Schuyler again.

The door in the roof creaks open, and I look up, seeing his long legs descend.

Shit.

I bolt up, move left and then right, see the PlayStation controller and grab it, unpausing the game I was playing earlier.

"Oh, come on!" I shout before I even move my char-acter, but he can't see the TV from that angle anyway, so whatever. "Oh, you bastard!"

I punch the button, zoning in on the screen, but I notice his every move as he climbs down the staircase. Long black shorts, sneakers, no shirt....

I move, jerking my body right and getting my character into his car. "No, go faster," I blurt out, glancing up. "Hey."

He doesn't stop or look at me, though. He simply passes by the couch, and my stomach twists as he opens the fridge door and then closes it.

"Now, go get the bag of money," I yell at the TV.

I'm sure he can see through me. Like I haven't been in the hideout obsessing about what he's doing, where, and with whom.

It's fine, though. He's safe. That's all that matters.

He wasn't with Green Street. He wasn't with the cops.

He was...with a girl. *Cool*.

I rage drive, the tips of my fingers charged and my thumb jerking the joy stick. Barreling though the city streets, I purposely side-swipe cars parked on the curb and then skid around the corner.

"Whipping the controller around doesn't make your character go any faster," Hawke tells me.

Yes, it does.

But I don't respond out loud. Now that I know he's safe, and he's talking to me, I'm going to let him wonder what I've been up to instead, having a fine time here without him.

"Turn right," he tells me.

He drops into the seat next to me, laying his head back, and I keep wanting to look at him out of the corner of my eye to check for hickeys or lipstick, but I don't care. And if he corrects me again, I'm gonna hit him.

"Raising the controller in the air isn't going to help you climb the stairs faster, Aro."

"Shut up."

"Use the knobs and buttons." He launches over and grabs for my controller, but I scoot away, breaking into a laugh. "You're wasting valuable energy," he shouts.

"I promise I'll live."

"Aro..." He reaches for me.

"No!" I pull away.

But he loses patience and picks me up, controller and all, and hauls me over into his lap. I laugh, steering like I'm driving a car as he wraps an arm around my waist, holding me tight.

"Just stay still," he orders. "That's always your problem. You get too worked up too fast. Use the damn buttons."

I play, moving in his lap, leaning and jerking, and he rests back against the couch, taking a swig of his beer.

The scent of whiskey drifts through the air, but he doesn't seem drunk enough for all the time he's had in the seven hours since I left him. He wasn't drinking for all that time.

I swallow, entering the club to go get my money. "So?" I broach.

"So, what?"

I hit the buttons, keeping my eyes ahead. "Who was it?"

I keep my voice light and gentle, fighting to sound like Kade or his other friends if they were asking him about his sex life.

"Schuyler," he finally says.

I get shot on screen, and I shudder, feeling it.

"And?"

He's quiet for a moment and then, "You really want to hear this?"

God, I want to puke. "Yeah," I chirp, steering my controller and trying to sound extra chipper. "If you want to tell me, that is. I need to live the teenage dream vicariously."

I smile, laughing under my breath, and I want to punch myself. Why am I doing this? I don't want to know.

But I need to.

His voice is quiet and raspy. "We went into the shower."

I square my shoulders, feigning interest in the game. "Did she wash you?"

295

"No, I washed her."

He looked at her. Touched her. Didn't think about anything else, did he? Nothing.

"With your hands or a cloth?" I ask him.

"With my hands."

I blink away the images in my head. "Did you like it?"

He breathes out a laugh and takes a drink. "I was a lot more relaxed this time."

Oh, fucking awesome. "Yeah, you're welcome," I spit out.

I'm really glad I could help you work through some of your hang-ups.

I punch the buttons, fighting to keep the scowl off my face. Why did it have to be her? Thinking about her gloating at their college campus earlier in the day and making sure I know that the two of them will be all on their own this fall, partying and screwing like animals... *Goddammit.*

"Anything else?" I ask, glaring at the TV screen.

But he just falls quiet, and another sinking feeling hits me. He's afraid to tell me something.

"What did she do?" I demand.

Just fucking say it.

His voice is quiet, but the only thing I hear as the video game plays. "She gave me a blow job."

My chin trembles, and tears wet my eyes. "In the shower?" I say, but it comes out as a whisper.

"Mm-hmm."

"Did you like it?" I ask him.

"Yeah."

Pain wracks my body, and I can't take it. I cry out and push myself to my feet, launching the fucking controller right at the TV. I hear the impact, but I'm whipping around and glaring at him before I see if it hit. "It's like second nature, isn't it?" I growl. "Giving it away to whoever is available for a good time? Congratulations, Hawke. You are finally a typical male, after all!"

He pushes off the couch, all of a sudden not so drunk and spitting words right back at me. "And what do you know... You do give a shit, *after all*." His eyes smile as he gloats, staring down. "You fucking little liar."

What?

"You seriously stood there at that party and told me to go screw someone?" His eyes blaze as he digs in his eyebrows and looks at me like I'm shit. "'Just don't forget your con-dom', like you're my fucking mother? Are you serious right now? No wonder I have trust issues with women! You're not doing me any good. Just playing with my head more!"

He advances on me and I stumble back.

"Do you have any idea," he shouts, "how much it hurt for you to want someone else to have me? To just pass me off like that? Like what we've been doing means nothing?"

But before I can respond, he's gone. He storms off down the hall, and a second later, I hear a door slam shut.

Okay, so maybe I underestimated our relationship. Something tickles my cheek, and I wipe it, realizing I'm cry-ing.

But I'm not the bad guy here. I want him, I act like I don't, but I do care.

I charge after him, passing the empty surveillance room, and seeing his bedroom door closed now. I throw it open, seeing him sitting on his bed, and I stalk up to him. "You know what? Screw you!" I say, tears welling again. "I don't want to care! You're a smart guy. Figure out why!"

He surges to his feet, coming at me. "Get in my bed."

"Fuck you."

"Get in my bed!" he yells and lifts me into his arms. My heart drops to my feet as he holds me by the backs of my thighs, and I push at his shoulders, his mouth inches from mine.

"What are you going to do?" I gasp. "Make me blow you so you can compare?"

"I'm going to kiss you," he says.

And he dives in, covering my mouth with his and cutting off my breath. His lips pause on mine, both of ours partially open, and fire spreads over my mouth, across my cheeks, into my hair and down to my toes. My clit pulsates, and I whimper, needing more. I move over his lips, soft, but he groans, diving in and taking me full force. I wrap my legs around him, and he slides one hand up the back of my scalp, kissing me again and again.

"You think I would let her touch me?" he whispers, hefting me up high. "Only you're allowed to touch me."

I look down at him as he carries me to his bed, dipping down for another kiss. And then another.

We fall to the mattress, and he thrusts between my legs, covering my mouth with his again.

"I thought you were going to come back," he tells me. "Or text me and tell me not to do it."

A sob catches in my throat. "It's going to be hard to leave you when the time comes, you know?" I press my forehead to his. "You're my only friend."

He slips his hand down the back of my underwear, grabbing a fistful of my ass and grinds himself into me, holding me flush with his body. "Friends can do this, right?"

"Yeah," I whimper, a light sweat already covering my body.

He comes down, pinning my hands above my head and kissing me. Slow. Firm. Playful. Biting my lips, his breath getting ragged as the heat from his tongue makes the room spin. I can't stop. I squirm into him, inching up to kiss him back, but I want to touch him.

I tip my head back, inhaling and exhaling as he trails down my neck, trying to calm myself down. I don't want him to stop, but we're going too fast.

He didn't touch her. I look down at him. *Thank God.*

Only I'm allowed to touch him, he said. I smile to myself, loving that.

"Is this mine?" he asks.

I feel myself float back to Earth and focus in on him pinching the T-shirt I'm wearing between his fingers.

I smirk. "Friends can do that, right?"

Share clothes?

But he gives me a mini-scowl. "It's dirty."

I shrug. "It smelled good."

He chuckles and sits up, gazing down at me. "Take it off."

Bubbles pop under my skin. His bedroom light is still on. He'll be able to see me like that first night on the couch, and his eyes burned everywhere they touched.

I sit up, drop my eyes, and pull his shirt over my head. Cool air hits my chest, and I set the garment aside. I lie back down, feeling him watch me.

But when I meet his eyes, he's not staring into mine. His gaze lingers on my blue underwear, which thankfully aren't trimmed in lace or some shit. I'd have to thank Dylan someday.

"Take those off too," he says.

The flesh of my nipples pebble, and he sees it, his mouth twitching with a smile.

Slowly, I slide my hands inside and push the panties down, watching him watch me the whole time. I can barely breathe, seeing his body go rigid when I'm all naked and lying on his blanket.

He sits there, and he doesn't leave, but he doesn't come back in either. I know he's worried about what will happen. How his head will never let him have what he thinks he wants.

"Turn on your phone," I tell him.

He looks at me, puzzled.

"Don't record, but watch me through the camera," I instruct. "Like you're watching something you can't touch."

The detachment makes him feel safe. Maybe he'll be less nervous if he can pretend that I'm not really here. That he's not really here...

"Aro..."

"It's okay, Hawke," I whisper. "Let's just see if you like it."

He takes his phone out of his pocket, and I can tell by the pinch between his brows that he's not sure this is right.

But he raises his phone, pointing it at me, and I start. I slide my hands down between my legs, my breasts plumping out and sitting high on my chest, and he stares at me on his phone, his breathing already getting shallow.

I rub myself, my finger over my clit again and again, bending up my knees and spreading my legs just a little.

The camera moves up, and I lick my lips, biting them to hold back the smile, but it comes out anyway. My skin warms with embarrassment, but I kind of like it. I like him watching me.

I slip my left hand down farther, thrusting my middle finger inside, and before I know it, I'm lost in this.

And so is he. He doesn't blink, a fire lighting behind his eyes as he watches every move, slowly moving the phone up and down my body, taking in every inch.

I close my eyes, pushing against the bed, again and again as I fuck with my left and rub with my right, performing for him.

My tits bounce back and forth, and I moan. "Hawke," I breathe out. "Record it. Do it."

I don't care. I want him to have this of me for as long as he wants. I want to know that when he fantasizes, it's to me.

I arch my back, pretending he's on top of me. "Hawke." I rub myself hard, adding another finger and moving it so fast, about to come. "Hawke..."

He doesn't answer though. I open my eyes, seeing him still holding the phone, but he's not looking through it anymore. His eyes are downcast as he watches my fingers, need written all over his face and in the glow of sweat on his neck. The camera's forgotten. He's just watching.

Did I go too fast? Does he not like it?

I stop, pulling my hands away, and sit up, grabbing his face. "Hawke."

But he just drops his phone, zones in on me, and takes the backs of my legs, yanking me down until I'm on my back again.

I gasp, but then he's there. His mouth between my thighs, licking so slowly.

I throw my head back and grab hold of his, holding him to me. "Oh, God."

Taking my nub softly between his teeth, he sucks it hard and then flicks it with his tongue. He strokes his tongue all over, reaching up and squeezing my breasts in both of his hands as he eats me.

He moves his mouth up and down, getting quicker but steady, and I feel it building.

"Hawke, just like that," I cry.

He sucks, licks, sucks and licks, and I move with it, fucking him back, again and again, until...

I go still, the orgasm exploding and spreading through me, up into my belly and down my thighs. I cry out, shuddering as he sucks me all the way through it.

I gasp and fall back to the bed, shaking and all my warmth sinking between my thighs.

Oh, God...

I'm afraid to open my eyes, so I don't, just feeling his mouth on my stomach, my breasts, and then my forehead before he wraps me into his body and I fall asleep.

Friends can do this.

I wake up in the dark room, my body curled into his and my head on his shoulder.

I look up at him, the light from the hallway illuminating the room just enough that I make out the sharp ridge of his jaw, the Adam's apple I licked last night, and his mouth. I reach up, brushing it with my fingers. Does he taste like me? I want to kiss him to find out, but I don't want to disturb him. I like him like this.

"When I die, I hope it's with this view," I mouth, gazing at his face that's home.

I smile and slowly sit up, careful not to disturb him. I'm being silly. In a few months, we won't know each other anymore, but whatever view I end up having some day, I hope it's like him. He's a good kisser.

I dress in some of Dylan's leggings, a tank top, and a hoodie, the morning chill seeping through the cement and my socks, and I grab my phone off the charger, heading out of the room to let him sleep in peace.

I tap out a text to Bianca, checking in and letting her know I'll see her soon, and then I head out to make something to eat, but I stop.

Veering back down the hall, I pass Hawke's room and enter the gym. Padding over, I jump on the exercise bike, no clue what I'm doing or why, but something surges inside me, like I'm ready to go. About to attack.

It's a good feeling.

I start up some music on my phone—"Esto No A Termi-nado"—and pedal, slowly at first and then faster. Five min-utes pass, my limbs are warm, and after ten minutes, I'm rising up out of the seat and pedaling as hair comes loose from my French braids and sticks to my forehead.

I slow after thirty minutes, feeling like I could go lon-ger, but my feet hurt on the pedals. I need sneakers.

Hopping off, I throw in a load of laundry, make some breakfast, and tidy up the great room, seeing the dent in the TV. I wince, gently running my hand over the splintered screen.

I hadn't realized I'd actually hit it. I walk back into the kitchen, dragging my guilt with me.

Somehow it seemed worse, the idea of him touching her than her touching him. If he'd really laid a hand on her, my head would've exploded. I don't care that I told him to do it. He knows me well enough by now to know I'm full of shit.

"Hey, what's that smell?"

I look up from my seat on the island, my knee bent up as I paint my toes with the black polish that I borrowed from Dylan last night.

"Empanadas." I let my eyes fall to his stomach that peeks out as he stretches his arms and yawns. "You didn't have beef, so I made apple."

I tear my gaze away and continue painting as he drifts into the kitchen, yawning again.

He picks up a pastry, taking a bite. "Shit," he blurts out, and I hear him chew. "That's really good."

Damn right, it is. You're not going to see those at his cousin's bakery.

Or is she his aunt? I think I heard that Quinn Caruthers is technically the aunt of the others she's pretty much the same age as, so...

He takes his laptop that I had open and twists it around, looking at the screen. "GED?"

I glance up, seeing him staring at me. I go back to concentrating on my task. "Just seeing what I'm in for, in case I want to get it."

And then I shut up, hoping he drops it. I didn't mean to leave that out for him to see. He'll think he's motivating me or some shit. Thank God, he didn't see me working out this morning. He would've beamed with pride.

I quit school about a month into my senior year, so while Hawke and I are the same age, I'm behind. There just wasn't a point anymore. I couldn't go to school and give a shit about the French Revolution or Virginia Woolf when Bianca was calling me in tears at my foster home because Mom was too tired to take Matty to preschool and she had a math assignment to get done before her own classes.

Which she hadn't gotten done the previous night because my stepdad had a party. She couldn't leave to go somewhere quiet because there was no one to watch Matty. They needed help. I had to work.

"A high school diploma is better," Hawke says. "Not every college accepts a GED, and you won't be eligible for some financial aid."

I dip the brush into the polish.

I'm not going back to high school. I still don't give a shit about the French Revolution.

But he doesn't press more, finishes his empanada, and grabs another as he pours some of the coffee I made. I glance up at his bare arms and neck, immediately flushing with heat. What would he look like if he'd grown up in my town?

That back would be covered in tattoos, for sure. Not a bad image, actually. The cords and muscles would look phenomenal covered in ink.

I blow out a slow breath and brush the paint on my toes, thankful I have something to do to distract myself. He hasn't touched me yet this morning. I know we're friends, but a little reassurance that he liked last night would be awesome because I'm starting to feel guilty.

I mean, his head was between my legs eight hours ago.

I sigh, the brush slipping over the top of my toe, painting it black. *Son of a bitch.*

I go to grab a napkin, but he's there, sliding the stool up to the island in front of me and sitting as he takes my foot and the polish.

I only resist a little, but then I let him. I lean back on my hands as he pinches my toe between his fingers and cleans up my mess. Dipping the brush in and wiping it free of excess, he chews and paints, and I stare at his mouth, still wanting to see if I'm still on his lips.

"I want to do that to you," I say in a quiet voice.

"Paint my nails?"

I remain silent, because he knows what I mean.

I want to taste him.

When I don't answer, he looks up, and I see the realization. His lips twitch, trying to keep the smile away.

"You gonna push me away if I try?" I press.

He shrugs a little, moving to the next toe. "I don't know. I usually don't know that I don't like something until it's too late."

That's the conundrum. I like that he feels comfortable with me, but pushing too hard could ruin everything. And I don't know how hard is too hard.

I shift my eyes, scared to ask but needing to. "Did you like it? What we did last night?"

He finally raises his eyes, and then in two seconds he tosses the brush and hauls me into his lap, pulling my hips into his body. "If you were still in bed when I'd woken up," he says over my lips, "you would've found out how much I liked that."

I can't hold back the smile.

He grazes my mouth with his, saying, "How much I liked your lips."

"Labios," I whisper the Spanish word, wrapping my arms around his neck, my mind easing.

He dips his head down, grazing my throat. "Your neck."

"Cuello."

He grips my ass and pulls me up, biting my breast through my clothes. "And your breasts."

I tip my head back, tingles everywhere. "Chichis," I tease.

"And your cunt," he murmurs, looking at me and sliding a hand between my legs. My clit begs for more.

I kiss his forehead. "Concha," I instruct him.

We kiss, and I settle back in with him between my legs and my head spinning. Is he just having fun? I need to keep it fun. I can't fall for him. What if he didn't fall for me? I can't be the hurt one.

"You can say cunt but not tits?" I ask.

He smiles, pushing me back up onto the counter. "One of my many mysteries."

Both the English and Spanish words are pretty vulgar, but I'd let him say them to me. Just him.

He works on the rest of my toes, blowing on the black paint, and I'm glad I'm wearing leggings and a sweatshirt, so he can't see the chills all over me. I've never seen a man do this for a woman before. I suddenly want him to wash my hair now.

"When did you get that Green Street tattoo?" he asks.

I lean back on my elbows. "When I was fifteen. Hugo, Nicholas, and Axel were in the same foster home. Hugo was aging out, but he was already at work. For a time—a short time—it just felt like..."

"Family."

I nod, sad thinking about it. "I was naïve."

At the time, I felt like I belonged to no one and nothing, and they were giving me a purpose. Everyone is searching for an identity, young people especially. It didn't take me long to realize how small that world really was.

I take a bite of his second empanada. "Why do you ask?"

"Just curious."

I sit back up and trace the words inked underneath his collarbone under his T-shirt. "When did you get this?"

He smiles up at me. "As soon as I turned eighteen. My dad has the same quote tattooed on him. He got it when he was falling in love with my mom."

These violent delights have violent ends.

"It's not a very hopeful quote," I tease.

More like something I'd get tattooed after a breakup.

But he jerks his chin, gesturing behind me. "Vivamus, moriendum est," he recites the words on the wall back there. "I think the two quotes mean the same thing in a way. One warns that passion that burns too hot can be destructive. The other reminds us that no matter what we do..." He levels his eyes on me. "Everything is eventually destroyed anyway."

So, fuck it. We're only here once, and it goes so fast. Love as much as possible.

He finishes the last nail. "My father feared how much he loved my mother, but he couldn't not have her."

"Why did he fear his love for her?"

"Because we can lose ourselves in other people."

He twists the cap back on the nail polish, and I gaze down at him, remembering last night. How lost he seemed. How he didn't even seem in his mind. He was out of control.

"And then..." He rises, relaxed with a playful look on his face. "The next thing you know, you're having duels where you kill her cousin and four other people die, and all because you had a wild time at a party one night and fell in love with a pretty face after only ten minutes of knowing her." He plants his hands at my side, getting in my face. "Now you're dead."

I smile, connecting the *Romeo and Juliet* reference to the quote on his skin.

"Dylan has a race tonight." He slaps both sides of my ass. "Want to ride with her?"

I widen my eyes. Really?

CHAPTER TWENTY-TWO

He watches them leave, standing below as they climb the spiral staircase, and the boy lifts the door for her.

His heart pounds a little harder, and he closes his eyes, enjoying it.

He likes them. How the boy watches her when she's not looking. How she breathes, because she knows when he's looking.

He misses that feeling. It's consuming, the want. Sometimes he thinks it's better than the having, because when it's just a fantasy, you're in complete control. You get to wonder what it will be like to have her, and it's fun, because when you no longer have to wonder, the dream is gone.

The boy places his hand over the small of her back, not touching as he guides her up to the roof ahead of him. He quickly follows, the door slams shut, and the chamber echoes like empty things do. Like they cease to exist when we're not there.

But the tower is never empty.

The boy and girl leave behind ghosts whenever they go.

He walks to the boy's surveillance room and scans the cameras, seeing them scale down the fire escape and run to the right, back to the alley where his car sits.

Gazing around at the rest of the images on the screen, he verifies that none of them are recording the inside of the hideout.

Good.

The boy is smart. He'd almost caught him a few times.

Leaving the room, he passes hers, but he doesn't go in. Her scent hits him from here. But it's not the Rebel's. It's not like summer. This is an older scent. *Her* scent. A wispy spice. He draws it in. *It's still there.*

Unzipping his leather jacket, he lets the air cool his neck as he drifts into the other room.

Coming to the foot of the boy's bed, he drops his gaze, jealousy knotting inside of him. The mussed sheets and the smell of summer in here too.

God, he misses being young.

A figure stops at his side, and he watches a hand reach down to the sheets and loop a pair of blue silk panties with his fingers.

"Don't touch them," he tells Deacon. "The boy loves her."

Deacon drops it and doesn't argue. That's what's great about him. He doesn't understand, and he doesn't care to. He just does what he's told.

Deacon walks around him, the bourbon on his breath wafting through the air. "I don't know why we're skulking about," he grits out. "I don't care if they're here. We should've just come in and torn the place apart."

"Keeping the phones was your idea."

But Deacon raises his voice. "I had no idea anyone would find the place."

"Shut up," the man bites out, spinning around and leaving the room.

The two could come back anytime. He and Deacon have been sneaking in and out, looking for the phones, but while Deacon wanted to run out the trespassers, the man couldn't let them go. Watching, listening...he almost couldn't breathe.

Weston. The Falls.

Déjà vu.

They're meant to be here.

He and Deacon meander into the great room, the letters still on the wall and looming over all, and even though they'd been here a handful of times over the years, they look around as if everything is new.

"It's amazing how much he's pieced together," Deacon says.

"Some details were off," the man adds.

They'd listened to the story the other night. Their story. They'd been in here, close, hearing the latest version of Carnival Tower, and he was truly in awe of how captivating those two were. He wanted to stay. To listen to them in the bedroom.

But it would've been wrong. She's the boy's story. Not his. That must be respected.

He'd taken Deacon away and let them have the tower that night.

Pulling open the door to the Rivertown tunnel, they walk down toward it.

"He knows we've been here," Deacon says.

"I think so too."

The boy is smart. He doesn't fear them. Should he?

Should they fear him?

"You like this, don't you?" Deacon teases. "You want him to find us. You want him to find her."

The man stops in front of her picture. The one with her hair dancing around her and her eyes that always looked kinder than they actually were.

They pluck the portrait off the wall, staring at it. At the girl who hurt a Weston boy, and that was only the start of the carnival she would never escape.

Winslet.

"It feels like something is starting again," he whispers to Deacon.

After so long...

He closes his eyes and breathes in a lungful deeper than he has in years, starved of oxygen and no appetite, but he's hungry again.

Hellbent again.

Finally.

It's happening.

He lets Deacon leave first as he trails far behind and detours into the surveillance room once again, and to the drawer of phones he'd found three visits ago that he told Deacon weren't in here.

The phones they were looking for that he's always known where to find.

Pulling out a present, he adds another one to the pile—a new one. A gift for the boy.

He leaves, carrying the portrait and with hot blood rushing through his veins.

CHAPTER TWENTY-THREE

Aro

Hawke shuts the door behind him, cutting off the obnoxious honking going on outside. Footfalls pound down the stairs, his uncle Jared descending in a rush as he tries to pull on a shirt. But then he slips on something and stumbles down a few steps.

"James!" he shouts, grabbing hold of the railing to catch himself, and I look down, spotting a pair of kid's sneakers on one of the steps. "Your shoes!"

He barrels for the door, and we jump out of his way as he yanks it open. "Madoc, shut up!" he barks. "I'll be there in a minute!"

He slams the door, Hawke's other uncle starting to honk out "This Old Man" on his horn. Jared throws the door a glare.

But then someone behind me whines, "Dad..."

Jared looks up, a little breathless, and I follow his gaze over my shoulder, seeing Dylan glaring as the two girls beside her gape at her dad's half-naked body. He cocks an eyebrow, pulling on his T-shirt.

When he finally notices us standing there, he looks between Hawke and I. "You sure this is a good idea?" he asks Hawke.

"She'll stay in the car," Hawke assures him, "and I'll keep my eyes open."

Jared looks at his nephew, thoughts going on behind his eyes that he's not vocalizing. I don't know why I want to shrink away. Some of this is my fault, but not all of it.

Jared turns his attention to me, looking down like he thinks even global warming is my fault.

"I'm gonna cut you a break," he tells me, "because I got into a ton of trouble at your age, too, but if you pull any shit, we've got problems. Understood?"

"Yes."

"Do you know me?" he asks.

I nod.

"Then you know I don't fool around."

"I've heard things," I say, wanting to look away, but if I blink, then he'll feel all superior, and I'm guessing he's used to feeling like that with people a lot.

"Like how I don't make threats," he goes on. "I make promises. And if anyone messes with my family or my shit, I can be petty as hell when it comes to grudges."

"Yeah, I've heard." I try to hide my smile but not completely. "I heard you were sooooo petty in high school, some chick ran off to Canada or something to get away from you..."

"Oh boy..." I hear Dylan mumble.

Hawke rubs his forehead.

But I don't stop. "And that you were so obsessed with her that you continued your stupid grudge when she got home..."

Jared's eyes flare.

"But she was pretty sick of your shit by then," I tell him. "So, she humiliated you and destroyed your car in front of the whole school." I chuckle. "You cried—"

"I didn't cry!" he shouts. "Is that what people are saying?"

His eyebrows pinch together, kind of adorably.

"I didn't cry." And then over my head to his daughter. "I didn't cry!"

I fold my lips between my teeth so I don't laugh.

"And it was France!" he spits back. "Not Canada. And she destroyed my car for no reason. It wasn't even my fault!" He spins around. "I didn't cry. Tate!"

And then he storms up the stairs to his wife.

Hawke laughs at my side.

I scratch the back of my neck. "Wow, that was easy."

Hawke takes my hand, and we turn. Dylan stands there, color swatches spread on the coffee table and her friends sit around it, one of them making notes.

"You got this?" he asks her.

She gives him a salute, and he releases me, walking away, but not before I feel his hand slide up the inside of my thigh. I gasp, hearing his quiet laugh, and then he's gone.

I look up at the girls, but no one's watching.

Dylan jaunts over and grabs my hand. "So, you ready?"

"You have seatbelts?"

I'd feel better doing the driving, but that won't fly tonight.

She leads me over to the table, and I notice more than just swatches. A laptop is open to pictures of dresses and girls wearing tiaras, and one of her friends has a price list going, but I can't see of what.

"What's all this?" I ask.

A little early for prom. Dylan will just be starting her senior year soon.

"This is Socorro." She points to the dark-haired one, and then the redhead. "And this is Megan."

Socorro waves. "Coco," she clarifies.

I nod back.

"Coco's having her quince," Dylan tells me. "We're picking out dresses."

Coco looks at me. "Have you had your quinceañera?"

"No." I drop my eyes to the A-line ballgowns with sweetheart necklines, traditionally pale pink or white, but it looks like she's researching some blue ones. "Not in the cards for my family."

I honestly can't imagine going through the custom. At one time, I fantasized about it. Passed a limo on the streets, fancy people piled outside, and a girl who looked like a queen being fluffed and helped into the car. It was magical.

Now, I can't justify it. There are more important things to spend money on.

"I love the idea of it," Dylan says. "Seems so fun. I know sweet sixteen's and that aren't very progressive today, but it's a reason to party."

"And to get presents and money," Coco adds, smiling. "Which is why I finally agreed to have it two years later than I was supposed to. I was a little rebellious at fifteen."

She laughs, and I stand there while Megan just smiles.

Silence falls as they all shift a little, and I'm pretty sure I was supposed to say something to continue the conversation, but I can't imagine what.

Megan inhales and plants her hands on the table, rising. "All right, I gotta go. I'll let you get to it."

"Right behind you," Coco says, gathering her things. "Mani-pedi with my mom."

"Later, Dylan," Megan calls out.

Coco bumps Dylan's hip playfully. "Byeee. Good luck tonight. Nice to meet you, Aro!"

Mm-hmm.

They close the front door on the way out, and Dylan pulls me along. "Come on."

We head through the kitchen and out to the garage, Dylan grabbing her wallet and keys on the way. She grabs a couple of waters from the fridge out there, and we climb into her car, fastening seatbelts. On the left sits a black Tesla coupe and on the right another Mustang.

The garage door opens, and Dylan hangs something on the rearview mirror before she releases the parking brake and shifts into gear.

I stare at the small thumbprint fossilized into a white piece of clay hanging from a green ribbon.

Everyone knows about that charm. Jared's wife shared a story about it in a magazine once. It's worthless and priceless at the same time. I hadn't come to the house to steal it, but when I saw it...

"Sorry about that, by the way," I tell her.

"If I didn't get it back, you would've been sorry."

I'm sure. She pulls out of the garage, pressing the button above her to close it behind us, and we drive onto the street, slowly picking up speed.

The charm swings from the mirror, and staring at it, I'm actually not sure what I would've done with it if I'd made it home with it that night. Maybe given it to the Rebels to barter with during Rivalry Week. Maybe I would've sold it.

Maybe I would've kept it, because I like the story behind it, and maybe it would bring me luck like it has for their family for so long.

"Hawke seems happy."

"Don't," I murmur.

Whatever is between him and me isn't like she thinks it is.

But she presses. "We got our vaginas waxed together, Aro. We can talk about this."

"And who did you get waxed for again?"

She sighs but says nothing. I look at her and watch her do everything to avoid looking at me, and I almost smile, because she's keeping something to herself. What is she hiding?

"Dylan?" I fight my amusement.

"No one, okay?" She draws in a breath. "I just...wanted to feel like a woman, I guess."

"A woman?"

She twists her lips, and I can tell she's embarrassed. "Guys don't like me," she says quietly. "I talk too much or drive too hard or they're afraid of my dad, I don't know what it is." She continues moving her mouth, and at that moment, my amusement fades as I realize she's trying to disguise the tremble in her chin. "I just thought it would make me feel pretty, is all."

My gaze falls. A week ago, I would've mocked her. She dares to think she's not attractive with how her big blue eyes compliment her pore-less complexion and light, brown hair? With the happiness that's always in her smile? With how she embraces people and oozes female solidarity?

Geez, I'd love to have that problem.

But she's not feeling good, and I never would've known if I hadn't pressed her, because she keeps a fucking smile on her face. She loves Hawke to death, and she talks to me like we've been friends for years.

And I don't think she's admitted to anyone else what she just told me.

I clear my throat. "He's my friend," I finally tell her. "And that's all I'm saying, okay?"

"Well, I'm his cousin," she continues, tipping her chin back up and finding her composure again. "And I would've won that fight, so make sure you're a really good friend, or else I'll have to prove it."

Yeah, right.

She grins over at me. "He's a catch, isn't he?" But then she starts mumbling under her breath. "Until he starts talking about comets and the formation of galaxies and all his astronomy bullshit."

I jerk my eyes to her. "What?"

"Oh, just you wait." She smiles tightly. "The bore is coming. Every hottie has a downside."

"He's into astronomy?"

"Mmm." She nods. "He interns at the university. Helps run their planetarium."

Of course. That's why he'd have keys. I didn't even think to ask. Just assumed the whole town was his playground like it usually is for rich kids.

"Hawke loves mystery," Dylan muses. "Wants to spend his life in a tower under a telescope aimed at the celestial sky."

I drop my eyes and shake my head. And he sat there, listening to me educate him like I knew more.

But I'm not mad. *He likes astronomy.* I have a friend who likes what I like.

I smile. Oh, I'll let him have it next time. I'm not holding back. Nebulae, astrophysics, cosmology, evolution...let's go. My education may only be from Google and YouTube, but I bet I know just as much as he does.

By the time I've organized my 'for' and 'against' arguments for the theory of dark matter—depending on which stance he takes, so I can take the exact opposite—we're at the track. Cheers go off, and I snap back to reality, seeing all the people.

"Whoo!" Two guys pound Dylan's hood as she maneuvers the car into its pit.

"Hey!" she yells at them. "Assholes."

I look around, the bleachers filled and tons of girls everywhere. What the hell?

"Why are there so many people?" I ask.

"It's my last race."

I look at her.

"I want to ride bikes," she says, putting the car into *Neutral* and pulling up the E-brake. "My dad doesn't know, so if you could keep it quiet..."

"Well, if they all know, he knows..." I gesture to the crowd gathered.

"He will soon enough," she replies, unfastening her seatbelt. "Just not tonight."

"But he was a bike racer," I say. "Is he scared you'll get injured or something?"

She shrugs. "It's a boys' club. He doesn't want me to deal with all that."

I know what that's like.

"But I really love it." She sighs. "And I want to get there on my own. Not because of my name."

Great. Do all rich kids have this much character? I hate being wrong about people.

"To the line!" someone yells.

Dylan looks out, seeing some young guy flagging her down, and she nods. Pulling out onto the track, she stops at the starting line and idles.

"And these people aren't all here to see me," she admits. "Most of them are here to see Noah. My father's new *protégé.*"

But she says protégé with some attitude.

I've never met Noah Van der Berg, but I know who he is and I've seen him and Dylan together. They seem to get along. Maybe friends, even.

But there's something else. Maybe she thinks she should be her father's protégé. He doesn't want to train her, though. I guess that would piss me off, too.

"I gotta talk to people," she chirps. "Sit tight."

She leaves the car, the engine still running, and I turn up the music as I peer out her tinted windows. People loiter on the sides, and I can smell the hot dogs and funnel cakes from the food trucks off to the left. Leaning down, I check out the control booth, a cross between a small air control tower and a fire watch tower. Where the windows would be is open air, and it's no more than three stories high. Just enough to see all of Fallstown.

Motorbikes roar in the distance, and a tall figure looms front and center inside the tower.

Jaxon Trent.

I'm only guessing, I can't tell for sure. It just looks like Hawke, but I know it's not Hawke.

They look the same, though. Alone. Far back from everyone else, because they both like to keep apprised of everything in their domain.

If Hawke's mom feared her love for him, then Hawke is his father's son, because it's hard to not let him get to me.

I take out my phone, remembering my sister hasn't gotten back to me yet.

Text me back, I type out to her.

I haven't talked to her since the day before yesterday. Something feels wrong.

I tap out a message to my mother, but then I stop and delete it. I can't trust her not to give my number to Reeves or Hugo, and then they can find me anytime.

Instead, I text Hawke. He's here somewhere, but I just need to make sure, since Bianca won't reply.

My stepdad is still in lockup, right?

I need to make sure Bianca doesn't have to deal with him, at least.

His reply is almost immediate. **Yeah, why?**

Just checking. Thx.

And I breathe out a sigh of relief.

But then I look up. I spot a distressed, brown leather jacket off on the sidelines that's all too familiar.

I slouch down, bowing my head. *Shit.* I should get in the back seat.

Fuck.

Reeves moves in my peripheral vision, and while I don't have to worry about my stepdad, Reeves is still a threat. What the hell is he doing here?

But of course, he's here. If Hawke and I show our faces, this is where we'll do it.

Muffled laughter and music go off outside, and I pretend to play on my phone, like a sitting duck.

I stare at the screen, but he moves, farther to my left, and farther and farther until he's moving around the front of the car, and I close my eyes, feeling sick.

Son of a bitch. Dylan's door opens, and he slides into her seat, the commotion from the crowd pouring inside the vehicle, but everyone's too distracted to notice us here. He slams the door shut, cutting off the noise, and I squeeze my fists, itching to pull the handle on my door and run.

He turns down the music. "Hi, Aro."

I start to text Hawke, but Reeves grabs my phone.

"I don't get to see you like this much," he taunts.

I glance over, seeing him looking me up and down, the short jean shorts and hoodie, my hair in two French braids. Different from the jacket, jeans, and hats that I wore before. I didn't want attention at Green Street, especially his.

He gazes at my legs. "I knew it was there all along, though."

He tosses something into my lap, and I look down, picking up the tiny camera. Like the one Tommy planted at the garage.

My heart feels like it doubles in size, trying to push through my sternum.

"I'm guessing you put that at Green Street?" he asks.

Me, he says. So, he doesn't know about Tommy's role. I exhale a little.

"And since I was in on Wednesday, collecting, he has me on video, then." He stares out the front windshield, his hand on the wheel like we're going somewhere. "Right?"

I look over at him. What is he talking about?

He was in on Wednesday? Hawke has the leverage we need?

"He hasn't gone to my superiors with it," Reeves says, "so he wants something. What does he want?"

"I don't know what you're talking about."

He's lying. Hawke would've told me. It's been days. Why would he sit on that footage if he had it?

But Reeves shakes his head. "I have two choices here, Aro. Haul your ass to jail and let you disappear from there.

You'd rot the rest of your life away in a concrete cage with filthy women and face tattoos..." He looks over at me. "And Bianca all to myself."

Fuck you.

"Or you can come home," he tells me. "I won't kill you. I make nothing with a dead body."

"If you think I will ever let you slave me out..."

"Oh, Aro." He looks at me like I'm a child. "What tales have the boys been spinning? I'm not that evil."

Then what? If Hawke has him, then why isn't he going after Hawke?

"You're going to run Green Street," Reeves informs me.

I go still, and he smiles in a soft way I've never seen before. "I've always liked you," he tells me. "Hugo won't take it well, though, and while I know there's no love lost, you don't want him dead. So come home. You can protect him from me. Move back to your mother's house. You'll have the muscle to keep your stepdad away and the money to keep your mother happy."

"For what?" I blurt out. "What do you want?"

I don't want to run drugs anymore. I never did. And I certainly don't want Hugo's place. My life expectancy will decrease by half, and it's already not high.

He simply looks at me. "You just have to pay me back."

With what?

And that's when it occurs to me. He's not dealing with Hawke for a reason. Hawke can't know.

"I'm not stealing anything from JT Racing," I state.

But he simply shakes his head. "The mayor's house," he replies instead. "Grudge Night. You're simply going to get Kade to unlock the doors. Madoc Caruthers has some things I need."

"Money?"

"There are so many things more valuable than money."

He doesn't elaborate, but I can imagine, since Hawke's uncle Madoc is the mayor and a powerful lawyer with national political ambitions. Reeves hopes to find something that will put a politician in his pocket. If he gets Caruthers by the balls, no footage Hawke has will see the light of day. Reeves controls the mayor and me, and I control Hawke. Reeves will be safe. That's how he sees it.

"Do that, and you can come home," he tells me.

Home? What's home?

But then it starts to sink in. Matty and Bianca. My mother's house, with her off my back and my stepdad out of the picture. I'd have a little money. Influence. Matty would have all the drawing pencils he wanted. I could have all of that...or Hawke?

Grudge Night is in two days. And what if I don't agree?

"In a year, your life will be very different," he nearly whispers. "Power will intoxicate you." He slips a hand between my thighs, squeezing the inside. "And then you'll *want* to fuck me."

I bare my teeth, trying to tear his hand away from where Hawke's brushed less than twenty minutes ago.

But he pulls away before I can. "Grudge Night," he reminds me.

And he opens the door, music flooding in from outside as he climbs out of the car and slams it shut again.

Fury overtakes me, and I'm not sure if I know what the fuck just happened. I kick the car, punching underneath the dash with my feet. "Ah!" I growl.

Hawke has him. He's had him for days! Why give Reeves a chance to find the camera and come after us? Why would Hawke do that?

A knock lands on the window, and I jerk my head, seeing Hawke's jacket.

I roll down the window.

"You okay?" He leans down. "What the fuck? What was that?" He rises, twists around, and then comes back down, looking past me and through Dylan's window. "Where's he going? Did he hurt you? I just saw him get out of the car..."

But I just glare at him. "You have the footage we need on him?"

His face softens, and he falls silent.

And that's answer enough. I throw open the door and step out, looking up at him. "Why didn't you tell me?"

He avoids my eyes, looking off to the side, and exhales hard. I study him.

I can't believe this. Reeves wasn't lying. Hawke has him. He could've had him in custody days ago.

"What are you playing at?" I yell, and I don't care who hears me. "What do you want? Are you trying to make this worse?"

"It was just yesterday morning," he explains. "I..."

He drifts off though, not finishing. So, he noticed yesterday when he studied the footage. Thirty-six hours. What is he waiting for?

But he doesn't say more.

"What?" I shout.

"Aro, I... I just..."

"You lied to me." I sharpen my gaze, hurt. "My sister needs me. She's all alone with my mother and her bullshit. What are you doing? You got your own agenda here?"

He shakes his head, but still, he can't form the words. *For Christ's sake.*

"Ready?" Dylan calls out, leaping back up to the car.

I wait for Hawke for another second, but when he doesn't say more, I dive back into the car and slam the door, rolling up the window. "God, just drive," I breathe out. "Fast."

"That's what I'm talking about."

Dylan presses the clutch, and shifts into first, pulling up level with the other driver. The announcer's voice booms over the sound system. "Miss Dylan Trent versus Sammy Phuong!" The crowd cheers. "You know the drill. Ten laps, no rubbing, and—"

"Oh!" Dylan blurts out, turning to look at me. "We forgot to have you sign a waiver."

A waiver?

But she waves me off. "We'll make a verbal agreement. I hurt you, and you can't sue me, okay?"

I side-eye her. "You hurt me, I hurt you."

She turns, facing the track again. "That's fair."

But seriously...she's never been injured, right? Has anyone died here?

The red lights on both sides of the track start blinking, and Dylan fastens her seatbelt, looks over and checks mine, and then shifts into gear again. One hand on the wheel, she jacks up the music, "Problem" by Natalie Kills blasting, and I see Hawke off at the sidelines out of the corner of my eye, but I don't look.

The light changes to yellow, Dylan's hand on the stick shift tightens, and my stomach somersaults.

I look over, seeing the other driver in a helmet, and I... *Wait, are you supposed to have helmets? Do we need—?*

But the green light glows bright, Dylan hits the gas, and I shoot out my hands, grabbing the console and the door as she charges off.

"Whoo!" she cries, the music filling the car so loud I can't think.

Racing around the bend, I hold the handle above the door, the car tilting as she dips to the inside of the track, and we speed head-to-head with the GTO on my right.

Dylan kicks it into third and then fourth, punches the gas, and I hit the back of the seat, my heart leaping into my throat.

I break into a laugh, the argument with Hawke forgotten. "Shit."

She flashes me a smile, winds around the next bend, and keeps going, maxing it out in fifth.

A few raindrops hit the windshield, and I glance over at her to see if she's going to stop.

But she doesn't seem to notice, arm out in front of her, steel-rod straight as she holds the wheel, with the other hand gripping the stick. Her eyes zone in on the track like a laser.

"Hold on!" she shouts.

Huh?

I tighten my fingers around the handle, the next turn approaching, but instead of slowing her speed, she swerves down to the edge of the bowl as close to the inside as she can and surges forward.

My insides flip, my skin tingles, and everything feels like it did last night in the tunnel when I felt Hawke behind me.

"Dylan..." I gasp, but then I start laughing.

Rain starts pounding the car in heavy drops, the car next to us swerves behind, and Dylan smiles.

"I'm going to drift," she laughs. "Watch this."

"What?"

"When I tell you, rip the e-brake, okay?"

My eyes widen. "What?"

"Ready?"

"What?!" I dart my eyes down to the parking brake. What the hell? What is she doing?

"Do it!" she shouts.

I shake, panicking, but then I grab the brake with both hands and yank it up. She powers over to the left, the rear of her car spinning and we go gliding around the turn, kicking up the rain that has collected so far.

She screams, and something between a grunt of pain and a whimper escapes me, but I refuse to shut my eyes.

The other car speeds past, and I watch. "Dylan!"

"Oh, I don't give a shit about winning," she chuckles. "That was fun, and it'll piss off my dad."

She zooms ahead, picking up speed again, but head-lights flash in front of us.

A car flies toward us, and I suck in a breath, Dylan pumping the brakes, skidding in the rain.

The headlights are coming right for us. What the hell is that?

Our car fishtails, I grab the dash, and we slide sideways, just stopping in front of the Mercedes blocking the track.

"What the hell?" Dylan gasps.

Sammy Phuong in her blue GTO are far past the ob-struction, the tower and crowd far in the distance. We jump out of the Mustang, rain hitting my head, and get clear in case they try to ram us.

But then I recognize the vehicle. *Mercedes*. This one's white, but I know whose it is. His black one was totaled at the park that night.

Hugo steps out, grinning, but then the other three doors open. I watch Nicholas, Axel, and two of Hugo's other henchmen, Jonathan and Alejandro spill out.

"Shit," I murmur. Hugo's wearing the leather jacket he

stole when he was seventeen. It has three interior pockets. *Knife and brass knuckles, for sure.*

A crowd runs toward us, and I take Dylan's wrist, pushing her behind me.

Hawke stops at my side, and I'm sure Kade, and all of their friends are with them.

"Don't call anyone yet," Hawke says into a radio.

"Are you sure?" some guy asks.

Hawke ignores him, handing the radio off to someone.

We all stand there, Hugo and his crew coming to stand in front of his car while we inch in close to each other in front of Dylan's.

"Hey, baby." Hugo's eyes gleam at me. "You hanging with Pirates now?"

I'm definitely not hanging with Pirates, but I feel all the eyes of Green Street on me like they've been betrayed as I stand surrounded by two Trents and a Caruthers.

"The girl I raised doesn't need anyone to protect her," he says, "and she doesn't hide behind rich boys."

Rain spills down my face, and I feel Hawke try to take my hand, but I pull it away.

Yeah, Green Street fed me. Weston is my home.

And not one neighbor protected me growing up. Once I was old enough, Hugo tried to turn me out. What makes them any better? They think they're owed my loyalty?

Axel and Jonathan inch forward, pulling their hands out of their pockets, and I stop breathing for a moment before I realize they didn't take out any weapons. Not yet.

But they do ball their fists, Axel eyeing Kade and Jonathan eyeing Hawke. They widen their stances, readying.

"They don't want you." Hugo steps closer to me, and Hawke tenses. "And where are you going to go when he forgets about you?"

He glances at Hawke and then back to me.

I know he's right. Maybe not today or tomorrow, but he's right. I've not forgotten the alignment of stars it would take for my life to be okay. My family, my debt, my record, the warrants that are undoubtedly out for my arrest right now, my lack of education...

I'll embarrass Hawke. I know it's not a relationship.

We hid together out of necessity and bonded. I could never stomach him trying to save me.

"Your mom hasn't been home in three days," Hugo tells me.

I cast my gaze up to him.

His voice softens. "You need to come home."

Hawke takes my wrist. "Don't you fucking move."

"I don't know how much longer I can keep CPS from showing up," Hugo threatens.

That's why Bianca wasn't answering the phone. She was afraid I'd come home if I found out. *Goddammit.*

Axel tips back a flask, emptying it down his throat, and Alejandro blows out smoke before he flicks his cigarette at one of the Pirates on my left.

"Shit." The kid wipes the embers off his shirt.

Green Street closes in, the air changes, and the hair on my arms rises as the rain cools my neck.

"Hawke, seriously," one of the Pirates says. "They will tear this town apart. Give her back."

But Hawke doesn't move. Hugo grins.

I look over my shoulder for the first time, Hawke's friends staring at me, some of them like I'm the cause of all this. They can fight, but they don't want to fight for me.

Hugo gazes at me, and I turn my head, whispering to Hawke. "These aren't my people."

He squeezes me. "Hugo is using you as an excuse. They've wanted this for a long time."

"Your friends won't see it like that."

I don't want to leave him, but I can't live like this. I can't follow him everywhere. I need to be in control of my life and make my own way. A friend should make his life better, not worse, and Bianca needs me.

I pull myself free and walk for Hugo.

But Hawke pulls me back. "Aro..."

"I'm not worth all this trouble," I tell him, yanking free again. "I need to go home."

His eyes sharpen, but he lets me leave. I walk over to Hugo and turn, facing the Pirates.

Hugo laughs. "Someone likes Chicana girls," he says to Hawke. "Never boring, are they? I'll get you another one."

"I want that one."

I dart my gaze up to Hawke, the sudden hardness to his voice not like him. He looked worried and sad before. Now he doesn't.

His glower is all for me.

"Well, you can't have this one," Hugo retorts. "Not unless, you know what."

Huh? I look between Hawke and Hugo, realizing they've had another conversation without me at some point.

But Hawke's focus is all on me. "Come here," he says.

I don't.

His jaw flexes. "I asked you once before when all this shit started," he grits out. "And I'm telling you now. Come here."

I steel my spine, remembering the last time we were all together like this. That first night in front of his house.

He never saw me as equal, always less. The one who needed to be paid for, protected, guided...

A pet. A project.

I square my shoulders. "You don't get to save me, Rich Boy."

Hawke's face changes, his eyebrows relaxing, his chin

lifting, and the heat that was all over him last night and while painting my toes this morning has now gone so cold.

Hugo just laughs. "Don't feel bad—"

But Hawke doesn't give him a chance to gloat. He launches out and throws a fist right across my foster brother's face.

I rear back, howls erupt, and Nicholas flies in to pull Hawke off, but it's too late. Hugo is already hitting back, and Kade runs in, everyone losing their fucking minds.

"Kill 'em!" Axel bellows at the top of his lungs, and before I even see who it is, some girl in pink Chucks is grabbing one of my braids and yanking my face down into her knee. She slams it into my cheek, and it takes a second, pain spreading through my face.

But it's like riding a bike. Every muscle fires like an engine, and I spring into action. I throw my shoulder into her stomach, she loses her grip, and I shove her back, sending her onto her ass.

I whip around, finding Hawke getting punched by Hugo as Axel holds him, and I start to run for him, but he shoots out his leg, kicking Hugo and then elbowing Axel in the side.

Throwing him off, Hawke twists back around, his eyes sparkling like fireworks as he glares at me. But then a punch lands across his face, and he spins, plummeting to the ground. He lands on the hard concrete, and then flips over with a cut on his cheek dripping blood. He eyes Hugo, and I rush over, dropping down on him.

"Stop!" I tell him. "Just go home."

But he pushes me off and launches toward Hugo again. The rain pours down on us, and I wipe the water off my face, hearing a scream. I turn my head, seeing Dylan straddle Eva Kissinger, Eva's massive fake diamond ring turned to the inside of her hand. She rears her palm back, ready to give

Dylan a nice fat scar for the rest of her life, and I run over, grab Dylan under the arms, and yank her off. Eva misses her by an inch.

Lightning cuts through the sky, thunder cracking over my head, and everyone is punching and kicking.

"Cops!" someone screams.

A few of the fights slow, people looking up, and I search the entrance to Fallstown, seeing lights flashing.

Everyone scatters. People take off, running back to their cars, and Axel pulls Hugo off Hawke, Hawke wiping the blood off his mouth.

They stare at each other, and I look between them.

"I'll meet you at Aura's shop in ten minutes," Hawke growls, looking between Hugo and me. "I don't want her anymore, but I'm gonna take her just to make her pay for wasting my time!"

I clench my teeth, but my heart won't calm down.

Hawke walks back toward the bleachers and the lot, where his car is parked.

"Hawke!" Kade yells, chasing after him.

Dylan passes me, murmuring, "Oh my God."

Aura's shop? That tattoo artist?

I look to Hugo. "What the fuck did you do?"

FALLS

CHAPTER TWENTY-FOUR

Hawke

I burst into River City Ink—formerly Black Debs—seeing Aura wiping down the table as two guys pass me, comparing their new tats. They leave, and I whip off my jacket and T-shirt, climbing onto the table. "I need a tattoo."

She stares at me, the same blonde dreads she's had my entire life turning gray, and her full sleeves faded with time. But she still looks cool as shit.

She rolls her eyes, mumbling, "Your father sucks at making appointments too."

This place gave my dad and uncles their first tattoos. All of their tattoos, actually.

I see headlights pull up outside, blurting out, "The Green Street brand?" I tell her. "I need it."

"No."

"Aura..."

"Hawke." She looks at me, a sternness in her eyes that I've never seen. "I don't know what's going on, but there is no way I'm putting that tattoo on you without speaking to your dad."

Hugo and his guys make their way across the street, and I catch a glimpse of Aro trailing behind.

"If you don't do it, they will." I gesture to the crowd making their way in. "And at least I know your shit is clean."

She shakes her head. "Hawke..."

"Just please," I beg. "I'll make sure my dad understands. I have to have it. You can call him after, if you're that worried."

She knows the tattoo isn't just a tattoo, and I'd be concerned too, if I were her, but she has to trust me. I'm of legal age, and if she doesn't do it, someone else will. She's already inked me once.

And she tattooed my mother's bite marks on my father, for Christ's sake. Now that was a dumb tattoo.

Hugo and his two sidekicks drift in, the bell above the door ringing, and Aro follows, her eyes barely raising enough to meet mine. She doesn't seem to be confused about what's happening, though, so I'm guessing Hugo filled her in.

She just shakes her head and mouths to me, "Don't."

I lock my jaw, simply leaning back on my hands and staring at her as Aura gets the shit ready. The Green Street tat is old, its history reaching further back than when it was just a gang affiliation. The old-timers and river rats all have it from back in the day when steam and coal ruled the waterways. She'll have a template on hand, I'm sure.

Kade and Dylan burst in, and I immediately shake my head. Every muscle in Kade's face flexes, and I'm not sure if he wants to kill me or them. This ink on me will make him spit knives.

"I assume you called Reeves," I say to Hugo as Aura places the design on my neck. "Get Aro out of here. I know you care about her."

I don't look at her because I'm not inviting her into this conversation. I can handle Reeves. She can't on her own.

But Hugo shakes his head as he cleans his nails with a key on his chain. "Reeves isn't coming. I haven't called him."

Why? I don't ask, though. I'm not going to let him indulge in the pleasure of doing us any favors.

But why wouldn't he call him?

Aura peels the template away and holds up a mirror, but I wave her off. "Just do it."

I hear a sigh, and then she starts the pen, a second later, she's cutting the skin.

It's not a big tattoo. The word River etched down the side of my neck vertically and a dark green line drawn down through the middle of it.

She's done in about seven minutes, and I finally meet Aro's eyes, feeling stronger as the slight pain goes on. Funny how their world works. One tattoo and they'll let me have a whole human. As if she has no say.

At least this will get them off our backs for a bit.

Aura wipes the blood away and tapes on a clear bandage. She hands me instructions for care and says, "You know the drill. Wash with antimicrobial soap and—"

But I'm not listening. I hop up and pull on my shirt and jacket.

"She's yours now," Hugo tells me and then announces to the others. "No one touches her."

I put some cash on the table for Aura and head over to the Rebels. "Why didn't you call Reeves?" I ask Hugo.

He just smiles. "Seeing that tattoo on a Trent *and* a Pirate is such payment. My honor is restored. For now."

Yeah, I'll bet. My friends are going to have fun with this, and he knows it.

But he leans in, lowering his voice. "The drugs and money weren't mine anyway. Consider our beef settled," he tells me. "And if you want to get me a few more of those cameras you snuck into the garage..."

I rear back a little.

"I can help you with him," he says. "It's time for Green Street Emancipation. We'll talk soon."

Oh, fucking great. You've got to be kidding me.

He leaves, the others following, and I take Aro, pulling her to my side. I do not want to be in bed with Green Street any more than I am. *Goddammit.*

I tell Kade, "Make sure Dylan gets home."

And I pull Aro with me out the door.

"Why did you do that?" she finally chokes out.

I lead her to my car, hitting the locks as a light sprinkle starts to fall.

"If you ever go against him, he removes the tattoo, Hawke," she says. "You know how he does it?"

Yes, I know.

She pulls away. "Let me go."

"Where?" I back her into my car, glaring down. "He'll just send you back to me, because you're mine. I feed you. I clothe you. I protect you. Isn't that what you wanted in a man like those losers?" Isn't that what she was after? What only Green Street could give her? "Well, you've got it."

"I don't belong to anyone!"

I rip the bandage off my neck, growling, "Say it again."

I press her into the car. *I dare you.*

Her eyes flit between mine and the tattoo, her chest rising and falling hard.

I did this for her. I fucking did this for her!

Her eyes fill with tears, and all she can do is close them, but I want her to look. At my neck. My face. My cut lip and my bloody eye—all because of her!

I notice headlights moving down the street and look, seeing the ones on top of the roof too. *Police.*

"Get in the car," I tell her.

She looks like she's going to argue until she sees what I see, and we both climb in.

I start the engine, not waiting to see if they pass or don't, and take off. My face hurts, my neck aches, and I'm so fucking pissed right now, this isn't the time. *Please don't pull me over.*

Maybe Hugo called Reeves, after all.

I sweep around the corner, look in my rearview mirror, and see the police car follow. My chest caves. "Fuck."

I shift into a higher gear and wince, hesitating for a second. "This night can't get any worse."

Screw it.

I speed off, my heart still pounding from the race. From the fight. From losing her to getting her back, and from the new ink on my neck. I'm losing control.

I used to be calm.

I barrel down the street, flipping on the windshield wipers as I make a left, and see the sirens turn on, because I just made it obvious that I'm evading. I hit the gas, speeding ahead.

I make some lefts and rights, quick turns and immediate slips onto various streets before coming back to JT Racing and quickly parking the car. Running out, I take Aro's hand and pull her to the other side of the building, seeing the cop car pull into the lot and block in Madoc's car from the back. Carrying my keys, I unlock Jared's old Boss, and we climb in. I start up the engine, and she looks out the back window, seeing that they're coming around the side of the building because his fucking car is so loud.

I pull onto the street, drive, and make a few turns before we're safely on the highway, no one on our tail.

I can't believe I did that. What the hell am I doing? I glance over at her, see those brown eyes looking over at me with her braids, and she looks so...

Perfect.

Pure.

She doesn't say anything that's not true, and I always know that everything I get from her—every word, every kiss—is real. She wouldn't waste her time otherwise.

I drive for a while, slowing to the speed limit, and rain starts hitting the windshield again as the black sky looms overhead. I see the turn for my parents' summer camp and veer left, hitting the gravel, because I need some air. I need to stop, close my eyes.

I need to get my heart to stop pounding.

I pull deep into the woods, the empty cabins and mess hall and the dark lake and boathouse hiding in the shadows of the trees. I park under the canopy of branches and leaves, drops pounding the roof and hood.

Turning off the car, I stare at the wheel, my mind racing like it does when I'm on a girl. So many things.

I need to get back on track.

I want to go home.

I miss my parents.

I want her there too.

I need to take care of Reeves.

Because none of this feels like it's about him anymore.

I wish I could go back to not wanting anyone.

Wanting someone is worse.

But I don't want anyone else to touch me.

She's the only one allowed to lay a hand on me.

I love her...looking at me.

Realization hits. None of this is about Green Street or Reeves anymore. She's everything.

I need some air. I just need to breathe, and then I'll get my goddamn life back, and I'll get ready for school like I should be doing.

Opening the door, I climb out of the car, taking off my jacket and tossing it inside. I slam the door and fall back against it, closing my eyes and letting the rain cool me off.

I don't know why I came here. I just didn't want the cops to catch us, and I'm afraid of what will happen if we go back to the hideout. I want to fight, and I know I'll instigate one if we're alone down there.

How easy it was for her to choose them, like she's theirs and not mine, and I just need to cool down, because I'm fucking crazy angry, and I'll make it worse if I look at her anymore.

Water trails down my neck, the new tattoo stinging, and I feel my T-shirt start to melt to my skin.

I inhale and exhale. *She chose them.*

But deep down I know. *She chose her family.* Her brother and her sister, as she should.

Her life is the opposite of mine. All she's learned is that she's the only one she can count on. Asking anyone for help is too much of a gamble, and asking me would hurt. She believes she's a burden. She'll never ask me for anything.

My arms hang like weights at my side, my body tired now that the anger is gone.

I climb back into the car, water dripping off my face and arms, and she still sits there, quiet. I don't think she's moved at all.

"My mom and dad have the kids," I tell her.

I look down, but I see her turn toward me out of the corner of my eye. "What?" she says.

I don't want to argue. I just want her to know they're safe.

"I talked to them on my way to the tattoo shop," I mumble. "They went with an officer. Your mom wasn't there, so they're staying at my house until she can be found."

Aro might get mad law enforcement is aware of their situation, but if she's smart, she'll know it's better to have them with my family than taking a chance on a neighbor calling CPS and the kids disappearing into the system.

"My parents told them you'll be coming to see them in the morning," I say.

She doesn't say anything, and last night seems like forever ago. The way she wanted me. How good it felt to see her jealous when she thought another woman had me.

She doesn't need me, though. The last thing she needs is me. She needs security and a home, and I'm being selfish. "I'll take you to them." I start the car. "My parents will help you."

But she stops me. She puts her hand on mine as I fist the stick shift, and I pause, too tired to fight anymore.

Rising up, she holds my eyes and slowly climbs over the center console to straddle my lap.

My chest caves, and I drop my eyes, wanting to touch her so bad, but it feels so good, just like this too.

She takes my face in her hands, turning my head and inspecting the bruises and cuts. Her warm fingers graze over the small wounds, and my eyelids flutter closed, feeling no pain anywhere now.

She blocks out everything else, and while I'm not sure if that's a good thing, I honestly don't give a shit.

My voice is almost a whisper, "I saw the video yesterday, but I didn't want to use it. I just..." I struggle to find my voice. "I wanted another day or two with you. I didn't want it to be over." I take her face in my hands and pull her forehead down to meet mine. "You are fucking up my life, girl." I breathe her in. "And I like it."

I like you.

She kisses my eyelids, soft and gentle, caressing my cheekbones with her thumbs as "Dark In My Imagination" drifts through the speakers.

"Are you hurt?" she says in a small voice, kissing my face everywhere. Little pecks, and it feels better than anything.

She pulls up my T-shirt. "Take this off."

I lift my arms and let her pull the wet shirt off of me. She drops it into the back, and her eyes roam, following the trail of her hands as she checks my body in the dark car.

Her nails graze the brush burn on my ribs, and I draw in a sharp breath. *Shit.* I didn't feel that till just now.

She jerks her eyes to me, yanking her hands away. "Baby." She kisses my mouth, its corners, my jaw... "Where else does it hurt?" she asks.

Everywhere. Nowhere. My head. My nerves. My heart. My fucking gut.

She kisses the scratches on my collarbone. Flicks her tongue out and licks the cut on my lip and leaves the softest touches of her mouth on my neck.

My cock swells, and I groan, grabbing her ass and pulling her closer.

"Aro..." I whisper, the heat of her body seeping through my wet jeans.

"Does that help?" She kisses my forehead.

But we start grinding, and I can't feel anything past her on top of me. I grip her hips, mesmerized as I watch her body move. I don't want to ever look at anything else.

She rolls her body into me, holding the back of my neck as her forehead touches mine again, and I can almost taste her mouth.

She kisses my face, my cheeks, my temples, and I tip my head back, pushing her mouth to my neck. "Hurts there," I tell her.

Kiss me everywhere.

She nibbles and sucks, trailing the tip of her hot tongue up my neck to my earlobe. I slip my hands under her shirt, touching her smooth stomach.

"You like me?" She bites my ear so soft, chills crawl my arms.

I nod.

"You trust me?" she asks. "You trust that if I hurt you, I didn't mean to?"

Again, I nod. I know she wasn't trying to hurt me at the track when she chose them.

"Look at me." She tugs my bottom lip through her teeth. "Open your jeans."

I open my eyes, staring into hers, and heat floods my chest as my pulse kicks up a notch.

"Open your jeans," she tells me again.

This is the part where I always start to freeze up. Does she want sex? Does she want to get me off? I shouldn't take something when I'm not sure how much I can give back.

She presses her lips to my forehead, brushing them across my skin as she caresses my chest. "Open your jeans, baby."

Baby...

And I'm hers. I unbutton them at the waist, breathing hard as I pull down the zipper and watch her hand slip down inside.

She inches up off my lap and moves her hand up and down, stroking my cock. I grab the back of her neck as blood rushes to my groin.

"Look at me," she says.

I open my eyes and look up into hers as she wraps her fist around me. I grunt, straining to grow in the tight space.

"Friends?" she whispers.

"Friends."

She strokes me faster, harder. "And friends do this."

Fuck yes. I push my jeans down as I cover her mouth with mine.

"You ate me so good last night." Her lips move over mine. "I want to make you come too."

She brings her hand up, dragging her tongue over it, and then dives back down into my jeans and keeps going.

I blow out a breath, the heat of her mouth on my cock excruciating and amazing at the same time.

"You're so hard," she whispers, pulling me out of my jeans and letting me rise.

"Fuck," I groan.

"Say 'that's good, Rebel.'"

I smile, my muscles flexing. "That's good, Rebel."

"You like your Weston girl, don't you?"

"Yeah."

"'Cuz you like wild girls," she pants, moving her hand up and down my dick faster as she licks my lips. "The good boy and his wild girl..."

I squeeze her ass, pulling her into me and feeling it. My wild girl. The one who sets fires everywhere she goes. I was dead before her.

"And you like me. Say it," I growl, thrusting into her hand.

But she shakes her head.

Such a brat.

I pull the hoodie off of her, and I unhook her bra, throwing everything onto the floor.

Pushing her back against the steering wheel, I come down on her with my mouth, sucking her breasts. She arches her back, pressing herself into me, and I drag her nipple out between my teeth, biting, kissing, and licking. I move from one breast to the other, coming in again and again. The horn goes off as I press her into the wheel, but I don't give a fuck. My groin is on fire, I'm rock hard, and I want more. I don't know...I need to taste her again.

"God, Weston, you taste good," I tease.

I flick her nipples with my tongue, and she moans, letting her head fall back and the horn blares in the rainy night again.

"Don't stop," she whimpers.

She reaches down and presses my dick between her legs, stroking it against her jeans.

"It's too rough," I tell her, taking my cock in my hand. "Take 'em off."

She presses down on my shoulders, raising herself up, and I help her push down her jean shorts until she's just in her underwear. She settles back on top of me, and I yank her in, both of us going for it.

With just her panties between us, she rolls her hips, grinding into me and I help, moving with her and bringing her back in again and again.

Her breasts sit pretty as she arches her back and gives me something to watch as she moves, but everything is too tight. My jeans. The seat. I have no leg room.

"Get in the fuckin' back," I growl in a whisper, kissing her hard. "Fuck..."

She pants, and I didn't realize how close she was. *Shit.*

"Now," I bark, pushing her.

She crawls over the console and into the back seat, and I throw open the door. Climbing out, I push the seat forward and dive into the back, coming right for her.

She scoots, but I grab her legs and yank her down. "Hawke," she yelps, shock in her eyes.

But I need to move. I just need room to move. I close the door behind me, and come down on top of her, loving how she spreads her legs for me.

I thrust against her, looking down at that body, and she reaches down, pushing my jeans and boxers down over my ass.

She holds me, digging in her nails as she thrusts up, and I get as fucking close as I can without being inside of her. A wetness seeps through her panties, and I kiss her as I reach between us, feeling her through the damp fabric. I feel every fold, every nub of flesh. I want my fingers inside of her.

"I need more," I groan. "Closer. I need to feel you on me, okay?"

She nods quickly, a whimper escaping.

I need to feel her tender skin down there on me. Against me. Just that. Nothing more.

She squirms underneath me as I yank down her panties, but I can't wait for them to be off.

I thrust myself against her, no shield between our bodies, and she moans so loud I almost come. "Ah, Hawke!" she moans, stiffening.

She breathes hard, and I fall to her body, skin sticking to skin, and I hold her face, staring into her eyes.

What the fuck? My head spins, everything is so warm, and something is squeezing my cock, but my hands are on her and her hands are on my shoulders and...

Oh my God. I shake, my head floating and something wracking my body that feels so fucking good.

"Hawke..." She squeezes her eyes shut, arching into me. "Oh, God, Hawke. What? I..."

She squirms, biting her bottom lip and looking in pain, but it's not that. It's...

My head floats back down to my body, and I feel her legs spread wide, her panties still hanging off one thigh.

And I know. Without looking, I know.

I'm inside of her.

Jesus Christ. "Aro..."

I didn't mean to do that. Did I hurt her?

But she's gasping, her mouth hanging open, and she looks like she's feeling something amazing, and I can't stop. I kiss her, diving into her mouth, feeling her moan drift down my throat.

I gaze down, pull out, and then... I thrust back inside of her, feeling her knees come up more.

"Ah," she moans. "Oh, God. Yeah. Don't stop. Please."

She throws her head back but grabs my hips as I come in again and again. *Holy fuck, Aro.* I look down at her body as it moves, her breasts sway up and down, and the sweat on her back makes her stick to the leather, grinding every time I enter her.

"Hawke," she pants as I go faster. "You're fucking me."

I kiss her. "Hold on. It's my first time."

She sticks her tongue into my mouth, and I grab her breast. Goddamn, the wet heat... It's so tight. I squeeze her hip, holding her there as I pump between her legs, the need getting heavier. My body about to burst.

"Ah, fuck." She whimpers over and over. "Hawke, don't stop."

Her pussy contracts around me, and I can't breathe for a second, shuddering. What the fuck?

"Harder," she moans. "You can go harder, if you want."

Hell yes.

I grab hold of the safety bar and stare down at the little Rebel, watching her come and hearing her fill the car with her moans as she explodes around me. Her hair sticks to her face and neck and her thighs spread even more, because she wants it all.

My orgasm crests, she grabs my hips, and I pump inside of her, harder and faster, our moans and grunts filling the car as she takes it, waiting for me to come.

"Hawke, you have to pull out," she tells me. "I don't want you to, but I'm not on anything."

I groan. It's coming. *Fuck.*

"Baby," I say, every muscle tensing, and I know I'm there.

"Fuck!" I yell and rip myself away from her body, spilling onto her stomach.

Pain and pleasure sweep across me at once, her scent and warmth covering me in waves, and I've never felt anything this good, but...

Shit...

The orgasm spreads like liquid heat across my body, and I can't see straight.

Dazed, I slowly pull away, take my T-shirt and clean her, and I can feel her eyes on me, but I don't know, I...

I just had sex. In a car.

"Hawke?" I hear her call my name. "Are you okay?"

I sit back, taking the shirt and cleaning myself off too. I stare down at her all over me. "In a car..." I murmur.

I did it in a car my first time.

When I don't respond, she sits up, bending her knees up to her chest.

"Hawke, I..." I see her shake her head out of the corner of my eye. "It shouldn't have happened. I just couldn't stop. I'm sorry."

She's sorry...

"I'm sorry if you don't feel good about it." She touches my arm. "I just...I know things happened kind of..."

In a car. I always thought I'd care where it happened. How it happened.

But right now, I just didn't give a fuck. All that mattered was how I felt, and I was feeling everything.

And I want more.

She starts to tear up. "I know it shouldn't have been with me. It just happened so fast. It—"

I look up at her. "Can we do it again?"

She goes still, gaping at me. I want more of her. It wasn't the car. It wasn't necessarily the right time, while we're both on the run.

It's just her. I've never felt anything more right. I'm supposed to be here.

"I mean, can you?" I ask. "Can you go again?"

I wasn't sure if women got sore after a while or anything.

Her worried face turns disbelieving and she breathes out a little laugh.

"Can I?" she mocks. "Can you?"

And her eyes fall to my dick in my hand, hard again already. "Oh."

I want to feel her on top. Or from behind or backwards or in any of the empty cabins over by the lake or any one of all the ways we can still do it together.

I sit back against the seat and pull her into my lap, holding her as I kiss her. I lift her up and position myself underneath, ready to go slower this time.

But she laughs, looking down at me with stern eyes. "Hawke, you need to wear a condom this time."

Oh, right.

I dive behind her, holding her so she doesn't fall as I dig in the center console.

But of course, Jared hasn't needed to use a condom in the over twenty-plus years that he's been married, and I come up empty.

I let my head fall into her chest, about to fucking cry. "We have to go to the store."

She just shakes with a laugh and plants a kiss on my forehead.

CHAPTER TWENTY-FIVE

Aro

"I'm going to go talk to my dad for a minute," Hawke says, his lips in my hair.

He kisses my head, and I look down at Matty and Bianca fast asleep in a spare bedroom as he leaves.

It's after midnight, and the house is dark. We haven't seen his parents yet. He took me right upstairs, and there were several doors, but he seemed to know which room they'd be in. It kind of looked like a teenager's room, but not Hawke's style. Dark gray walls, lavender curtains, white bedding... Some plants and photography on the walls. A dreamcatcher, and a tidy white desk. The hardwood floors are beige, and there's a fur rug, which I'm sure is fake.

I step over, my clothes and hair still damp, but Matty lays curled into Bianca, the bed only made for one person, but they're small, and I'm guessing they didn't want to be separated. Glasses of water sit on the nightstand with a nearly empty bowl of leftover popcorn kernels.

I want to assure Bianca I'm here, but it'll wake Matty up too, and they should sleep. Hawke's parents got him down, and everyone needs rest.

I leave and quietly close the door behind me, passing another room on my way. I look inside the dark space, seeing the bed, the window, and the leaves blowing outside.

Hawke's room. Seems like so long ago we stood in that tree out there and he warned me not to come in here.

I smile to myself. If only he'd known he was stuck with me from that moment on.

I venture back downstairs, the moon glowing across the gleaming floor, and I listen for voices to tell where Hawke is.

But I don't hear him.

I move hesitantly around the stairs, peeking into the living room and trying to see out the windows. I inhale the light scent of jasmine and slowly make my way to the kitchen.

The paint is fresh, the floors are new-ish, and the appliances are about as top-of-the-line as I can imagine. The refrigerator is twice the width of an average one.

But I know this house is old. Hawke mentioned things about his uncle growing up here. It's been in his family for decades.

I trail through the kitchen and out the back door, coming onto the porch. Rain spills over the awning, and I close my eyes, breathing in the thick, cool air. The scent of green grass fills my nostrils, and I stop at the top of the first step, looking around the backyard.

A playset on the right. An outdoor rock fireplace and seating area on the left. No jacuzzi or pool. Just wide open space and plenty of room to do cartwheels.

A light glows off to the left, from the porch on the other side of the fence. Dylan's house.

But then I notice her, a woman sitting several feet away from me, wrapped in a blanket and bobbing a bare foot that peeks out of her silk pajama pants.

I turn, taking a step back.

"Hi," she says.

She stares at me, and I glance back at the house. Where's Hawke?

I look at the woman again, noticing the smile in her eyes and the way she kind of tilts her head. Hawke has his father's coloring, but he looks like her.

"Juliet Chase," I say, but it comes out as a mumble.

The author.

But she just smiles. "Juliet Trent at home. And you're Aro."

Yeah. I'm not sure if she knows about me from Hawke or from other people, but I really hope it's from Hawke.

It takes a moment, but I remember my manners. I reach out, offering my hand. "Hi."

We shake, but I pull away really quickly, because I don't know why. She's kind of a big deal in certain circles, but I also just took her son's virginity in a car, and she's looking at me like she knows that, but how could she, right?

I don't know. Parents know things.

"I feel like I should apologize for something," I ramble, "but there's been a lot, and I've lost track, so I'm really not sure..."

Surprisingly, she breaks into a laugh. "You remind me of someone."

I remain silent.

"Myself," she clarifies.

But she doesn't elaborate. The blanket spills off her shoulders, and I see she's wearing a delicate top with spaghetti straps underneath, really looking younger than I'm sure she is. Not that she's old—I have no idea—but she's beautiful.

I stand there for a minute, not sure what else to say. I mean, I'm sorry about the trouble. Has she seen any videos from the fight tonight?

I look around. "It's nice here," I tell her.

I've wondered once or twice why a semi-famous author and her brother-in-law next door, who's a huge name in his industry, remain living on Fall Away Lane. It's a decent enough neighborhood, but they can afford more space. Bigger houses. Gates, which would probably come in handy with crazy fans.

But I get it now. Family next door, quiet, the tree, sentimental value...it's pretty perfect.

"I am sorry if I caused a lot of trouble," I tell her. "I don't mean to."

Well...

"Well, not always," I point out.

Sometimes I mean to.

Mrs. Trent draws in a deep breath and rises, taking the blanket with her. She leans onto the railing, the rain still coming down in streams.

"What I've learned about trouble is that it all depends on the outcome," she tells me. "Trouble is only bad if it doesn't work out."

"And if it does?"

"Then it was just fun," she says. "A story you'll recap on holidays and laugh about, surrounded by people you love."

I smile, not sure most parents would admit that. Trouble is bad. Taking chances is bad. But yeah... It's like war. History remembers the ones who won as right, just like stealing that charm gave me Hawke. Incidentally, anyway.

So, I'm not sorry I broke into their house. At least not yet.

"Thank you for taking them in." I slip my hands into the pockets of my shorts. "I can take care of them on my own. The situation at the house with my mother was just a little—"

"I know you can." She stops me. "I know you can do it, Aro. But you don't have to. I just want to make that clear."

She turns to me in that way adults do when they want to handle me. I don't meet her eyes.

"Listen, I don't know what will happen yet, okay?" she says. "Maybe your mom will come around. Maybe she'll need help and come to get them in a year. Maybe Jax and I will talk and wonder if we're too old to keep up with Matty..." She laughs to herself. "It's been a while for us."

She sighs and looks back out at the rain.

"Maybe Bianca won't want to stay so far away from her friends..." she goes on. "There's a lot to discuss. None of this is permanent or fixed yet, but what I can assure you is that you're not alone anymore." And she looks at me again, and I meet her eyes. "We can help you make sure they're taken care of."

No one can take care of them like me. No one cares about kids who aren't theirs.

"But we've got them now—for a few days, at least—and you can breathe a little," she says. "Take some time to think. I can tell you; a few years seems like forever when you're young, but it goes by so fast. If you do end up taking them, you don't want to be working two jobs."

Yeah, she sounds like Hawke.

"They don't want to see you unhappy." Her voice softens. "Consider your education and your future. When you got out of college, Matty would still only be ten."

And a lot can happen in that time. He could get defiant, and they could decide they can't handle him. Bianca could run away. Their voices will only get louder as they get older. I'm the only one who can keep them on track. Safe.

A voice calls me. "Aro."

I look over, seeing Hawke in the doorway, and he comes over, seeing it in my eyes. The fatigue. His mother means well, but she doesn't know. She doesn't know how easily a kid's life can be destroyed. Everything I do will be to protect them. I'm the only one I can trust.

He takes my hand and looks to his mom but careful to turn so that she can't see his new ink. He probably told his dad, though, and will have him break the news to Mrs. Trent. "You got the kids?" he asks her.

She nods, and he pulls me away.

We head through the kitchen, down the hall, and toward the front door, but I immediately pull him to a halt. "No, can we stay?"

I know he wants to go back to the hideout. Be alone together, so his parents don't hear us, but...

"I want to be here when they wake up in the morning," I tell him. "It'll reassure Matty if he sees me."

He blows out a breath, and I kind of want to smile at how depressed he suddenly looks. "You're killing me."

He trusts his parents, so he's not worried about them taking care of my siblings, but I don't know them. I'm not leaving.

"All right." He leads me up the stairs, and I slide my hand up the back of his T-shirt, looking forward to holding him. He's always so warm.

But he takes me into his room, pulls out a clean T-shirt, and then takes my face, kissing me hard on the lips. "The shower is to your left." He points toward the door. "And I'll see you in the morning. Sleep tight."

What? He starts to leave, but I grab his hand. "Where are you going?"

"To the couch," he says. "I'm not going to be able to keep my hands off you, and my parents might freak if we're doing it right under their noses."

He pulls me in again and presses his lips to mine, holding my face, and breathes me in like he needs me to live. It goes warm down to my toes, and I wrap my arms around him.

But he pulls away. "I'll see you in the morning."

And I watch him go, trying not to smile at how tight his jeans suddenly look.

Two hours later, I'm still awake.

I mean, I want to be here when my brother and sister wake up, but I feel like I should've just gone back to Carnival Tower with Hawke.

Not like I'd be asleep yet anyway if I had, so I guess that's a consolation.

And why do they call it Carnival Tower? He never explained that. And is it really a tower? It has a great vantage point from up on the roof, but I don't know...

I shake my head, trying to get my head clear, my brain to stop working for a while, but all I keep thinking about is the race, the fight, the tattoo...

The car and the hours out at the lake.

I'd showered and cleaned, but I still feel him. His weight. His mouth. His warmth on my belly. I wish he'd been my first too.

I would've gotten the affection I deserved. The consideration, the time, the intensity... I didn't think it would ever feel like that. Like I *had* to have him. I would've known not to expect any less in my future, and I hope it was the same for him.

I throw off the covers and hop out of bed, opening the drawers to his dresser until I find a pair of green and black plaid boxer shorts. Slipping them on, I roll them over a couple of times and smooth out my hair over the black T-shirt he loaned me. Opening the door, I creep into the hallway.

The grandfather clock down in the entryway chimes, and I check all the doors, making sure they're closed. I don't want to run into his parents.

Stepping quietly down the stairs, I find him in the living room, sprawled out on the couch. He wears black pajama pants, no shirt, lying on his back, one foot on the floor and one on the couch. His arm hangs over the side, the other hand over his stomach.

My chest aches, and my body screams. Looking at him so vulnerable right now is like a feast displayed on a dining room table that I can't wait for.

I climb on top of him, dragging my nose up his stomach to his chest and grabbing his nipple between my teeth.

He gasps and jerks, and I shoot up, pressing my forehead to his. "I missed you."

His breathing hitches, but his eyes come into focus, and he sees me, taking my face in his hands.

I press my mouth to his, grinding my groin into him and feeling the hard ridge of his cock already.

"Are you hurting?" I ask, grazing my fingers over the cut on his cheek.

"No." He grabs my ass and thrusts up into me, but my knee brushes against something between him and the couch, and I look over, pulling out an iPad.

The screen illuminates. "What's this?" I ask.

He grabs for it. "Nothing..."

But I rear back, curious now. I swipe the screen, and a video is paused but the image is clear. What the hell?

I press *Play*, a man yanks a woman's hips back into him as he slides into her from behind. Moans pour out as she grips the edge of the kitchen table, her ass slamming back into him faster and harder.

"Are you serious?" I gape at him. "Weren't you satisfied?"

We did it three times in the car, and he comes home to immediately jerk off to porn?

"No," he blurts out, grabbing the iPad and clearing away the video.

No?

"I mean, yes," he replies. "It's not that. I was...researching."

"Researching?"

He sits up, and I sit back, but he won't meet my eyes for a second.

He shifts underneath me, like he's looking for his words. Finally, he asks, "Have you ever...done it like that?"

Doggie-style? I shake my head.

He drops his eyes again, and I kind of want to smile at the way he chews his lip to cover up how nervous he is. He's got to be six-one with a chest for days. A god, and he acts so shy.

"Would you like to?" he asks me in a soft voice.

Tingles spread up my spine. I'd love nothing more right now than to be back at the tower, the two of us in his bed, *practicing*...

But...

"What?" he asks when I don't reply.

I know he's going to be mad if I say it, but it needs to be said.

"I just feel like maybe you'd want to save some experiences," I tell him.

Maybe now that he's over the hump, things will be easier for him.

He plops back on his hands, staring at me and the softness is gone.

"I'm just being practical," I say, keeping calm. "You're not going to fall in love with a high school dropout. I can't pay for anything. Eventually, you'll meet someone else. Maybe save some of these adventures for her—"

"I'd rather know what I'm doing when I meet her."

I go still, not expecting him to say that. So, he already knows he won't fall in love with someone like me. He really is just practicing. *Fan*-tastic.

He pushes me back, and comes down over me as I lie on the couch. "I want to be good at this."

"You will," I whisper. "You've got a nice dick. She'll love it."

He smiles, but it looks bitter. "I should have found you ages ago. Guess they were right about Weston girls."

"And what do they say about us?"

He slips a hand under my shirt, kneading my breast. "Not for forever, but certainly for fun."

Prick. But I laugh it off. "Not as bad as what they say about Falls boys. 'Can pay the bills but can't make you come.'"

He edges back, pulls me up and twists me around, pressing me into the back of the couch from behind. My knees dig into the cushions.

He covers my back and breathes in my ear as he slides a hand inside the front of my panties, caressing me. "Did you come with me?" he breathes the words across my skin.

His fingers brush my clit, and my eyelids flutter. He covers my pussy with his hand, holding on, and I just want to grind into it.

"There's no reason to lie." He kisses my ear. "Did you come?"

I nod.

"Was it good?"

I nod again.

He takes his hand out, sticks his middle finger into his mouth, wetting it, and then slips it back between my legs. He toys at my entrance, and I hold his hand, keeping it there.

"You want more?" he asks.

I widen my knees a little. "Hawke..."

I pull off my shirt, bringing his other hand to my breast and turning my head to hover my mouth over his.

"Baby..." he breathes.

"Are you hard for me?" I roll my ass into him, feeling it. "Yeah..."

"Am I fun?" I taunt.

"Mmmm..."

I whip around, plant a hand on the side of his neck, and shove him down to the couch, coming down and straddling him. I sit up, his eyes on my tits. "Then I hope you can't stop getting hard in your jeans," I tell him. "When you take your little, pink blonde to the movies, but can't stop thinking about how much fun I was in the hot back seat of your car." I roll my hips on him. "You'll never fuck anyone else like me."

He reaches up, grabs the back of my neck, and pulls me into his mouth, both of us lost in the kiss. My nipples rub over his chest, and everything is perfect. The way my body molds to his. The way I only have to lower my chin for my mouth to reach his. The way he feels so good to hold.

I pissed him off, so he pushed back, and I don't care if

I'm right and he'll eventually realize that there are others better suited for him...or if I realize he's right and we should just let it be and see where this goes. I have to have him.

I rock my hips faster, moaning as he chews up my lips, and I'm about to rip off the rest of my clothes when the stairwell light brightens the entryway.

I pop my head up.

"Fuck," he whisper-yells.

He bulges between my legs, and I leap off of him, scrambling for my shirt. I pull it on, grab the iPad, and jump onto the sofa, curling up like I'm watching something.

He sits up and holds his head in his hands, breathing hard.

Footfalls hit the stairs.

"Hawke," I grit out through my teeth.

He adjusts himself, grunting like he's in pain, and grabs the blanket over the back of the sofa, covering his erection.

His father rounds the banister, sees us, and stops. He stands there in a gray T-shirt and jeans. His messy hair sticks up everywhere.

"Hawke," he says, nodding.

"Morning, Dad," Hawke says, barely opening his mouth.

Then his eyes flash to mine, and I smile tightly, but he hoods his eyes, looking amused as he walks away.

Because parents aren't stupid, and he's making sure I know that.

Another door slams shut upstairs, and I hear footsteps as the grandfather clock chimes six times.

I look out the window, seeing it's still dark but with hints of blue now instead of black. The sun is coming up.

I look over at him, not sure if he's okay or not. Is he mad? It wasn't really a fight, but I don't seem to be very good at reading him. I set the iPad down, about to rise, but he leaves the couch first, heading up the stairs.

No backward glance. No smile. No kiss.

He's mad.

I was just being honest. He gets so pissy. It's not self-deprecating to be realistic. Straight up, he's out of my league, and sooner or later, he's going to realize it.

I don't have much time to seethe, because small feet appear on the stairs, and I see Matty holding the railing with both hands as he takes each step one at a time.

"Aro!" he squeals.

His smile supersedes everything else. I run over to him and wrap my arms around him, lifting him up. "Did you sleep well?"

"Uh-huh!" He grins wide, his straight rows of perfectly white baby teeth flashing for me. "They have a jungle gym. We played on it last night. And the lady read me a story like you do sometimes."

On the rare occasion when my night is free and my mom or stepdad aren't home anyway.

"Where's Mommy?" he asks.

Good fucking question, dude.

But then Mr. Trent shouts, "Who wants pancakes?" and Matty's attention is gone as he squirms out of my arms.

Bianca trails down the stairs, dressed in shorts and a T-shirt, and she looks at me. She opens her mouth to speak, but Matty pulls her toward the kitchen.

I follow, the two of them pulling out chairs. I tuck my hair behind my ear, heading to the counter. "I can do it," I tell Hawke's dad.

"I know." But he doesn't look up or stop mixing batter, and I breathe out a laugh. His wife and him are soulmates—definitely.

Juliet strolls in, and I can't help but gape at the floor-length, black velvet robe with gold dragons embroidered on it. She looks regal, like she should be floating across the high balcony of a mansion or haunting a castle somewhere. I love a woman who just doesn't give a shit.

"I set a selection of clothes on the bed," she tells me. "Just in case you need them, but of course, you don't have to wear any of it."

"Thanks."

Jax pulls out plates and utensils, and I quickly take them before he can stop me, placing everything on the table and pouring the juice.

"Is everything okay?" Bianca asks me, keeping her voice low.

"I think so."

We need to talk, but not now and not in front of Matty.

But she looks away, and I see the worry.

"Hey." I catch her eyes again. "You're either staying here or I'm taking you home, and if we go home, I'm not leaving. We'll figure it out."

It sucks, I know. Being bounced around, losing what's familiar... Even if your home life is hard, at least it's the devil you know. It feels like everything is dark when you don't feel secure in your surroundings, or know where you belong. When everything is in limbo. She's never been in foster care. I know that feeling well.

"Just think of this as research," I say, taking a seat next to my brother.

"And what am I researching?"

"Is there a Falls boy cuter than your boyfriend?" I tease. "Inquiring minds want to know."

She rolls her eyes, but her shoulders relax a little, and I spot a smile peeking out. Hawke's dad chuckles behind me, and Juliet places a mug in front of me. "Coffee?"

"Thanks." I grab it.

The kids eat, but I keep checking the hallway, waiting for Hawke. Maybe he's showering.

My insides twist a little. I don't regret what I said, but him unhappy doesn't make me happy. I can't leave Matty and Bianca, but I kind of miss the hideout now.

"We're going to the water park today," Jax announces. "If you and Hawke want to be here around six, we'll order some pizza tonight."

"Okay."

"Or you can come," he says. "You're invited, but I have a feeling my son has things to do, so I wasn't sure what your plans were."

At that moment, Hawke enters the kitchen in joggers, still no shirt, and AirPods in his ears. He carries his phone.

"Hey," his dad says.

Hawke fills a glass with water and gulps down the entire thing. I sit there, waiting for him to say something.

But he just tells his parents, "I'm going for a run."

What? I jerk my head, watching him walk back down the hallway and then open and close the front door.

"Uh-oh," his mom mumbles.

"What happened?" his dad asks.

I look at both of them.

His mom shakes her head, starting to clear plates. "No idea."

"What's wrong?" I ask.

Why do they think he's upset?

"Hawke hates jogging," he explains. "He only does it when he needs air."

Great.

An hour later, everyone is gone and Hawke still isn't back. I empty the dishwasher, and then I sift through the clothes Juliet set out, pretty sure I'll just put Dylan's clothes

371

back on from yesterday, but...

There are a few cute things, actually. I pull on some black jeans with rips in them, and slide my arms into a black and gray flannel that's not really a flannel. The fabric is light, and I button it all the way up to the neck. It's tight and rides up on my stomach, just a little. I want him to look, but I don't want it to look like I'm trying to get him to look.

I sift through his drawers, hesitating only a second before invading his privacy. If he had anything to hide, he wouldn't have put me in here. I find a drawer with hats and gloves and pull out a black beanie. I cover my head, my hair falling down my back.

"Hey!" I hear someone call.

I look around, catching flailing out of the corner of my eye. Dylan stands in her open French doors on the other side of the tree.

Walking over, I lift the window and lean down. "Hey, you okay?"

"Yeah." She smiles, and I see people behind her.

"Sorry about last night," I say.

But she waves me off. "I didn't die."

I laugh to myself, but then I see the faces of the people in her room, one of them Hawke's ex. She looks over her shoulder, listening to Dylan as Coco, Megan, and another girl I don't recognize try on clothes and blast music.

I try not to wish that Hawke would walk in right now. It's shallow and petty to want her to see me in his room with him.

Before they're off to college together anyway.

"So, are you staying?" Dylan calls out.

"I'm not sure."

The girls laugh, and Dylan winces a little, looking guilty. "I would've invited you, but it was a spontaneous slumber party, and I had a feeling Hawke wanted to have a discussion after the tattoo shop last night."

"You could tell that, huh?"

She gives me a loaded look. "So, did you have a discussion?" she prods. "But not like a discussion. I mean a 'DISCUSSION'."

And she does air quotes. I roll my eyes, like I'm going to discuss anything with her. Or with anyone. "Shut up," I grumble.

But then she stands up straight, her face falling as she looks behind me, and the next thing I know, someone is pulling me back from the window and slowly closing it again. I look over my shoulder, seeing Hawke with a towel around his waist as his bare chest covers my back. He reaches up, pulling the cord for the drape to descend, and I look out the window one last time, seeing Schuyler behind Dylan, watching us disappear behind the curtain.

When did he come in?

"I don't want anyone else touching you while we're messing around," he says behind me. "You understand?"

I pause.

What is he doing? I said the same thing to him, and he agreed quickly, but it feels colder, him asking me.

Not to mention, he said he already knew I wouldn't mess with anyone else.

"Get on the bed," he murmurs.

My stomach drops a little, and my pulse quickens, but I hesitate. I like the words. I don't like how he's saying them.

"I thought that's what you wanted," he taunts, touching my hair. "Some fun. Some practice."

I wanted a friend with benefits. He's not acting like a friend. He's behaving like an asshole.

"Maybe you're right." He sighs. "Maybe none of this is real. Maybe I should find out if I can finally screw Schuyler now. Should I find out?"

I don't give a shit.

"Pump her in the back seat of my car tonight?"

My hands shake, the images coming unbidden. He could have anyone he wanted. And he's good. For a recently deflowered virgin anyway.

"Maybe my naughty little Rebel cured me," he coos in my ear. "Good girl. You were useful."

Fuck off. I spin around, locking my jaw so hard my teeth ache, but in one swift movement, he wraps his arms around my thighs and lifts me high.

He comes in hard on my lips, moving over my mouth like he's starving, and my body floods with heat. *God.* I slip my tongue in, and his growl travels down my throat as we nibble and hold each other tight.

We fall onto his bed, me straddling him, and I'm whipping off my hat and quickly unbuttoning the shirt.

"Don't touch her," I say, looking down at him.

He pulls the shirt down my arms and then sits up, unfastening my bra. "I don't want to touch her." He breathes hard over my lips. "Only you're allowed to touch me. I want to do it all with you."

I wrap my arms around his neck, and we fall back down, my jeans and underwear getting pushed down my legs and his towel is gone.

He reaches into his nightstand and pulls out a condom, and I don't ask at what point he slipped those in there, but I'm hoping he has them in his car and in the hideout now too. Or will anyway.

I shift off a little, and he rolls it on, stroking his dick. I grab it from him, fitting him inside me, and he scoots up, leaning back against his headboard and gripping my hips as I start to slide him all the way inside me.

"Aro..." he groans.

I can't go slow. Not right now. I rock into him, moving him in and out, faster and faster. My hips roll back and forth, and he comes up, sucking on my breasts. A moan escapes, and I let it, not trying to be quiet for anyone.

"Fuck..." I whimper, the head of his cock hitting deep inside. "It's so hard, baby."

"Fuck me, girl," he growls. "Goddamn."

I lean forward, holding the headboard behind him, and bounce, the wooden frame banging into the wall. My orgasm builds, and I start rolling again, chasing it as he pulls my ass in again and again.

"Hawke..." I moan. "I'm coming."

I grind so fucking hard, getting him deeper and deeper, until the orgasm explodes. Sparks spread through my belly and down between my thighs, and I ride it out, crying out over and over. "Oh, God..." I jerk into his body, and then slam my mouth down on his, thrusting my hips and not slowing for him.

"Aro," he whispers, grunting. "God, don't fucking stop."

And I can tell he's close.

He digs his fingers into my ass, and his stomach flexes. His eyes squeeze shut, he freezes, and I climb off him, yanking off the condom.

"Aro!" he shouts.

But I bring my mouth down on him, sucking him down my throat and bobbing up and down.

"Oh my God..." He grips the back of my hair, thrusting up, pumping my mouth one, two, three, and... "Fuck!"

He spills into my mouth, and I hesitate a second, but then... I swallow it, and I keep going, sucking and finishing him off.

His chest rises and falls hard, but his hips slow and his

grip in my hair relaxes as his orgasm subsides.

"Jesus..." he whispers.

I look up at him, loving the way every muscle is defined and how tense and good he came. I keep my eyes on him and lick his cock, playing and loving how he feels on my tongue.

I'd never done that before, and I never wanted to. I just wanted it all in this moment. I still do.

I come up and curl into his arms, draping my leg over his body.

"Friends do that, right?" I ask.

He shakes with a laugh, but he's too spent to tease back.

I kiss his jaw, and we stay like that for another hour before I drag him back into the shower. Again.

FALLS

CHAPTER TWENTY-SIX

Hawke

I hold her hand, heading down the sidewalk and feeling a few people stare. Maybe they think I'm still wanted by the cops. Maybe they know she's a Rebel and from Green Street. Maybe they're wondering if I have a girlfriend.

I guess she's my girlfriend now. Not that I have a problem with it. But I honestly don't think of it like that. It just feels good to need her. To finally feel everything with one person and know that it lived up to the hype.

Why did it suddenly work with her?

She pulls her hand out of mine and stops. "I don't want to do this."

I reach over and take her hand again, leading her to Rivertown, but she digs in her heels.

"Your mom is ordering pizza," she argues.

"I don't want pizza." I pull her along. "I want a burger."

"But they're going to think the tattoo is because of me."

I open the door to the hangout. "It is because of you."

"You know what I mean."

I pull her inside, and she lowers her voice as eyes turn on us.

"They're going to think I initiated you into a gang or something," she grits out between her teeth.

I see an empty table and drag her to it. "Not *something*. It's a gang, Aro."

People watch us as we pass their tables, and she groans as my friends and former classmates look up from their phones and turn away from their meals to follow us with their eyes.

Their gazes drop to our entwined hands.

I pull out her seat for her, and she slams her ass down, the legs scraping across the tile as she pulls out the menu.

I hold back my laugh. I actually wouldn't have minded pizza. Or to just take her directly back to the tower and continue having her to myself, but Reeves knows I have him, so he'd be stupid to come after us. We're free, and I'm taking her to dinner where everyone can see.

I take a seat, and Annabelle Foy comes up, placing coasters down for us. "Hi, Hawke," she says. "Medium rare, gouda, dressed?"

I nod, but Aro shoots her a dirty look. Pursing her lips, she stuffs her menu back between the ketchup bottle and the napkin holder. "Same, I guess," she mumbles.

I can't contain my smile that time. I like her jealous.

"Two lemonades," I tell Annabelle.

She nods and leaves, and I sit back in my seat, slipping my hand into Aro's that lays on the table.

"Now you know my burger order too," I tease.

"Whatever."

I really shouldn't like how territorial she is, but it means she's afraid of losing me. I like that, because that was the exact reason that I didn't tell her we were in the clear when

I knew I had the evidence on Reeves. I just needed to keep her another day. *Maybe two.*

I thread my fingers through hers, in awe of her hands. How small and smooth they are. Like I half expected them to be made of grit and iron with how she uses them.

I graze the raised skin over the back of her hand that disappears up the sleeve of her gray and black flannel. "How did that happen?" I ask.

"I don't want to talk about it."

She pulls her hand away, and I watch her, barely noticing Annabelle setting the lemonades down on the table. Aro unwraps her straw, sticking it into the glass.

"Do Hugo, Nicholas, and Axel know?" I press.

She meets my eyes.

"No one should know you better than me," I tell her.

I understand if she doesn't want to talk about it, but she has talked about it. She's not telling *me* because she's embarrassed for me to know about her life. She wasn't with her foster brothers. That won't do.

"My grandmother," she says finally. "My father's mother. She got tired of my shirts always being wrinkled. Lost her patience one Sunday before church and ironed the sleeve while I was wearing it."

I look down at the scar again, knowing her sleeve wouldn't have extended that far down her hand. I picture the woman holding her down, Aro screaming.

"Jesus Christ," I say, taking a drink. "How old were you?"

"Seven."

When I was seven, I was bummed, because I didn't have grandparents. Not blood-related anyway, although Jared's mom and Madoc's dad did a good job of stepping in.

My dad's mom abandoned him when he was a kid, his dad was in jail, and my mom never let me visit her mother unsupervised. She said the woman was unstable. Now I'm grateful they protected me. They knew some parents were bad, and we were better off without.

"It's okay," Aro assures me. "I still remember the pain, but I never had to see her again, so that was good. My mom came through that time." She gives a sad smile. "She let the bitch have it."

You almost can't see the tears in her eyes.

"It wasn't that bad," she says, "but the scar got even worse over time. As I grew, the skin stretched, I guess. Got a little gnarly."

"Where was your dad?"

She takes in a breath and exhales. "He joined the Navy before I was one. Saw him a few times after that, I'm told, but I don't remember. He got drunk and died in a car crash in Hawaii when I was nine. That's where he was stationed."

I hold her hand, thinking about how lucky my cousins and I are. How lucky Quinn is. But our parents, like Aro, didn't have it so great. Jared and my dad were neglected and abused. My aunt Tate lost a parent, and my mom was alone so much. So alone before she found my dad.

They found a life, because they found each other. People save people.

"Does it ever hurt you?" I ask her.

She shrugs. "There's some nerve damage, so parts of it are a little numb, but I can use it just fine."

"No," I say softly. "I mean, does it ever *hurt* you?"

Her eyes dart up to mine, and I hold her gaze. I told her all that shit about my head, the girls, how I freaked out every time someone wanted intimacy, and I couldn't do it. She knew exactly what to do. She just stayed. She touched me. She never pushed.

I want to know everything.

A small smile pulls at her mouth. "I used to have to look up all the time. I didn't want to see most of what was around me." She looks up at me and leans down to suck on her straw. "I like my view right now."

And she winks. Everything warms under my skin, and I squeeze her hand, satisfied.

She sits back, and I let her hand go. "You haven't asked me what Reeves said in the car last night," she says.

I wait.

She crosses her arms over her chest. "You wanted to see if I'd tell you."

"Asking you would mean that I didn't trust you to tell me," I retort. "I knew you'd tell me."

"Ugh, you're so infuriating." She rolls her eyes. "You did not."

I chuckle. "Honestly, once Hugo showed up, you've taken over my head, and I haven't thought about anything else since. You've either had me pissed off or naked, so I've been distracted."

Her face falls, and I swear I see a blush.

"What did Reeves say?" I ask her officially.

But then someone pulls a chair up to the table, and Kade straddles it, sitting between us on the side. "Yes, what did he say?"

Dylan shows up on my right, taking a seat, and Annabelle sets the food down, Dylan immediately snatching one of my fries.

Aro eyes me, looking apprehensive to talk in front of them, and I get it. They're both live wires.

She picks up the mustard. "He wants me with you all on Grudge Night." Then she looks at Kade. "He wants me to get you to unlock the doors to your house."

Kade shoots me a look.

"Money?" I ask her.

"He doesn't need money." She lifts her bun, squeezing on the condiment, and I take it from her before she sets it back down. "And if he did, there are less high-profile people with a lower-tech security system to rip off."

I go through Reeves's train of thought in my head. He found the camera. He'd told Aro as much last night.

"He knows we have footage of him at Green Street," I say.

She nods.

"So, he needs something better to guarantee his freedom," Kade adds.

I look at him. "What would he have on your dad that he could use?"

"Nothing." Kade looks at me like I should know better than to ask that. "My dad returns the shopping cart to the bay every goddamn time, in case someone is filming and they try to accuse him of being unfit for mayor or senator, because he endangers property or children in cars or the environment or some shit," Kade goes on. "He's scared to death of Twitter. My dad is clean."

"I know." I take a drink. "Why does Reeves want inside the house then?"

We all sit there for a minute, thinking. Kade will host the Senior Sleepover on Grudge Night. It's different than the Senior party he threw. The Senior Sleepover welcomes anyone in the school—not just seniors. We stay together. Safety in numbers and all that. A tradition that started with the birth of the Carnival Tower legend.

Even though the Marauders don't exist, and Weston never actually breaks into houses, we still get together for fun. We pretend that it's real, because it's exciting to think they might show up.

But with everyone there, the house will be packed. Aro can easily be there, get Kade to unlock the doors, but that still means Reeves would have to get by unnoticed. Which, if everyone is drunk enough, would be possible, but...

"Maybe he doesn't want inside the house," Aro says, looking up at me. "He knew I'd tell you. He knew he couldn't trust me."

I hold her gaze, realization dawning. "A decoy..."

"Huh?" Dylan looks between us, still not understanding.

Kade tells her, "He told her he'll be at my house, so we're all at my house, waiting for him, and not where we can see what he's really up to."

Her mouth falls. "What do we do?" she asks me. "Grudge Night is tomorrow night."

"Nothing," I reply. "I turned in the Green Street footage. They brought him in an hour ago for questioning."

Everyone at the table stops, and I squirt ketchup all over my fries.

"That's what I talked to my dad about last night," I tell Aro. "We have more on him than just the footage, too."

Her eyes light up, and the three of them look between each other and then me and then each other again.

"So, it's over?" Aro asks. "Nothing is that easy."

I laugh under my breath, because she's good. "Green Street is on the video too," I inform them. "And Weston will protect its own. Grudge Night could get...ugly."

Immediately, Dylan breaks into a smile, and I don't even have to look to know that. I feel it. "Why does that make your eyes light up?" I ask her.

Kade and Aro laugh a little, Aro taking a bite of her burger.

"We get the kids," I tell them, "including James and A.J., tucked in safe, and we be ready. That's what we do."

We eat, Dylan steals all of my fries, and Kade orders his own burger, before we leave about an hour later. Dylan has a gameplan in the notes on her phone, and Kade will be making sure his parents are out of the house, just in case.

We walk onto the sidewalk. "And the Senior Slumber Party? Should we still have it?" Dylan asks.

We step over the curb, behind Dylan's Mustang. "Do you think that's a good idea?"

"God, no."

But when I look up, she's smiling, because she loves bad ideas.

I shake my head, but okay. If she wants some fun, I think she's going to get it.

Kade crosses the street and gives us a nod before he climbs into his car, and I follow, taking Aro to mine. We'll go check on her brother and sister, but then we're coming back to the tower. I need some rest before tomorrow with just her around and not my parents.

But then a vehicle is there, screeching to a halt in the middle of the street. I barely have time to make out Dirk and Stoli before they're rushing and shouting.

"Grudge Night, bitches!" Stoli howls, and Dirk grabs Aro and hauls her into the convertible. She falls in with him, and I hurry over, but they're already speeding off. Tire smoke fills the air.

"It starts now!" Stoli yells. "No fraternizing with the enemy, Hawke!"

"What the fuck?" I growl, watching them peel away with her.

Dylan and Kade run over, and I hear Aro scream in the back of the car.

"We'll take good care of her!" a voice booms, followed by laughter fading away as they disappear around the corner.

"That was Falls." I breathe hard, digging in my pocket for my keys.

And I thought the biggest threat would come from Weston.

CHAPTER TWENTY-SEVEN

Avo

"**T**his isn't funny!" I yell, thrashing in their arms. "Let me go!"

One of them has my wrists, and I kick against the door, the dark-haired one laughing. I remember him. He's one of the guys who was in the park that night and in the hideout later. Stoli or something?

"Is he following us?" the blond one next to me asks the driver, and I look around as we zoom past streetlights, driving far above the speed limit.

Stoli pulls me up onto his lap, laughing, and the driver's eyes flash in the rearview mirror. "Of course, he's following."

"Then let the fun begin!" Stoli roars into the night.

The guy next to us wraps something around my wrists, and I pull them away, but I'm too late. He yanks the strap, binding my hands with a cable tie, and I growl, kicking and whipping around. "Dammit!"

My hair flies into my face, and I'm about to launch forward to grab the driver, but Stoli wraps his arms around my body like a steel band, no doubt guessing that I'm capable of anything.

Probably a bad idea to attack someone while they're driving anyway, but I've never been accused of good ideas, so...

They cruise past the last stoplight, turn left, and hit the highway toward Weston.

But then I look over, seeing the other person in the seat next to the driver.

"Hey, Aro," Schuyler says, rolling on some lip gloss and meeting my eyes in her mirror.

I flinch. *Oh, what the fuck?*

"We're just going to give you a ride home, okay?"

"Thoughtful."

"I mean, you can come back," the driver tells me, and I see his white teeth flash a smile. "We're just teasing Hawke."

Stoli tips back a silver flask, and I look down, seeing his legs cross over mine, locking me in.

"Well, she'll have to walk, Dirk," Schuyler tells him. "River rats don't have cars."

Bitch. Did she plan this? Get a little pissed when she saw me and Hawke in his room this morning?

But I keep calm, replying, "Someday I will have a car." I look at her. "Might have a job, too. A career. A family. A little money maybe. A Caribbean vacation." I pause. "Maybe a cruise. Hey, anything is possible, right?"

She turns her eyes over her shoulder, staring at me.

"But having none of that shit equals being happy," I tell her. "As you *well* know."

Hawke has probably been the only thing to ever escape her. She's used to getting what she wants.

"I get it," she goes on. "Hawke is your meal ticket. If I were in your shoes, I wouldn't blame you for targeting him."

Targeting him? I don't need Hawke. Any woman with half of a brain should bank on paying her own bills. And being a single parent. *Hope for the best, plan for the worst.*

"Some women can only grow by men," she muses.

Whatever.

Stoli lifts his flask again, and I smell the alcohol. "Why do they call you Stoli?" I ask.

"It's a mystery."

Yeah.

The driver—Dirk, she'd called him—increases his speed, and I look behind me, seeing Hawke disappear behind the turn we just sped around.

Shit.

Dirk winds around turns, the tires screeching, and I grab his headrest to keep upright. "Slow down!" I shout.

But Stoli speaks up. "Hey, Weston!" he sings.

I look and see he's holding out his phone, pointing it at us in selfie mode and recording.

"Got one of your own!" he announces. "Let's get this party started!"

Idiot.

I look behind me again, but I don't see anything. Where is Hawke? I can't go back to Weston. My brother and sister are in Shelburne Falls, and I have nowhere to stay if I go home.

"So, have you guys done it yet?" I hear Schuyler ask.

I don't look at her.

"I wouldn't be surprised," she admits. "Maybe that's what Hawke needed. To slum a little. Get himself excited with someone who will only ever be a hot piece of ass."

"Jesus, Schuyler." Dirk laughs, glancing at her, then back to the road. "We're having fun. Don't be a bitch."

But she just keeps going. "If he hasn't touched you, don't worry about it. He'll probably be a virgin forever. His dick is broke."

It was hard enough in my mouth this morning.

I don't tell her that. Instead, I lean forward, ball my fists tight, still held together with the zip-tie, and jerk my chin. "Hey."

She turns her head, and I punch her right in the goddamn nose.

She flails, but I launch myself out of Stoli's lap, grab her in the front seat, and hold her hair as the car swerves.

She screams, and they try to pull me off.

"Hawke is worth a hundred times of every other man you've ever met," I grit out in her face. "If I hear one more piece of shit about him leave your mouth, you'll need surgery to fix your face."

"Hey!" Dirk yells, trying to drive and rip my hands off her. Stoli wraps his hands around my waist, yanking me back, but the more he pulls, the more I bring her with me over the fucking seat.

"Ah!" she cries, and I spot a line of blood dripping out of her nose.

The car rocks side to side, we tumble, and I pull her as I kick the back of Dirk's seat.

He slams on the brakes, swerves to the side of the road, and the car screeches to a halt. Everyone loses their balance, and Stoli releases his hold just long enough. I throw myself out of the car and fall to the road, breaking my fall with my arms. I gasp, climbing to my feet.

I don't wait to look where I am. If he just posted that video and the Rebels see me back in Weston, they'll keep me there.

I run.

With my wrists still tied in front of me and my hair flying in my face, I race across the road and into the woods. I see headlights approach, but I don't stop to see if it's Hawke.

"Aro!" Stoli yells.

Digging in my heels, I run as fast as I can, through the trees, down an incline, and across a dirt road.

"We're going to get you!" someone sing-songs.

"Get her!" I hear another shout.

Shit. Sweat dampens my face, and I don't know when I lost my hat, but it's probably still in the car.

I fall into a tree, breathing hard and looking around.

"Aro!" Stoli shouts. "I've got vodka!"

And I laugh, surprising myself. I know they're playing—well, maybe not Schuyler. She'd probably chop off all of my hair for making her bleed twice.

But I can't go back to Weston. Not while things are still unsettled with Hugo and Reeves, and especially not without my sister and brother.

Something shines ahead, and I peer around the tree trunks, making out moonlight on water.

Blackhawk Lake.

I run, seeing racks of canoes that haven't been put away yet, the dock, and dark buildings barely visible around the water and under the shadows of the trees.

The camp. Hawke and I didn't go inside any of the cabins last night, and they're probably all locked, but I race for them anyway. I can hide in between.

But just then, a figure runs out in front of me, and I suck in a sharp breath before I recognize that it's Hawke. I smile, but he looks pissed. He swoops down and picks me up, throwing me over his shoulder. He runs, and I grunt, his shoulder digging into my stomach.

"I *can* run, you know?" I tell him.

Why the hell is he carrying me?

He climbs a small set of stairs, I hear a lock twist, and we're inside an enclosure, the scent of campfire and Axe Body Spray heavy in the small space.

He slams the door and whips around like he's scanning the cabin for danger. I try to hold in my laugh, but it escapes.

He came after me.

He always comes for me.

God, I love him. I—

I freeze, still hanging there on his shoulder.

I love him...

The words are only a breath in my head, but my heart swells so hard it hurts.

I close my eyes. My arms feel too empty—everything feels empty when he's not around, I...

I was ready to kick that bitch to the moon for talking about him that way. I couldn't allow it. It should never happen. She's not fit to know him, and I'm sick to think she ever got to touch him.

I can't love him.

But I do.

"Fuck," I mumble.

"You okay?" he says, hearing me.

He sets me back on my feet, and I shake off everything in my head and the stupid, damn epiphany that I just had. "Yeah, they're just fooling around," I explain.

I hold out my wrists, and he pulls out his keys, slicing off the plastic band. "He was going ninety miles an hour, Aro. I'm going to kill them."

"Four against two?" I remind him. "They're trying to take me back to Weston."

He frowns.

We hear shouts in the night, and Hawke walks to the window, peering through the cracks in the shutters that are already secured over the windows for the winter ahead. The moonlight hits the tattoo on his neck, and I'm paralyzed. Was he thinking he'd get it removed someday? Does he already regret it?

Or maybe he'll keep it forever, always having a reminder of me. That once, we were here together.

The words are soft but clear, and I don't even try to stop myself. "I love you," I tell him.

He turns his head away from the window, toward me, but not all the way.

I take a step toward him. "Don't say anything," I blurt out. "Please. I don't want to know if you don't love me too, and if you say you do then I'll worry you're just saying it because I said it. I just..."

I can't breathe all of a sudden. A week ago, I wouldn't have thought I'd be the first person to ever say 'I love you', but when he goes off to college, I want him to know this was real. That he was important to me.

"I want to crawl inside of you sometimes," I whisper. "Sometimes I want you to be all that I can see and hear. So that nothing exists in the world to me but the feel of you."

Something passes by the cabin—a rustle of leaves, someone running, an animal—but neither of us register it enough to hide.

Hawke slowly turns, and I can just make out his blue eyes in the shadows.

"I'm scared, Hawke. I'm always scared." I take another step. "You don't see it yet, but your life will change, and I won't be able to keep up. I know this will end, but I need you to know that you're incredible and you'll be my favorite memory. I'll miss you so much."

I stand there, my stomach in knots because I'm dying to know what he's thinking, but a weight's been lifted off my shoulders now too. I'm always hiding, but I needed him to know that.

He doesn't speak, though.

Instead, he rushes me, and I catch him in my arms, both of us grabbing for each other as he backs me into the wall.

He catches my lips between his teeth. I can't breathe. *Hawke...*

"This is all there is," I gasp, tears filling my eyes. "You're all there is, and I can't stop no matter how much my brain is telling me to."

He squeezes me, pressing our bodies together so close and our lips hovering over each other. I inhale his scent, wanting to keep it on something I own—anything—and never wash it off.

Let us live, since we must die.

I wrap my arms around his neck and gaze up into his eyes. "We're kicking and screaming when we come into the world and kicking and screaming when we leave it," I tell him. "Death is never peaceful or painless. In most cases, we know it's happening. We're frightened and suffering and hopeless, because all we can feel is the agony, and we won't be able to think beyond it, because we're so scared. We don't want to go."

He kisses me, and I kiss him back, memorizing everything I feel.

"We won't be able to remember everything that was wonderful," I whisper. "We won't think of this. It's what's between that's the good part. Between birth and death. Every breath. Every heartbeat. And all the ones that were for you." I bite his bottom lip softly. "I want your arms around me, because I don't know if they ever will be again. I don't know if tomorrow will come or if you'll think of me when it does, so I want it now. Hold me. Hold me as tightly as you can. I fucking love you."

He grips my hair at my scalp. "And I'm never going to let you stop."

He covers my mouth again, his friends outside forgotten as he slips his tongue inside and the feeling reaches down to my goddamn toes.

I groan, pulling off his shirt as he unbuttons my jeans. I push them down my legs, shimmying out of them as he takes my face and kisses me harder.

"Hawke..." I flick his top lip with my tongue. "I want to feel you for the next five fucking days. Fuck me hard."

He growls, pulls me to the table in the center of the room, and comes down on my back, forcing me over. I hit it, moaning and so damn wet I'm practically melting.

He yanks down my underwear, and then I hear him unwrap a condom. I bring my knee up, laying it on the table at my side.

"Aro..." He fists my hair with one hand, crowning my entrance with his dick in the other, and then says in my ear. "Let me know if this doesn't feel good, okay?"

He slides inside of me, groans, and in less than two seconds, he's pounding away.

I tip my head back, close my eyes, and smile, just hanging on as he hits deep. He squeezes my hips, and I prop myself up on my elbows, gripping the other side of the table, feeling him enter me again and again.

"Aro, God," he groans, but it almost sounds like he's in pain.

"Don't stop." I moan with every thrust. "Go harder and faster. Please."

I want to feel him when I wake up. I want him to see it on my face. I will never forget him.

"Weston can't have you back," he tells me. "You're mine."

He leans over me, planting his hand on the table, and pumps harder. I cry out, his groans fill the cabin, and his cock slides so deep I feel it in my stomach. I can fucking taste him. We're unstoppable.

"It's too loud," I pant. "They're going to find us."

"I don't give a shit."

I smile again and feel the orgasm cresting. "Hawke, Hawke...I'm coming."

He pumps again and again, and I hold my breath as it bursts open. Spreading through my tummy, and making my entire body freeze, he fucks me, and I ride it out, letting it course under my skin.

My body bounces as he rides me. *God, I love him.*

But then we hear someone's voice. "Oh, shit!"

I pop my head up, Hawke stops, and I see Stoli standing in the doorway.

But only for a split-second. Hawke comes down on me, covering my body and face, and then I hear Stoli shout, "Sorry, Hawke!"

And he slams the door.

"They're busy!" We hear Stoli yell to someone. "Super busy!"

"Seriously?" Dirk says outside the door. And then a shout, "Way to go, Hawke!"

I try not to, but I snort. His friends are so supportive.

But Hawke isn't laughing. "I'm going to kill them."

I rise up, propping myself up on my hands and looking over my shoulder. "Tomorrow," I tell him, backing up into his dick. "I want to take a bath in the lake and then come back in here and ride you until you sweat."

He growls and wraps his hand around the front of my neck, making my back arch and my ass press into his cock. "Look up, baby."

I do, seeing the skylight and the stars. He moves inside me, the ghost of my orgasm still there as he chases his.

I feel him—only him—every sense and every breath filled with him, because for the first time ever, I'm exactly where I'm supposed to be.

And the sky is looking back.

"I want to stay here forever," I whisper.

I lean over the console, burying my nose and mouth in the sleeve of his shirt. I peer up at him, in love with the sight of me all over him. The hickey on his neck. His hair all over the place, because he swam, we played in the water, and then we fucked and played again.

Then we woke up and played some more.

But he shakes his head, one hand on the wheel and the other holding mine. "Girl, don't give me that look." A smile pulls at his lips. "We need to eat. And I need a shower."

I sigh. I know. Me too.

The sun shines through the trees, waning as the late afternoon warmth soaks into my skin. We'd stayed out at the lake all day, neither of us wanting to ever leave.

My thighs tingle, and an ache throbs between my legs, because I'm a little sore, but I love it. I love loving him with my body. I like sex. With him.

We park the car and sneak up to the roof, descending through the door. It's only been a couple of days, but the place looks different. Still the same comforts, though. Hidden, quiet, safe.

He picks me up and carries me to the shower, and I kiss him the whole way, laughing as we stumble to get our clothes off.

I wash my hair and rinse, both of us unable to keep our eyes off of each other.

We don't have long before school starts for him. Dylan and Kade won't go back for a couple of weeks, but college starts earlier. His aunt Quinn had left to get resettled in her Notre Dame apartment before I even came to live in the tower, he'd told me.

"Is it an option for me to stay here after this is all over?" I ask him.

He remains silent.

"I mean, just in case," I blurt out. "Like if the kids stay in the area, and I want to be close to them, and maybe until I can earn enough to get a place for them and me?"

I don't know who owns this place, or if Hawke has plans for it once school starts back, but knowing I have a place to live for the next few weeks would help. I'm asking. It's what he wanted.

He rubs water over the back of his neck, turning away. "We'll talk about it tomorrow, okay?"

I narrow my eyes. Why tomorrow? It's not that hard. Yes or no?

I knew I shouldn't have asked.

"I don't expect anything for free," I assure him. "I was just seeing what my options are. Never mind."

I turn away, but I hear him behind me. "What are you going to do with a GED, Aro?"

Huh?

"You should want more options," he explains.

Is that his business? My plans for my future?

I rinse off the rest of the soap. "Or maybe you just want a girlfriend who won't embarrass you."

He's going to have a PhD, eventually. He can't wind up with a high school dropout. I turn away, but in a moment, he's there, twisting me around and taking my face in his hands. "Don't ever say that again."

Tears sting my eyes, and I don't know what to think anymore. I want what he wants. In a perfect world, sure.

But that's not going to happen for me. There are more important things. I just can't.

I pull away, and we finish washing, but we don't say more. I wrap a towel around me, heading into the tunnel, but as soon as I step into the dim hallway, I see Dylan and Stoli.

Hawke comes out behind me, charging toward his friend in only the towel around his waist. Stoli starts to run, but Hawke grabs him by the T-shirt.

"Dude..." Stoli gasps. "It was all in good fun!"

Hawke pushes him up against the wall.

"I'll never touch her again!" the moron shouts, holding his hands in front of his face. "I promise! I promise!"

Hawke holds up his fist but doesn't punch him. Dylan scoffs, sauntering toward me in black shorts, a long-sleeved, loose black top that cuts up in the front a little, showing her stomach, and sheer black tights. She wears black boots with a wedge heel, making her a few inches taller. "You guys almost ready?" she asks me.

I dive into my room. "I have to get dressed."

We leave the boys to it, and she follows me inside, carrying a bag.

I pull out some clothes, slipping on some underwear under my towel.

"I saw something you might like." She holds the bag out to me. "I had to get it."

"What is it?"

But she just smiles.

I take the bag and peer inside, pulling out something that looks like a shoebox. I drop the bag to the floor.

Peeling open the lid, I see a pair of boots, kind of like hers, but hers have straps that let her foot peek through, whereas these are completely covered. There's a heel, but the sole is rubber. I love the buckles and the zipper.

"Coco says that sometimes they give young women their first pair of heels at their quinceañera," she tells me, "and you said you didn't have one, and I never had a sweet sixteen, because they're sooooo archaic—but maybe I would've liked to have one—maybe..." She pauses and then rejoins her original train of thought. "Anyway, I thought we could wear heels tonight."

I glance at hers again and then mine, remembering the custom. She's right. Sometimes, your quince is when you get your first pair. A symbol of being a woman, etc.

I've actually had heels. These wouldn't be my first pair, but... I pick one up, examining it. *I would wear these.*

I smile to myself. *She's not bad.*

"We might have to run at some point," I point out.

It's entirely possible.

She just looks at me, her bottom lip kind of sticking out. "But I want to wear heels."

I laugh. I guess it's pointless to argue.

She picks up the bag and digs inside, pulling out the jersey I didn't see.

It's a blue and black Rebel football one. I gape at her. "Where the hell did you get this?"

I grab for it, but she snatches it away. "You gotta wear the heels, though."

I snatch it out of her hand and roll my eyes. "I'm going to break an ankle," I grumble, taking the jersey and new shoes to the bed with the rest of my clothes. "But fine."

I dress, and she lends me some makeup from her purse. Once my hair is dry, I pull it up into a high ponytail and tease it up, feeling like I'm putting on armor for war.

I pull on my new shoes and look down at myself, legs looking so much longer in jean shorts and heels. The blue on the jersey brings out my skin tone, and I'm excited for Hawke to see me done up a little. I loved how he looked at me at that pool party.

But...

Something's off. There's nothing exactly wrong, but it's not my style. Dylan stands at my side, and I look at her, and she looks at me, and she says, "I feel like we should switch."

Oh, thank God. Black is my color.

We giggle, whipping off our clothes. She gives me her tights and shirt, and I toss over the jean shorts—which are hers anyway. I pull out my hair, dab on a little more plum lipstick, and when we emerge, Hawke and Stoli are already waiting in the great room.

"Dylan, what the hell are you wearing?" Stoli barks.

She sashays past, pulling her hair up into a ponytail with the huge Weston football jersey hanging on her lean body.

But all I see now is Hawke, sitting on the couch and looking over his shoulder at me. His eyes trail from my new heels all the way up to my face.

I feel the tight shorts and the way the shirt grazes my stomach like it's his fingers.

I stare at him, my hair hanging over both sides of my face. Heat rises in his eyes.

"Take it off!" Stoli yells at her.

"Nope," she chirps. "It'll be funny."

We leave through the bakery and out the front door this time, the sun already set and High Street in full evening craze. The streetlights glow, cars drift past, and a line forms at the movie theater. Packed restaurants sit diners at the outside tables, and I look up, the stars like confetti across the sky.

Grudge Night.

It's only six, and the sun won't be up for twelve hours.

Twelve hours.

An '82 El Camino drifts past us, and I know Hawke and Dylan don't know who's in the car when the passengers look at us and we look back at them, but they know those are Weston kids inside. They hold my eyes a little longer, one of them swiping his finger across his throat, smiling while he does it.

The Rebels are already here.

"Did you warn Hunter?" I hear Hawke ask Dylan.

Her reply is clipped. "He saw the message."

I draw in a deep breath, feeling the balmy night in every pore, and the hot cement under my heels. The smell of flowers from the potted plants that decorate the storefronts fills the air, and I can hear my pulse in my ears.

"Let's go," Hawke says.

But then I hear a rumble, spotting a black car with rust around the edges of the doors and the paint worn through, revealing the old blue underneath.

I grab Hawke, stopping him. "1972 Dodge Charger," I whisper.

He follows my gaze, seeing the classic vehicle crawl past us, the tinted windows hiding who's inside.

The hair on my neck rises, and I turn, looking up at the roof of the hideout. A form stands there, their face hidden in the trees, but I make out the arms and the hood. I know they're looking down at us.

"Marauders…" I say, remembering Hawke's story.

But Hawke retorts. "That story isn't true. It inspired, but it's not accurate."

"I think it might be," I reply, turning back toward the street. "There's a reason there's bad blood between Pirates and Rebels. And something woke them up."

The tower has new residents, and someone has noticed. It's starting again.

FALLS

CHAPTER
TWENTY-EIGHT

Hawke

"**W**hy Madoc's?" Aro asks. "They could be going any-where."

I turn right, watching the Charger continue straight, and I speed ahead to get to the highway and the shortcut to Madoc's house.

"You think Reeves is sending them?" she inquires.

"If Madoc has something that can protect him or that Reeves can use as leverage, he'll need it more than ever now," I tell her.

It's his style to get angry teenagers to do his dirty work for him. They're dumb enough to take the fall for him. That's why he built Green Street in Weston. Because the parents there aren't connected, the younger population is desperate.

"And if they're just here to play," I add, "Madoc's is where everyone is at."

Either way, the fun is at Kade's house tonight.

Stoli and Dirk follow, Dylan taps away on her phone in the back seat, and Aro sits next to me, her eyes peeled for the other car. I punch the gas, trying to get there before them.

"Tie them up..." she says under her breath. "Hold them hostage...other things if people are into it..."

She repeats my words from the Carnival Tower story. I never really knew if it was all true or not. My parents didn't seem to know much, and around the time I was born, the stories seemed to disappear altogether. According to my research anyway. The rivalries went on but all very tame. No violence, no breaking and entering, no threats, definitely no murder...

If that's what happened to Winslet anyway.

Aro is right. Something is happening again, and it's hard to ignore that Carnival Tower is a story that just might be somewhat true.

I glance in my rearview mirror, seeing the Weston jersey still on her. "Dylan..."

But she purses her lips. "No."

She doesn't even look at me, just shakes her head.

"They will take it off of you," I grit out. "You have other clothes in that bag. I know you do."

But she refuses to look at me, probably texting Kade and her friends to warn them that a shit-ton of trouble is on the way.

She's going to be a senior this year, and from the looks of it, a whole new shit show is on the way.

And she just races toward trouble. Every damn time.

I won't be there to watch out for her, and I don't trust Kade to have her back. He just encourages her.

I look over at Aro, seeing her watching me. "And whose side are you on tonight?"

But I say it with a small smile, so she knows I'm teasing. Kind of teasing. There's a lot more to her home than just Green Street, and the only thing she has here is me. It's hard to be sure what she has to fight for.

But instead of saying Falls or Weston, she just says, "Yours."

My chest tightens, and I look back at the road, knowing we have no time for me to pull over and kiss the hell out of her.

She told me she loved me last night. I never thought in a million years she'd be the one to the say it first. I'd wanted to say it since that night she crawled into bed with me and just slept.

And then she woke up the next morning and hopped out, going off to make coffee.

No pressure.

No expectations.

Just there for each other.

Not that women were always so all over me that I had to fend them off or anything, but in that moment, I knew I needed her in my life—as a friend or anything really—because it was the first time I knew I was never going to be alone again. As long as I could keep her.

Of course, my family is amazing, and I'll always have them, but I loved Aro that morning and how she seemed to understand that I had just needed someone to talk to. I told her stuff I would never tell my family or friends, because I knew she wouldn't laugh at me.

I loved her in that planetarium and when we made pizza for breakfast and when I saw her standing alone at my college and watching the other students. I wonder if I might've even loved her on the fire escape in the rain that second night.

I don't want her to ever speak another word again that I can't hear.

But she thinks this is going to end. She even seems resolved to it failing when we part ways for school. Like she doesn't even want to try.

Her history with Green Street is tough to compete with, because even though she hates it there, she's comfortable with Hugo and the rest of them. She knows what she's in for. Nothing is unexpected. They all grew up the same—she feels equal.

Expecting her to change nearly her entire life is a lot to ask, but she'd better get on board, because I'm not losing her.

"This won't be just Weston," she tells Dylan and me as we fly through Madoc's open gate. "Green Street will be there." And then after a short pause, "They'll be in charge."

Most people in Weston aren't affiliated with Green Street, but every person in Green Street *is* from Weston. Except Reeves, the real boss, a fact I'm sure Hugo resents.

Still, though…many of the Rebels idolize the gang, and they're easily manipulated to help cause trouble whenever Green Street needs them.

Cars pack the driveway and the lawn, tire marks ripping the grass and creating puddles of mud. The fountain in the center of the driveway overflows with soap suds, and I hear a crash inside as some Trent Reznor song blasts over the speakers.

I pull in behind two other cars, blocking them in, and take my phone, dialing Kade. It'll take forever to find him in there. I need to call him.

We climb out, all of us scanning the road behind us for any sign of the Rebels' headlights.

The music blasts, the phone rings in my ear, and I shake my head. "Kade, pick up the phone. Goddammit."

He probably can't hear it.

What am I saying? He probably doesn't even have it on him.

I take Aro's hand, glancing at Dylan. "You don't leave my sight." And then to Aro, "Stay close."

We head for the house, and I swing open the door, music hitting my ears like a needle. I flinch.

People loiter around the entryway and linger on the stairwell leading to the second floor. Jasmine Cavanaugh is pressed against the wall underneath the Caruthers' family photo being felt up and kissed by someone I don't recognize.

We make our way past the living room where air mattresses cover the floor, and half of the students dance around in their pajamas, drinking, laughing, and cuddling.

But then I look ahead and stop.

"Jesus," I whisper.

Dylan laughs, and I don't have to see her face to know she's delighted. I shove open the patio doors and blink long and hard. "Madoc's going to kill him."

Foam machines spill suds all over the pool deck, the pool, and onto the lawn, reaching about three to four feet high in certain areas where it piles up against the rock walls and fences.

Our friends and classmates—hell, the whole fucking school—is here, dancing thigh-deep in the suds, drinking, and falling in the pool that they can't see because it's covered with foam, just like the deck. Blue and green strobe lights make it hard to make out anything, all of the other lights off.

Madoc spends a fortune on landscaping, and I don't want to be Kade tomorrow when his friends have trampled his petunias because they can't see what they're stepping on.

I search the area, looking for his blond hair.

But someone calls my name, "Hawke!"

I jerk my eyes over, seeing Dirk head my way. "Have you seen Kade?"

"No, man. Call him."

I already did.

I just shout. "Kade!"

Aro and I spin around, looking, but then I tell Dylan, "Go make sure Madoc's office is locked."

She nods and runs. Madoc keeps his office secured when he knows a lot of strangers will be in his home, so it should be off limits tonight, too.

But we need to make sure.

"We should shut this down," I tell Aro.

She shakes her head. "No. The crowd will slow them down. You don't want them to have free rein of the place. The Pirates outnumber them anyway."

"The Pirates will think it's all in good fun," I fire back. "They won't fight back."

"You want to put drunk people on the road?" she asks. "They're here for a slumber party, Hawke. They're in for the night."

"I know th—"

But all of a sudden, the house goes dark, every light inside dying.

What the hell?

"Ohhh!" people cheer around us, but I look at Aro and she looks at me.

"Where the hell is Kade?" I murmur.

And Dylan...

Shit.

Everything out on the patio still runs—the decorative torches, strobe lights, and foam machines. They're on a separate breaker.

The chatter inside the house gets louder, and then we hear screams. I barely start to move before Aro is clutching my arm. "What is that?" she asks.

We both look to the patio doors, watching as dark figures emerge from the house. Some wear face paint, others wear nothing to hide their identities, and I spot Farrow Kelly sliding a backward baseball cap over his blond hair as he strolls in shirtless to show us all how badass his tattoos are.

He's the Weston quarterback. If he sees Dylan in that jersey, I'll be spending my night trying to get her out of his fucking trunk.

Hugo, Axel, Nicholas, and a couple of their Green Street cronies drift in, and then T.C. Wills takes Farrow's side and holds his hands around his mouth. He shouts up into the night air. "Grudge Night!"

Everyone at the party turns, noticing them at the doors, and I walk with Aro to cut them off before they come any farther. No one speaks as they watch Weston invade, the music dead and silence taking over the entire house.

Farrow looks to Hugo—his future employer—no doubt. "You want to take this?" he teases with a smile.

But Hugo just shrugs, looking amused. "Have at it, kid."

I take Aro's hand, trying to shift her behind me, but she refuses to go.

"You after something?" I ask Farrow.

"Oh, we're just dying to see how the other half lives."

"Be careful or we may cross the river to do the same."

His eyes gleam, and Dirk and Stoli take my side.

"We'll just have to take off our Rolexes first," Stoli adds.

I laugh, turning my head. "You got a Rolex?"

"Dude, my dad is overcompensating since the divorce."

Aw... I fix my gaze back on Farrow, seeing how well he's holding it together, or trying to. The dude is dumber than a brick. All he has are his fists.

He turns his eyes on Aro at my side. "Hey, baby. Been missing you at school."

Nicholas shifts, and it grows quiet, the tension thick like someone is about to move.

But then we hear Kade's voice. "She's not missing you," he tells Farrow as he finally joins us with a cup of something in his hand. "Pretty boys are nice, but pretty doesn't last. Your girls always make their way over here when looking for someone to pay their Visa cards for the rest of their lives."

Aro whips her head toward Kade, takes a step, and I reach out and grab her, rolling my eyes. "He's kidding," I tell her.

I level him with a look.

He wasn't talking about her. Or really anyone in particular. Just flashing Daddy's wallet to make Weston feel inferior, which is a low blow, but hey, it's Kade.

Farrow approaches Aro. I tighten every muscle.

"We saw the video last night," he says.

"Both of them," Hugo adds. "And you still owe a debt to me."

Both of them. The one Stoli posted after kidnapping her, and the one I handed off to the police proving Reeves is a dirty cop. That one hasn't gone out to the public, but Hugo would know about it by now.

"You know I'm a feminist, Aro," he points out. "I will hold you just as responsible as I would any man."

He's not talking about the shit we found in the trunk that night in the park by the fish pond. He's talking about her betraying Green Street. She was safe when she became mine at the tattoo shop, but that changed yesterday when the Reeves video proved they were running drugs in Green Street. Now we're enemies again.

Aro shifts next to me, and I follow her gaze, seeing white and blue hair peek out from between all the Weston kids.

Tommy Dietrich.

Whatever that kid's looking for, she's finding it with Green Street.

But then I hear Kade's low bite. "Tommy..." he grits out. Then he jerks his head, gesturing for her to get her ass to his side. "Now!"

Her eyes flit anywhere but at him as she swallows.

Scared. Nervous. As always.

But then...

Her jaw tightens, she raises her eyes, and she lifts her chin. "Or what?" she asks him, meeting his gaze. "What will you do?"

"You're Falls."

And to my surprise, she steps forward, almost like she's following orders. But she stops. "Then give me a ride home. On your motorcycle." The kid doesn't blink. "Take me home."

Kade doesn't say a word. Just stares at her.

"How about a game then?" Farrow smiles. "And then we'll leave, okay?"

T.C. and another guy I don't know hold up their hands, several sets of silver handcuffs dangling from their fingers.

"All you gotta do is run," Farrow tells us, looking around at the crowd.

"Ohhh," someone laughs behind us.

Excited chatter starts to fill the patio, and everyone shifts, ready to move.

Tie them up, hold them hostage. Other things if people are into it.

Yeah, tie up the Trents and Caruthers, so we won't stop them from looking for whatever it is they're really here for.

T.C. shouts at the top of his lungs. "Get 'em!"

Screams go off, frantic laughter and squeals, and everyone runs. I look to Aro. "Hide," I tell her.

"Shit!" Dirk cries, and I whip my head around to see someone taking him down with cuffs in their hand, but they both disappear into the pile of suds.

I look around. "Dylan!"

But then I catch a flash of blue as Dylan runs back into the house.

"Get off me!" I hear Aro cry.

I look to see her shove some Weston chick in the chest, the girl falling into clouds of foam and then we hear a splash. I can't help but laugh, because that was the pool. She should be glad for the soft landing, I guess.

"Let's go!" I grab her hand, because of course, she didn't go hide like I told her. We run back into the house, and I don't see Kade anywhere, but people race and laugh as Rebels catch girls, tying them up, and throw guys down on the ground.

This is ridiculous.

But then I hear a scream. "Farrow! We got a Rebel jersey on a Pirate here!"

I look over to see Nicholas on top of Dylan, my cousin fighting him off as he tries to cuff her.

"Goddammit," I bite out.

"This one's insane!" He laughs as she swats at him, thrashing.

I grab him by the hair and haul him back, hearing him grunt as I throw him down on the floor.

I drop down on him, my knee on his neck, and lock one cuff on his own wrist, trying to get the other one on.

Aro pulls at me. "Hawke, stop!"

But then she's gone, and I look to see Schuyler yanking my girlfriend off of me.

Aro shoves her into the wall, anger etching both girls' faces.

Well, this has stopped being fun, I guess.

"Bitch!" Schuyler yells.

I give up on Nicholas and climb off, scowling down. "You don't touch her!"

But Aro is there, helping him off the ground as he smiles.

"Hawke, relax," Aro says, standing with him. "Nicholas is a good guy."

His grin grows bigger and he puts his arm around her, the cuffs still dangling from one wrist. "Trust her," he chirps. "She's known me a lot longer than she's known you."

I stare at them, hit with the reminder that they've lived together. For a lot longer than she's lived with me.

"Hawke, let them have her!" Schuyler yells. "She's trash!"

But I ignore her.

Chaos whirls around us as people give chase and laugh, others already tagged as they sit on the floor. I notice Weston people out of the corner of my eye bringing in the foam machines and small water tanks. Suds spill out inside the house now, but all I feel is the need to kick his ass and give her a head start back across the river before I chase her down and fuck her on her own turf.

"Come here," I tell her.

She straightens, lifting her chin as Nicholas stands at her side. "I don't have a Visa card," she says.

He snorts, burying his forehead on her shoulder.

But all I see is the glint in her eyes. *God, I love how much trouble she is.*

I barely notice how the commotion has died down and Rebels grab me, locking my wrists together as I watch her to see what she's going to do.

Dylan and Kade stand close, being secured, and Schuyler stands next to the wall, watching us.

Farrow approaches, phone out and snapping pictures. "This is excellent."

Kade drops his scowl, not giving them the satisfaction. "Watch your back," he taunts, but it sounds like a promise.

But then someone else approaches. They walk up, standing with Weston and wearing a mask. No one else wears a mask.

A backwards cap covers his hair, and he wears a white mask with blacked-out eyes.

Farrow looks over at him. "Where were you?" he asks the stranger.

Whoever he is doesn't answer. He just walks up to Kade, looks to Dylan at his side, and then gestures to both.

His crew must know what he wants, because the next thing I know, the guys are fastening one cuff to Dylan and another to Kade, locking them together.

Kade thrashes. "No!"

"What the hell?" Dylan jerks, trying to free herself.

The masked one, whom I'm sure is Reeves, leaves, disappearing out the front door.

How the hell did he get out of jail?

Laughter echoes all around Weston, and I shake my head, looking to Aro and waiting for her to tell her people that we've had enough fun for the night.

But Aro just grabs Tommy and yanks her away from them.

"She'll just come back to us," Hugo says.

But my girl isn't having it. "You need to leave."

"And why would we do that?"

"Because I can pay her ransom."

I jerk my eyes to Aro. *Ransom.* As if Tommy Dietrich is a hostage too.

But she is thirteen, and she shouldn't be with these people.

"You pay me, it won't just be once," Hugo warns her, and I know what he wants.

I jerk against my cuffs. *No one touches her.*

Aro approaches him, ignoring me. "Yeah, it will. Because I have your money."

Aro, Jesus. Don't give him that fucking money. We can't trust him. He'll always think she owes a debt, no matter how much she gives him.

"The bridge," he commands. "Thirty minutes." And then he looks to Nicholas. "Go with her."

So she doesn't run...

Weston drifts by with bottles of liquor and trays of food they've liberated from Kade's party, one of the dudes carrying a girl over his shoulder.

"This one wants to come with us," he announces.

"Coco!" Dylan shouts.

The girl hanging over his shoulder pops her head up, and I recognize Dylan's friend. "What?" She grins. "I want to see their party."

"Seriously?" Dylan tries to yank free of Kade, but he just grunts, pulling her back.

I arch an eyebrow, looking at Aro, and the knowledge that Weston is taking another Falls girl doesn't escape either of us.

They leave, their engines firing up outside, and Hugo shoots Aro a warning look before he closes the door behind him.

Nicholas heads for the driveway, Aro turns and backs away, holding my eyes as she goes.

I shake my head, warning her.

But she purses her lips, trying to hide her damn smile.

Stopping, she heads back over to me, glances around, and fixes her gaze on Schuyler. Walking over, she plucks a bobby pin out of Schuyler's hair, the girl scowling as she jerks in her cuffs.

Aro straightens the pin, reforming it, but I meet her gaze and can't look away.

Pressing her body into mine, her scent hits me, and liquid heat rushes through my veins as her mouth hovers over mine. She reaches behind me, and I hear the bobby pin slip into the lock of my cuffs.

I brush her nose with mine.

"I've been detained before," she whispers as everyone in the room watches. "A few times..."

I almost laugh. *Seven times, actually*. I've seen her record.

She moves the bobby pin around, taking my bottom lip between her teeth. "It's actually not that hard once you get the hang of it," she teases.

I nod. "So, what you're saying is handcuffs won't work on you."

She smiles. "Maybe duct tape."

I graze my lips over her forehead, brushing her hair with my mouth and dying to have her in my arms. "I love you," I say.

"I know, baby."

The lock clicks, the cuffs open, and I pull out of them, letting them fall to the ground.

She slides the pin into her pocket and backs away as I rub my wrists.

"Aro," Dylan calls out, holding up the bindings she shares with Kade.

But Aro only watches me.

I take a step, watching her get closer to the open door and the car with Nicholas and Tommy waiting.

"Don't..." I tell her. "Don't cross that river."

But she doesn't stop.

"Let us loose!" Kade demands.

Aro holds up her thumb and index fingers, forming a frame with Kade and Dylan in the picture, and studies it.

"Mmmmmmm, no." She drops her hands. "That'll be funny."

"Aro!" Dylan screams.

Followed by Kade. "Aro!"

She spins around and runs away, and I start after her
but stop, knowing I can't leave Kade and Dylan behind. Aro
jumps into the waiting car and speeds away, and I twist
around, digging into the side table for Kade's motorcycle
keys.

CHAPTER TWENTY-NINE

Aro

"**W**hat's the plan?" Nicholas asks me.

Tommy climbs into the back, Nicholas taking the passenger seat next to me, and I hit the gas of his old Nova, speeding back to High Street.

"Get them out of town," I tell him, "so you two shitheads don't get arrested, and no Pirates get killed tonight."

I check my rearview mirror, not seeing any lights yet.

But I will. Hawke will be coming, trying to stop me, I'm sure.

I zoom past trees and dark turn-offs, the sign for their high school ahead, but I jerk the wheel left and head toward the main area of town.

"You love him?" Nicholas inquires.

I try to keep my smile to myself, but I feel it escape. Nicholas is the only "brother" I ever really trusted. Well, I trusted that he never wanted to hurt me, at least. He was always apprehensive when Axel got aggressive, or Hugo tried to coerce me into doing things I didn't want to do.

But he only put up so much of a fight. Ultimately, he did what he was told, and I was always on my own.

Until Hawke.

"What do you think, kid?" I glance at Tommy in the rearview mirror. "Should I love a Falls boy?"

"I think he wants you bad."

I squeeze the wheel, trying to contain the flood of warmth and happiness. "He does, doesn't he?"

Mr. Class President is my everything.

Tommy leans over the front seat. "If he comes to the bridge, you should be his girl."

"That easy, huh?" Like playing 'He loves me, he loves me not'?

"It shouldn't be any harder, that's for sure," she says.

I watch the road, her words making more sense than they would've two weeks ago. *Let us live, since we must die.*

Fuck it. If he comes to the bridge, I'll follow him anywhere.

Two bright circles appear in my mirror, but I turn onto High Street, losing sight of them. Could be anyone.

But as we make our way down the avenue lined with businesses and restaurants, I hear the town clock chime, the echo of the bell the only noise. Fog drifts in, clouding the street, and while I see patrons inside Rivertown, the sidewalks are now empty of al fresco diners, and everything is eerily quiet.

I pull over to the curb and park, looking around. "Does something feel off to you?"

Nicholas and Tommy just look around, but neither respond.

I open the door. "Stay here."

But Nicholas grabs my arm. "He said to stay with you."

I jerk away, climbing out of the car. I don't give a shit what Hugo said. "Stay here."

I'm not going to run. Where would I go?

Running around the corner, I leap up, grab the ladder, and pull it down. Climbing the fire escape, I run up the three flights, hop over the ledge, and race across. But instead of going to the door, I stop at the edge and look down onto High Street.

Carnival Tower. Whoever they were in that story Hawke told me knew what they were doing. Especially if they were from Weston. A hiding place right in the middle of a rival town with a vantage point to see trouble coming.

This is a great spot.

I turn my head, seeing figures through the fog in the middle of the street about fifty yards down.

Something flies over the banner strung up over the street, and I see the form of a body being hung by the neck.

It's a mascot. A pirate costume stuffed with filling to look real.

The Rebels cackle and jump back into their car, tossing eggs at vehicles as they pass. I watch them trail past Nicholas's car and down the street, but then I see it.

The buckets strung up over an identical banner at the other end of the road.

One Pirate on each side climbs the pole, yanks their cords, and tar spills onto the Rebel car.

Shit.

I need to get to the bridge before the police show up to block our exit. This is going to get out of hand.

But just as I turn to head down into the tower, I realize it's too late. Cops spill down the street just as fights break out and Rebels jump out of the truck.

I jerk my gaze back to my car, seeing Tommy and Nicholas get out of the Nova, and I run back to the fire escape, scurry down, and race back onto High Street. Nicholas shoves Tommy back into the car, and I yell, "Keep her in there! Dammit!"

But he barely has time to look up at me and acknowledge before I hear, "Hey! Stop!"

I twist around, seeing a cop heading my way.

Oh, no.

"Aro Marquez," he says, hand resting on the firearm on his hip.

How does he know my name?

Well, they all probably know my name. Or worse, he works with Reeves and is looking for me.

I shake my head. *You've got to be kidding me.*

I run, diving into Rivertown as Rebels chase Pirates and the cop chases me inside.

"Stop!" he yells.

Not a chance. You can arrest me tomorrow for whatever I did. Not tonight.

I race into the hangout, pushing through people, but commotion breaks out as a noise outside grabs everyone's attention. People shoot out of their seats, and I push through them, trying to escape through the back of the place before he catches me, but I don't know where the kitchen is.

Instead, I race down the tunnel.

People pour out of their booths, knocking me in the shoulders as they rush past to go see what's happening out in the street, and I whip around, looking behind me.

He's not there. Yet.

"Shit," I whisper.

I back up farther and farther, more and more people heading out, and then I spot him. The top of his bald head as he rounds the corner, just visible over the sea of others.

No, no, no...

426

I slam into the wall, unable to go any farther. He weaves in and out of the crowd, I search for a way out, but he catches sight of me and pushes through people.

I squeeze my eyes shut, but then I lose my balance, falling backward.

I gasp, déjà vu hitting me as someone catches me, hauls me back into their arms, and the mirror closes, cutting us off from the cop.

"What the f—"

But a hand covers my mouth, and I whimper, squirming in their arms.

Then I stop.

The cop clears the crowd, halts, and looks left to right, not seeing where I was just a moment ago. Confusion spreads across his face, because I'm suddenly gone, and he doesn't know how.

The person holding me stands as still as I do, watching him. Waiting for him to reconcile in his head that I must've slipped past him in the chaos.

He looks to the mirror and approaches, studying it. Placing his hand on the surface, he presses, and we hear the latches creak against the pressure, but it doesn't give.

I'm in Carnival Tower.

Hawke?

But it isn't his voice in my ear. "You know why they call it Carnival Tower?" the man behind me asks in a low voice.

Chills spread up my arms. That's not Hawke's voice.

"Because freaks play here," he replies.

I swallow, my heart jackhammering in my chest. *Oh my God*. Who is it?

The cop frowns, looks around again, but eventually, he just turns and walks away. He disappears around the corner, and I clench my thighs, more scared now.

I almost want him back.

But then the guy behind me whispers, "You're welcome, kid."

And he whips me around, spinning me away from him, and I stumble back into the tunnel, nearly falling.

"What?" I breathe out. "I..."

I find him just in time to see a tall figure in a faded leather jacket slip through the mirror, the back of his dark hair moving quickly through Rivertown and around the same corner the cop went.

Gone.

What the fuck was that? *Who* was that? Has he been in here before? I grip my hair at the top of my head. *Son of a bitch...*

I don't have time to worry, though. I have to go. I run down the tunnel, briefly noticing the portrait of the blonde isn't on the wall where it was. Hawke must've taken it down.

I barrel into the great room and dig out the bag of money Hawke and I had stuffed into a kitchen cabinet. We weren't sure what to do with the cash, but I'm glad I still have it.

Looping the bag around my neck, I keep my eyes peeled for anyone else lingering in here and race for the bakery. I guess I shouldn't be scared. He helped me, didn't he?

It's just so super creepy. It was kind of fun to believe the mystery that the other caretakers of Carnival Tower were still out there somewhere, their memories still haunting the hideout, but to know he can fucking get in and out anytime he wants... Are there others?

I've been naked in the great room. Hawke's door wasn't closed when he went down on me the other night.

Mierda...

Climbing through the mirror, I run through the kitchen, out the back door, and into the alley.

"Aro!" someone shouts.

I look left, seeing Dylan and Kade. Dylan flags me down. Did they drive?

I run to the end of the alleyway and keep going past the fire escape and onto High Street. They follow.

I lead them to Nicholas's car. "Where's Hawke?" I ask.

"He was on Kade's bike," Dylan says. "We lost him."

I climb into the car, and Kade whips open the passenger side door. "Back seat," he tells Nicholas.

My foster brother looks at me, and I just start the engine. "We've gotta go! Come on."

Jesus Christ, I don't have time for this.

Nicholas huffs but steps out and slides into the back.

Dylan scoots in next to me, followed by Kade, their wrists still bound.

I pull away from the curb, take the next right, and then I veer left.

"You drove here," I tell them. "You could've just met me at the bridge."

But Kade yanks their arms up together. "Handcuffs!"

I snort. *Oh, right.*

I slip the bobby pin out of my pocket and toss it at him. "YouTube it."

He scowls, bringing up his phone and trying to concentrate.

"Hawke sped off," Dylan tells me. "But we saw this car as we passed by, so we stopped."

Where the hell is Hawke? Is he thinking he'll confront the guys at the bridge, or cut them off before they even get there?

He needs to let me handle this. I have to do it myself.

I want my freedom from Green Street. I can't let Hawke take care of this for me.

I rush onto the quiet highway, a dark tunnel lit only by headlights and encased under a canopy of trees. I check my rearview mirror, waiting for something, but I don't know what.

It's like I know something is going to happen.

The scattered streetlights of Weston appear to the right, and I look over, seeing a stream of white moonlight across the river. Slowing just a little, I turn right and race across the bridge.

I roll down the window, dig out a penny from Nicholas's ashtray and whip it out the window, over the hood, and hopefully over the side of the bridge.

"Why'd you do that?" Dylan asks.

Kade works the bobby pin into the cuffs.

I roll the window up again. "Pay to pass."

"Huh?"

"Rivalry Week…" I remind her. "The prisoner exchange… You don't know this story?"

She pinches her eyebrows together.

I shake my head. "Someday, when there hasn't been a lot of rain kicking up the mud on the river bed and the water is really clear, look over the side," I tell her. "You'll see the car way down there."

"The car?" she blurts out.

I nod, exiting the bridge and turning left.

"Why don't they bring it up?" she asks.

"Because it's her grave."

I can feel her eyes on me, and I just laugh. There really is a car down there, and everyone in Weston knows the legend behind it. I'm surprised she doesn't.

The Legend of Rivalry Week. Just like Carnival Tower, we have our stories too.

It's probably not true, though. Just something that happens when people are left to their imaginations. Rivalry Week every October is full of fun that people like to pretend is dangerous.

Maybe it was once. The car is down there, after all.

But then Dylan asks, "Weren't we supposed to stop there?"

"Not that bridge," I state. "The train bridge."

Kade growls, jamming the bobby pin in over and over like more force is the trick.

Kind of like how I play video games, I guess.

"Can we drive on that bridge?" Dylan inquires.

I let out a sigh, glancing at Nicholas in my rearview mirror. He looks back, both of us knowing why Hugo specified that location.

"No," I tell Dylan. "We can't."

She's going to find out soon enough what's in store.

The train bridge runs parallel to the main bridge, less than a mile up. The overgrown brush lines the sides of the road, the tar worn and filled with potholes, much less manicured than the Falls' side.

But still, I like it out here. You can smell the mud in the water, and you can't buy this kind of wild. Air that you can eat. It's like a city fifty years after an apocalypse. Rundown warehouses surrounded by tall grass and everything falling apart, because there's no money.

But everything is alive. Especially at night. In the fall and in the winter.

Pulling over to the side, I park and step out of the vehicle, taking the bag with me.

"Aro!" Kade bites out, and I know he still needs help with the cuffs, but I can't take my eyes off the bridge.

We walk, and I hear everyone leave the car.

I stop at the start of the tracks, looking across the bridge and see Hugo with his people already standing in the middle. Trees loom on the other side, their headlights lighting up the bridge, and I feel the heels of the boots Dylan gave me dig into the gravel. The balmy August air sits on my stomach. I look around for Hawke.

Where is he? Not that I need him right now, but if he's not here, then something happened.

We walk up onto the bridge, the wooden planks between each track spaced about six inches apart. The ground appears below, but if I keep going, it'll be water instead of dirt. Ripples. Light then dark, because it'll get deeper, and my hands shake. I grip the strap of the bag with both hands.

"What's the matter?" Dylan asks.

I open my mouth, bile rising instead of words. "Nothing," I finally reply.

Forcing my feet to move, I step from one plank to the other but keep my gaze ahead on Green Street and my fellow Rebels. Shoulders squared and chin up, I don't want Hugo to have the satisfaction. He chose this place because he knows it scares me.

We stop about ten feet away from them, and Hugo holds out his hand for the bag.

But I squeeze my hands around the straps. "No."

He eyes me, waiting.

"I don't trust you," I tell him. "What do you want?"

He drops his hand, Axel, Jonathan, Farrow Kelley, and a few others shifting behind him. They outnumber us, four to eight. I'm not counting Nicholas as being on my side as much as he wants to be.

"I want the money," he states.

"What do you really want?"

His brown eyes gleam. "What do you got?"

I need my freedom. I don't want to live like this. I can't go back to Green Street. Not after having Hawke. I love him.

Hugo needs to let me go.

"The video Hawke turned in screwed you," I point out. "You're afraid Officer Reeves will roll over on your entire operation to save himself."

"And?"

"And that won't happen," I say.

I'm going to do what was so impossible to do, but it'll be the one thing that saves me.

I'll ask for help.

I'll get Hawke to take me to his uncle, Madoc Caruthers. I'll get him to not allow Reeves to cut a deal. I'll get him to protect Green Street.

For my sake.

"Are you connected, girl?" Hugo teases. "Already?"

"Just say okay."

He stares at me.

My stomach rolls, and my eyes start to sting. "Say okay," I grit through my teeth.

"Okay." He holds out his hand.

But I turn my head toward Dylan. "What time is it?"

She pulls out her phone. "A little after nine."

"What time is it *exactly*?"

"Why?"

I pin her with a look.

"Um..." She fumbles with the phone. "Nine-oh-eight."

I look up at Hugo again, hardening my eyes. "I want my freedom," I bite out, still holding the money. "And I want your word in front of all of these people that I owe you nothing further. You'll leave my family and me alone."

"I promise I'll leave your family alone. And you owe me nothing more."

I don't move. That wasn't what I asked him.

"But I can't leave you alone, Aro," he says. "You're part of my family. I can't just let you forget that."

A high-pitched whistle echoes in the distance, and I drop my head.

"What if I miss you?" he taunts.

He could've just lied. He could've just lied and said he'll let me go, but he didn't. I guess I should be grateful for that, at least.

With my heart like a fist in my chest, clenching and unclenching, I step over to the ledge, the river flowing underneath.

I pull the bag off and hold it over the side, locking my knees to keep them from shaking.

His gaze flashes to the bag suspended over the water.

"My freedom," I demand.

But he just snickers. "You can drop it, Aro. We'll find it."

The bag has air in it. It'll float for a little while.

He doesn't want me. I'm not family, and he doesn't love me. This is his pride talking. He can't let everyone see he let one go.

He can't let anyone go.

The whistle pierces the air again, and I fight to not look down the track for what I know is coming.

"Tell you what." Hugo smiles, and I want to punch him in the throat. "Weston versus the Falls. The last one who leaves the bridge wins you."

"Fuck...off," I damn-near gasp with a sob lodged in my throat. God, I feel sick. I knew he was going to do this.

"The train will come," Hugo explains. "The last one—Pirate or Rebel—who leaps into the water wins you."

"Everyone?" Kade asks.

Tommy passes by, switching sides, and stands with Hugo.

Kade glares at her. "Get...your ass...back over here." He bites out every word, but I don't even care. I don't want any of them doing this for me.

I look down, starting to feel the vibrations of the train as the wind blows the water down below.

Hawke...

My chin trembles.

But then, I tip my head back and look up. And for the second time in twenty-four hours, I feel it.

I'm supposed to be here.

"You can't swim," Hugo says.

I tip my head back down. "And you can't kill me."

A hand slips into mine, and I know it's Hawke before I even look.

"Go back to the car," he tells me.

I look up at him, but I don't move a muscle. "I didn't know if you'd come."

His eyes dance a little. "You all didn't specify which bridge."

I almost laugh.

But I don't.

I should've known. He'll always come.

"I will fight him every day to keep you," he whispers.

"I know you will."

But I don't want you to. I don't want to fight every day. I want to make his life better, otherwise, what's the point?

"All of you," Hugo announces. "Against all of us. Last one standing."

The bridge shakes under us as the train rounds the bend, ringing its bell to alert people it's coming. I see it out of the corner of my eye. Lights bright, big and yellow, and my hair blows as I stare up at Hawke.

All of Hugo's people step up to the ledge, excited laughter going off.

"Go," I mouth to Hawke, begging.

Please.

But he shakes his head. "No."

I jerk my glare to Dylan and Kade. "Go. Please."

Kade looks to Dylan, but Dylan just looks at the water.

Is she actually smiling?

Kade grasps her hand and shoots me a look. "You're Hawke's," he says. "We stay with Hawke. Under a black flag..."

The train powers toward us, everyone stepping onto the other side of the track, and my legs wobble underneath me.

I glance over at the kid. "Tommy, you just jump, okay?"

I don't want to risk her getting thrown by the force of the train. She doesn't need to prove anything.

No one has died doing this. We're off the track and won't get hit, but the power when it goes past—hell, when it even approaches—is too much force. I've seen people do this.

The bridge shakes, and everyone eventually loses their footing, plummeting to the water below.

The bet rests on which crew has the last one standing.

The platform starts to bounce, and I let out a cry under my breath.

Hawke clasps my hand. "Kick hard. Don't let go of me!"

The train races toward us, rolling onto the bridge, the sound filling my ears.

"Don't let go of me!" Hawke yells again.

I squeeze my eyes shut.

The whistle blares, the bridge bounces, and I cry out, fighting to keep my balance.

"Fuck this!" I hear one of Hugo's crew bellow. Someone flies over the edge, falling with his knees bent up and his arms flailing. "Ahhh!"

He enters the water, but we don't hear the splash. I look down, realizing I'm digging my nails into the back of Hawke's hand.

"Look at me!" he says.

Tommy crouches down, and I think she's going to jump, but she straddles the beam instead. Closing her eyes, she holds on.

"Look at me!" Hawke shouts again.

People start spilling off the side, Hugo holds out his hands, widening his stance to maintain balance, and I jerk my eyes to Hawke.

And he smiles. "We're going to laugh about this someday!" he says.

I gape at him, and he just starts laughing.

"This isn't funny!" I bark.

"It will be when I get you drunk later!"

I slap his arm. "Hawke!"

What an... I grit my teeth. He's just like his mom. *Trouble is only bad if it doesn't work out. Blah, blah, blah...*

The train charges toward us, my stomach drops into my feet, and I watch as Jonathan, Axel, and Nicholas all dive over the side.

Tommy bobs up and down on the beam, but then she can't hold herself anymore. She tips over, hitting the wooden plank next to her, and then sinks like a dead weight.

Did she hit her head?

I look at Hawke. "Someone has to go after her!"

But it's Dylan I hear. "She's just a kid!" she yells at Kade.

She tries to yank free of the cuffs, but of course, they're still attached, and it's no use. Kade just glowers at the water. Frozen.

I look down, not seeing her. I don't want to jump. I don't want Hugo to win, but if anyone gets hurt...

I don't have time to leap, though. Kade takes Dylan over the edge, plummeting into the water below and going after the girl.

The engine fills the air, and I start to shake with the force, unable to stop. I shouldn't have worn heels. I knew that.

Hugo, Hawke, and I stand on the edge, the seconds like a lifetime as the train rushes, almost on us. Hugo glances to the train and back to us, and I see the light in his eyes and know that look immediately.

No...

He moves toward us, Hawke sees him, but instead of Hugo forcing us both, Hawke grabs him first, and they both fall over to the edge. Hugo drops like a bullet, but Hawke catches the beam. I scream and crouch down to try to help as he hangs there.

But there's no way I can pull him up.

He gazes up at me, and the train speeds past.

"It's okay!" I yell. "Let go!"

His eyes hold mine, trying to stay for me, but he falls, crashing to the water.

My hair goes wild, and I hug the bag to my chest, so fucking scared.

But as I look left and then right, I see I'm the last.

I'm the last.

I can jump. It's over.

But I can't. I see them below, Kade and Dylan helping Tommy as they swim for the Shelburne Falls shore. Hugo and the others for the Weston shore.

And Hawke there, wet and treading water, waiting for me.

It's not that far. Maybe twenty feet, but...

The force makes me stumble, but I don't want to fall. I'm not going to fall.

That's not how Hugo gets to end this.

"Fuck!" I cry out.

I leap, bag in hand, and my heart lodged in my throat.

I suck in a breath and crash into the river, immediately reaching for something—anything—and thrashing, because I feel like I'm sinking.

But I do what Hawke said. I kick. And kick some more and more until I feel hands grab me. I clutch him, and he pulls me up. I take a breath, but he cuts it off with a kiss.

"We're teaching you to swim before next summer," Hawke gasps. "How the hell did I miss that when we were out at the lake? Goddammit."

I laugh, but I can feel hot tears on my face over the cold water.

"Get on my back," he says. "And don't kick anymore."

I hold onto his shoulders and he swims us to shore. I watch Kade and Dylan climb to their feet on the muddy beach, Tommy walks off, dripping wet, and disappears into the brush.

We reach shallow water, and I stand up as Hawke grabs the bag from me and throws it back into the river. "Go find it, you son of a bitch!" he yells to Hugo on the opposite bank.

I look over at the Rebels and Green Street, some of them smiling and howling, others flipping us the finger.

But we don't have long to wait. I hear sirens in the distance, and Hawke takes my hand, pulling me out of the river.

I toss the keys to Nicholas, liking him even more now. He chose my side, with Dylan and Kade. "Get them home, would you?"

He nods, looking tired and breathing hard.

Kade tries to pry the cuffs off him and Dylan with the bobby pin again.

I step over, take it from him, and finagle the lock, hearing it give. The cuffs release, and Kade nearly growls with happiness.

"Damn," Dylan whines. "It wasn't that bad."

He just cocks an eyebrow. "Let's go."

They run off, and before I know what's happening, Hawke is sweeping me up into his arms, carrying me into the shelter of the woods.

"I can walk," I tell him.

But he just replies, "You don't have to."

He runs, holding me close.

I'm free.

His.

I bury my face in his warm neck. The first of a million more times I look forward to doing that.

FALLS

CHAPTER THIRTY

Hawke

The train fades away, disappearing down the track and into the forest. Nicholas speeds off with Kade and Dylan, and I have no idea if they grabbed Tommy or not. She's probably already making the trek on foot, but our phones are fucking wet. I'll try to call her when we're home.

I hold Aro to me, seeing the red and blue flashing lights through the trees. The conductor probably called the police when he saw us jumping.

Sirens ring in the air, and Aro kisses my mouth. "Baby, stop," she tells me. "Stop."

I take us to the ground, the police cars streak past us, and I come down on top of her. I hold her face.

"I really love you," she whispers, gazing up at me.

My eyes sting, and I'm not sad or upset, but I know why all the same. Reeves is gone. Hugo and Green Street are off our backs—at least for now.

She loves me.

I smile. "I know," I reply, just like she did at Kade's house earlier.

"Why did you do that?" She shakes her head at me. "Don't you see? I'm going to kill you eventually. I'm a mess."

I laugh. And then I come down on her mouth, sliding my fingers into her wet hair as I kiss her. I move slow so I can feel her, taste her, breathe her in...

"You're the only time I've ever felt it," I say.

"What?"

I rise up a little, looking down at her. "Live or die. You or nothing." I brush her cheek with my thumb. "I have to have you."

I kiss her again, taking control and sliding my tongue past her lips.

She moans, and I slide my body in between her legs.

"You're crazy now," she whimpers. "What have I done to you?"

"This." I rub my hardening cock between her thighs and her hand to my chest, my heart thundering inside. "You're doing this to me. I'm finally fucking alive."

After about an hour, we make it back to Kade's, and I call Tommy, but she doesn't answer. I don't want to go look for the kid—I'm exhausted—but luckily, she texts me back before I have a chance to head back out.

Home safe.

I send her a thumbs up, feeling like I should say something else, but I'm not sure what. I could tell her to stay away from Green Street until I'm blue in the face, but I won't be around this fall to babysit her.

And Kade won't go near her. We've all got a ton of shit happening.

But by the next morning, we all just wish we were dead.

At least for a minute.

"You little shits!" I hear Madoc shout.

I startle, waking up on the couch in his library, Aro in my arms.

I open my eyes to see him launch his overnight bag up the stairs and then try to find his way through the sea of kids all sleeping in his entryway and kitchen.

I spot Kade passed out on his stomach in the middle of all the air mattresses.

Oh, shit.

It takes a second for the fog to clear and to connect the dots.

When we'd gotten back last night, we saw that the Rebels brought in the foam machines when they tied people up. But we ran out of here before we had a chance to notice. By the time we got back, the party was still going, drunk people not giving a shit that the Caruthers' living room was under three feet of suds.

And to be honest, no one had the energy to clean it up. We tossed out the machines and the tanks, moved the air mattresses and what bedding we could salvage into the entryway, and put some people for the sleepover up on the landing at the top of the stairs. Kade stayed up to get drunk with friends, Dylan disappeared to a spare bedroom by herself, and I curled up on a couch with Aro.

I thought we'd have enough time to erase some of the damage before Kade's parents got home. We were all just too tired last night.

"You know..." Madoc grits out, trying to get to his kid without stepping on someone else's. "Just when I start to think you can't come up with anything worse, you surprise me every time!"

Kade hugs his pillow to his body, mumbling, "I'm an overachiever."

Madoc yanks off his son's comforter. "Get up!"

"Why?" Kade pops his head up. "Is breakfast ready?"

Madoc's eyes flare, and he launches himself at his son.

But Kade's mom pulls his dad back. Madoc struggles, his black suit jacket coming off his shoulders as he tries to pull away from her.

Kade's grandfather, Jason—who's kind of a pseudo grandpa to me too—chuckles as he walks past with our grandmother, Katherine. "I said you were going to have one just like you," he tells Madoc.

Fallon tries to soothe her man, not nearly as upset that expensive furniture and carpets are still spotted with remnants of the water and foam. "It'll be a story someday," she tells him, still trying to pull him back. "Just remember that. We'll laugh about this."

"I'll be dead before this is ever funny!" Madoc yells.

He pries himself loose and swoops down to grab his kid, but Kade laughs and scurries away, hopping over another mattress. Some of our friends start to wake up, others are already awake, either laughing at the spectacle or shielding their eyes and ears to nurse their hangovers.

"No!" Kade crawls away and disappears down the hall.

"Get him, Dad!" A.J., Kade's nine-year-old little sister, eggs their father on.

"A.J., you're supposed to be on my side!" Kade cries.

But I hear him laugh. Fallon shakes her head, veering off to the kitchen and letting her husband and son go at it, and I kiss Aro's hair, slipping out from underneath her. She sleeps, and I follow Madoc to explain. It's not exactly *all* Kade's fault.

Although, the foam party was his idea.

"Noooo!" Kade bellows as his dad comes down on his back, and they wrestle to the floor. "Get off!"

I stop next to A.J. as she giggles.

Then Madoc stops.

He looks up, into his office on the left.

Light from the window spills across his face, and he holds Kade down as his son continues to wriggle underneath him.

"Where's my laptop?" Madoc suddenly asks.

My face falls. What?

I walk up to the open door and peer inside, Madoc's office is pristine, except for a few loose papers on the floor. His laptop, which usually sits on his desk, isn't there.

He rises and walks in, Kade's smile fading as he climbs to his feet. He, A.J., and I follow their dad.

"Your laptop?" Kade chokes out.

"Yes." His dad looks at him. "The office was locked. Did your friends get in here?"

Kade looks at me, and I glance back. "Oh my God," I murmur.

I was right. The fucking Marauders. It was all a decoy.

"Reeves," I tell Kade. "They came here to get the laptop for him."

But Madoc breaks in. "What do you mean? What's going on?"

"Drew Reeves," I tell him. I should've warned him about what he had asked Aro to do. "He was planning on breaking in here—"

But then A.J. interrupts us. "Daddy, your painting," she says.

We all stop.

"What?" Madoc glances behind him to the wall behind his desk.

"The painting is open," she tells him, pointing.

We all move for the framed pastoral scene, seeing it's indeed apart from the wall on one side, cracked open like a door.

Madoc uses the painting to hide what's behind.

"Could they have gotten into the safe too?" I ask.

Everyone in the family knows it's there, but I doubt anyone would give that information away.

Madoc twists the dial, pulls the lever, and cracks open the safe, hesitating just a moment as he looks inside.

Then, he reaches inside...and pulls out his laptop.

He holds it up, looking to Kade.

"I didn't put that in there," his son says.

"Are you sure?"

"I wasn't drunk, Dad."

Madoc cocks an eyebrow, studying the computer. "Well, your mom and A.J. were with me..."

And the only other person who knows the combination is...

"Hunter," I say under my breath. I glance at Kade. "He was here."

But when? It had to be before they came, or...when they came, to hide it from them in time.

Kade's fear fades, and something else settles in his expression. His eyes harden, and he goes rigid. He grabs the laptop and stares at it, his brow furrowing. "How did he know they were coming for this?" he asks me.

I shake my head. *I have no idea.*

"Will you come in with me?" Aro asks.

The Maple Room sits beyond, outside her passenger side window, and I gaze over at her.

I wish she knew she never has to ask that.

It's been two days since we faced Hugo, and I've been trying to put myself in her shoes. Her entire life is in limbo now, and I would hate it. Changing towns, changing schools, changing homes... I don't think I'll ever know how hard this is for her, but I'm doing everything I can to make sure I'm the one constant.

In a week, she'll feel a little more comfortable in Shelburne Falls.

In a month, she'll have a routine.

And in six, she'll be smiling at her life without having to try. I hope.

I squeeze her hand. "Yeah."

We walk into the bar, the scent of wet wood and cigarettes permeating the air as I look around at the pool tables half-filled with daytime drinkers. Kevin Hayes, the owner, works the bar. The guy's gray ponytail always seems greasy, and I swear he has an endless amount of Fort Lauderdale Spring Break T-shirts, because he's always wearing one.

He's a good guy, though. His life goal is to retire and be a beach bum in Key West, so he works this place seven days a week to pay for it someday.

He eyes us as we walk in. "How are you doing, kid?" he asks Aro.

She nods at him, but he must see she's not here for fun. He looks into the bar and calls out, "Carmen."

I follow his gaze, finding Aro's mother. She stands behind some guy I don't recognize, her black apron tied around her waist and wearing a tight top and jeans. The silver jewelry in her belly button sparkles in the dim light.

She pulls off the man—not her husband—and stares at Aro, hesitating.

"I'll be okay," Aro tells me, stepping forward.

Her mom approaches, only meeting her daughter's eyes in short glances. I stay back.

She stops in front of Aro.

"Just don't talk for a minute, okay?" Aro tells her. "I don't want to fight."

Her mom stands there, her shoulders squared, because she's used to being in trouble and knows her daughter isn't here for anything good.

"Thank you for leaving them with Mr. and Mrs. Trent," Aro says. "I know you didn't do it for them, but still..."

Everything is still up in the air, and no paperwork has been approved, but I'm pretty sure my parents are prepared to take the kids. Aro and I will help.

"And if they miss me?" Carmen asks.

"They've always missed you. But they'll get over it."

Pain hits her mother's eyes.

"The only hard part about all of this is they're going to think you don't love them," Aro tells her, "and that's why you gave up." She shakes her head, softening her voice. "I know you love them, Mom. I'll make sure they know it, too. Just do me a favor, okay? Don't show up in six months and try to get them back because a guy dumped you and you're lonely. Let them start their lives. Have parents and pancakes and playdates. Matty has taken to Jax."

I want to smile at that, but I don't. My dad had to take the kid to work with him at JT Racing today, because Matty wouldn't get off his back. Like literally.

"You'll see them," Aro assures her. "Just let them be. Don't take them back unless you're giving them something better. Please."

Her mom doesn't say anything, but her eyes say enough. They water, despair coming through. Did my grandmother look like this when she let my mom walk away? What was my dad's mom thinking when she left him?

When she doesn't say anything, Aro turns, and we start to leave.

But then we hear her behind us. "I never..."

Aro stops, and I look to see her mom approach again. "I never thought I would be like this," she tells her daughter.

Aro's lips tremble, and I don't know if she's sad or angry, but whatever it is, she doesn't want to let it out. "I know, Mom," she says with her back still turned. "Life just does things to people."

We leave, heading out to the parking lot, and I wait for her to take my hand before I kiss her head.

I think about my dad's mom a lot, hating her for never trying and not being there to protect him from all of the things that happened to him.

But then I wonder if she just would've been worse. Another abuser. Maybe it hurt my dad not to have her, but maybe it would've hurt more to love her and be disappointed.

I open the door for her, and she turns to look at me before climbing in. "You sure your parents are up to taking in three strays?"

I raise my eyebrows. "Three?"

I was confident she was staying, but I didn't have a confirmation. She is eighteen after all, so she's no longer obligated to be anywhere.

She shrugs. "It's time to break the cycle," she says. "And it's just for a year, right? A year to finish high school."

My chest fills up with something, and I don't know what it is, but there's a lot of it and it feels good.

"Are you sure?" I ask her.

I want her to have everything, but she has to want it too. I just want her to know she can have anything she wants, if she fights for it.

She nods.

I touch my hand to her face. "Solo un año," I tell her.

Just a year.

But her eyes flare. "You actually speak Spanish?" she yells.

I hold back my laugh. "I told you I spent a lot of time outside of America growing up."

She slaps my arm. "Hawke!"

I pull away from her attack, chuckling. "What?"

She knew I understood her when she called me 'motherfucker'. I guess she just assumed I only understood some swear words and nothing else.

"You should tell someone you speak their language!"

"Why?" I shove her into the car and close the door. "You only spoke Spanish when you didn't want me to know what you were saying, which is rude," I say through the window. "You deserved it."

I walk around the car and climb into my seat. But in a second, she's immediately straddling me and holding my neck with both hands.

She glares, but I can tell she's playing.

"I'm sorry, baby." I smile, brushing her nose with mine. "Te amo."

"What?" she demands.

"Te amo." I catch her nose between my teeth before her lips. "Te amo, Aro Marquez."

She starts breathing hard and gives in, kissing me. "Oh, that's hot. Speak more Spanish, Hawke."

I snort. "Back at the tower. Let's go."

She drops back into her own seat, and I race well above the speed limit to get us back to the hideout. It's only been a couple of days, but I've missed being in here with her. I almost wish we could cook up some more trouble so we could stay.

We come down through the rooftop entrance, and as soon as she reaches the bottom of the staircase, I snatch her into my arms and pull her into my body.

"We have to be quick," she gasps, pulling off my shirt. "Matty will be waiting for me."

We crash onto the sofa, and I toss the PlayStation controller to get it out of the way. I peel off her tank top, she pulls her hair out of its ponytail, and she starts to unfasten my shorts.

But I jump off of her. "Condoms," I groan.

I hurry to the surveillance room, already hard with the blood rushing to my groin. I'd dumped some provisions in here when I came to delete any possible footage of us on the bridge two days ago.

But Aro calls out, "Just one!"

"Maybe."

I hear her laugh. She thinks I'm kidding. I open the grocery bag on the desk, digging out the box and pulling a couple of packages out. I stuff them in my pocket and start to leave, but I see one of the drawers cracked open.

The drawer with the phones.

I slide it open all the way and immediately spot the new addition. It's a twenty-year-old Nokia like most of the others, but this one is black and a slightly updated 6210.

I pick it up and press the *Power* button. The screen lights up, and my heart skips a beat. "Aro?" I call out. "Come here!"

I wait for the phone to go through its start-up process, and after a few seconds, I hear her shuffle in behind me.

She stops at my side. "What is it?"

"Did you put this in here?"

I look down at her, seeing she holds my T-shirt to her body, her shorts still fastened. I show her the phone.

"It's a phone that wasn't here before," I point out.

"I've never seen it." But then she draws in a sharp breath. "There was someone here, though. I completely forgot to tell you."

"What?"

"He grabbed me on Grudge Night, pulled me in through the mirror in Rivertown before a cop caught me. He saved me, actually. I thought it was you at first."

"And?" I blurt out.

"And nothing." She shakes her head. "He left. He just said 'You know why they call this place Carnival Tower? Because freaks play here.' And then he was gone."

What the hell?

I look back down at the phone. Someone knows we're here. I mean, I kind of knew that, but he's been coming in and out while we've been here. He left a new phone.

Whoever he is, he's having fun with us.

I should've realized something was wrong when I noticed the portrait missing in the other tunnel yesterday. I just assumed Aro moved it.

I tap the *Menu* and find *Messages*, clicking on the only thread I see.

I told you she always liked me more.

I hold it between Aro and me, so we can both read.

You think? the owner of the phone replies. *Maybe she likes your face. Maybe she fantasized it wasn't actually you.*

Aro looks up at me, and I try to make sense of what they're saying. *She* likes his face. Winslet?

Did she think it was someone else she was having sex with?

"Twins?" Aro says.

I stare at the phone. The story says one friend died, the other avenged him. The legend says one friend *faked* his suicide, while the other joined him in taunting her.

But both are mistaken.

"They weren't friends," I say out loud. "They were twins."

Identical, from what it sounds like.

"That'll narrow it down," Aro tells me. "How many sets of twins have been in Weston?"

Not many, I'm sure.

I want her in the tower, Person B says.

I do too, the owner of the cell phone replies. *But I have a better idea first.*

I always love your ideas.

You want more of her?

Hell yes.

You want me to have her? the owner asks.

I'm dying for it.

My blood races but it's cold as ice.

Rivalry Week, our man says. *A new tradition. Hostages.*

I'm listening...

We'll talk at home, he tells his brother.

And the conversation ends.

I exit, double-checking for more, but that was the only discussion.

I toss it back into the drawer, standing there with Aro.

"They were twins," I murmur.

She could've easily slept with one, who pretended to be the other. Maybe the obsessed boy got her after all. How much more diabolical to get revenge on an unrequited love than to fake your own suicide and pretend to be your brother—the one she really wants?

"And it didn't end with Carnival Tower," Aro says.

"Rivalry Week..." I mumble.

She stares up at me, amazement in her eyes. "The prisoner exchange was their idea?"

Hostages, they'd said. Sounds like the prisoner exchange we have every October before Rivalry Week between St. Matt's, Shelburne Falls, and Weston—three rival schools.

I sift through the other phones in the drawer. There's a hell of a lot more to the story, and someone involved in it knows we're here and is now participating.

And Rivalry Week is coming. "We've gotta get these other ones working," I tell her.

EPILOGUE

Aro

"I should go in alone."

Hawke side-eyes me, and I can practically read his train of thought.

I don't think that's a good idea. He'll be nicer if you're with me.

But I get it.

You don't want to hide behind your boyfriend. Got to own up, get his respect. Yada, yada, yada...

After all, I did break into Jared's house, steal his property, and kind of tear apart his town.

Maybe I shouldn't go in, after all.

But I stop and shake my head. *No, I should.* He's related to Hawke. We've got to get past it.

Hawke sighs, unhooks his seatbelt, and gives me a tight smile. "I'll be here if you need me."

I plant a peck on his cheek and step out of the car, carrying my piece of paper. I head across the lot, glancing over

459

my shoulder and seeing him watching me. I pull open the door to JT Racing.

A roaring engine hits my ears, and I look over to the back corner on the right, a tech working on one suspended in the air at his eye level. I look around, scanning the rest of the area. Employees, two cars sitting front and center with their hoods up, and then the fridge, counter, and offices behind. To the left, a red stairwell leads to an office upstairs, its windows allowing for viewing down into the shop. The floor shines, and of course, I've always liked the smell of tires.

A man approaches.

"Is Jared Trent in?" I ask.

He nods, shouting, "Jared?"

I look up and see Trent appear at the top of the stairs. He wipes his hands with a shop towel and starts down, holding my eyes the whole time.

"Everything okay?" he asks.

He probably thinks I harmed his nephew or daughter.

But I nod. "Yes."

He walks up to me, and I simply hold out my résumé. "You have a part-time position open for an assistant," I point out.

His eyebrows shoot up. "And you want to work here?"

It's not a question, just a statement, like he doesn't believe me.

"I want to work," I tell him.

Here is as good a place as any.

He stares at me, takes the résumé, and I watch his eyes move over it before he starts laughing. "Debt collection." He looks up at me and then continues reading. "Sales. Security. Investments... I've never seen someone say extortion, fencing, assault, and embezzlement in such nice words before."

"I've got gifts."

"You do," he says, reading over the document some more. "Back in the day, we probably would've been friends."

But not now. He's looking at me with different eyes, and I get that. He has things to lose now, and for a while, I assumed I'd eventually lose anything I did have anyway. Judging from the stories, he lived rather recklessly once upon a time too.

I'll just lay it out. "I know the job is cake," I tell him. "Evenings and weekends. Run and get food, make coffee, sort mail, clean up...I don't care. I'll be on time, and I'll do it right the first time you ask."

"And when someone leaves their wallet laying around?" he asks me. "Or you want to take one of the cars on a joyride one night, or a competitor comes and offers you ten-thousand dollars to steal my passcodes and my plans for my new engine...?"

I look away. *Yeah, I get it.*

I'm going to run into this problem every time I apply for a job or college or a loan... I have a record, and it'll be around a while. References will help, but I need to get those.

Which means I need a job.

"I'm not going to steal from you," I tell him.

He says nothing.

"I like it here," I explain. "I like my siblings being in this town and with Jax and Juliet. I'm not going to ruin that."

He cocks his head but remains silent. He hasn't said no, which means he wants to say yes. He knows as well as I do, we'll probably run into each other a lot, since I'm dating his nephew, but he doesn't trust me.

I stare at him, unblinking, as his workers drop tools, slam doors, and shout at each other across the shop behind me. I clear my throat. "There's a camera on me from the southwest corner, up by the window that's painted shut with

461

the dead fly stuck to the screen," I tell him. "Another one at the southeast corner, but I really wouldn't trust that one, if I were you. It's blinking red right now which indicates it's offline."

His eyes dart up, glancing behind me to the camera that's dead.

"There are also seven witnesses in the shop, other than you," I go on, "and while I'm pretty sure Mullet Mike back there is high, since his pupils are as big as black marbles, four of the others made direct eye contact with me when I walked in and will remember they saw me here today."

Trent's gaze flickers, but I remain still, my hands at my sides.

"There's also the woman walking in right now, carrying her dog," I point out. I saw her reflection in the glass wall behind Jared a moment ago.

He looks around, seeing old Blue Hair enter the shop holding her brown-chihuahua-cocker-spaniel-mix. *Chipaniel?* I have no idea.

He looks down at me again, slightly unsettled.

"If I steal from you," I tell him, "you won't see me."

His jaw flexes.

"No one will."

He may not believe I'll never commit another crime, but he can be damn sure I won't commit one here. That would be stupid.

Thirty seconds later, I'm running back out to Hawke.

"I got the job!" I beam as I climb into his car. "I start this weekend."

"Congratulations." He grabs me and kisses me. "Let's celebrate." He shifts into gear. "Rivertown."

I slam my door shut but put my hand on his before he shifts into gear. Inching up, I lean over the console and start nibbling his neck. "Lake."

I bite his lobe.

"You start school tomorrow," I remind him. "Don't you want to have some last-minute fun with your high school girlfriend?"

He does a little laugh-gasp, but when I slip my hand between his legs, feeling him already hard, I don't have to ask twice.

"Seatbelt," he growls, shifting into second and peeling out of the lot. "Now."

Two Weeks Later

I look out my window, seeing Dylan through the tree as she lies on her bed. She's on her stomach, feet bobbing behind her as she scrolls through her phone and listens to music on her headphones.

My stomach fills with a weird feeling. Nerves and apprehension, but also anticipation and...

Warmth.

Matty is ecstatic—loves Jax. And Bianca, aside from the whining over the distance from her boyfriend, sleeps and smiles more now. She's worried about fitting in at our new school, but I'll be there, and I'm really hoping everyone knows that before they fucking mess with her.

I look around Hawke's old room—which I'm told was once his father's and then Jared's before that—but I didn't change much because I like Hawke's smell on everything as it is. I want to cry a little.

But I won't. It's so weird.

I have a room of my own, a job, a college boyfriend, Matty and Bianca are fine and fed, and I have a tree that connects me to my first female friend.

I look out the window again, and Dylan looks over, immediately breaking into a smile and hanging her tongue out in a funny face.

I laugh. She's got me excited for the school year, as much as I hate to admit it. The first football game is in two weeks. Rivalry Week is in seven weeks. We have the senior ski trip and her birthday sleepover. I've gone full-on suburb.

A knock hits my door. "You all set?" I hear.

Hawke walks in, and I look behind me, my stomach dropping. I hate it when he dresses like this, especially when his parents are home.

Black joggers, no shirt, bare feet. Like he doesn't even live here anymore. Does he purposely remove half of his clothes when he visits from the dorms, just to drive me nuts? Thankfully, we still have the hideout, although we can't get to it as much as we want. School, work...

I nod. "I think so."

He wraps his arms around my waist and I circle his neck.

"You'll have Dylan and Kade." He stares down at me. "No one will mess with you."

"I can take care of myself."

"Exactly, and I would rather you didn't," he retorts. "I know how you handle females who get on your nerves."

I laugh, remembering both times I handled Schuyler. And Dylan. I should probably apologize for that one at some point, actually.

But he tugs at me. "I'm serious. You get suspended or expelled, and I'll have to start dating someone more mature."

I jump up, and he catches me in time as I wrap my legs around him. "Need I remind you of all the very mature things you like to do to me, Pirate?" I whisper in his ear.

And he whips us around and lays me down on the bed, hovering over me. "They're burned into my memory, *Pirate*."

"Oh, that's right." I wince. "Shit."

I'm a Falls girl now. Technically speaking. *Under a black flag we sail. Woohoo.*

"Seriously, though." He kisses my nose. "Cut yourself some slack. And cut them some slack. A lot of students haven't had the experiences you have. They'll be a little shallow and ignorant, but someday, they'll understand everything you do. Their behavior is not your problem."

"Okay."

I say it like 'yes, sir'. I know he's right, although it might be hard to remember it in the heat of the moment when they piss me off.

Either way, I'll put his mind at ease. "It's only a year anyway," I tell him.

"And then you'll be with me."

Maybe. If I can get into college, that is. I'm trying not to think too far ahead yet.

But it's hard. I keep thinking about being where he is, freedom, and having all night.

"Until then, I'm going to enjoy you sneaking time with me whenever you can," I say, pulling him down.

He kisses me, his tongue dipping into my mouth and reaching down through my body. I moan.

"Hawke, out," someone says.

He jumps off me, and I suck in a breath, sitting up. His mom stands in the doorway, holding the door handle.

"Now," she orders.

But he's gaping. "Why?"

"She has school tomorrow."

"I'm not going to keep her up all night."

She gives him a look, lowering her voice for the kids getting ready for bed. "I know what you're here to do," she whispers.

I bite back my smile, my eyes vollying between Hawke and his mom.

"We're eighteen," he points out. "And we were alone in the hideout for lots of unsupervised nights."

"Well, now she lives here."

"Mom!"

"She's in our care, Hawke!" Now she shouts. "And in high school. How would it look if my son is slipping in and out of her bedroom whenever he wants? Now out!"

He scowls, but he doesn't argue further. Leaning over, he kisses my lips and says, "I'll pick you up from school tomorrow." And then he looks at his mom and heads out the door, brushing past her. "The ride home will take several hours."

I struggle to hold back my laugh.

His footfalls hit the stairs, but Juliet pokes her head back in the door before she closes it. "*I'll* pick you up from school tomorrow," she tells me. "I think we should go to the gynecologist."

"Mom!" Hawke yells.

But she closes the door, her voice still carrying from beyond. "You're not allowed to make me a grandmother until Matty is in middle school, Hawke!"

I crash back on the bed. *Oh, boy.*

It's going to be a fun year.

THE END

Thanks for reading Falls Boys!
Pirate Girls is next in the series.

Rivalry Week is coming!

AUTHOR'S NOTE

I debated writing this letter to you, but I guess it's best to be me and to just go with it. If you've been a reader of mine for a while, you know I'm kind of open about some things.

Heroes in the Romance genre typically get more love. We dream, we swoon, we live vicariously, but as a writer, my stories were always the heroine's stories, to be honest. Not that the hero is a side character, but he's definitely a catalyst for *her* journey.

And Aro is one of my heroines who's very close and personal to me.

We grew up in similar environments. I'm also the oldest, from a broken home, and raised by an addict. We didn't have a lot of money, and whenever we got some, it disappeared pretty quickly. Rent was always a struggle, we never paid all of our bills in the same month, and we ended up being homeless for about a month when I was sixteen. I scrounged for money, I stole groceries, I missed weeks and weeks of school...

Now I don't tell you this for pity. So many of you have had similar experiences. We've all been through shit, and I have a beautiful life now. I'm very lucky.

I tell you this, because Aro's struggle of not feeling like she could leave is not often talked about. That poverty is a cycle, because children of struggling parents are relied upon to raise their younger siblings. They drop out of school, settle for jobs that fit their "parenting" schedule, and then that's it. That's their life. One year becomes five and five becomes ten very quickly.

I remember my freshman year at college, walking by a room with an open door and hearing the young women inside talking about me. My birthday had been that week and—as is customary—the house leader had decorated my door, boldly blasting the fact that I was turning twenty-one when most of my housemates were still only eighteen. "I had no idea she was so old," I heard one of them say.

I felt bad about it at the time, because I felt like a failure for having to wait three years post-high school to start college, but looking back... God, I was lucky to get there at all, you know? I could've easily never left my hometown. I could've fallen into the cycle.

In fact, I almost didn't leave. My mom had been unwell for most of my life, and I practically raised my little brother, like Aro looked out for Matty. What would happen to my brother if I left for college? Who would get up with him in the morning? Who would make sure he went to school? Who would make sure he didn't have to eat McDonald's every day?

Older siblings can feel trapped. They don't want to report a parent, because wherever their sibling is sent could be worse. You could lose track of them—never see them again. Who knows what would happen? No matter how bad things are, you don't want your family split up.

So, you stay.

But I got out. Eventually. I hated not knowing what was going to happen to him without me there, and maybe I should've stayed, but I knew what would happen to me if I didn't go. And thankfully, I had help. I was raised on the charity of taxpayers and family members, and I went to college on loans. Not something I recommend if you don't have to do it, because student loans suck, lol, but I wouldn't have gotten out if I didn't have that help. I didn't do any of it alone.

And years later, my sister and I returned and took custody of my brother. He's a man now and doing great.

Now, I don't want this to appear like I'm bashing my mother. I know she wishes she had a different life, addiction is a disease, and who she became is not who she wanted to be when she was a kid. Her story is not mine to tell, but she does have one and I know that. I just wanted to relay that a child's lot in life is often situational. Not a matter of them being ignorant or lazy. They're dreamers too. They want what you want. It's often more complicated than we assume it is.

I think this is why I write heroines who always seem to be fighting back against something. I love to see them rise up and defeat the odds. Rika, Tate, Fallon, Juliet, Banks, Winter, Emory, Tiernan, Easton, Jordan, Ryen, Clay, Liv, Castel, Alice, Aro, Kat... I get to relive something hard and be the person I wanted to be a lot earlier.

For me, it's hardly ever about what the hero is doing in a book. It's always about creating a situation where the heroine is forced to fight, because it took me so long to learn how to do that.

And maybe I'll find another way to create those situations for my heroines that doesn't involve combating the hero. I have every confidence in my ability to evolve. But we all start somewhere.

Looking back, I'm honestly grateful I grew up the way I did. Like Katherine and Quinn, my mother showed me what I didn't want. I learned vicariously. Of course, I still made some of my own mistakes, and I hope my daughter learns from me too.

I hope this letter didn't sound political. That wasn't my goal. We all come from our own experiences, but this is what I learned through mine, and I write about it in every book.

People change people.
And sometimes, people save you.
Ask for help. Be willing to give help if you can. We're only here once.
And every now and then, look up.

Thanks for reading, and thank you for everything!

Turn the page for a surprise sneak peek of *Pirate Girls*.

*Please make sure you've read *Falls Boys* first. This scene takes place six weeks after the end of *Falls Boys*.

Kade Caruthers crosses the road, the night air turned chilly now that it's October. School had started over a month ago, and they'd been seniors for weeks.

But now the real fun starts.

Rivalry Week.

The Prisoner Exchange.

One of many traditions between the rival schools in Shelburne Falls, Weston, and St. Matthew's, the wealthy suburb of Chicago. Instilled to foster harmony and peace between communities, it gives students a chance to bond with their rivals (and hopefully bring that awareness and newfound tolerance back home with them).

It's very simple. They each take hostages, a family in that community hosts the "exchange students," and they attend the rival school as a guest for two weeks.

Countries used to do this as a way to guarantee peace. Kings and emperors would offer up family members, knowing that if anyone broke the treaty, you were endangering your mother or your son or whomever you'd given to the enemy as a hostage.

"Kade Caruthers." Beck Valencourt grins, walking over with his crew.

Kade looks to Dylan, and she crosses her arms over her chest as Stoli, Dirk, and a few others gather around to present a united front for the Pirates.

"How's it going over in Shitburne Falls?" Beck asks.

Kade laughs. "You know who my grandfather is, right? They would never find your body."

Beck flashes him a genuine smile—knowing of Kade's retired gangster grandpa and the stories surrounding him—but he's used to Kade's jibe. The friends shake, coming in for a quick hug.

"Will we see you on the slopes this year?" Beck asks.

"You bet." Kade nods. "Iron Mountain."

"Hell yeah."

Like the Falls is just a little bit better than Weston, St. Matthew's is a little more affluent than the Falls. The rich CEOs and stockbrokers in Chicago created a nice, little oasis close to the city, but not too close. Kade's maternal grandfather lives there, and Kade actually gets along with Beck Valencourt and his friends when they run into each other on weekends up at the ski resort. They'd all been snowboarding together since they were thirteen.

College would even things out, but until then they had to play their roles for their respective high schools.

Kade looks to the right at the cars parked in the middle of the country road, searching the black windshields for a familiar profile.

"I can try to accommodate your request," Beck says, holding out his hands. "You just can't have my girlfriend."

Kade chuckles. "Actually, I just want a football player."

"I knew that about you."

"Shut up." Kade glances to the right, seeing the bridge to Weston and Farrow Kelly on his way with his whole fucking entourage. "It's only for two weeks," he tells Beck. "You'll get him back in almost the same condition."

"Well, we want Trent," he says, pointing to Dylan. "Agree to that and we'll give you a player. We want to see what she can do on our track."

He grins at her, but she rolls her eyes. "I don't want to go to St. Matt's," she tells Kade. "They're stuck up."

She flashes Beck and his guys a look, and Beck laughs.

But Kade shrugs. "You can have her."

Dylan jerks her head to Kade, and he can feel her glare.

"Just give us Hunter," he tells Beck. "If Hunter comes here, she can go there."

Dylan drops her eyes.

But Beck looks confused as he glances to the friend at his side and then back to Kade. "Hunter? Your brother?"

Kade stares at him.

"Hunter checked out weeks ago," Beck explains. "He's not attending St. Matt's this year."

Kade takes a step into him. "What do you mean?"

"Yeah," Beck says. "I don't know what to tell you. He's a loss. Definitely. And he left us high and dry without a tailback at the last minute too. But don't you worry." He smiles wide. "We'll be ready."

"What the hell are you talking about?" Kade blurts out. "Where did he go?"

"I had assumed he came back here."

Kade searches his brain, trying to figure it out. Neither he nor Dylan had heard anything, and Kade's grandfather would've touched base with his parents if his twin was missing.

Did his parents know his brother left St. Matt's?

What the hell is going on?

"Can we still have Trent?" Beck asks.

Kade shakes his head. "Fine, whatever."

But then Dylan breathes hard, stepping up to Farrow Kelly instead. The captain of the Weston team. "You guys race bikes?"

The corner of his mouth lifts in a smile as he looks her up and down, the Green Street tattoo already etched on his neck, even though he's still a full-time student. "Yeah, but we don't have a track, honey. Can you handle it?"

"I can handle it," she snips. "Can I be your prisoner? I need to get out of here for a couple of weeks."

He laughs, looking to Kade. "Did I really just get this lucky?" But he doesn't wait for an answer, looking back to Dylan. "Daddy gonna be okay with this, Baby Trent?"

"Do you care?"

He holds her eyes, rising to the challenge. He pulls out handcuffs, binding her wrists in front of her as a young woman with three roses inked on her left hand rips off a piece of duct tape and plants it over Dylan's mouth. It's all a part of the ceremony of being a prisoner.

The young woman smiles at Dylan. "This won't be fun, honey. Brace yourself."

He watches as they pull Dylan across the bridge, coins flying over the side and into the water as they go. Kade shakes his head. He needs to get home and talk to his parents.

"We'll take Stoli then," Beck says. "Who do you want?"

"I don't give a shit."

Kade's whole fucking plan has gone to hell without Hunter.

Beck tosses someone over, everyone moving to their cars to make the trek to the hostage's house for clothes, personals, and phone chargers before being taken to whatever family and student is fostering them for two weeks.

Kade turns to leave with their prisoner, but Jaden, Beck's running back, stops him. "Hunter's been AWOL for a while," he warns Kade. "Been spending a lot of his weekends in Weston. We figured he had a girlfriend there or something."

"Weston?"

But the guy turns, and starts to leave, vehicles racing away.

Why would he spend time in Weston?

Wait...

Kade runs to the bridge, crossing it but stops halfway as he peers over the side. Down below, on the Weston dock, he watches them load Dylan into a shiny, black 1950s pickup truck. It starts up, headlights on, and backs away from the warehouses and bars. It peels off down the street and out of sight.

But as soon as they leave, he sees the car parked on the street behind.

And he sees him.

Hunter.

His brother leans on the hood of his '68 Camaro dressed in jeans and a black hoodie, his blond hair—same shade as Kade's—windblown as he watches the truck drive off with Dylan inside.

It takes a few seconds, but Hunter turns and meets Kade's eyes.

Kade can't see the smile on his brother's face, but he knows it's there.

"Shit," Kade grits out.

He was at the foam party. He was the one in the mask.

Hunter is with the Rebels.

And he has Dylan all to himself in Weston for two weeks.

PIRATE GIRLS IS NEXT!

ACKNOWLEDGEMENTS

To the readers—it has been an incredible year. I've never really felt imposter syndrome before. I love what I write, and I've never felt shame to share it or face my family and friends with my work.

But over the past year, with the amazing support of Booktok and Bookstagram, I've gotten so many new readers, and the attention is more than I'm used to. All of a sudden, I'm starting to think "Wait, why is my book on the same Barnes and Noble table as *Dune*?" or "I seriously owe _____ an apology, because her books are the standard and she probably hates seeing them grouped with mine."

These books and authors have that thing that makes them great, and I don't belong there.

But...I decided to be grateful for whatever lucky star I was born under and make the most of however long I get to keep writing. Lol. So, thank you. It's nice to feel heard and worthy, and since I'm lousy at marketing, thank you again for promoting, sharing, reading, and reviewing. I absolutely could not still be here after nearly ten years without your support.

To my family—you're amazing and supportive. I know I can be consumed in my head with stories, often mumbling conversations I need to write down, and leave you with all the errands, renovations, and laundry, but I promise I can relax a little now. At least until it's time to prepare for *Motel's* release! Then we're in the trenches, again. Sorry, guys.

To Dystel, Goderich & Bourret LLC—thank you Jane and Lauren for being so readily available and helping me grow every day. I couldn't be happier.

To the PenDragons—love you! Excited to hear your theories on what's to come in the series!

To Adrienne Ambrose, Tabitha Russell, Tiffany Rhyne, Kristi Grimes, Lee Tenaglia, and Claudia Alfaro—the amazing Facebook group admins! Not enough can be said about the time and energy you give freely to make a community for the readers and me. You're selfless, amazing, patient, and needed. Thank you.

To Christine Porter, Elaine York, Ashlee O'Brien, Hang Le, and Cassy Roop—not enough thanks exist for doing great work and doing it quickly. I know I'm not easy to work with. I often need things quickly and come back for changes, so thank you for being flexible, and as always "I'll try to get the next book done WAY in advance for you to do your work. I promise I'll really try this time."

To all of the book bloggers, bookstagrammers, and booktok accounts—thank you, thank you, thank you. I've never believed authors are the best people to sell their own books. Readers won't trust me telling them why they should read my book. They'll trust other readers. You've changed the game. We can write and make a living, and you're helping the indie community thrive like never before. So much has come in throughout the past year, and I know I haven't nearly acknowledged every tag, but I want you to know you're appreciated. Your beautiful pictures, your hot (or funny) TikToks, your time writing reviews... I know it won't last forever, but I'll enjoy it for as long as I can. Thank you!

To every author and aspiring author—thank you for the stories you've shared, many of which have made me a happy reader in search of a wonderful escape and a better writer, trying to live up to your standards. Write and create, and don't ever stop. Your voice is important, and someone out there needs to hear it.